Also by Savannah Carlisle

The Library of Second Chances

The Summer of Starting Over

If I'd Have Known

Praise for Savannah Carlisle

". . . Savannah Carlisle is now one of my go-to authors for heartwarming, Kleenex-clutching, feel-good romance!"—**Annie Rains, *USA Today* bestselling author**

"A charming, inspiring, and empowering second-chance summer romance that will make your heart sing!"—**Karen Schaler, Emmy award-winning screenwriter** on *The Summer of Starting Over*

"Carlisle's novel is thoughtful, with well-developed characters who move beyond common small-town girl and big-city boy tropes. Instead, she pulls together two characters who turn out to have far more in common than they think."—***Kirkus Reviews*** on *The Library of Second Chances*

"I was completely enchanted by this charmingly sweet beach read and just adored the letters exchanged in the Little Free Library."—**Teri Wilson, *USA Today* bestselling author** on *The Library of Second Chances*

"Fans of *You've Got Mail* will swoon over Lucy and Logan in this charming romance that celebrates the splendor of small-town living."—**KJ Micciche, author of *The Book Proposal*** on *The Library of Second Chances*

". . . Savannah Carlisle's debut is sure to delight. The author's vivid descriptions put me right in Heron Isle along with the characters and had this city girl longing for the cozy and picturesque small-town life she masterfully depicted."—**Meredith Schorr, author of *As Seen on TV* and *Someone Just Like You*** on *The Library of Second Chances*

"100% recommend this for your summer (or anytime) TBR!"—***The Book Nerd Mama*** on *The Library of Second Chances*

Where We Belong

Where We Belong

SAVANNAH
CARLISLE

HARPETH ROAD
PRESS
Nashville

HARPETH ROAD PRESS

Published by Harpeth Road Press (USA)
P.O. Box 158184
Nashville, TN 37215

Paperback: 978-1-963483-44-4
eBook: 978-1-963483-43-7
Library of Congress Control Number: 2026931949

Where We Belong: A Warmhearted, Uplifting Romance

Cover Design by Sarah Hansen
Cover images © Shutterstock, Adobe, Deposit Photos

First printing: March 2026

To my husband, Chadd, who has always supported every entrepreneurial adventure I've dreamed up and been my cheerleader, sounding board, chef, housekeeper, and anything else I've needed while I work feverishly at my desk. You inspired that side of Michael, and I'm forever grateful for your support, friendship, and love.

Chapter 1

Chloe

Hiding in the storeroom of her café, Chloe Beckett read the email for the third time. Her hands trembled with excitement because she still couldn't believe what it said.

Dear Ms. Beckett,

We're thrilled to invite you to the final round of interviews for The Next Great American Entrepreneur. You are scheduled for Friday, March 6 at 10:00 a.m. at 308 W. 38th Street, New York, NY 10018.

From there, we'll schedule hometown visits for the remaining finalists and select our cast by the end of March. Filming will take place during the months of April and May.

Please contact Trina Richards at 212-555-5282 to book your trip to New York, and complete the attached questionnaire before your arrival to ensure we have the information we need should you be chosen to proceed.
We look forward to seeing you then!
Sincerely,
Penny Shelton
Assistant to Executive Producer Mark Landis

It was all she could do not to scream out loud, but she didn't want to draw attention to herself. She was one step closer to getting her business featured on a national television show. Even if she didn't win the $750,000 grand prize, she'd basically get free national advertising for her café, Island Coffee. It was a win-win.

Now all she had to do was make it through the final round of interviews. How many people had they invited to New York? She knew the plan was to cast ten entrepreneurs, with one getting voted out each week until they were down to four, then a winner would be crowned at a live finale. It was a brand-new show, so other details were sparse. Would they be voting each other out like on *Big Brother*? Or would there be judges? Maybe even an audience vote like *Dancing with the Stars*?

Since the focus of the show was on small businesses—where the owner was still actively involved in the day-to-day—small film crews would be sent to follow each contestant through the weekly challenges in their hometowns before the final four would convene in New York for the live finale.

Her friend Madison over in the tourism department was

going to die when she found out. A television show filming on the ground on Big Dune Island would be amazing for the whole town.

Chloe took a deep breath. She was getting ahead of herself. She still had to make it through the final interview.

"What are you doing back here?"

Iris Fisher's voice startled Chloe, and her phone clattered to the tile floor. Iris was her right-hand at the café. She'd been the first employee Chloe hired, but she was so much more than that. Iris filled a grandmother-shaped hole left in Chloe's life by her own Grandma Sophie, the inspiration for the café who sadly hadn't lived long enough to see Chloe open it.

Chloe bent to retrieve her phone, smoothing the apron tied at her waist as she straightened. She wasn't ready to share her big news with anyone yet. "I was just checking my email to see if we had any new orders. The Millers need a cake for Theo's birthday party next week."

"Let me guess," Iris said, putting a finger to her chin like she was thinking hard. "Baseball-themed?"

Chloe nodded, laughing. "We're gonna hit this one out of the park. It'll be a homerun. A grand slam, even." With a former Major League Baseball player as a brother, Chloe had a slew of baseball-isms she could throw out, pun intended.

"Sam can't wait for the party. He bought Theo new batting gloves with his chore money," Iris said, referring to her grandson, who played Little League baseball with Theo on the team Chloe's brother coached.

"That's so sweet. What a thoughtful little man you have."

"I'm biased, of course, but I agree," Iris said, smiling as

she grabbed a stack of freshly laundered napkins to roll silverware before the end of her shift.

Chloe followed Iris back out into the café and spotted her brother, Austin, talking to a group of older women who were regulars several afternoons a week. She grabbed a pot of coffee and walked over to say hi to everyone.

"Stop flirting with the ladies," Chloe kidded as she gave her brother a side hug with her free arm. "After all, you're an engaged man now."

"It's going to be the wedding of the century," Tammy Perkins, a retired schoolteacher who'd taught both Austin and Chloe, said. She lifted a teacup adorned with tiny purple pansies to her mouth for a sip.

All the cups, plates, and bowls in the café were donated from families around town, usually after elderly parents had passed and the children decided they didn't need or want their formal china. It had been Chloe's idea, as a way to honor their memories and give the coffee shop a personal touch. In addition to using the pieces to serve the guests, shelves all around the café held additional cherished porcelain. Combined with the rattan chairs and tranquil blue, aqua, and white décor, it had been important to her to create a space that felt warm and homey.

The table buzzed over the impending nuptials, everyone offering their ideas, from the flowers to the song for their first dance. Austin was recently engaged to his childhood friend Gigi Franklin, who ran a law practice less than two blocks away.

"It's going to be great, as long as my beautiful fiancée and her mother don't kill each other first," Austin joked.

The two women had very strong personalities, and they rarely seemed to agree. Ms. Myrtle, as Gigi's mother was known to the younger generation, ran multiple boards and organizations on the island and was known for both her impeccable taste and impossibly high standards for everything, including her daughter.

"I bet Myrtle is thrilled to finally have a wedding to plan," Lottie Jefferson said, who was married to the town doctor. "And who would have guessed Gigi's perfect match was right here under her nose the entire time?"

It was no secret that Ms. Myrtle had spent years wishing Gigi had started a family instead of a law practice. Now, Gigi was getting a ready-made family, joining Austin and Luke, the boy she'd helped him adopt a year earlier.

Alice Barker, president of the garden club, was sitting closest to where Austin stood and reached over to touch his arm. "It's just so lovely that you both came back home after you went off and had your adventures. Gigi to open her law practice and you to help open this café. I don't know what the town would do without you two."

Chloe hoped no one had seen her wince at the reference to her brother's involvement with the café. But of course they hadn't, because she was invisible when he was around.

"Oh, I can't take any credit," Austin said. "This place is all Chloe."

She appreciated her brother's efforts, but she saw the looks on all their faces. They knew he was just being modest and that Chloe could never have opened this place without him.

And it was true. She had needed Austin to provide the capital to open the café because she didn't have any collateral to offer a bank for the business loan she'd applied for first. Then he'd gone one step further and helped her buy the building that housed the café to ensure she wouldn't get priced out of the place. She'd forever be grateful to him for his investments in her dream, but it was her café in every other way. Everything in it, from the heirloom china to the unique baked goods, which she made herself, had been her idea. Making that known was exactly why she needed to get on *The Next Great American Entrepreneur.*

Winning would mean she could buy him out and stand on her own. Austin was the last person who would try to steal the spotlight from her, and she was racked with guilt when she thought about wanting to buy him out. He wasn't just her brother; he was one of her very best friends. She just wanted to be known for something of her own. To stop living in Austin's shadow.

The ladies continued peppering Austin with questions about the wedding, and Chloe excused herself. As she went back to the register to ring up a young couple's purchases, Chloe wondered if she should talk to Piper about the final interview for the show.

Piper Presley was local country music star Callie Jackson's publicist. Although she was based in Nashville, she spent almost as much time on Big Dune Island these days thanks to her work with Callie and a younger local musician, Sienna Leighton, who Callie had helped land her first record deal. The president of their label had even moved to the island and married Callie's uncle, essentially establishing a satellite office on the tiny island they all called home.

Piper could probably coach her on what to say. The interview wouldn't involve the media, but it seemed like the same skill set. Chloe had a tendency to get overly excited and gush when she was nervous.

Chloe really wanted to do this all on her own, though, which was why she hadn't told anyone on the island she'd even applied for the show. Now she had to think of an excuse to be out of town and make sure Iris could cover her at the café. She hadn't taken a single vacation since opening her business seven years ago, so she knew there would be questions from Iris, Austin, her parents—everyone.

"Can I have those last two slices of strawberry cake?" Austin asked as he approached the glass case by the register that showcased the café's baked goods. "Luke aced his spelling test yesterday, so I promised something special for dessert tonight."

Chloe raised an eyebrow. "Don't you need three?" Although Austin and Luke weren't moving in with Gigi until after the wedding, she knew they all ate dinner together most nights.

Austin rolled his eyes. "Gigi says she's not eating anything with sugar until after the wedding. Apparently, Ms. Myrtle implied at the last fitting that Gigi's wedding dress was too tight."

"Yikes. Could you imagine our mother ever saying something like that?" Chloe shook her head.

"No, but don't you remember Dad making me drink those terrible banana protein shakes all the time in high school to put on weight because I was 'too scrawny'?"

She scrunched up her nose in disgust. Chloe might have been overlooked, but Austin had experienced the opposite: intense scrutiny. Their dad had been really tough on Austin growing up, all but forcing him to become a Major League Baseball player to realize his own unfulfilled dreams. Austin's relationship with their dad had been improving since Austin became a dad himself, but there were some things Austin would never forget, even if he did forgive.

"Take Gigi these," Chloe said, using tongs to grab two peanut butter cookies from the case and sliding them inside the bakery box with the two slices of strawberry cake. "I started making these for the ladies on the keto diet who come over after yoga. They're sweetened with dates, so she can indulge without the processed sugar."

Austin grinned as he took the pink box from her. "You're the best. I really don't know what this town would do without you. I'm really proud of you, sis."

It wasn't pride she felt at his statement, though. It was guilt. How could she explain to him that she wanted to buy him out of the café?

She could worry about that later. No sense in stressing over something that was so unlikely. She'd have to get herself on the show and then actually win against nine other entrepreneurs. If she managed to do that, *then* she could think about how to tell him.

"Tell Luke congratulations on acing his spelling test," she said, waving at Austin as he backed away to make room for another tourist couple to approach the cash register.

After she cashed them out, Chloe opened the email on her phone again. She only had ten days before she had to be in New York. As she racked her brain for excuses for leaving town on such short notice, her favorite New Yorker, Michael Russo, walked through the door.

He was on his phone, but he smiled and nodded in her direction as he headed toward his usual table along the wall near the back of the café. His short black hair was swept mostly to one side with just the right amount of product to hold it in place. The most formal person there, he wore a black suit jacket and a white button-down shirt with jeans and highly polished black dress shoes.

Michael was an investor in a local construction company, Thomas Construction, owned by Austin's best friend, and Callie's husband, Jesse. When Michael had first become involved with Jesse's company years earlier, he'd only dropped into town a few times a year to check in on things. Jesse didn't have a formal office, so he always met Michael at the coffee shop. Chloe had been immediately smitten with him, even if he was ten years older than her. He was smart and confident, and everyone paid attention when he entered a room. No one questioned his business acumen.

Every time Chloe saw him in action—meeting with Jesse or taking other business calls—she wondered what it would be like to command that sort of respect. In the beginning, it seemed like Jesse had been a little afraid of him, but now they were more like buddies when they sat at the table together. Because of his close involvement with Thomas Construction, Michael had been spending an increasing amount of time on the island over the past couple of years, so much so that he'd stopped staying at one of the hotels and bought a condo in a newer development on the south end of the island.

Chloe considered confiding in Michael about the show. He was the closest thing she had to an outside opinion since he was the only person in her circle, outside of Piper, who wasn't born and raised on Big Dune Island. Plus, he was a successful businessman.

She thought about it as she made his usual, a soy latte with an extra shot of espresso. He came into the café frequently when he was on the island, and they'd run into each other around town and chat, but she hesitated to call him a friend. He didn't seem to let anyone get that close.

Chloe was pretty sure he wouldn't tell anyone if she asked him to keep it confidential, but she also felt a little silly. He didn't strike her as the reality television type. Would he think she was ridiculous for wanting to participate in something like that?

He'd told her several times that she reminded him of his kid sisters, which was why she'd resigned herself to the fact that he'd never see her as a grown woman or someone he might want to date. He still made her heart flutter whenever he walked through the door, though, immediately placing a goofy smile on her face, but she knew it was one-sided. Being on what would probably amount to a stereotypical cheesy reality show certainly wasn't going to help things.

Nope, this was her secret to keep. Maybe the first big secret she'd ever kept in her life. Of course, if she got picked, the whole town would know. But that was a problem for future Chloe.

Here-and-now Chloe had coffee to serve and travel plans to make. And maybe just a second or two of ogling the most attractive man in town. It didn't hurt to look, right?

Chapter 2

Michael

"I hear congratulations are in order," Michael said as Chloe approached his table with his usual order.

Her eyebrows knit together. "Congratulations?"

"A little birdie told me you made it to the final interview round for *The Next Great American Entrepreneur*."

"Shh," she hissed, looking around the café before sliding into the seat across from him. She leaned forward. "How do you know that? I haven't told anyone."

He resisted the urge to chuckle. Chloe was known around town for her inability to keep secrets, so he couldn't believe she'd keep something this potentially life-changing under wraps.

"One of the producers is a friend from college. He knows I spend a lot of time down here and that it's a small town, so he asked if I knew you or had ever been to your café."

"And what did you say?" she asked, her big blue eyes frantically searching his face for any clue.

Michael shrugged. "I told him I grab a coffee here now and then." He kept his face neutral so she wouldn't know he was just teasing her.

Her face fell like he'd just told her Santa Claus didn't exist, and he instantly regretted toying with her emotions. She had that effect on him, though. He was always more relaxed when he was on the island, but Chloe made his day feel even lighter with her perpetually sunny demeanor.

"Don't worry," he said, giving her a reassuring smile. "I told him it's my favorite coffee shop on the entire East Coast."

Her face broke into a wide grin. "Only the East Coast?"

"Well, you know, I don't spend a lot of time anywhere else." He leaned back in his chair as he sipped his latte.

Chloe looked around the coffee shop again. It was quiet this afternoon, only a couple of tables by the front windows occupied by locals Michael recognized. He always opted for a table further back along the wall, so he and Chloe were safely out of earshot of the other patrons at the moment.

"Can we keep this between us?" she asked.

Us. Why did that one little word make the air feel like it was suddenly charged with electricity?

What had begun as a feeling of big brother protectiveness over Chloe, like he had for his own sisters, had been morphing into something more over the past year. His business partner Jesse was the one who'd clued him in to Chloe's flirting a few years earlier. But at thirty-seven years old then, Michael had been ten years her senior, and that had felt like a gulf that was too wide to bridge.

However, she'd changed a lot in the years since. The giggly, gossipy girl he'd met when he'd first started visiting

Big Dune now seemed like more of a mature woman and peer and less of a kid.

She'd grown into a savvy businesswoman too. He'd paid attention to how she'd introduced new concepts into the coffee shop, like increasing her baked goods since there was no other bakery in town and even offering wedding cakes. Chloe had also added personal touches, like the heirloom china and, more recently, a little section of merchandise with customizable serving platters and cutting boards. Island Coffee was far more than just a coffee shop—it was the center of the community. Which was exactly what he'd told his friend Chris who was casting the show.

Now, Michael mimed locking his lips and throwing away the key. "Done, but why the secrecy?"

Chloe looked down, playing with the hem of the floral-print apron around her waist. "It's going to sound bad."

"Let me be the judge of that. What is it?"

"I don't want to hurt my brother's feelings. The main reason I want to do the show is to be able to buy out his share in Island Coffee if I win."

"You two not getting along?" It was hard to imagine. He'd never met two siblings who got along so well, and he said that as someone who had four sisters he adored. Austin and Chloe were both incredibly upbeat, positive people. He'd never seen them bicker or fight like he did with his siblings. They were like puppies bounding around after each other.

She shook her head. "No, it's not that at all. You know Austin, he's the best."

"What then?"

Chloe glanced at the table full of local women near the front door, and he followed her gaze, waiting for her to reply.

"I don't feel like anyone around here takes me seriously. They all think this is Austin's café and that I just work here."

Michael frowned. Sure, he saw Austin in here all the time, but he was usually just raiding the bakery case or chatting it up with some of the locals. Michael had never seen Austin actually do any work in the café.

"He's more of a silent partner, right?" Jesse had once told Michael about how Austin had helped Chloe with the start-up capital.

Chloe sighed. "Yeah, he's really great as far as partners go. He lets me run the café however I see fit. He really just helped me out with the cash I needed to start the place."

"But he's kind of the golden boy, huh?" Michael asked.

"Exactly." Chloe nodded. "Everything he touches turns to gold. Always has."

"I'd say it runs in the family." He smiled when he saw Chloe blush. "You've made this place pretty successful. And clearly, I'm not the only one who's noticed. Making it to the final interviews for the show is no small feat. My buddy said it was really competitive."

Chloe was beaming now, her blue eyes lit up with their usual zest for life. He'd cheered her up, which made warmth spread across his body like the sun had come out from behind a cloud.

"Well, now that you know," she leaned in like they were planning a coup, "maybe you could help me figure out an excuse to go to New York next week for my interview. I never go anywhere, so everyone is going to think it's suspicious. I just don't want to tell them about the show until I've made it to the final stage with the hometown visits. Then I'll have to come clean."

"Have you ever been to the city?"

She shook her head.

"Well, we definitely have to fix that," he said, pausing to think. "What could you need to go to the city for?"

"All I could think of was a conference for café owners or women entrepreneurs or something like that, but they'll wonder why it's so last minute."

Michael sat up in his chair, a smile creeping across his face. "I've got an idea. My firm recently acquired a new hotel in Brooklyn. It's a little boutique place, and it has a coffee shop on the ground floor that's in desperate need of a makeover. We'll hire you to come consult with us for a few days."

She frowned, her brow furrowing. "No one is ever going to believe that. Why would you hire someone who owns a tiny coffee shop in a small town like this to tell you what to do with a café in New York City?"

"The hotel is in Park Slope, which is like a small town. It just happens to be near the city. We were already planning on hiring a consultant because reimagining hotels isn't our usual forte. We're usually opening something new, but The Perry has been in Park Slope for decades. A hotel consultant only knows how to make rooms and fancy restaurants profitable, not necessarily community oriented. You know how to do that, and that's what we need. I want it to feel like this place, so neighbors drop in, not just hotel guests. You're exactly what we need."

Skepticism was still painted across Chloe's face, but her blue eyes were taking on a sparkling gleam. She looked like she wanted to be excited, but he could tell she didn't feel confident enough to let herself believe she could do it.

"Chloe, you can do this. I would ask you to do it even if you didn't need to be in New York for the show. I just hadn't thought of it yet."

Her mouth opened, then closed, then opened again. "Wait, are you saying you actually want me to consult with you? This isn't just a cover story. You really want me to do it?"

"Yes, that's exactly what I'm saying. I'll have to check our budget, but we could probably pay you in the neighborhood of twenty-k for consulting services. You could stay for a couple of days after your interview to look at the place, and I'll show you around the city. You can't come to New York for the first time and not see the sights."

She was staring at him open mouthed now. "You'd pay me twenty-thousand dollars? To do what, Michael? I don't even know what a consultant does."

"Honestly, I don't know what they do half the time either, other than send me a bill for their services." He smiled, trying to put her at ease. "We'd go see the space, and you'd tell me what kind of furniture you'd buy, how you'd arrange it, what we should serve. That sort of thing. We could spend some time in the neighborhood so you get a feel for it, and then you could help me figure out how to engage the community there the way you have here."

"I mean, it sounds amazing," she said, shaking her head, "but I'm totally not qualified. Won't you get in trouble with your partners for hiring some rando?"

He laughed. "No, I won't get in trouble for hiring a 'rando' because you're not that. You're a very successful café owner who's created something that's an integral part of her community, and that's exactly the kind of expertise we need. Don't worry. No one questions my decisions. I know what I'm doing."

"Okay, I guess," she said, her face finally returning to normal. "My interview is on Friday morning, so maybe I could stay through the weekend? I just have to make sure Iris can cover the café while I'm gone."

"Is the show covering your travel?"

"Yeah, they gave me the name and number of someone to call, but I haven't done it yet. I was still figuring out how to pull it off."

Michael pulled his wallet out and extracted one of his business cards. "Do you have a pen?" She fished one out of her apron and handed it over. He flipped the card to the blank back side and wrote the name and number of the woman who handled travel at his firm. "Call Jeanie and tell her to book you a hotel for Friday and Saturday night. I'm assuming the show will put you up on Thursday night so you can interview Friday morning, then they'll probably want to fly you back that day. Tell them you're staying the weekend and covering your own costs and ask if they can book your flight back for Sunday instead. If they give you any trouble, just tell Jeanie to book your flight back."

He held the card out for her to take, and her hand brushed against his as she reached for it. She fumbled the card, dropping it on the table. Did he make her that nervous, or was she just questioning herself? She was going to need to be more confident in her interview if she wanted to make the show. He probably should have talked her up more to Chris, but he still had time for that.

"Thanks," she said, holding up the card. "I seriously can't believe the day I'm having. It's kind of incredible."

"You've earned it," he said, holding up his cup to toast her. "We're going to have a great weekend in the greatest city in the world, and you're going to get yourself on that TV show."

We. He'd just referred to them as a *we.* He hadn't referred to himself with any woman as a *we* in a long time.

Women were pleasant distractions from work for a date or two, but he never let himself become part of a *we*. Too messy.

"From your lips to God's ears," Chloe said, her smile spreading wide. The local women from the front table were approaching the cash register now, so she stood. "I'll let you know when I've made my travel arrangements."

He nodded before she turned and scurried off to the register. One of the older women in the group was giving him a disapproving stare now, an eyebrow raised.

He knew the locals were all a little suspicious of him and his motives, even if he had helped save Thomas Construction, one of their beloved local businesses. If he'd learned anything in his years of visiting the island, it was that these people watched way too many Hallmark movies where the guy from the big city only showed up to bulldoze buildings or wreak havoc on Main Street. He'd seen the movies too. He had four sisters, after all.

But he'd saved a business here, not closed one. Maybe that wasn't what the disapproving stare was for, though. Maybe it was that Chloe had been sitting with him.

He'd once remarked to Jesse that she was like the community's granddaughter because of all the older men and women who congregated in her café daily. There was a group of retired men who had coffee there at the same time every morning, and the garden club and book club both met there as well. He could tell by the way they doted on her that they all still saw her as a child. Maybe the television show would change that and show them what an incredible businesswoman she'd become.

Picking up his phone, he figured it wouldn't hurt for him to be a little more direct with Chris. He snapped a photo of Chloe interacting with the women at the ornate, antique brass register, a smile lighting up her face. The angle was wide so Chris could see the ambience of the cozy café, with its cabinet filled with homemade baked goods, antique china lining shelves on the walls, fresh flowers on every table, and original pressed tin ceiling.

> You gotta come see this place for yourself.
> If she makes it to hometown visits, do you
> travel with the crew? I'll show you around.

Michael hit send, feeling like he'd done his good deed for the day. If Chloe wanted to be on the show, he'd do everything he could to get her there and help her win.

Chapter 3

Chloe

When Michael had first said he knew a producer on the show, Chloe's heart had leapt. Could that help her get on?

But she'd dismissed the thought almost immediately. She didn't want anyone's help with this. She wanted to prove to herself, and everyone else, that she could do it on her own.

She was thankful, however, that she didn't have to tackle New York City on her own. Michael was providing her with the perfect cover story, and she still couldn't believe he was really going to pay her to give him some ideas for his hotel café. Maybe if she didn't make it onto *The Next Great American Entrepreneur*, she could become a real consultant and make enough money to buy out Austin that way.

From inside her apartment above the café, Chloe heard

the clack of heels climbing the staircase outside, and her heart started thumping in rhythm. She'd decided to tell her best friend Reagan Hartman about the show tonight so she could help Chloe pick out clothes for her big trip.

The door was open since Chloe was expecting her, and Reagan entered holding a bottle of rosé.

"I come bearing wine," she said, opening her arms to hug Chloe.

"Good, because we might need it," Chloe laughed, moving into the small kitchen to grab two glasses.

"Trust me, after the day I've had, I definitely need it." Reagan unscrewed the top off the wine and poured them each a generous portion.

"Tough day at the office?"

Reagan had been working as Gigi's legal assistant since she'd opened her law office on the island about five years earlier. Chloe knew she loved her job, but it could also be really stressful.

"Just some crazy deadlines, but we made it."

Reagan flopped down on Chloe's pale pink couch.

Chloe came to sit near her in a vintage floral-upholstered armchair she'd thrifted from one of the island's antique stores and re-covered. The apartment had a separate bedroom area, but the living room, kitchen, and dining room were one large space with high ceilings and exposed beams. Large windows filled the wall overlooking Main Street.

Chloe loved that she only had to stumble downstairs in the morning to start baking fresh goods for the day, and the rent was reasonable since her brother now owned the whole building. Well, all but the one percent interest she held thanks to her much smaller contribution, although she was proud that she'd been able to do that. He'd still have his investment in the building, even if she bought him out of his interest in the café. The building had several other tenants, and she'd still be paying him the rent they'd agreed on for both the café and her apartment.

"So, what's the big news?" Reagan asked, interrupting her thoughts. "Did you score a cake for a big destination wedding? I heard bookings for weddings here are up like, triple, after Callie's wedding was splashed across *Vogue*. I bet we'll get even more celebrities coming to the island to get married."

"No, it's not that. Although we are getting more cake orders now that everyone's seen Callie's wedding cake." It was yet another success Chloe had trouble claiming as her own, since it was her famous friend who'd gotten her into a magazine for her cake design. It made it hard to say whether the cake was featured because of its artistry or simply because it was *the* Callie Jackson's wedding cake.

"So spill. What is it?" Reagan asked.

Chloe took a deep breath. She needed to just get it all out at once, so she said in a rush, "I applied to be on a new reality show for entrepreneurs, and I've made it to the interview round. I leave for New York on Thursday for one last interview, and then they'll come here for a site visit if I'm selected and filming will start soon after. The winner gets $750,000 for their business, and I need you to help me figure out what to wear."

Reagan had stopped sipping her wine and was staring at Chloe in astonishment. "Clo, that's amazing." Her wine nearly sloshed over the rim of her glass as she got up and set it on the coffee table and then fell on top of Chloe in a giant embrace. Now it was Chloe's wine that spilled everywhere.

She laughed as Reagan climbed off her and perched on

the edge of the sofa. "Tell me all about it. How does it work? How many people are left?"

Chloe told her what she knew about the show.

"Is it just for cafés?"

"I don't think so," Chloe said. "The initial application was just for small business owners, anyone under one million a year in revenue."

"Why didn't you tell me you applied? I'm so proud of you, Clo."

"I didn't think I'd get this far. I didn't want to tell anyone in case I didn't make it."

"Well, of course you'd make it," Reagan said, picking up her wine glass again to take a drink. "Island Coffee is a pillar of the community."

"I don't know about that." Chloe had never really thought of it that way. Ms. Myrtle was a pillar of the community. Big Dune Island wouldn't be the same without her. She made things tick. But Island Coffee? She just served people absurd amounts of caffeine and sugary treats.

Reagan nodded, frowning at Chloe like she was clueless. "Umm, right. It's where every important thing in town gets dreamed up and hashed over. It's somehow magically both a place for locals and a must-see for visitors. It's the heart of Main Street, Clo. Don't you know that?"

Blushing, Chloe looking down at her wine glass, intently studying the pink reflection staring back at her. Reagan and her other friends frequented the café, but no one had ever talked to her about it like this.

"Well," Chloe said, "I'll be sure they talk to you if they do a hometown visit. I need all the cheerleaders I can get."

"You've told Callie and Piper, right? With their endorsement, you're a shoo-in."

It was then that Chloe realized it was probably the

publicity from Callie's wedding that had even gotten her this far. If the producers had done an internet search on the café, the articles on Callie's wedding would have been first to come up. She couldn't help being a little deflated at the nagging idea that maybe she'd only gotten in because of that. That's something the producers would have done, right? She hadn't mentioned it in her application, but of course they would have searched all the businesses online. It wasn't even her café's website that came up first in search results—it was articles from *Vogue* and *People* that mentioned the wedding. She'd looked.

Too late now to change that, though. She'd just have to show them her café was more than one celebrity wedding cake.

"I actually didn't tell them about Callie and Jesse's wedding cake. I kind of wanted to get in on my own merits, you know?"

Reagan nodded. She knew how Chloe felt about living in Austin's shadow and wanting to prove herself. "I get it. You've earned this all on your own, even without that."

"What I really need help with is figuring out what to wear for this interview. My closet looks like it exploded. Help?"

"I've got you," Reagan said, standing up. "You need something that conveys your unique charm but shows them you mean business."

"I'm not sure if I have clothes that say that." Chloe laughed, following Reagan into her bedroom.

"It's going to be cold up there this time of year, so layers are key." Reagan was already starting to sift through piles on the bed.

In the end, Reagan chose a knee-length dress with blue and purple flowers on a black background and told Chloe she'd loan her a black leather jacket and black suede booties to give an edge to the otherwise feminine look. It really did sound perfect.

"So when are you going to tell Austin and your parents?" Reagan sat on the edge of the bed as Chloe changed out of the dress.

"There's no point in telling them unless I get the hometown visit. Michael actually gave me a good cover story to explain to my family this weekend why I'm going to New York." She replayed her talk with Michael and the offer to have her consult on his hotel project.

"Finally," Reagan sighed. "It's about time you two are going to stop flirting and just do the dang thing."

Chloe shook her head. "It's not like that. It's all business. He's just helping me out so I have a cover story."

"You said he offered to show you around the city, and he got you a lucrative consulting gig like he was ordering a glass of water. The man is into you."

"He is not. He sees me like a little sister. I think I'm actually the same age as his youngest sister. We have absolutely nothing in common." Even as she said the words, a little part of her hoped she was wrong but was certain she was not.

"It's a tale as old as time." Reagan shook her head. "The brother's best friend always falls for the younger sister eventually."

"Well, he's not even really friends with Austin, and he definitely treats me like a kid sister."

"You'll see." Reagan pointed her wine glass in Chloe's direction. "You two will get to New York, on his turf, and he'll make his move."

Chloe felt a tingle all the way from the top of her head to her fingertips and toes. It really did sound like a movie, and she'd give anything for the starring role. Her business dreams and her more personal ones all coming to fruition over the course of one weekend? It was too good to be true.

Throwing a stray blouse from her dresser at Reagan, Chloe laughed it off. "I just want to get on this TV show and collect my consulting check. Anything else is just icing on the cake."

"So you're open to the possibility?" Reagan wiggled her eyebrows suggestively.

"Get out of here." Chloe pointed at the door, smiling. "My alarm will be ringing before I know it."

Reagan gathered her belongings, promising to drop off the jacket and booties over the weekend.

"Good luck with the fam," Reagan said as she hugged Chloe on her way out the door.

Closing the door behind Reagan, Chloe leaned against it. She'd heard all the clichés about New York being the city where dreams come true, and in that moment, she found herself hoping it might happen for her too.

Chloe's family had lunch together after church every Sunday, and it was usually the only time she got away from Island Coffee since it was closed that day. This week, she was with her parents, Austin, Gigi, and Luke at Captain Kellers, a casual seafood restaurant with a large deck overlooking the intercoastal waterway. They were seated outside, enjoying the early March weather that within a month would turn too hot, humid, and mosquito-infested for outdoor dining.

After everyone placed their orders, Chloe cleared her

throat. "I wanted to share some exciting news with everyone."

They all turned to look at her, each face telegraphing their surprise that she would have anything new to report that they didn't already know. After all, it was a small town, and they generally saw each other multiple times a week when the others came into the café to grab coffee or snacks.

She dove in before she lost her nerve. "I've been offered an amazing opportunity to consult for Michael's firm on a coffee shop he's redesigning in a hotel the firm just bought in Park Slope," she said in a rush. When no one said anything, she added, "That's in Brooklyn, and I'm going to be traveling up there next weekend to see it in person."

Gigi was the first to jump in. "That's incredible! Which hotel is it?" She'd lived in Manhattan for the first few years of her legal career before returning home to Big Dune Island.

"The Perry," Chloe replied. She'd studied every picture she could find of the hotel online. There were photos of the current coffee shop space, and she already had some ideas for how to redesign it so it was more welcoming. It looked like a dark, uninviting place in the few photos she'd found.

"You're traveling to New York alone?" Her mother's face was immediately etched with concern, lines forming between her eyebrows. Although her parents had traveled extensively across the country to watch her brother play baseball over the years, they were both born and raised on Big Dune Island and still harbored some stereotypical beliefs about the safety of larger cities.

"No." Chloe shook her head. "Michael will be there too." She didn't mention that she was going up Thursday night and wouldn't see him until after her interview on Friday. The show had offered to reimburse everyone for cab fare, but Michael's assistant had booked her a car and told Chloe someone would meet her in baggage claim to help her with her luggage. It was like something straight out of a movie.

"No," her dad said. "You're not going to the city with some man we barely know."

"Dad," Austin interjected, "we all know Michael. I feel comfortable knowing he'll be watching out for her up there."

Their father frowned. "He's a man, Austin. That's all the information I need to know. I don't want my little girl off on a trip with him."

"I'm not a little girl, and we're not going on a trip together," Chloe said, but she didn't think they heard her as they continued sparring back and forth. Aside from Gigi, no one had even celebrated the fact that she'd been asked to consult on such an important project.

"I was younger than Chloe when I moved to the city. She'll be fine," Gigi said, grabbing a hushpuppy from the basket in the middle of the table and turning to Chloe. "Just walk with purpose like you know where you're going, and maybe don't ride the subway alone. Not on your first trip, anyway. I wish I could go with you. I miss the city."

Chloe's father frowned at Gigi, no doubt irritated that she'd undermined his position.

"You miss the city, huh?" Austin teased his fiancée, putting an arm around her and squeezing her closer. "What does it have that we don't have here?"

"Good Thai food," she said, smiling up at him before turning back to Chloe. "If you have time, make Michael take you to The Thai Palace in Hell's Kitchen. It's divine."

"I don't like this," Mr. Beckett said flatly. "Why would

he want you to consult on a coffee shop in Brooklyn? It sounds suspicious to me."

Chloe tried not to let the hurt show on her face. Was it really that hard to believe that she might be able to help Michael with the café? Admittedly, she'd wondered the same thing at first, but it stung more coming from her dad. Like she'd been right to doubt herself, because her own father didn't even believe in her.

"He wants her help because she runs one of the most successful businesses in town," Austin told their father before turning to her. "I think it's great. I'm proud of you, Clo."

"Think he needs advice on how to run a hotel?" Luke asked, looking up from the game he'd been playing on his Nintendo Switch since they'd sat down. "Tell him I run a very successful B&B."

This lightened the mood around the table, everyone laughing and shaking their heads at the ten-year-old's offer. Luke had inherited the Salty Breeze B&B from his grandmother a year and a half ago, and although it was held in a trust until he was eighteen, Austin and Gigi were teaching him about running the business little by little.

"I'll be sure and tell him you're available," Chloe said.

Luke nodded and went back to his game.

Chloe's mother turned to her now, the initial shock of the announcement no longer visible on her face. "I'm sure it's a wonderful opportunity, honey. I just worry about you traveling alone with a man we barely know. Just be careful."

"I will be, Mom. I'm not a kid. I'm thirty." She directed the last part at her father.

"You'll always be my little girl," her dad grumbled, sitting back in his chair and folding his arms over his chest. "Sue me for wanting to protect you."

"I appreciate the concern, Dad. But I promise I know what I'm doing. It's going to be great. I've always wanted to see the city."

Gigi launched into a laundry list of all her must-see, must-eat New York recommendations, and the conversation at the table took a more pleasant turn. By the time they finished their meal, she had the blessing of her entire family. Not that she needed it, but it was still nice to have. She loved her family, and she just wanted to make them proud. To make them see her as competent and capable. And yes, successful.

Next stop: the City of Dreams.

Chapter 4

Michael

"You hired the woman who works at the coffee shop on the island to consult on the Park Slope hotel?" Michael's business partner, John, asked after he called to say they'd be up for the weekend.

"She doesn't just work at the coffee shop. She owns and runs it, and it's the busiest place on Main Street," Michael told him. He knew John wouldn't tell him no, which was why he hadn't cleared it with him first.

Michael's track record spoke for itself. It wasn't the first time he'd gone out on a limb with his partners either. The last time was to allow Jesse the chance to restore historic homes on the island a few years ago, and that had turned into a whole new division for Thomas Construction that was both profitable and busy.

John harrumphed into the phone. "It's probably the only place in town to get coffee."

Outside of the few hotels on the island with their own kiosks, that was true, but Michael knew that wasn't why Island Coffee was so successful. Chloe was the reason, with the way she'd made it feel like the town's living room, where everyone was invited and welcome. And that's what he wanted to replicate in Park Slope at The Perry.

"And we want the café at The Perry to feel like the only place in town to get coffee, even if it isn't," Michael countered. "We want to be an extension of the neighborhood. A cozy, friendly place where moms can get together after school drop-off."

"Fine," John said. "Just take Alessandra with you. She's going to handle the design work on that one."

Alessandra was the designer they used for all their high-end projects. He and Alessandra had dated briefly several years back, but neither had been in the market for a long-term relationship. Since then, they'd taken each other as plus-ones to industry events, weddings, and social gatherings as a way to avoid getting too serious with anyone else. She was the perfect plus-one because she didn't want anything more and could work a room. He'd done some of his best networking with her by his side. She was, however, territorial, and didn't appreciate it when he took someone else to a function instead of her. The time he spent on Big Dune Island had given him some much-needed perspective, which had made him realize how shallow and performative she could be.

The idea of Chloe and Alessandra meeting gave him pause. They were opposites in nearly every way, from their height to their personalities, and Alessandra was not going to like sharing his attention. Left to her own devices, Alessandra would steamroll right over Chloe. Thankfully, he'd be there to ensure that didn't happen.

"Did you get the numbers I sent you on the warehouse project in Jacksonville?" Michael asked, changing the subject.

John said he and the other partners had approved the budget on the warehouse the firm had purchased out of foreclosure the previous week. "I guess that means you'll be spending more time working from down there?"

That was exactly what it meant. Where he'd dreaded visits to the tiny island ten years ago when he'd first started checking in on their investment in Thomas Construction and its associated development projects, he now enjoyed the time he spent there and considered himself a part-time resident.

"Yeah, we have those two new rehabs on Victorians downtown, and we still need to finish up the last few houses in that development on the south end. By the time Jesse finishes the rehabs, the warehouse project should be in full swing. He'll come down and work on the plans and then hire a local crew to work on the build-out."

The plan was to renovate the long-vacant warehouse into industrial-style lofts in downtown Jacksonville. Although the building wasn't on the Historic Register, Jesse had made the case that it was still an important part of the neighborhood. They'd leave exposed brickwork in the units, along with exposed ducts in the high ceilings. There was nothing else like it in town, and it would serve the growing number of professionals who didn't want to live farther out of the city at the beach and commute into town every day.

From where he sat at his desk in his condo on Big Dune Island, the ocean stretched out before him, just beyond a line of dunes and a wide stretch of sandy beach. The blue sky seemed to stretch on forever from his perch on the sixth floor. Sunlight didn't even make it into the windows of his twenty-sixth floor condo on the Upper East Side most days thanks to the towering buildings around his that blocked the light.

"Sounds like you have it under control down there."

"Yep, we're all good here."

Sure, there were things he missed about the city. Especially his mom and sisters. He really should bring them down to visit. He'd been saying that for years, but admittedly, he found it difficult to slow down long enough to do anything outside of work. He always did Sunday dinner with them when he was in the city for the weekend, though, and he was looking forward to seeing them this weekend to catch up.

Michael's phone vibrated on the desk, and he looked down to see an incoming text from Alessandra.

> I hear we're going to be working together on Saturday. Dinner at Chez Vincent after? I'll make a reservation. See you soon.

He would normally say yes to Alessandra's invitation so he could get the latest scoop on who was looking to poach whom from which firm and which projects were about to go out for bid. Not this time, though. He had the entire weekend mapped out for Chloe so he could show her his favorite parts of the city. Alessandra, however, was not going to take that well, so he thought of how to word it without lying to her. That wasn't something he did.

> Sorry, can't this time. Our consultant is only in town for the weekend, and I have to get everything squared away before I head back to Florida on Monday. I'll see you Saturday at The Perry.

There. What he'd written was all true and hopefully wouldn't ruffle any feathers. Alessandra wasn't someone who heard "no" very often.

When his phone buzzed again seconds later, he expected it to be Alessandra but smiled when he saw Chloe's name instead.

> Just landed!

Included was a photo of the city skyline from an airplane window. Michael could imagine her squealing when she saw it, her big blue eyes lit up with excitement. She'd probably scared the people around her on the plane. He had some regret that he hadn't been able to fly with her, but there was a planning board meeting in Jacksonville that evening he couldn't miss.

Leaning back in his chair, he smiled as he texted her back.

> The city isn't ready for you! Get a good night's sleep so you can kill it tomorrow. I'll see you after, and we'll start our grand tour.

He'd asked Jeanie at his office to get Chloe a car from the airport. Although he was certain she could navigate getting her own cab or rideshare, he wanted her to experience feeling like the red carpet was being rolled out for her. She'd shared how much her family had revolved around her brother and his ascent to the major leagues, so now it was Chloe's turn to feel special.

His phone buzzed again on his desk, and he didn't miss how his excitement waned when he saw Jesse's name instead of Chloe's.

I'm downstairs.

Michael texted back that he'd be right down before closing his laptop and gathering the initial renderings they'd worked on for the warehouse. When he got downstairs, he noticed Jesse was dressed much more casually than he was. Leaning against his truck, typing something on his phone, Jesse had on khaki pants with a pale blue polo tucked in. Michael was in a full suit.

"Too much?" Michael asked, gesturing at his clothes as he approached.

"For a funeral? No," Jesse laughed. "For the City of Jacksonville planning board? Yes."

Sure, meetings like that on the island were fairly casual. He'd learned that lesson early on. This was the first time they were working on a project in Jacksonville, though, and he'd assumed it was more like New York. Jacksonville had an international airport, and he'd been surprised to read that it was the largest city in the country by land mass.

Michael groaned. "I should change, huh?"

Jesse nodded. "If you don't want to look like a big corporate developer who only cares about the bottom line, yes."

Michael turned to walk back to the condo building, Jesse on his heels. Life really was so much easier when he was indeed a big corporate developer who only cared about the bottom line. Okay, maybe not as personally fulfilling, but definitely easier. He understood people who negotiated with spreadsheets and profit and loss statements, making decisions based on numbers alone. When you had to factor in emotion and sentimentality, the formulas weren't as cut and dried.

"You realize I've had to buy a whole new wardrobe just for here?" Michael asked as they entered the elevator.

"I think you've even gotten some color in your face," Jesse teased. "You looked like a vampire when you first started coming down here."

"Yeah, my skin cancer odds have probably increased tenfold in the past ten years." Michael was being sarcastic, but it was probably true.

"I bet your Vitamin D levels are up, though," Jesse countered.

Michael didn't tell him that his Vitamin D levels really had been low on some blood work a few years ago. Refused to give him the satisfaction.

Less than ten minutes later, they were in Michael's Audi A8 on the way to Jacksonville for the meeting. He'd splurged on the car when he'd bought the condo, knowing he'd be spending more time on the island. It was the first time in his life he'd lived outside of New York City, even if it was only part-time, and the first time he'd needed to own a car. He'd joked it was a mid-life crisis, although he hoped being forty didn't actually mean he was middle-aged.

He and Jesse had moved on to discussing the parking variance they would be requesting at the meeting when Michael's car announced an incoming text from Chloe. And then another. And another. Rapid-fire, at a rate now only surpassed by the staccato of his heartbeat.

He could feel Jesse looking at him as he punched at the screen in the console to dismiss the messages. Glancing in his direction, Michael saw Jesse had raised an eyebrow but couldn't read the rest of his face.

"Just some questions for our big trip to the city this weekend, I'm sure," Michael said. Jesse had already heard the news from Austin earlier in the week.

Michael had been pleasantly surprised by how supportive both Austin and Jesse had been about Chloe consulting with him. That they trusted him with their sister —Jesse had always said she was like the sister he never had —meant a lot. They'd probably feel differently if they knew how his feelings for her had recently begun changing, however.

"It's a big opportunity for her," Jesse said. "Would you have imagined when you first visited Big Dune Island all those years ago that you'd be taking advice on your business from one of us?"

"Probably not." He most definitely would not have.

"What do you do when you go to New York?"

"What do you mean?" Michael asked as they drove over the bridge that would take them through a series of barrier islands before dropping them onto the interstate into Jacksonville. "I go back up there when there's work to do."

"I mean, what's the one thing you have to do every time you're back in New York? Is there a bagel place you miss or something like that?"

Michael laughed. "Why does everyone think all of us New Yorkers have a special bagel shop we can't live without?"

"Because you argue about it with every New Yorker we run into."

"The correct answer is Best Bagels on West 35th."

"I wouldn't know," Jesse said. "I've never been to the city."

"We'll have to change that one of these days. Maybe the whole gang can come up for a weekend when the hotel reopens so you can admire Chloe's work on its café."

"Sounds good to me. Callie will probably be going stir-crazy in a few months." Jesse and Callie had welcomed a baby girl—Clara, named after Callie's mother—a few weeks earlier, and Callie was taking a break from touring to stay home with the baby.

"I go see my mom and my sisters," Michael said quietly. Thoughts of Jesse's little girl reminded him of the four younger sisters he'd helped raise after his father's passing. "That's the one thing I always have to do when I'm back in New York."

Chapter 5

Chloe

From the air, the city had looked even bigger and more imposing than Chloe had imagined from seeing it on television and in movies. Soaring steel-and-glass buildings were crammed together, jutting up at competing heights like the straws she jammed into the glass container on the café's counter. She'd read somewhere that Manhattan was roughly the same size as Big Dune Island in terms of land mass, but it couldn't look more different.

She'd been to Atlanta to watch Austin play baseball, and cities like Nashville and Chicago for bachelorette parties, but there was just something different about New York City. She had felt the buzzing energy of the city from the time her plane landed at JFK to meeting up with the driver holding her name on a little white sign by baggage claim. It was going to be an amazing weekend, whether she made the show or not.

Ricardo, her driver—she had a driver!—took her carry-on luggage from her and escorted her out to a waiting black Cadillac SUV, opening the door for her like she was a visiting dignitary.

"There's water in the cupholder for you, miss," he said as she climbed into the car. "You can also control the temperature there." He pointed to controls built into the back of the console.

"Thank you." She settled into the black leather seat, buckling her seat belt as he closed her door and went around to the back to load her luggage.

Ricardo told her it would be about an hour before they got to her hotel, which surprised her because the city had looked so close as the plane came in to land. It wasn't long before she figured out they'd be in traffic the whole way, inching along in a sea of yellow cabs and other assorted vehicles.

Chloe decided to review her notes for the interview until they got closer to the city. After she'd confirmed her trip with the coordinator, she'd received an email with more information about this final round of interviews, which included news that the show would have three judges. It would be the first time she'd be in front of them, which meant they could ask her anything about her business, even basic stuff she'd already covered in previous rounds. Fortunately, she knew her business inside and out, and she'd rehearsed her elevator pitch in front of the mirror at least four dozen times over the past week.

Since *The Next Great American Entrepreneur* was in its first rieason, she'd done an internet search for people talking about casting on other business shows like *Shark Tank* and *The Profit*. She'd been pleased to find people who had gone through the casting process and then posted about their experience, including lists of questions they'd been asked. From there, she'd pulled together a list of nearly one hundred questions, which she began to rehearse in her mind now.

She was about a dozen questions in when she looked up and realized they were about to enter a tunnel. After a minute or two in the tunnel, she could see daylight ahead.

Looking at her in the rearview mirror, Ricardo said, "We just went under the East River, and now we're in the city." She'd told him when they'd met in the airport that it was her first time in New York.

As he expertly navigated between cabs and pedestrians darting across crosswalks, Chloe leaned to look out the window and followed the vertical lines of buildings that seemed to reach endlessly toward the sky. The tallest buildings on Big Dune Island were just three stories high, thanks to the local height ordinance meant to prevent development like this.

The energy here was palpable as they glided down the streets, people walking with determination, just like Gigi had told her to do, and cars zipping around them when they slowed to make a turn. Everyone was in a hurry. Like they all had somewhere to be, something important to do. It was exciting and overwhelming all at once.

Chloe couldn't believe how many corner markets there were—"bodegas," Gigi had called them—their produce piled up in bins outside on the sidewalks. There was one on nearly every corner. Then every few blocks, there was a florist shop with flowers of every color billowing from stacked stands. Between them were coffee shops, drug stores, souvenir shops, and restaurants serving Indian, Thai, Greek, Italian, and everything in between. And, of course, dozens of the city's famous New York bagel stores.

Every storefront on every block they passed for the next twenty minutes in stop-and-go traffic was occupied. The sheer number of restaurants and stores in the limited area was incredible. She couldn't even fathom how many people had to live here to keep that many places in business.

Ricardo pulled up outside her hotel, the Arlo Midtown, and told her to wait until he came around to help her out. After he handed off her luggage to a bellman, she was escorted into the hotel and directed to the front desk for check-in. While the woman at the desk programmed the keycards for her room, Chloe glanced at the people who milled around the lobby. Were any of them her competition? The show had probably put them all up in the same hotel.

After the woman told her about hours for the restaurant and bar, the location of the gym, and how to access the room service menu, Chloe made her way to the bank of elevators nearby. The lobby of the hotel was very nice, but it was nothing compared to the room she entered on the twenty-fourth floor. The room itself held a king bed with crisp white linens and a dark wood surround. She walked across the plush carpet and took in the enormous bathroom with its glass shower and double sink before continuing over to the closet to store her luggage on the provided stand.

On the far side of the room, huge windows along one whole wall made the room light and bright, and a door led out onto a terrace with a hammock. This high up, she thought she'd have more of a view, but taller buildings rose all around her.

Walking out onto the balcony, however, the view improved as she looked up and down the street and took it all in. Even up here, a cacophony of sounds filled the air—horns honking, the whine of a siren, and the sound of a jackhammer somewhere nearby. She hadn't been able to hear any of it inside the room, so at least it wouldn't affect her sleep. Main Street in Big Dune was practically dormant outside her own apartment window at night.

Lying in the hammock, just to try it out, Chloe reveled in feeling like she was right in the middle of all the action. She could see how you could get used to the soundtrack of the city. It was probably hard to feel alone in a place like this, with so much life all around you. She thought it would make her feel small, but she was surprisingly energized by it all.

Chloe considered snapping a photo of her terrace to send to Michael but rejected the idea. She'd already texted him a photo of the city she'd taken from the airplane window and then a few selfies from around the airport with fun travel quotes on the walls and an "I love New York" store filled with T-shirts and other souvenirs with the iconic phrase. She'd probably gone a bit overboard.

She should let him know she'd arrived okay, though, right? Just one more wouldn't hurt, even though he'd only replied to her first photo of the aerial view of the city. Snapping a photo of the balcony that showed off the hammock and her view down West 38th Street, she shot off a quick text.

Made it, and I even have a balcony!

Disappointed when the three little dots didn't appear to show he was replying, Chloe went back inside. She needed to finish looking through questions, review her financials so they were fresh in her mind, order room service, and get to bed at a decent time.

If she didn't get cast for the show, it wasn't going to be

because she wasn't prepared or hadn't tried her hardest. She was going to leave the interview tomorrow knowing she'd done everything she could.

Chloe had hardly slept, but she was so excited—and nervous!—for the day ahead that she was wide awake as she walked out the front door of the hotel. She'd mapped out the walking route on her phone, and it was only a few blocks to get to the building where the interviews were being held.

The cool morning air nipped at her cheeks, and she pulled her coat a little tighter as she started out. Warm weather had already arrived on the island, and in a few weeks, the spring break tourists would begin arriving to lie on the beach and wade in the water. In Manhattan, however, it was still winter. The leather jacket Reagan had loaned her was meant more for fashion than for warmth, so she'd borrowed a wool peacoat from Gigi. The video screen in the hotel elevator had said it was only thirty-eight degrees outside, and it felt every bit that cold. She was very thankful for the fleece-lined tights she'd ordered to go under her dress after checking the forecast a week ago.

Chloe smiled at people coming toward her on the sidewalk but noticed no one made eye contact. Most had ear buds in or large headphones stretched across their heads, backpacks or large tote bags over their shoulders. They were all singularly focused, like they knew exactly where they were going and were ready to get there.

Well, so was she. A left on 8th and then a right on 39th, and Chloe had arrived at the address she'd been given. She gave the guard her name and was directed up to the ninth floor.

Once in the elevator, she checked her reflection in the mirrored doors and smoothed her shoulder-length brunette hair, which she'd styled with loose flat-iron curls. When she arrived on the ninth floor, she followed the signs down the hallway to a door marked with the show's logo. She paused, taking a deep breath to calm her nerves. This was it—her big chance. Pushing the door open revealed a plain square room with no windows and stark white walls. There was no artwork, no décor of any kind. At a folding table directly in front of her, a young woman sat with a few papers spread before her. Behind her, only one other woman sat in one of the half dozen folding chairs against the wall.

"Good morning," Chloe said, smiling as she approached the table. "I'm Chloe Beckett."

The woman ran a finger down a list that appeared to have about twenty names on it. Chloe hadn't known how many people they would call back for interviews, but if that was it, she might have as good as a fifty percent chance of making it. Excitement surged through her, and she was glad she'd limited herself to one cup of coffee that morning. She had a tendency to talk too fast and get a little overly bubbly when she was enthusiastic—or nervous—about something, and caffeine would only have made it worse

"I've got you all checked in," the woman said. She seemed bored with the task she'd been assigned, unwilling to offer any additional information or encouragement. "You can take a seat, and they'll call you back when it's your turn."

Unlike everyone else Chloe had encountered since walking out of the hotel, the woman in the folding chair along the wall gave her a big smile. "Hi, I'm Brianna," she said, holding out her hand.

"Chloe," she said, reaching to shake Brianna's hand. "Nice to meet you."

Brianna looked to be about the same age as Chloe, maybe a little older. Her face was warm and friendly, and she was wearing a pair of wide-legged black pants with a fuchsia sweater. Definitely on par with the dress and black leather jacket she and Reagan had picked out. Chloe had been a little worried she'd show up to find everyone else in full business suits.

"I was starting to think they weren't going to let any of us meet," Brianna said quietly, like she didn't want the woman who'd checked them in to overhear. "Like maybe they staggered our times so we wouldn't run into each other."

"You haven't seen anyone else yet?" Chloe asked as she shrugged off her long winter coat and laid it across a chair before sitting one seat over from Brianna to avoid being right on top of her.

Brianna shook her head. "I think someone is already in there." She nodded her head toward a closed door on the side of the room. "They were just going in as I got here."

"It's all so secretive," Chloe said. "I feel like I don't even really know what I've signed up for."

"Same. But you know what they say, 'All publicity is good publicity.'" Brianna shrugged.

"What kind of business do you have?"

"I own a hair salon in Atlanta. What about you?"

"I have a coffee shop and café on Big Dune Island down in Florida."

"Oh, I love Big Dune," Brianna exclaimed. "My family used to vacation there all the time when I was a kid. I

haven't been in probably ten years, but I remember everything there was just so beautiful."

"I grew up on the island and never had any desire to live
anywhere else. Most of my friends went off to college and
settled down in bigger cities, but I love our little town."

"Why not?" Brianna said, like it was an obvious choice.
"You get to live somewhere other people vacation. Sounds
ideal to me."

"I love Atlanta too, though," Chloe said. She almost
added that her brother had played for the Braves—after all,
she was proud of him—but it felt like an unnecessary flex.
She didn't want to come off like she was bragging, and this
whole experience was supposed to be about becoming her
own person, separate from her brother.

"It has its perks, as long as you live close to where you
work and don't have to sit in traffic every day."

"It didn't look like there were many names on her
sheet," Chloe nodded toward the woman manning the table
at the front of the room, who had put in earbuds and was
now watching something on her phone.

"I know," Brianna said, her eyes lighting up. "I mean,
maybe they're doing more than one day of interviews, but if
that's the whole list, we probably have a one-in-two chance
at being cast."

The women chatted about their previous interviews
and the lack of information they'd been given on the details
of the show's format and how a winner would be selected.
Chloe realized Michael might have been able to get more
details, but she hadn't wanted him to get involved and work
his connection on her behalf. She knew she was being stub-
born—cutting off her nose to spite her face, Grandma
Sophie would have chastised her—but she needed to do this
her way.

A man in a full suit, who appeared to be in his late thirties or early forties, exited the door Brianna had pointed to earlier. He never even looked in their direction on his way out, striding confidently past the table and into the hallway.

A woman stuck her head out the door from the other room. "Brianna Alexander?"

"That's me." Brianna started to rise before the woman stopped her and asked her to give them a minute to reset.

"Give me your phone," Brianna said to Chloe, holding out a hand. "I'll put my number in if you want to grab a drink later."

Chloe didn't tell her she'd probably be busy with Michael later, simply handing over her phone. She was happy to have made a new friend, and maybe they'd be able to connect later to talk about their interviews. It would be nice to know someone else going through the process who she could talk to about things.

"Good luck," Chloe said.

"You too." Brianna reached over and squeezed her hand just as the woman reappeared to call Brianna into the room.

Once she was alone, Chloe's mind began to race with all the things she'd memorized. Her elevator pitch, profit margins, future projections with the wedding dessert business picking up, why she'd started her business, what she wanted to do with it in the future. She was prepared for anything they might ask.

Or so she thought.

Everything went well for the first fifteen minutes or so. After Brianna exited, giving her a thumbs-up and a big smile, Chloe was led into the room and introduced to the show's three judges: Andie Matthews, who owned a successful chain of cupcake shops across the Midwest and had been the winner of a popular reality baking show; Thad

Windemere, the heir to the luxury Windemere Hotel fortune; and Nathan Marks, who'd co-founded a premium tequila with Hollywood heartthrob Gavin Keller. She'd wondered who the judges might be, but she'd pictured investors like Michael, not household names like this. It was a little intimidating, but Andie had a warm, friendly personality that helped Chloe ease into the interview.

Chloe answered their questions about why she'd started the coffee shop, the types of items served, average daily sales, the growth of the bakery side of the business, and several questions about the town and the percentage of locals versus tourists she saw daily.

"So tell us about what you'd do with the money if you won," Andie prompted.

Chloe explained her brother's initial investment and her plans to buy him out, which would take roughly half of the prize money. The rest she'd like to reinvest in the business as needed, replacing chairs and tables, buying some additional kitchen equipment to help her expand the bakery side of the business.

"Think bigger," Thad said.

Chloe waited for him to elaborate, but he didn't. Andie glanced at him as if she too were waiting for him to give a better prompt, then turned back to Chloe.

"I think what Thad means is that we're really looking for businesses that want to expand or innovate in their fields."

"What I mean," Thad said, leaning forward to put his elbows on the table in front of him, "is that you can get a business loan for all that." He waived a hand at her like her ideas were just pesky flies. "I'm challenging you to think bigger. You made it this far, which means the producers saw potential in your business. What is that unrealized potential?"

For perhaps the first time in her life, Chloe was at a loss for words. This hadn't come up in the previous interviews. She wasn't sure how you innovated when it came to running a coffee shop. The basic premise was pretty well established. That left expanding. She thought of the café she was going to help Michael with in Brooklyn, mentally reviewing the hotels on the island. The ones that were big enough to support something already had their own coffee kiosks, and the B&Bs made coffee and pastries for their guests.

Then she remembered Morgan Hatfield, the young woman from nearby Cypress Shores, who'd stopped by the café recently to ask questions about how Chloe got started. The coffee shop in their town had been closed for a couple of years, and she was interested in reopening it. Unfortunately, she'd texted Chloe later and told her she'd been turned down for the business loans she'd tried to secure. She remembered what it had been like to be in Morgan's position, but Chloe had been lucky enough to have Austin's assistance.

"I'd franchise Island Coffee," Chloe blurted out. She went on to describe the other small towns nearby that lacked their own coffee shops or that only had corporate stores in nearby commercial areas. She thought about what Michael had told her about why he'd wanted to hire a consult for his project. "Each location would run on the same business model, but the interior and other touches would fit each individual community. You know how families tend to gather in their kitchens? It would be like that, where everyone would feel like they belonged."

"I love it," Andie said, smiling broadly. "Franchising my business was the best move I ever made."

"Franchising is smart," Thad nodded. "There could be an Island Coffee in every small town in America. It would need a rebrand, of course. You can't put a place called Island Coffee somewhere landlocked, but rebranding is fairly painless when you only have one location so far."

Chloe didn't let the disappointment show on her face. They wanted her to change the name of her business?

"Have you thought about getting your liquor license so you can sell alcoholic coffee beverages?" Nathan asked. "You could stay open later in the day and even into the evening. I bet in some markets that would really play out well."

Now they wanted her to turn her coffee shop into a bar? Was that how these shows worked? They made you change your entire concept? Sure, she'd seen the "sharks" give advice to business owners on their show, but those hadn't seemed like complete overhauls the way this was beginning to sound.

The three of them continued to bat around ideas for things that might work in different markets. They asked her questions about how she decided on new beverages, pastries, and desserts to try and about the small groups and events she hosted, like the book club and garden club, which then led them to more conversations about how to tailor those to each franchise. Thankfully, they didn't go back to the idea of adding alcoholic beverages or the name change, so by the time she left the room, Chloe had almost convinced herself that franchising was the way to go.

"Move over Starbucks," Andie said, smiling as she escorted Chloe to the door after the two male judges had said quick goodbyes before crossing the room to a small beverage station. "There's a new coffee shop coming to town."

Had she been this enthusiastic and encouraging with the other entrepreneurs? Did this mean Chloe was in?

She thanked Andie, waiting until she was alone in the hallway before doing a little celebratory skip down the hall. Not only had Chloe saved the interview with the franchise idea, she was pretty sure she had a real shot at making the show.

Stepping onto the elevator, she texted Michael.

> Done! I think it went well!! Let me know when and where to meet you.

As nervous and excited as she'd been for her interview earlier that morning, she was even more so now at the thought of spending the entire weekend with Michael. As she pushed through the door out onto the busy sidewalk, she couldn't help feeling like she was living someone else's life.

But it wasn't someone else's life. This was the new and improved Chloe Beckett. Watch out world.

Chapter 6

Michael

Michael checked his watch as he strode into the Arlo hotel's sleek lobby—3:15. Chloe's message had said she'd be down at 3:30, after she'd finished a video call with a bride about a cake for her upcoming nuptials. Just enough time to get a drink and shed the lingering tension from his delayed flight. He'd had their afternoon and evening all planned out, and he'd been worried the delay would ruin it all and leave Chloe to wander the city on her own. Thankfully, they'd been able to secure another plane and had taken off only an hour late.

The lobby bar was intimate, with low-slung chairs and leather couches along the windows and a long marble bar that ran the length of the room on the opposite wall. He chose a seat with a clear view of the lobby so he could watch for Chloe, shrugged out of his coat and ordered a scotch, neat, from the server who appeared. The familiar pace of the city settled around him, but something felt different. Usually, his first hours back in New York were filled with pitch meetings or investor calls. Instead, here he was, having a late afternoon cocktail like a tourist.

He took out his phone, rereading her earlier messages about the interview. Chloe's enthusiasm practically bounced off the screen, even in text form. When he'd texted to tell her he'd landed and looked forward to hearing about the interview, she'd responded within seconds.

> Can't wait to tell you! I think I have a real shot!! See you soon!

He'd never met anyone who doled out exclamation points with such abandon, but it was exactly how she spoke. Chloe loved life, and she made no effort to contain her enthusiasm for everything and everyone—nor should she. She was like sunshine in human form.

Michael had just finished scrolling through emails and was taking the last sip of his scotch when he looked up to see her walking toward him. Her face lit up when she spotted him, and he found himself standing because the energy surging through him was too strong to stay seated.

She launched herself into his arms, greeting him with a hug that caught him off guard. They'd never embraced like this, but he didn't mind it. He caught a whiff of vanilla and coconut and chuckled softly. You could take the girl off the island, but you couldn't take the island out of the girl.

"What?" she asked, stepping back and cocking her head in curiosity.

"You smell like a piña colada," he said.

She smiled brightly. "It's my shampoo. I swear, I could eat it, it smells so good."

"Alright, island girl," he said taking his wallet from his

back pocket and removing enough cash to cover the drink and leave a generous tip. "Are you ready to tour the big city?"

"I am so ready," she said, bouncing on her toes. "Where are we off to first?"

"We'll cab it up to the west side of Central Park so we can walk through a little of it, then we'll come out by the Plaza, check out the lobby, then head over to the Rock— Rockefeller Center," he said when he realized she might not know its nickname, "where we can pop into FAO Schwarz and go up to the top. How does that sound?"

"So basically, we're reenacting scenes from *Home Alone 2*?" she teased.

She wasn't wrong, but there was a reason all those things were in the movie. They were iconic New York City attractions.

"It's one of the only sequels that's better than the original," he said with a smile, shrugging. "Is there somewhere else you'd rather go?" Maybe he should have asked her what she wanted to see.

"It sounds perfect," she said, threading her arm through his. "Let's go."

She'd done it as a friendly gesture, but it felt intimate. They'd gone from chatting at the coffee shop and when they saw each other around town to hugging and linking arms. He'd have pulled away from her on Big Dune Island where gossip spread through town like the jasmine that grew everywhere and wound its way up trellises. But they were in New York City, where they could be completely anonymous. So he confidently strode right out the door and onto the busy sidewalk with Chloe on his arm like it was the most natural thing in the world.

The afternoon passed in a whirlwind of NYC moments. Chloe's eyes went wide at the Plaza's opulent lobby ("This chandelier probably costs more than my entire café!"), and she charmed the doorman into telling stories about celebrities he'd encountered. At FAO Schwarz, she couldn't resist playing "Heart and Soul" on the floor piano, coaxing Michael to join her for "Chopsticks" despite his protests. He was still grinning as he snapped her picture with the toy soldiers flanking the entrance.

The observation deck at Rockefeller Center was quieter than usual for a Friday. As the sun began to set, shades of amber and rose tinted the city in a warm glow, and Michael watched Chloe take it all in. She pressed her hands against the glass, drinking in the endless grid of streets and towers stretching out before them.

"C'mon," she said, motioning him over, "let's take a selfie."

He pushed aside thoughts of looking like a tourist, the desire to indulge her enthusiasm stronger. Taking the phone from her hand, he turned around so the view would be behind them. She squeezed next to him, and he put his arm around her without even thinking. Her cheeks were rosy from the cold, but her big smile looking back at him from the phone's screen made him feel a warm buzz he usually only got from a glass of scotch. He was so busy looking at her that he almost forgot to take the picture.

Grabbing the phone from him, she switched to the album to view the photo. "It's perfect," she said. "It looks like we're on top of the world."

And, if he was being honest, he kind of felt like he was.

As she turned back to snap more pictures of the skyline

through the glass, Michael checked his watch. "We should head to our next stop, or we'll never get in. They don't take reservations, but it'll be worth the wait."

Chloe raised an eyebrow. "What kind of place is it?"

"It's called Bemelmans Bar. It's in The Carlyle Hotel, and the piano bar there is legendary. And the murals . . ." He trailed off, not wanting to spoil the surprise. "You'll see."

They caught a cab uptown, and Michael found himself stealing glances at Chloe as she watched the city scroll past their window. The energy she'd maintained all afternoon was softening into something quieter, more contemplative. He wondered what she was thinking about. Was she replaying her interview in her mind? Or maybe, like him, the unexpected afternoon they'd shared?

He shouldn't think like that. They were basically on vacation. This wasn't real life. In real life, he was ten years older than her, and they were two completely different people. He was all spreadsheets and bottom lines, and she was the very definition of footloose and fancy free.

The cab pulled up in front of The Carlyle, and he followed her out onto the sidewalk after paying the fare. Inside, there was a line down the hallway to Bemelmans, like there was every night. It would be mostly tourists hoping to grab a table to enjoy the live jazz and admire the art on the walls.

Michael came by often when he was at home in the city, so he took Chloe's hand and led her down the hallway. Her hand was cold because she hadn't been wearing gloves, and he wrapped his warm one around it tightly. He could feel the people in line glaring at him and heard one murmur about cutting the line, but he ignored them. Sure, it was kind of a douche move, but they knew him here. He was a regular, so he always got a table or a spot at the bar.

At the door, he was greeted by one of the servers he'd known for years, who shook his hand and ushered him inside. There weren't any tables available, so he steered them toward the bar and invited them to get a drink until something opened up.

The bartender reached over the bar between patrons to shake Michael's hand. "Good to see you, Mr. Russo."

"You too, Paul."

Someone flagged Paul from the other end of the bar, and he promised Michael he'd be right back for their order. Michael grabbed a menu and handed it to Chloe. She'd barely looked at the list when her eyes got big. "Thirty dollars for a drink?"

Michael laughed. "New York prices. Besides, we're celebrating."

"What are we celebrating?"

"Your interview, of course."

"We don't even know how it went."

"Sure we do. You said it went great."

"What do I know?" She shrugged. "I'm just glad it's over."

"I'm sure you did great. So pick a drink, and let's celebrate it being over." He'd texted his friend the producer earlier to ask how she'd done, and he'd said he couldn't reveal much but that she'd held her own. Michael didn't want to get her hopes up by telling her, but it seemed like a good sign.

Chloe pointed a pink manicured fingernail at the menu. "The Jackie O."

"The Jackie O it is," he said, reading the ingredients. Two kinds of vodka and champagne, with some fruit and herbs for flavor. She might need Jackie O's big black sunglasses in the morning if she had more than one of those.

After Paul took their order, Michael steered Chloe toward a single seat that was opening farther down the bar so she could sit while they waited.

"So you were able to cut in line, and the bartender knows your name," Chloe observed. "Come here often?"

"It's my favorite place in all of Manhattan. Of course, I try to come on weeknights when it's a little less crowded, but I couldn't let you visit New York without experiencing Bemelmans. Did you notice the walls?" He gestured to the illustrations that ran around every wall of the large room.

"Yes, it's interesting," she said, leaning around the person next to her to get a closer look at the adjacent wall. "Is that all hand-drawn?"

He nodded. "Did you ever read the *Madeline* books as a child?"

"Yes," she said, recognition dawning. "It's the same artist?"

"His name was Ludwig Bemelman, hence the name of the bar. He lived in the hotel with his family for a period back in the 1940s in exchange for painting the hotel's new bar." He watched her eyes light up with wonder as she swiveled in the chair to look around the room. "There's Central Park in all four seasons and even a cameo from Madeline herself." He pointed in the iconic little girl's direction. "We can walk around after we eat. Maybe it will have thinned out a little by then."

Paul returned with their drinks just as Jefferson, the server who'd ushered them inside, came to tell them a table was opening across the room. They moved over to a cozy two-seater tucked in the corner of the room as the pianist started playing.

"This place is amazing," Chloe said, taking a sip of her cocktail. The drink was pink and bubbly, just like the woman holding it. "Wow, and this drink is absolutely incredible. I see why you like to come here."

"It's a bit of a family tradition. My dad actually proposed to my mom here, and then my sisters and I each celebrated our sixteenth birthdays here." He saw her head tilt as she gave him a questioning look. "What?"

"I just didn't take you for the sentimental type," she said, pausing like she was trying to decide whether to reveal more of her thoughts. "It sounds like this place means a lot to you. Thank you for introducing me to it."

As she said the last words, she reached across the short distance and put her hand over his. He resisted the urge to turn his hand over and wrap it around hers.

Jefferson returned with the bar's signature snacks, cheese straws and two kinds of nuts, and Chloe pulled her hand away. "I haven't seen you in here lately, Mr. Russo. Thought maybe you'd forgotten about us," Jefferson joked.

"Never." Michael shook his head. "I've just had more business down south. This is my friend, Chloe Beckett." He motioned toward her. "She owns a coffee shop and café down on the island where I have work, and she's come up for the weekend to consult on a new hotel we acquired over in Park Slope."

"Well, any friend of Mr. Russo's is a friend of mine," Jefferson said, bowing his head. "It's lovely to meet you Ms. Beckett. I'll give you two a few minutes with the menu."

Ready to steer the conversation to something less personal, Michael nodded toward the menu open in front of Chloe. "Everything here is good, but you have to try the East Beach Blonde Oysters. They're different from what you have on the island," he told her. "We can order a few things so you can try a little bit of it all."

"Why don't we just order your favorites? It all sounds delicious."

Jefferson returned, and Michael ordered the oysters and a charcuterie board to start, as nothing more would fit on the table.

"I see he talked you into the oysters," Jefferson said to Chloe. "They're Mr. Russo's favorite."

Chloe smiled at him when Jefferson left to put in their order.

"What?" he asked. "You're surprised I'm a creature of habit? I do get the exact same thing every time I'm at your place too."

"It's not that. I'm just surprised things aren't so different here. I always thought people were pretty anonymous in a big city, that you didn't get those same personal touches you get in a small town."

"It's more like a series of dozens of small towns here," he said. "There are little pockets all over the city, and within those, it really isn't all that different from Big Dune. I have a dry cleaner and a barber and a newsstand that I frequent, and a few bars and restaurants like this. All those people know me, and I know them. Jefferson, for example, has a wife and three grown children. They're all in their twenties. His son ended up in San Francisco, but his daughters both came back to the city after going away for college."

"Wow, you really do know him. So your place is nearby then?"

He nodded. "Just a couple of blocks away. Welcome to my neighborhood." He held his scotch up to toast. She clinked her glass to his, and they both said, "Cheers."

"So this is your version of Island Coffee," Chloe said, gesturing to the bar's warm ambiance. "The place where everybody knows your name."

"I never thought about it that way." Michael considered it. "But I guess you're right. Though your regulars are more likely to share family recipes than stock tips."

"Hey, Earl Watson brought you that tip about the marina property," she pointed out, eyes twinkling.

"Over your grandmother's coffee cake recipe, as I recall." The memory made him smile. "You know, I used to think success was all about the numbers. Projected growth, market share . . ." He trailed off as Jefferson arrived with their oysters.

After Jefferson left, Chloe picked up one of the shells. "And now?"

"Now I'm not so sure." He watched her try the oyster, an *Mmm* indicating she enjoyed it. "Take today's interview. On paper, you might not match up to candidates with MBAs and corporate experience. But you understand something those kinds of people probably don't. You know how to make people feel like they matter."

"Like how you matter to the people here," she said softly. "They're not just being nice because you're a good tipper. They genuinely like you. I can tell."

Something unspooled in his chest at her words, and he tried to ignore the sensation. "You say that like you suspect there are people who only pretend to like me," he teased, hiding behind humor. "Like I'm some kind of big bad corporate grim reaper."

"I don't think that," she said, reaching for another oyster. "Okay, maybe a little when you first came to Big Dune to work with Jesse, but that was before I knew about your secret life as a regular at piano bars with children's book murals." She smiled at him, and the candlelight bathed her face in a warm glow that felt intimate.

Taking another sip of his scotch to try and chase away

the thoughts he absolutely should not be having about her while they were on the eve of a new business partnership, he turned their conversation back to the show.

"You haven't told me about the interview yet," he said. "Tell me more about how it went. What kinds of questions did they ask?"

"Well, they wanted to know about my background and how I started the café." Chloe picked at the napkin sticking out from under her drink. "But they seemed most interested in my revenue projections and growth strategies. I tried to explain how every cup of coffee or baked treat comes with a story—like the china people donate to commemorate loved ones, or how we serve family recipes from locals—but they kept steering me back to numbers."

Michael nodded. "That makes sense. At the end of the day, the success of a business rests on its ability to financially support itself. Your community approach is great for customer loyalty, but they'll want to know how it translates to the bottom line."

"See, that's where we're different," she said, but her tone was warm, almost teasing. She told him about Morgan coming to her for advice on opening her own café in Cypress Shores and how she'd used that to suggest franchising Island Coffee during the interview. "When Morgan approached me, my first thought wasn't about profit margins or even what I could get out of helping her. It was about how she lights up when she talks about creating a space where people feel at home, just like I did with Island Coffee."

He watched her face animate as she talked about helping this other woman who was a virtual stranger to her. "But you still need capital to make that happen. That's why winning this competition could be huge for you. The prize money could fund developing your franchise model, creating franchise agreements, and even hiring people to help support franchisees like Morgan. You could use her location to prove your model can scale. Heck, you could even offer her financing on the franchise so she doesn't have to depend on a traditional business loan."

"I only understood about half of that, so I definitely have a lot to learn if I go in that direction." She fiddled with one of the dangly earrings she wore. "I just hope I can convince them that success doesn't exist on spreadsheets alone. Sometimes it's about that perfect cup of coffee on a bad day, or being the place where someone writes their novel, or . . ." She gestured around the bar. "Being someone's favorite spot in all of Manhattan."

The pianist started playing "As Time Goes By," and Michael caught himself wanting to reach for her hand but resisted. "Well, you've convinced me. And I'm a pretty tough sell."

The way she smiled at him then made his chest tight. He reminded himself this was just one weekend, that they lived in different worlds. But sitting there in his favorite bar, watching Chloe charm everyone around her just like she had back on the island, those worlds didn't feel so far apart.

Chapter 7

Chloe

The hotel room was so dark when Chloe woke up on Saturday morning that she had no idea what time it was. The blackout curtains made it feel like a cave. A very luxurious cave, with the most perfect pillows and a billowing duvet that felt like sleeping in a cloud.

Turning the alarm clock away from where she'd pointed it at the wall to dim its brightness, she saw it was seven o'clock. For anyone else that might seem early, but she never slept that late. She was usually downstairs baking for the day by 5:30 a.m. Even on Sundays when the café was closed, her body clock still woke her at five daily.

Michael wasn't picking her up to head to Brooklyn until nine, so she had time to order room service and enjoy having someone else cook her breakfast for once.

After her order was placed, she pulled on the plush

hotel robe and padded into the bathroom to wash her face and brush her teeth. Coming back out into the room, she opened the curtains and raised the shade, squinting in the sudden brightness of the sunlight pouring into the room. It looked to be another beautiful day in Manhattan.

She'd hardly had time to scroll social media when room service knocked on her door, wheeling in a cart with a tray that held fresh-squeezed orange juice and a large plate covered by a silver dome. Chloe signed for her breakfast, leaving a generous tip for the woman who'd delivered it.

Taking the tray across the room, Chloe decided to treat herself. She'd never had breakfast in bed before, but she was indulging in the fairy-tale vibe of the weekend.

The previous afternoon and evening with Michael had been perfect. New York was everything she'd hoped it would be and more. Central Park was much larger than she'd imagined, the Plaza even more opulent, and the view from the Top of the Rock even more stunning. And Bemelmans had been pure magic. It all contributed to feeling like she was living inside of a movie.

Chloe's phone buzzed on the bed next to her, and she finished chewing the last of her chocolate chip banana pancakes before she accepted the video call from Reagan.

"Chloe Beckett, are you still in bed?" Reagan asked as she walked around her house, bending down to pet her golden retriever, Maple.

"Even better," Chloe said, holding the phone out farther to show the tray in her lap. "I'm eating breakfast in bed."

"Yas, queen. I love it. Now, tell me everything. I want to hear about your interview, sightseeing with Michael, everything."

Chloe had tried to call Reagan when she'd returned to the hotel after her interview the previous day, but Reagan and Gigi had been wrapped up in some sort of legal documents that had to go out by the end of the day. Then by the time Reagan had called her back, Chloe was already out with Michael. Now, she started by giving Reagan a blow-by-blow of the interview, including some of the details she'd left out in the version she'd told Michael, like how Thad had made her feel like she was just running some sort of mom-and-pop shop that wasn't impressive in the least.

"Pompous jerk," Reagan said. "But it sounds like he came around once you told him about your franchising idea."

"Yeah, but I'm not even sure if that's what I want to do."

"That's okay, right? It's not like you committed to anything. When will you hear if you made it?"

"I think any day now. They weren't real specific, but they did say we needed to be ready for a site visit in the next couple of weeks if we were selected."

"That's so exciting," Reagan said as Chloe watched her go outside with Maple. Reagan chucked a ball across the backyard before she sat down in one of the chairs on her patio. "But enough about work. Tell me about Michael. Where'd he take you? What was he like in his natural environment?"

Chloe took Reagan through everywhere they'd gone and everything they'd talked about, leaving virtually no detail out. Reagan was like the sister she didn't have, and they told each other everything.

Reagan sipped from her coffee mug before replying. "That sounds like a date."

Shaking her head, Chloe moved the tray off her lap and pulled her legs up to her chest. "It wasn't like that. He was just keeping me company and showing me around."

She thought about the electricity that had raced from

her fingertips across her whole body when he'd taken her hand and led her through the crowd outside Bemelmans. She had left out that detail when she'd told Reagan about their visit to the bar. Even sisters had some secrets, right?

That was all it had been, though. Sure, they'd had conversations that went a little deeper than their usual short, casual talks at the coffee shop, but it wasn't like he'd tried to kiss her at the end of the evening or anything. He hadn't even invited her to see his place, which was close by. He'd simply hailed a cab for her and told her he'd pick her up in the morning. He'd been very gentlemanly, but definitely not flirtatious.

"He was not just showing you around," Reagan disagreed. "He took you to his favorite spot. He let you into his inner sanctum."

"His inner sanctum? What is he, a church?" Chloe joked, but she remembered how he'd told her about his parents' engagement and his family's tradition of dining there for each child's sixteenth birthday. She wasn't ready to admit to Reagan just how intimate the evening had felt at times. Glancing at the clock on the nightstand, she realized it was 8:15 already. "I should probably start getting ready. Michael's picking me up at nine to head to The Perry."

"Ah yes, time to go be a serious business consultant." Chloe watched Reagan's golden retriever drop a slobbery tennis ball in her lap. "Maple, gross." Reagan chucked the ball across the yard again. "Are you nervous about it?"

Chloe stood, propping the phone on her breakfast tray as she carried it to the desk. "A little. I mean, he obviously thinks I have something valuable to contribute, but what do I know about luxury hotels? The fanciest thing about Island Coffee is the vintage china we serve everything on."

"That's exactly why he asked you, because you understand how to make people feel at home, no matter where they are." Reagan stopped and stared into the phone like she was looking directly into Chloe's eyes. "Chloe Beckett, you deserve to be there. You earned it. Now don't forget to act like it."

Chloe smiled. "Scout's honor," she said, holding three fingers up in the Girl Scout sign they'd learned together as Daisies in kindergarten. "I'll call you later and tell you how it goes."

"You better. Good luck!"

At precisely nine o'clock, Chloe watched from the lobby windows as Michael climbed from the back seat of a black Cadillac SUV like the one that had picked her up from the airport.

"Good morning," he said, grinning as he came through the hotel's front door. "Ready to be a high-powered consultant?"

"As I'll ever be." She followed him outside just as Ricardo exited the vehicle and came around to the passenger side. "Ricardo, good morning. It's nice to see you again."

"You too, miss," he said, opening the door for her.

Once they were both in the car and it was pulling away from the curb, Michael explained they could use the car service today since they were technically on the clock with his firm.

"Did you sleep well?" he asked her.

"Like a baby. Those beds are heaven." She watched the city scroll past her window, still mesmerized by the endless succession of storefronts and restaurants. "How long until we get to Brooklyn?"

"About thirty minutes, traffic permitting. Which it never does." Michael shook his head as Ricardo expertly navigated around a delivery truck double-parked in their lane. "We're meeting Alessandra, our interior designer, at ten. That gives us time to explore the neighborhood a little bit first so you can get a feel for it."

Michael spent the rest of the drive telling her about the history of The Perry, how it had fallen into disrepair, and all the work his firm was doing to renovate and reopen it. He pulled a tablet from the seat pocket in front of him and swiped through renderings of the rooms and lobby to give her an idea of the overall design of the hotel.

"I'll show you around, but none of the wallpaper or flooring or furniture is in yet."

When they turned onto the tree-lined streets of Park Slope, she marveled at the beauty of the neighborhood. Stately brownstones stood shoulder to shoulder, bay windows bowing out in perfect symmetry on each floor. Young mothers pushed strollers, couples walked dogs, and kids on scooters zoomed past cafés and boutiques.

"This isn't what I pictured when I thought of Brooklyn," she said. "It has a real family feel."

Michael nodded. "That's exactly why we bought The Perry. Park Slope is actually the oldest historic district in the city. Prospect Park is just up there," he said, pointing out his window, "along with the Brooklyn Botanic Garden. Hey, Ricardo," he said, leaning forward. "Can you take us over to Washington Park?"

Ricardo nodded, flipping on his turn signal and easing onto a side street to go in the opposite direction Michael had pointed for Prospect Park.

"There's something I want to show you," he said, his

eyes twinkling. It was the same look he'd given her when he'd taken her to Bemelmans the previous evening.

When they pulled up to the park, Michael told Ricardo they'd be right back. Chloe followed him a short distance into the park, past a playground to a stone farmhouse. It was perhaps the most surprising thing she'd seen the whole trip.

"This is the Old Stone House," he said. "It's a replica of a Dutch farmhouse similar to one that originally stood in this area."

"Wow, it's hard to imagine this all as farmland. I love that this sort of history has been preserved. The brownstones are great, but this is really unexpected."

"Ooh," he said, putting a hand on her arm to guide her past the house. "You're going to love this too."

He led her to a green garden shed with a brightly painted mural on the side. At the top, it read, "Garden Train Tool Lending Library."

"A tool lending library?" she asked. "That sounds fun. What is it?"

"The Garden Train is a volunteer organization that started and maintains gardens at all the schools in this district. And when the kids or parents or teachers need tools to work on the gardens, they can borrow them from here."

"What a great idea. It's like a Little Free Library but for tools." She followed him as he turned down the path back toward the car, passing a dad pretending to chase a little girl down the sidewalk, her pigtails swinging wildly as she giggled at him trying to catch her.

"It's a really special neighborhood," he said. "It's why I want The Perry to be part of the community and not just somewhere you put up friends or family when they come to visit."

"Is this where you grew up?" she asked as they got back in the car.

He chuckled. "Not even close. I grew up in Queens. My dad died when I was ten, and then it was just my mom, my four sisters, and me." He was quiet for a moment, then added, "We didn't have much. My mom worked two jobs so my sisters could take dance classes. Our neighbors Mrs. Amato and Mrs. Gallo would take turns watching us after school until I was old enough to look after my sisters on my own."

The vulnerability in his voice made Chloe's heart flutter. This whole trip, Michael had been showing her a side of him she'd never seen before. He'd come a long way from those humble beginnings.

"Do you still have family in Queens?"

He nodded. "My mom and my oldest sister, Maria, and her family live about two blocks apart. My other sisters are all married too. One lives over in Hoboken and the other two moved out to Long Island and live on the same street."

As Ricardo drove them down streets lined with more brownstones back toward the hotel, Michael told her a little about each of his sisters, their husbands, and his six nieces and nephews.

"That is a big family," she said. "I love being an aunt. Luke is the best. He's crazy smart, and he's such a happy kid." Luke had easily folded into their family after Austin adopted him, and it was almost hard to remember what it had been like without him.

"Here we are," Michael said as Ricardo pulled up in front of a four-story brick building that featured a rounded frontage on the corner where two streets met. It was a gorgeous building with cream-colored stone accents along each of the building's corners. No wonder Michael's firm had decided to snap it up.

"The Perry" was spelled out in ornate gold letters above the entrance. Inside, the hotel's lobby was dusty and littered with scaffolding and construction equipment, but she could imagine what it would become. Elaborate crown molding ran around the top of the walls, and marble floors were visible through the sawdust.

A worker breezed through the lobby to grab a tool, and the sound of a saw could be heard from somewhere deeper in the hotel. Michael held up a hand in greeting, eliciting a nod from the man, who was gone again as quickly as he'd appeared. Then Michael steered Chloe toward a doorway to the left.

The coffee shop space could be entered from the lobby or the street. It had been cleared of whatever furniture had previously been there, leaving a large room covered in dust and debris. Currently, it was dark and uninviting thanks in part to the paper that covered the windows and the broken light fixtures overhead, only about half of which lit up.

"The previous owners used it mainly as a breakfast spot for hotel guests," Michael explained. "It's a nice big open space, though, and those floor-to-ceiling windows will let in a lot of light. What do you think?"

Chloe walked the perimeter of the space, her mind already racing with possibilities. The room had good bones —high ceilings, large windows, and the same marble floors as the lobby. "All of this window space is huge," she said, peeling back the paper over one window to peek at the view. "Everyone fights over the two tables I have by the windows, but here you can fit so much more. I think we could create some cozy nooks here like they have at the Arlo. If you position couches and chairs just right, you can create intimate little living room spaces for friends or family to gather."

She turned to find Michael watching her intently. "What?"

"Nothing. I just always marvel at people who can look at a space like this and imagine what it could be. All I see is a big empty room. I mean, I know it has some great historic details, but I have no ability to picture what it could be without someone like you pointing it out to me."

"The ceiling height is fantastic too." She looked up at the original tin ceiling. "Actually, it reminds me of—"

"Island Coffee," they said in unison, then laughed.

"Great minds," Michael said. "I thought the same thing when I first saw it."

"We could do a mix of seating as you move away from the windows. You need some tables for people who want to sit and work or meet to discuss business." She turned back toward the wall that held the door to the lobby. "I'd put the counter and register along there, and what if we commissioned an artist to do a mural on that wall to celebrate the neighborhood's history? Like how the Old Stone House preserves the story of what used to be there."

"Exactly. Like how you display the china at Island Coffee. Each piece tells a story."

They were bouncing ideas back and forth, completely in sync, when the sharp click of heels on marble announced a new arrival. A tall woman in stilettos and a perfectly tailored black dress stood in the doorway, her dark hair swept into a sleek chignon. Her red lipstick was the perfect color for her olive complexion—the kind of perfect shade of red lipstick some women spent their entire adult lives trying to find.

"Michael, darling." She air-kissed his cheeks, then

turned to assess Chloe, raising her perfectly arched eyebrows. "And you must be the consultant."

"Chloe Beckett," she said, extending her hand. "It's nice to meet you."

"Mmm." Alessandra barely touched her fingers before turning back to Michael. "I've already drawn up preliminary plans. Very modern, very fresh. Clean lines, minimalist aesthetic. The Park Slope crowd is quite sophisticated these days." She started clicking on her tablet, angling it so only Michael could see.

He barely looked at it before turning his attention back to Chloe. "Actually, Chloe and I were just talking about making things a little cozier. A little more personal. A community gathering place." He went on to tell Alessandra about Island Coffee, the heirloom china, and the family recipes Chloe used for some of the baked goods.

Alessandra's smile didn't reach her eyes. "How . . . quaint. But we're creating a luxury hotel experience here, not a small-town diner." She turned to Chloe like she'd just remembered she was there. "No offense."

"None taken," Chloe said, though something in her gut twisted. "But luxury doesn't have to mean impersonal."

"Chloe's right," Michael jumped in. "We want to strike a balance. Like how the lobby combines historic elements with contemporary design."

A contractor poked his head through the door and asked Michael if he could come look at something, leaving Chloe alone with Alessandra. As she watched the woman hold up the tablet to take photos of the space, she pointed to the wall they'd just been discussing and told Alessandra about her idea to commission a mural.

"I think what makes a neighborhood special is how it honors its history while embracing the present."

"You've spent a lot of time in Park Slope then?" Alessandra turned, a condescending look aimed at Chloe. She asked it like she knew the answer but wanted Chloe to have to admit it.

"No," Chloe confirmed, tucking her hair behind one ear. "But Michael's told me a lot about it, and we toured the neighborhood this morning."

"Yes, well, I grew up nearby. I know the kind of people who live here and what they're looking for." Alessandra waved her hand dismissively.

Chloe was momentarily stunned into silence as Michael reentered from the lobby. Alessandra claimed his attention immediately.

"Now, I'm thinking chrome and glass, perhaps some industrial elements . . ." She tapped the tablet back to life and held it out to Michael.

As Alessandra commandeered Michael's attention with her sleek designs, Chloe thought about what he'd told her about growing up in Queens, about neighbors helping look after him and his sisters. The kind of community where everyone knew each other, just like Big Dune Island. Just like Park Slope appeared to her to be.

Chloe might not have known about luxury hotels, but she knew how to make a place become part of the fabric of the community. And that's what Michael had said The Perry needed. She reminded herself what Reagan had said earlier about how she deserved to be there.

For the next hour, Alessandra dominated the conversation with talk of trending design elements and luxury finishes. Every time Chloe offered a suggestion about community engagement or ways to make the space more welcoming, Alessandra would redirect with phrases like "elevated experience" and "upscale clientele" as if she hadn't even spoken.

When Alessandra pulled Michael aside to discuss some technical specifications for the lighting, Chloe wandered over to the windows, peeling back the paper again. Outside, a group of mothers with strollers had stopped to chat, laughing as they jostled babies and coffee cups. One woman pointed at The Perry's facade, gesturing excitedly to her friends. Chloe could hear her grandmother's voice telling her, *People don't just want somewhere to go, they want somewhere to belong.*

"Well," Alessandra's voice cut through her thoughts, "I think we have everything we need. I'll update the renderings to incorporate what we discussed."

"Actually," Michael said, "I'd like to hear more of Chloe's thoughts on the seating layout and that community wall concept."

Alessandra's perfect smile tightened almost imperceptibly. "Of course. Though perhaps we should focus on the broader design vision before getting into decorative details."

"The details are what make a space special," Chloe said quietly, but firmly. "They're what make people feel at home."

"This isn't meant to be anyone's home, dear. It's a luxury hotel." Alessandra checked her watch. "I have another appointment. Michael, call me later about those light fixtures?"

After she left, Michael turned to Chloe. "Ready to grab some lunch? We can talk more about your ideas without interruption."

As they headed out, Chloe took one last look at the space. Despite Alessandra's dismissive attitude toward her ideas, she could still see its potential. The question was, could she convince everyone else to see it too?

Chapter 8

Michael

"I'm sorry about Alessandra," Michael said as Ricardo navigated them back toward Manhattan. "She can be a bit . . ."

"Intense?" Chloe offered with a small smile.

"That's one word for it." He watched her profile as she gazed out the window. She'd been quieter since leaving The Perry, and he couldn't help feeling responsible. He'd anticipated the clash between Alessandra's sleek minimalism and Chloe's warm, personal approach, and he should have done more to help validate Chloe's position.

"You don't have to apologize," Chloe said, turning to face him. "She obviously knows what she's doing. I mean, the renderings she showed us were beautiful, even if they're not my style."

"Beautiful, but cold." He shook his head. "We've done a dozen brand-new hotels that look exactly like that, and I should have said so. What made me want to buy The Perry was its historical significance and the potential to make it feel like it belongs to the neighborhood. Like Island Coffee belongs to Big Dune."

"I don't know." Chloe's voice trailed off while she twisted a ring on her finger. "Maybe Alessandra's right. The Park Slope crowd probably is more sophisticated than what we have on the island."

"Hey." He waited until she looked at him. "Do you know why I really showed you the Old Stone House and that garden shed this morning?"

She waited for his reply instead of guessing.

"Because this neighborhood isn't about being sophisticated. Sure, you have to be well-off to live here, but it's actually one of those neighborhoods where everyone knows everyone. The moms who meet for coffee after school drop-off, the old guys who've been playing chess in the park for decades, the families who volunteer in those school gardens —that's what makes Park Slope special. Just like the regulars at Island Coffee are what make it special."

Some of the light returned to her eyes. "That's what I was trying to say about the community wall. We could feature photos and stories from the neighborhood."

"Exactly. And before you start doubting yourself again, remember that *you* are the one who actually runs a successful coffee shop. Alessandra designs beautiful spaces, but then she moves on to the next project. You know how to make a local business work and how to integrate it into the community."

He'd have to find a way to handle Alessandra, to make her understand that this project needed to be different. He had to delicately balance his firm's relationship with her and what he wanted for this particular project. Alessandra had been right that hotel guests would expect a certain level of luxury, but he believed they could still deliver on that while giving the neighborhood something special too.

"She didn't seem to think my experience counted for much," Chloe said.

"That's her problem." He caught himself reaching for her hand, then thought better of it. "Listen, why don't you take the next few days to think about the space and what you think would work there, and we'll sit down when I get back to the island and talk it over."

She nodded. "Sure, that sounds good."

"For now, let's just enjoy the rest of the afternoon. We have time to grab a bite to eat before the show. What are you in the mood for?"

She told him about the Thai place Gigi had recommended, and he found the address for Ricardo. From there, they'd head to a matinee of *The Great Gatsby*. He couldn't let Chloe visit Manhattan for the first time and not make it to a Broadway show. He'd also promised to show her Times Square before he had to head to a work dinner.

The Thai restaurant lived up to Gigi's recommendation. Chloe gushed about the array of flavors in her Pad Thai and insisted he try her mango sticky rice dessert. He found himself watching her during their meal, captivated by how she approached each new experience with genuine enthusiasm.

The Great Gatsby was the perfect choice for her first Broadway show. The stage design was spectacular, with moving set pieces that transformed the stage from Gatsby's mansion to the Valley of Ashes in seconds. During the song "Beautiful Little Fool," he glanced over to find tears streaming down Chloe's face. She caught him looking and laughed, dabbing at her eyes with a tissue.

"What?" she whispered. "I'm a sucker for tragic romance."

Times Square was exactly the sensory overload he'd expected. While he usually avoided the tourist hub like the plague, seeing it through Chloe's eyes made it almost magical. She insisted on taking photos in front of the giant electronic billboards, with costumed characters, and in a dozen other places around them.

When they arrived back at the Arlo to drop her off, she hugged him tightly on the sidewalk outside the hotel door. He held onto her, suspended in the moment, oblivious to everyone rushing past them. Unlike the first hug the day before in the bar, which had been unexpected and quick, this one was long and intentional. He didn't want to let her go, but he had a work dinner he now resented having to attend.

In the cab on the way home to change for his meeting, he couldn't stop thinking about the way Chloe's face had lit up when he'd defended her vision for The Perry. Or how naturally she'd fit into his favorite places in the city, as if she'd always belonged there. He wished they had one more day together before going back to reality on Big Dune Island, but he was booked solid with breakfast, coffee, and lunch meetings on Sunday, and Chloe was flying home.

Michael's phone buzzed with a text from his sister Maria, bringing him back to the present.

.Can you bring the wine tomorrow? Ma's making Sunday sauce.

Right. Family dinner. Maybe it would help clear his head, remind him why mixing business with pleasure was never a good idea.

But first, he had to survive dinner with potential

investors without letting his mind wander to a certain café owner who was probably exploring more of the city without him.

"Michael!" His mother's voice carried out the open front door and down the brownstone's front steps the next evening as his nieces and nephews spilled out of the house to greet him. "You're late!"

"By two minutes, Ma." He shook his head.

His sister Cristina's twin girls, Sophia and Isabella, raced down the steps to greet him, followed by Maria's son, Anthony, who was excitedly detailing his latest baseball game. The scent of his mother's Sunday sauce wafted out the door, making his mouth water.

Inside, controlled chaos reigned as it did every Sunday. His youngest sister Gina's toddler was climbing the baby gate while her husband, Marco, tried to wrangle him. His sister Angela was setting the table around Cristina's youngest, who was doing homework he'd apparently forgotten was due tomorrow.

"Here," his mother said, taking the wine he'd brought and handing it to Maria. "Now come taste the sauce."

In the kitchen, she held up a spoonful of deep red tomato sauce. It was the same ritual every time he was there, with him tasting first just like his father used to do. His brothers-in-law were all in attendance too, but she never let any of them have the first taste when he was there.

"Perfect, Ma. Just like always." He leaned down to kiss her forehead.

She patted his cheek, studying his face. "You look tired. Did you work all weekend?"

"Actually, I was showing someone around the city. A consultant for The Perry project." He tried to keep his voice casual as he grabbed a piece of bread to soak up more sauce.

"Someone?" Maria appeared in the doorway, eyebrows raised. "You spent your whole weekend playing tour guide?"

"It wasn't like that. She owns a coffee shop down on Big Dune, and we're planning to have her help design the hotel's café space."

"She?" His other three sisters were all suddenly in the kitchen too, like sharks sensing blood in the water.

"Chloe Beckett," he said, immediately regretting offering the name when he saw the looks they exchanged. "It was strictly business."

"Sure it was," Angela said, grinning. "That's why you're blushing."

"I am not—"

"You took her to all the tourist spots?" Angela asked. "That doesn't sound like you. You hate playing tour guide."

"Where'd you take her?" Cristina asked.

He rattled off everywhere they'd been and realized they'd really packed in a lot in the two days they'd had together.

"You took her to Bemelmans?" his mother asked, pausing with her wooden spoon midair.

The room went quiet. Bemelmans was practically a shrine to his family, and he knew it was significant to them that he'd taken Chloe there. Their father had proposed to their mother at Bemelmans, saving tips for months from his restaurant job at the time to be able to afford to take her there.

Michael had made it his mission to recreate that night for his mother on her fiftieth birthday, piecing together the story from her old friends and his father's former coworkers. He'd also taken each of his sisters there on their sixteenth birthdays, telling them the story of their parents' engagement, making sure a piece of their father lived on in this small way.

"You're the man of the house now, Michael," his father had said to him as he'd reached the final days of his battle with pancreatic cancer. *"Take care of your mother and sisters for me."*

Michael had been ten when his dad passed. His mother had gone from stay-at-home mom to primary breadwinner practically overnight. She'd gotten a job as a checkout clerk at the neighborhood grocery store, and a friend who cleaned offices after hours had found her work several evenings a week.

He'd gotten his first job a couple of years later, delivering groceries for the market where his mom worked. As a teenager, he'd stocked shelves at night. His mother had tried to tell him to focus on school, but he'd seen how tight money was. Besides, she'd been working two jobs herself.

"Well, what did she think of our spot?" his mother asked.

"Who doesn't like Bemelmans?" Cristina asked.

All his sisters began talking at once, rattling off their favorite things about the bar and how long it had been since they'd each been there, allowing Michael to avoid answering his mother's question. Maria wanted her husband to take her there for their anniversary, but he was balking at the expense.

He watched his mom cross the kitchen to fill a pot with water for the pasta.

"Ma, there's a pot filler over there. That's what it's for," he said, pointing to the arm of the brushed nickel faucet that was built into the backsplash above the stove.

His mother huffed. "A pot filler. So ridiculous. Who's so lazy they can't walk across the kitchen to fill a pot?"

He shook his head. His mother had finally relented and let him buy her a brownstone a few years back when the building they'd grown up in was getting razed, forcing her out. But her favorite pastime had become mocking all the luxury amenities.

"Mr. Big Shot Investment Banker over here, probably," Angela laughed.

"Private equity," his other sisters corrected in unison, then dissolved into giggles.

"Alright, that's enough," their mother said, but she was smiling. "Michael, tell us more about this Chloe. What did she think of the city?"

He thought of how Chloe's face had lit up at the Top of the Rock, her tears during the show, and her infectious laugh at lunch. "She loved it. Everything was exciting and new to her. She even made Times Square feel magical instead of tacky."

When he looked up, all five women were staring at him with identical knowing expressions.

"What?"

"Nothing," his mother said innocently, turning back to the stove. But he heard her mutter under her breath, "Sounds like someone else is excited too."

"Ma—"

"Uncle Mikey, come see our dance," Sophia said as she appeared in the doorway with her twin, Bella, saving him from further interrogation. "We've been practicing it all day for you." The girls took ballet and loved performing for him when he visited.

Grateful for the escape, Michael headed for the family room, but he could hear his sisters' whispered conversation behind him.

"Did you see his face when he talked about her?"

"Strictly business my foot."

He was never going to hear the end of this. But somehow, he couldn't bring himself to care.

After he'd clapped and praised the twins following three dance routines, Michael's mother called everyone into the dining room for dinner. The adults took up all the room at the large formal table, the kids fighting over who sat next to who at card tables set up in the adjoining sunroom.

The constant flow of voices at dinner would make an outsider believe his family never saw one another as they talked over each other to tell stories about neighbors, people at work, and the parents of their children's friends. There were always at least three conversations going on at once, making it difficult to follow any one storyline.

"Can you pass the bread?" Maria's husband, Steve, asked quietly next to him. Michael studied his brother-in-law as he handed over the basket. Steve had been unusually subdued all evening, none of his usual jokes or animated stories about his plumbing business.

"How are things going with that big project?" Michael asked. "The one with the affordable housing units?" Steve's plumbing company had put together the winning proposal for a major project in Astoria.

Steve pushed pasta around on his plate. He glanced at Maria, who reached over and squeezed his hand. "I had to pull out of the project. In fact, I'm . . ." He paused. "I'm shutting down the business."

The clinking of forks against plates stopped as everyone turned to look at Steve. The company had been around for more than forty years, having been started by Steve's late father.

"What happened?" Michael asked, though he had a sinking feeling he knew. Steve had always put people before profits, taking on projects others wouldn't touch, hiring guys who needed second chances, and extending payment plans to clients going through hard times.

"The Marshall project killed us," Steve admitted, referring to a large hotel that went under before it opened. "Then the Parkers couldn't make their payments, but they had a new baby and medical bills, so I let them delay paying and tried to float the material costs myself. Then the Chen family needed emergency repairs after that storm." He shook his head. "Before I knew it, I couldn't make payroll."

"Why didn't you say something?" Michael asked. "I could have—"

"That's exactly why I didn't say anything," Steve cut him off. "I wanted to make it work on my own. I really thought I could turn it around."

Maria wiped at her eyes with her napkin. "I told him we should have come to you. But Steve wanted to help all these families, and I supported that. It felt like the right thing to do."

The rest of dinner was subdued. Michael watched his nephew Anthony pushing his food around his plate, probably wondering if this meant he'd have to change schools. Michael remembered that feeling, the constant worry that came with financial instability.

Later, as he helped his mother load the dishwasher, she touched his arm. "There's more," she said quietly. "They've been living paycheck to paycheck for months. They're three months behind on their mortgage."

Michael closed his eyes, remembering the constant knot

of anxiety in his stomach as a kid, watching his mother count pennies at the grocery store, hearing her cry at night over bills.

"Why didn't they come to me? I can catch them up. Give them some breathing room."

"You know Maria. Proud, like your father." His mother handed him another plate to load. "Steve's a good man. He leads with his heart."

Michael thought of Chloe, of her passion for community over profits. Of how quick she'd been to doubt herself when Alessandra had challenged her vision for The Perry.

"Sometimes good intentions aren't enough, Ma."

"No," she agreed softly. "I'm just thankful his dad isn't alive to see him shut down the business." Michael's family had known Steve's since he and his sisters were kids growing up in the same neighborhood.

He nodded, but his mind was already running numbers, figuring out how to help Maria and Steve without wounding their pride. He couldn't let his nephew face the same anxiety he and his sisters had known. This was exactly why he'd worked so hard to build his success, to protect his family from ever feeling that vulnerable again.

Chapter 9

Chloe

Monday morning had been busy at Island Coffee thanks to a malfunctioning espresso machine and an unexpected group of ten in town for a conference who'd decided to have a breakout session in the coffee shop.

Chloe was exhausted from her big weekend in the city. Although she'd initially been disappointed Michael couldn't spend time with her Saturday night or Sunday morning before her flight, she'd ended up hanging out with Brianna. It had been nice to debrief with someone who understood what the interview process had been like and to speculate about how the show might play out.

Plus, it was Brianna's first trip to the city too, so they'd knocked a few more spots off their sightseeing list, including a trip to the top of the Empire State Building on Saturday night and walking the High Line with their coffee on Sunday morning. They'd promised to stay in touch and cheer each other on, no matter what happened.

At 10:30, Chloe was finally taking her first break of the morning when she felt her phone buzzing in her apron. It was a New York number. Chloe was so nervous that she bobbled the phone in her hand, nearly dropping it, as she rushed back to the kitchen where it was quieter.

"Hello?" she said, hearing the nerves in her voice as she tried to play it cool. Was this *the* call? Did she make the show?

"Is this Chloe Beckett?" a male voice asked.

"It is." She began pacing the short length of the kitchen.

"Hi, Chloe. This is Chris Paulson. We didn't get a chance to meet this weekend, but I'm a producer with *The Next Great American Entrepreneur*. Do you have a minute to talk?"

Thankfully the group of ten had just left, so she did. "Sure."

"We've all been really impressed with you and your business throughout this process so far. The judges had some great comments about you following the interview this weekend." He paused, and Chloe could hear the shuffling of papers.

Was he letting her down easy? This sounded like the business version of an "it's not you, it's me" speech.

"I'm calling today to set up a site visit, because you've been selected as one of our potential contestants. We'd like to get down there on Thursday. Does that work for you?"

Potential contestant? What did that mean exactly? She thought making it to the site visit meant she'd made the show, but she tried to tamp down the excitement bubbling to the surface in case she was wrong.

"I hope you don't mind if I ask a question, but what did you mean exactly when you said I'm a 'potential contestant'?"

"I'm sorry, I should have explained," he said. "You have been selected for the show, but nothing is final until after the site visit. We've selected two alternates in case we discover anything on our site visits that might preclude a contestant from participating. We don't expect any issues, but you never know." He half-laughed as he continued. "I was casting for a dating show one time, and we made a surprise visit to a contestant's hometown to film B-roll before the show started filming, and it was us who were surprised when her husband answered the door. Turns out they'd agreed she could go on the show to try and grow her social following to boost her skincare business."

"Well, I'm not married," Chloe joked.

"We just want to make sure contestants have truthfully represented their businesses. It's simply a necessary precaution. Can we put you down for Thursday? The network has moved up our premiere date, so filming would begin in a few weeks."

Everything was suddenly happening so fast. She had to be ready for a crew to visit the café in three days, and they'd be filming for real in less than a month?

"Okay," Chloe said. "Thursday it is. Do I need to do anything to prepare?"

"We don't want to interrupt your business," Chris said. "What are your hours, and when are you busiest?"

They worked through the logistics. Chris and two of his colleagues would come into the café during the morning rush just to observe. Then they'd come back after she closed at three o'clock to discuss their thoughts on how future filming would work. He said they'd also be trying to get in touch with someone from the city to get permission to shoot B-roll around town they could use later in the season. She gave him a couple of names and numbers of people she knew over at city hall but asked him to give her the afternoon to give people a heads-up.

When Chloe ended the call, it all sank in. She'd made it! She was going to be on *The Next Great American Entrepreneur*!

She had a little skip in her step as she stuck her head out of the kitchen door and gave an exaggerated wave to Iris to come to the back. Chloe had filled Iris in on the show when she'd asked her to cover the café while she traveled for the interview, swearing her to secrecy. She'd been relieved that the older woman was as excited as Chloe about the potential spotlight on Island Coffee.

The door hadn't even swung shut behind Iris when Chloe ran over and nearly tackled the older lady in a hug. "I did it," she said, squeezing her. "I got on the show!"

Iris pulled back, holding her by the arms to look at her. "Really? The show is coming here?"

Chloe nodded so fast she was afraid she looked like a bobblehead doll that had been shaken too hard. She was sure her smile stretched all the way from ear to ear.

Iris tugged her back into an embrace. "I'm so proud of you. I wish your grandmother were here for this."

Tears sprang to her eyes. Chloe ached for her grandmother, the woman who'd taught her to bake and be a good host while her parents were off with Austin at baseball tournaments somewhere. She'd passed a few years before Chloe opened the café, but there were little things that reminded her of Grandma Sophie every day, like the cutting board her parents had given her with Grandma Sophie's buttermilk biscuit recipe engraved on it.

When Iris backed away and noticed a tear sliding down Chloe's face, she said, "I didn't mean to upset you." She reached up and wiped away the tear. "Sophie is up there watching us right now, and you know she wouldn't want you to waste a second being sad when there's so much to celebrate. Why don't you knock off early and go tell your family?"

"Are you sure?" Chloe asked, swiping at both eyes and smiling again. "I need to go tell Molly over at the city that the producer is going to call about shooting B-roll, and I thought I'd stop by and tell Reagan and Gigi while I'm over there. Then I'm going to hunt down my parents and Austin."

Iris nodded. "Go on. I've got everything here under control. Cassidy will be in any minute to help with the lunch crowd." The third member of the café's team, Cassidy, was a college student working part-time two afternoons a week and on Saturdays so Iris could help with her grandson.

Chloe told Iris about the people coming on Thursday, and Iris volunteered to come in early the next morning so they could do a little spring cleaning and put together a plan. After taking off her apron and hanging it on a hook in the back, Chloe fished her purse out of her desk drawer and headed over to the city to try and catch Molly before she left for lunch.

The city hadn't even had a policy for filming in town before Callie moved back. However, interest in her comeback had drawn entertainment reporters and other media to Big Dune Island, so Molly said they now had forms that had to be filled out and the mayor had to approve filming locations. Technically, they required five business days' notice, but Molly said she was sure the mayor would be thrilled for the exposure for both Island Coffee and the island itself and would sign off on it before Thursday.

Molly promised to call Chloe once they heard from the production company and keep her posted on the approval, so Chloe headed a few doors down to Gigi's law office to share the good news and see if Reagan had time for lunch.

Gigi's law office was located in a historic house that had been converted by the previous attorney who'd run a practice there. Reagan sat in the front area that had once been a living room, while Gigi occupied a bedroom-turned-office in the back. The dining room was now a conference room, and there was another bedroom-office that sat empty, waiting for Gigi to expand her practice with another attorney.

Reagan was on the phone and held up a finger when Chloe entered to indicate she should wait. When Chloe opened her phone to text her parents and Austin to ask if they were free for dinner, she saw Michael's name near the top, from when he'd asked if she'd made it home safely on Sunday afternoon. She'd rather tell him the big news in person, but he wasn't due back for a couple of days. Should she shoot him a text to let him know she'd made it, pending only the site visit? After all, he was the first person she'd even told about the show.

Before she could decide what to text, Reagan had hung up and turned her attention to Chloe. "Were we supposed to have lunch today?"

Chloe usually managed to get away from the café once a week to have lunch with Reagan somewhere on Main Street where she could get back to the shop quickly if needed. Today was not planned, however.

Chloe couldn't hide the smile spreading across her face. "No, I just have some big news—"

Reagan cut Chloe off before she could finish. "Omigosh, did you make the show?" She was already leaping out of her chair and coming around the desk.

"I did." Chloe beamed as Reagan rushed over to hug her and the two of them began jumping up and down.

"What is going on out here?" Gigi asked, emerging from her office down the hallway.

"Chloe is going to be famous!" Reagan said before Chloe could answer.

Gigi's eyebrows knit together in confusion, and Reagan slapped a hand over her mouth. "I'm so sorry, Clo. I got so excited I forgot she doesn't know."

"Know what?" Gigi asked.

Chloe filled Gigi in on the TV show and the real reason for her visit to New York.

Gigi's eyes got big, and her face lit up. "And you just found out you got on the show? Congratulations!" She rushed over to make it a group hug, all the women squealing as they bounced up and down.

"Have you told Austin about all this yet?" Gigi asked as she pulled back, smoothing the skirt of her dress. "He's going to be so excited for you."

"Not yet. I was just going to text him and Mom and Dad to see if we could all do dinner."

"Good idea. I won't breathe a word of it. I'll let you tell him," Gigi said, moving her fingers to her mouth to mime zipping her lips.

Chloe explained to Gigi and Reagan how the show had backup contestants, so there was still a chance she might get cut after the site visit. They assured her that wouldn't happen.

"Send me over anything they ask you to sign and let me

review it first, okay?" Gigi said. "I mean it. They'll probably send you all sorts of contracts and releases. I want to make sure you and Island Coffee are protected."

"Thank you, I will," Chloe promised as Gigi ran back down the hall to answer a phone ringing in her office. Chloe didn't mention that she didn't really know what she'd signed when she'd filled out her application. She remembered some legal mumbo jumbo in small print at the bottom, but it had all sounded pretty standard.

"You have time for lunch?" Reagan asked.

"I was going to ask you the same. Iris is watching the café for the rest of the day so I can tell everyone and start getting ready for the site visit on Thursday."

"They're coming on Thursday?" Reagan asked as she went back around her desk to grab her purse.

Chloe shared what she knew about the site visit on the walk over to lunch at Mack's Diner. Reagan had to run to the bathroom after they ordered, which gave Chloe time to send a message in her family's group text about dinner, and another to Michael, which she kept short and simple.

> A producer called . . . I'm on the show pending a site visit on Thursday! Thanks again for all your support!

Her heart raced as she watched the three little dots dance on the screen, indicating he was writing a reply. When they stopped without a new text appearing, her shoulders slumped. He was probably just in the middle of something else, but she couldn't help being a little disappointed.

Chloe slid her phone into her purse as Reagan returned to the table so she could concentrate on celebrating with her friend. They talked about what she should wear on

Thursday and the most impressive treats she could bake to show off her unique offerings. By the time they'd finished lunch, her head was swimming with ideas. She knew the judges wouldn't be there, but she was going to knock the socks off whoever did show up. After all, it couldn't hurt to have production in her corner, right?

Energized by lunch, Chloe was excited to see new messages in their family group text from everyone saying dinner tonight was on. She was just lamenting that there was no text from Michael when her phone buzzed with an incoming alert. Finally, it was him!

> Congratulations! I knew you could do it.
> We'll celebrate soon.

She was so busy grinning at her phone like an idiot that she nearly ran right into Mr. Herman rolling the mail cart down the sidewalk. Apologizing, Chloe stopped to ask how his wife was doing and made him promise when he stopped by the café to tell Iris to give him some of the petits fours Chloe knew Mrs. Herman loved, on the house. His wife had recently been given a clean bill of health after a lengthy treatment for breast cancer, and it sounded like she finally had her appetite back.

Chloe's next stop was the tourism bureau at the end of Main Street to give them a heads-up about the show. Though there was a risk of the news getting to her family before she could share it herself, with so little time to prepare, she was left with no choice. She had to let the mayor's office and the tourism bureau know what was happening.

Nellie and Emery, the town's two-woman tourism department, were thrilled to hear about the free publicity the show would bring Big Dune Island. They asked if she'd talked to Piper about helping with PR, and Chloe wondered if it was time to bring her into the fold. After all, Chloe had made it onto the show on her own. Piper could just help manage her image and ensure Island Coffee was presented in the best light.

After swearing Nellie and Emery to secrecy until she could tell her family that evening, Chloe fired off a text to Piper asking if she was in town. When she replied that she was, Chloe arranged to have a drink with her before dinner with her family that evening.

Everything was coming together. Was this what it felt like when you realized your dreams were coming true?

Piper was thrilled to learn about the show and promised Chloe any help she needed, even volunteering to come meet with the crew on Thursday afternoon with her. When Chloe told Piper about her desire to win or lose this one on her own merits, Piper assured her she understood. She'd simply help coach Chloe from the sidelines, make sure she came off well on television, and prep her for any media interviews.

From there, Chloe went to dinner with her parents and Austin. There was some initial shock about the television show and why she'd really gone to New York over the weekend, but overall, they were supportive. Her mother's initial reaction was to say how great the opportunity would be for *both* of her children, a disappointing reminder that they saw Austin as being just as integral to the café as Chloe, but she tried to shrug it off. And although her father had a lot of questions, mostly out of concern for how she might be portrayed—"after all, those reality television people make their money by creating drama"—he surprised her by ordering a bottle of champagne for the table to celebrate. Chloe chalked it up as a win and vowed to change the way her parents saw her—as a successful, independent businesswoman—by the end of the show, win or lose.

A text came in from Brianna later that evening saying she'd made the show as well and that she'd asked the producer if Chloe made it so she could congratulate her. Chloe felt bad she hadn't thought to do the same, but she was glad they'd be continuing on the journey together. They promised to text each other if they needed a pep talk or just to vent, vowing not to let the outcome of the show change their budding friendship.

On Thursday, the sky outside was bright and clear, the kind of perfect spring day that kept tourists coming back to the island year after year. Chloe had been up since four that morning, determined to have everything perfect before the crew arrived. Fresh flowers adorned every table, display cases were filled with her best-selling treats, and the entire café gleamed.

Several groups of regulars were settled at their usual tables, and Chloe could tell by the way they watched the door that they were hoping they'd catch a glimpse of the television crew. People had been asking about it all morning as she buzzed around refilling coffees and delivering baked goods to tables.

"They're here," Iris whispered, nodding toward the door. She and Chloe had looked Chris up on LinkedIn that morning to inspect his photo so they wouldn't miss him.

Chloe's heart skipped a beat as she watched Chris and two others—a woman with shoulder-length brown hair and a man with a black baseball hat—settle into a corner table.

She'd known they were coming to observe during the morning rush, but her palms still went slick with nerves.

"Morning, Chloe!" Earl Watson called as he entered with his usual crowd of retirees.

"I'll go get them started with something," Iris said, nodding toward Chris's table. "Give you a minute to settle your nerves and let them observe you in your natural element."

Chloe went behind the counter and looked for the mugs she knew her regulars preferred—Earl's was from his great aunt Sadie's china, Bob's was from his mother's, and Jim liked a Christmas pattern, no matter the time of year.

"How was pickleball yesterday?" Chloe asked as she set a cup of coffee in front of each man. She hoped they didn't notice her hand shaking. Chris and his crew were two tables behind her, but close enough to overhear the conversation. She tried to focus on Earl and Jim's argument about who won pickleball instead of wondering what the TV crew was writing in their notebooks.

Taking a deep breath as she stepped away from the table, Chloe made her way to over to her observers.

"Welcome to Island Coffee," she said, flashing them a smile.

Chris introduced himself, then Sarah, the show's DP—whatever that was—and then Huey, one of the show's cameramen.

"So lovely to meet you all," Chloe said, shaking each of their hands. "I see Iris already got you all something to drink. I'll bring you over a selection of our baked goods so you can try a little bit of everything."

"I'm trying to stick to my keto diet," Sarah said, "but did I hear that woman over there order a strawberry piña colada muffin?"

"Yes," Chloe nodded, "It's one of my original recipes that's become a real hit with visitors and regulars alike."

"I think it all sounds good," Huey said.

"Great," Chloe said, "I'll put you together a little sampler."

Chloe arranged nearly a dozen baked goods and breakfast items on a few plates, then delivered them to the crew's table. This elicited stares from a few regulars and hushed whispers as they seemed to figure out these were the special guests.

"These all look incredible," Sarah said.

Chloe pointed at each item as she named them off: a strawberry piña colada muffin for each of them, plus items to share that included a banana-cream croissant, her grandmother's buttermilk biscuits, one of Ms. Tilley's giant cinnamon rolls—a recipe from her grandmother's best friend—a slice of fried green tomato quiche, hash brown casserole, and a few more traditional items like a blueberry muffin and a plain croissant.

"I can already tell this show is going to be bad for my waistline," Sarah said. "The things I do for this job—" She cut herself off as she popped a piece of strawberry piña colada muffin in her mouth. "Mmm," she practically moaned. "This is everything I dreamed it would be."

"There's more where that came from." Chloe smiled. "You just let me know if you want another one."

"Hey, I think my mom had plates like this," Huey said, running a finger over the pattern on the plate in front of him.

"That's a Wedgwood pattern called Royal Albert Old Country Roses," Chloe explained. "It's a very popular pattern that's been around for decades and is still in production." She explained how families donated items to the café when their loved ones passed as a way to preserve their legacy. Nodding to where Earl, Bob, and Jim sat, she told them about how the men were drinking from mugs from their own families.

"That might be the sweetest thing I've ever heard," Sarah said. "We should get a little vignette or two on that." She directed this comment at Chris.

"There's a lot to work with here," Chris agreed. "Chloe, we'll let you get back to work. We just want to observe for a while. We can all sit down and talk after you close up today."

"That sounds good. Enjoy," she said, gesturing to the food. "And let me or Iris know if we can get you anything else."

The rest of the morning passed in a blur of familiar faces and practiced rhythms. Ms. Myrtle, Gigi's mother, stopped in for tea with a couple of the other ladies from the Junior League. Chloe might have been imagining it, but she thought Ms. Myrtle was glaring at the television crew with a disapproving stare. She probably wasn't imagining it, though. Ms. Myrtle was known for her impeccable taste and impossibly high standards. There was no chance she'd ever watched a minute of reality television, and it seemed like just the sort of thing she'd deem unsavory.

Around ten, Mrs. Herman came in, practically glowing. "Chloe, dear, I had to come thank you for those petits fours. They're the first sweets I've truly enjoyed since finishing treatment."

"I'm so glad," Chloe said, coming around the counter to hug her. "How are you feeling?"

"Better every day. And having something that actually tastes good . . ." Mrs. Herman's eyes welled up. "Well, it makes me feel like myself again."

The crew stayed a couple of hours, taking notes and occasionally whispering among themselves. Chloe tried not to eavesdrop but couldn't help overhearing snippets about someone named Carson.

". . . automated ordering system in every location . . ."

". . . app tracks customer preferences . . ."

". . . five locations in three years . . ."

Chloe's stomach clenched. They were talking about another contestant. One who was clearly more tech-savvy and focused on rapid growth. Was it another coffee shop? She hadn't considered they might take two businesses of the same type. She wasn't mentally prepared for that sort of direct competition.

She and Iris took turns keeping their coffees refilled and asking if they needed anything else to eat. Eventually, they said they were going to go explore the town and that they would return at three. They tried to pay, but she insisted it was on the house.

Promptly at three, just as the last customer was leaving, Chris and his team reentered the café. "Ready to chat?"

Chloe nodded, untying her apron. Iris squeezed her shoulder as she passed.

"This place is incredible," Sarah said. "The personal touches, the way you know everyone's story. This will tug on the heartstrings of our viewers."

"Yeah," Huey said. "Middle America will eat it up."

"But," Chris added, "we also need to make sure you stack up against your competition. I don't say this as criticism, but your business is the smallest on the show in terms of staff, revenue, and just about every other metric. You mentioned franchising in your interview, though. Tell us more about your plans for that."

"Well . . ." Chloe twisted a ring on her finger. "There's

this young woman, Morgan, in Cypress Shores. She's interested in opening her own café, and I've been mentoring her a bit."

"Perfect!" Chris leaned forward. "We'd love to film that mentorship. Maybe even feature her as your first franchisee?"

"Oh, I don't know." The idea of putting that kind of pressure on Morgan made her uncomfortable. Besides, she hadn't even told Morgan she might be willing to franchise Island Coffee or that her name had come up as part of the casting process. Heck, Morgan didn't even know about the show. "We haven't really gotten that far," Chloe said, hoping to hold off on the discussion.

"But that's what makes it perfect for TV," Sarah said. "We could follow the whole process. Carson—another contestant—is already successful with his kombucha chain. You'd be showing a more personalized path to growth."

There it was. Carson, with his automated systems and multiple locations. Everything Chloe wasn't.

Chloe took a deep breath. "I want to be honest. I'm not sure franchising is the right path for Island Coffee. The whole point of this place is that it grows from the community it serves. I'm not convinced that can be replicated."

Chris's brow furrowed. "Then why did you pitch franchising in your interview?"

"Because the judges asked me to think bigger," she admitted. "But maybe bigger isn't always better? I mean, Mrs. Herman doesn't come here because we have the fastest service or the most advanced ordering system. She comes because we remember her favorite treats and notice when she's having a hard day."

The bell above the door chimed, and Chloe looked up to see Michael entering. Her heart did a little flip even as anxiety bubbled in her stomach. What was he doing here? He knew what time they closed.

Michael flashed a smile at Chloe before he turned to Chris. "Hey man!" Michael strode over, grinning.

The producer stood, embracing Michael like an old friend before stepping back and studying him. "Island life looks good on you."

Ahh, Chris must be Michael's college buddy at the show. Chloe hadn't even considered it. She'd been too busy preparing for the visit.

"I was hoping to steal you for dinner," Michael said to Chris—who said, "Sounds good"—before turning to Chloe. "You should join us. That is, unless you're still doing official show business?"

"We've basically wrapped," Chris said. "Though I do have a few more questions about the franchise idea . . ."

"Actually," Sarah interrupted, "I think we have everything we need. This place has something special. Something authentic." She smiled at Chloe. "Sometimes the best way to think bigger is to dig deeper into what already works."

Relief flooded through Chloe. She looked at Michael, who was watching her with warmth in his brown eyes. Dinner with the producer wasn't crossing some sort of ethical line, was it? After all, she was already on the show, right? "Dinner sounds great," she said. "Just let me change first."

"You all are welcome to join us too," Michael said to Sarah and Huey.

"Nah, we still have B-roll to shoot before it gets dark," Huey said.

"And I'm still full from breakfast." Sarah laughed, patting her stomach.

Chloe told Sarah and Huey it was nice to meet them

and that she looked forward to working with them once filming began. As she headed upstairs to her apartment, she heard Chris asking Michael about some mutual friend from college. She wondered how much Michael had leaned on his friend to consider Island Coffee. Was he the real reason she got on the show?

Chapter 10

Michael

"Remember Julie Thompson?" Chris asked as their waiter cleared their appetizer plates. "She's a producer on the West Coast now."

Michael nodded, though his attention kept drifting to Chloe. She'd changed into a sundress printed with tiny blue flowers, and her cheeks were flushed from the glass of wine she was nursing. Dune & Brine sat right on the water, and the setting sun shining through the windows cast everything in a golden glow, including Chloe.

"Did she ever marry that guy from the campus radio station?" Michael asked, forcing himself to focus on Chris.

"Yeah. Divorced him two years later. Classic man-eater." Chris shook his head. "Speaking of man-eaters, how's Alessandra?"

Michael nearly choked on his scotch. "She's—" He glanced at Chloe, who was suddenly very interested in her wine glass. Chris had met Alessandra a couple of times in the city when Michael had taken her as a date to an alumni social or a friend's wedding. "Our relationship is strictly professional."

"Right." Chris's knowing smile said he wasn't buying it. "So Chloe, tell me more about the family heirlooms in the café. Are there a couple of regulars you think would do well on camera? I think we could build a whole episode around that."

As Chloe gave a couple of suggestions, Michael found himself remembering the plates his mother had carefully wrapped and moved with her to the new house. His parents had never had fancy china, just a simple white set with blue trim that they'd received as a wedding gift. But his mother had treasured it, using it for every holiday and special occasion.

". . . don't you think, Michael?"

He realized Chloe was looking at him expectantly. "Sorry, what?"

"I was saying how the dishes and recipes are about preserving memories. Like your mom's lasagna pan."

He smiled, touched that she'd remembered that detail from a story he'd told her over the weekend, about how his mom still used the same lasagna pan her grandmother had made the family recipe in back in Sicily. "Exactly. Though in my mom's case, it's more about refusing to accept change."

"Your mom sounds amazing," Chloe said. "The way you talk about her reminds me of my grandmother."

"You'd like her," he said without thinking. "She'd probably try to feed you until you burst, but she'd love having someone appreciate the traditional ways of doing things."

He'd almost forgotten they weren't alone at this dinner until Chris spoke.

"What about the recipes?" he asked. "Didn't you say the cinnamon roll today was someone else's recipe?"

Chloe nodded. "My grandmother's best friend, Ms. Tilley. My grandmother would have all her friends over every Tuesday, and each woman would bring a dish. Ms. Tilley always brought her homemade cinnamon rolls. Some days they'd sit around and knit, sharing stories while they worked. Other times they would play cards or try out some new crafting project. Everything I know about hosting and baking is from my grandmother."

"So it's another way you honor people in the community," Chris said.

"Yes, it's sort of become an Island Coffee tradition. When someone who was known for a secret or special dish passes, their children bring me the recipe to make in the café, but only on the condition I don't share the recipe. Sometimes we only make it right after they pass as a one-time thing to honor them, but sometimes it's so popular that I ask if I can continue making it on a more regular basis."

"You want to be in town for Mrs. Grover's lemon bars," Michael said. They were his favorite.

Chloe smiled at him. "I'll make sure they're on the menu when we start shooting."

"Listen, Chloe," Chris said, "I know you're worried about the franchise angle, but I think you're overthinking it. Carson's automated kombucha bars are one path to growth, but your community-based model could be just as successful. Different demographics, different approaches."

"I just don't want to promise something I'm not sure about," Chloe said. "Especially to Morgan."

"You could just use the show as a way to explore the

idea," Michael suggested. "Tell Morgan it's something you'd love to do if you can figure out how to make it work and win the money, but that nothing is guaranteed."

"Exactly," Chris said. "Viewers will relate to someone wrestling with real questions about growth versus authenticity. Not everyone wants to be the next Starbucks."

"The judges seemed pretty focused on scale," Chloe pointed out.

"Trust me," Chris said, "in ten years of producing business shows, I've learned that the most successful contestants aren't always the flashiest ones. They're the ones who know who they are and stick to it."

Michael watched Chloe absorb this, saw some of the tension leave her shoulders. Their conversations from the weekend had revealed she was worried about measuring up to the other contestants, but Chris was right. Her authenticity was her strength.

The waiter appeared with their entrees—locally caught grouper for Chloe and Chris, steak for him. As they ate, the conversation drifted to lighter topics. Chris told stories about disaster contestants from the dating shows he'd done before, and Chloe shared tales of recipe mishaps at the café. Chris questioned Michael about island life, and he admitted that the place had grown on him.

"I barely recognize you," Chris said. "The Michael I knew in college would never have invested in a small-town construction company, let alone stuck around to become part of the community. Please tell me you don't own a pair of flip-flops."

"People change, but not that much," Michael said, laughing.

After dinner, Chris excused himself to take a call from the network. Michael and Chloe stepped out onto the restaurant's deck, the warm breeze carrying the salt scent of the ocean.

"Do you really think I can do this?" Chloe asked as she turned to face Michael. "Compete against people like Carson with their fancy apps and multiple locations?"

"I think," he said carefully, "that you've already built something most business owners only dream of—a place that matters to people. The rest is just details."

She looked up at him, and for a moment he thought she might hug him again like she had when they'd said goodbye in New York. He was disappointed when she didn't, but he wasn't willing to be the one to initiate it either. He didn't want to lead her on, and he had no intention of starting anything with her right now. She needed to focus on the show, and he had plenty of work he should be focusing on.

"What?" she asked when he didn't look away.

"Nothing," he said. "I just think the show's lucky to have you."

Chris returned then, and they said their goodbyes to Chloe. Michael watched her walk away until she'd disappeared around the corner toward the stairs that would take her down to street level.

"Come on," Chris said, clapping him on the shoulder. "Let's grab a nightcap at that place across the street, The Salty Dog. You can tell me what's really going on with you and Chloe."

Michael considered protesting, but it had been a long time since they'd been able to catch up. "Sure, but just one drink. I have a packed schedule tomorrow."

The Salty Dog was busy for a Thursday, probably due to a fishing tournament that had brought extra boats to the marina. They found two stools at the end of the bar, and

Michael ordered another scotch while Chris went for bourbon.

"So," Chris said once their drinks arrived, "how long have you been falling for her?"

"I'm not—" Michael stopped at Chris's raised eyebrow. "It's complicated."

"Because of the show?"

"Because of everything." Michael stared into his glass. "She's ten years younger than me. We have nothing in common. And yes, there's the show, and The Perry project, and the fact that I'm her brother's best friend's business partner and don't even live here full-time."

"That's a lot of excuses for someone who isn't falling for her."

Michael sighed. "You saw her tonight. The way she lights up talking about the café, how she remembers every customer's story. Being around her is like drinking liquid sunshine."

"Meanwhile, you're more like choking on a spreadsheet?" Chris teased.

"Basically. You remember my brother-in-law Steve? The plumber?"

Chris nodded. He used to come home with Michael for the weekends in college, so he knew the whole family. Michael hadn't meant to bring up his brother-in-law's situation, but it had been weighing on him. He filled Chris in on the failing plumbing business.

"Sounds like he tried to run his business with his heart instead of his head," Chris said.

"Like Chloe does?" Michael took another sip of scotch. "But she makes it work. Somehow, she balances the books while still treating everyone like family."

"Maybe that's why you need her," Chris suggested. "To

show you there's a middle ground between cold efficiency and bleeding heart."

"Or maybe I'd just ruin what makes her special by trying to turn it into a case study for a business textbook."

Chris leaned back, studying him. "You know what I think? I think you're scared."

"Of what?"

"Of admitting that maybe all those spreadsheets and profit projections aren't enough anymore. That maybe success can be measured in other ways."

Michael thought of his mother's face when he'd bought her the brownstone, how proud she'd been that her son had "made it." He'd spent his whole life trying to ensure his family never felt the financial insecurity of his childhood again. But lately, he found himself thinking more about his father. Not the memory of his death, but of his life. How he'd known every neighbor's name, helped at church festivals, made everyone feel welcome.

"You know what the craziest part is?" Michael said finally. "For the first time in my life, I'm not sure what the smart business move is. The Perry could be just another profitable luxury hotel, or it could be something that actually matters to people. Like Island Coffee matters."

"Like Chloe matters?"

Michael didn't answer, but he didn't have to. Chris knew him too well.

"For what it's worth," Chris said, signaling the bartender for another round, "I think you're both in your heads too much. You're worried about ruining her authenticity, and she's worried about measuring up to bigger businesses. Meanwhile, anyone who spends five minutes with you two can see you balance each other perfectly."

"It's not that simple."

"It never is." Chris slid a fresh scotch in front of him. "But maybe that's the point. Life isn't a business plan, Michael. Sometimes you have to lead with your heart and trust that the numbers will follow."

Michael's phone buzzed with a text from Jesse about the warehouse project in Jacksonville. Another property that could either be just another deal or something meaningful to the community. He was starting to think there might not be any going back to his old way of doing things.

The text from Jesse turned into a long phone call the following morning about the numbers not working for the warehouse project. After the feedback from the community, they'd hoped they could reserve some space at street level for artist studios to fill a gap in town created by the closure of a nearby art co-op.

"I talked to some of the artists to find out more about what they were paying in the co-op, but to meet those rates, we need to be able to charge a lot further below market for rent than we thought," Jesse explained. "Even if we found reliable tenants, we'd be looking at a significantly lower ROI than if we went with standard retail. We could still try to limit our tenants to local businesses, though—no chains—to help keep that community-focused feel."

Michael pinched the bridge of his nose, studying the spreadsheet on his laptop that Jesse had emailed over the night before. He'd been up late running different scenarios, trying to make the numbers work. "What about tax incentives for historic preservation?"

"Already factored those in. Along with the enterprise zone credits." Jesse sighed. "Look, I love the idea. The arts community would go crazy for it. But you know John and the other partners. They're not going to sign off unless we can show stronger returns."

He was right. Michael had built his reputation on delivering consistent profits. It was why his partners trusted his judgment on projects like The Perry, and why he had the freedom to spend so much time on Big Dune Island.

"Give me a day or two to think on it," Michael said.

After hanging up, he stared at the rows of numbers on his screen. Five years ago, this would have been simple. He'd have leased the ground floor to whatever national chain would pay top dollar, gotten them to commit to sponsoring a 5k race or donating ten percent of every Wednesday night's sales to a children's charity, thrown some vague "commitment to the community" language in the press release, and moved on to the next deal.

But now he couldn't stop thinking about what the warehouse could mean for the neighborhood. About all the artists who'd lost their workspace when the co-op closed. About how spaces like Island Coffee brought people together in ways a chain store never could.

His phone buzzed with an email from Alessandra containing her latest renderings for The Perry café. They were sleek and modern, with chrome accents and minimalist furniture. Everything designed to maximize efficiency and turnover. She'd included wallpaper designed by a local artist as her nod to the neighborhood—her idea of a compromise on Chloe's idea of a mural—but it had the same neutral, forgettable style as what she'd put in every other space they'd done together.

And that wasn't what he wanted for this space.

Michael closed his laptop. He needed coffee, and not the kind made by the fancy automated pour-over machine in his condo's kitchen. He needed the real thing, served in a mismatched mug by someone who remembered exactly how he took it.

Island Coffee was busy when he arrived, but Chloe spotted him immediately. She was behind the counter talking to Austin, who'd apparently just picked up his youth baseball team's uniforms for the upcoming season and was showing off the Island Coffee sponsorship patch he'd added to the sleeve.

"First game is Saturday," Austin was saying. "And before I forget, the air conditioning guy was here yesterday, and he found some issues with the HVAC system while he was doing the regular maintenance. We need to get him in here before summer to replace a few parts so we don't risk it going out, and he wants to clean the ducts at the same time."

"Can't it wait until after the show is done?" Chloe asked. "It's only six weeks of filming. I've just got so much on my plate right now getting ready."

"No rush." Austin shrugged. "It can wait. It's not urgent."

Michael watched their interaction and wondered for the first time what sort of arrangement they had. He knew Chloe had invested a small amount alongside her brother when he'd bought the building and that Austin had given her the start-up capital. He'd heard her mention having a good deal on the rent for the café and her apartment upstairs, but he hadn't wanted to pry by asking for details.

"Your usual?" Chloe asked in his direction as she delivered a danish to a table nearby.

"Please."

As she went back behind the counter and reached for his preferred cup—a simple design with delicate blue flowers that reminded him of his mother's wedding set—he watched her work. Everything about the café was an extension of her. It was warm, inviting, and personal. But could that be replicated in a franchise?

She set his latte in front of him with a smile that chipped away at his sour mood from a morning spent pouring over spreadsheets. "You look like you're stressed about something."

"Just trying to make some numbers work on a project," he said. He took a sip of his perfectly prepared latte. "How are you feeling about filming starting soon?"

"Excited. Nervous." She sat in the chair across from him. "I keep thinking about Carson's kombucha empire and wondering if I'm in over my head."

He didn't mention the revelation he was having about the unique financial circumstances that might make replicating her model more difficult for franchisees. Maybe he should, so she'd be prepared if it came up on the show. But looking at her hopeful face, he couldn't bring himself to add to her doubts. Not now. Not when she was about to start filming.

"You'll be great," he said instead. "Just be yourself."

It wasn't until he was walking back into his condo, the warehouse spreadsheets weighing on his mind, that he realized the irony. Here he was, trying to find ways to make community-focused projects work within standard business constraints, while Chloe operated in a bit of a bubble where she hadn't had to face those same constraints.

Things were always more complicated than they seemed on the surface.

Chapter 11

Chloe

The kitchen looked different in the glow of television lights. Chloe had walked into this space before dawn nearly every day for the past seven years, but today it felt surreal. Her normal routine of starting the morning's baking while the world was still quiet had been replaced by the hum of equipment, the murmur of crew members, and the sharp brightness of professional lighting.

"Could you do that again?" the cameraman asked. "But this time, move a little slower when you pour the batter."

Chloe nodded, picking up the mixing bowl again. She'd already redone this shot twice, but she understood they needed to get it right. At least they'd arrived early enough that she wasn't behind schedule yet.

"And remember to smile," Sarah prompted from where she stood reviewing footage on a small monitor.

Chloe thought about pointing out that no one actually smiled while pouring muffin batter at four-thirty in the morning, but she kept that observation to herself. Instead, she focused on the familiar motion, trying to find a balance between natural and camera-ready.

"Perfect," Sarah called. "Now let's get a shot of you putting them in the oven."

"They need about two more minutes to rest first," Chloe said. When Sarah raised an eyebrow, she added, "It helps them rise better. Creates a better texture."

"Really?" The sound guy perked up. "I didn't know that."

"There's a lot of little tricks like that," Chloe said, falling into her natural rhythm of sharing kitchen wisdom. "My Grandma Sophie taught me most of them."

Sarah's eyes lit up. "That's great. Can you tell us more about that while you work? Just talk about your grandmother and baking."

It felt odd, sharing stories about her grandmother while the camera rolled, but Chloe found herself relaxing as she worked. Baking and sharing stories were already things she did every day. She was just doing it in front of a camera today.

The morning progressed in a pattern: bake, film, repeat. By the time Iris arrived at six, they'd captured what felt like hours of footage but had somehow managed to stay on schedule with the morning's baking.

"How's it going?" Iris asked, tying on her apron. Her eyes widened at the array of equipment and people filling their usually peaceful kitchen.

"It's . . . different," Chloe said, smiling. "But we're making it work."

"Alright, everyone," Chris called from the doorway. "Time for the challenge reveal."

Chloe's stomach flipped. She'd been so focused on managing the morning's filming that she'd almost forgotten this was a competition. Chris held up a tablet, and suddenly the judges' faces filled the screen.

"Good morning, entrepreneurs," Andie began. "For your first challenge, we want to see how you'd take your business to the next level. Create a signature product or offering that captures your brand's essence but could work across multiple locations. Good luck."

The tablet went dark, and Chloe felt her mind racing. A signature product that could scale? She glanced around her kitchen at the morning's fresh-baked goods. Everything here was made from scratch, with care and personal attention. How did you package that?

"We'll give you some time to work," Chris said. "But we'll need to film your process, your attempts, and maybe interview a few regulars about what makes this place special."

Chloe nodded, already moving toward her recipe box. She had dozens of original creations, family recipes passed down through generations both from her own family and those of her patrons, even special treats she'd developed for regular customers. But which one could work beyond these walls without losing what made it special?

The bell above the front door chimed as their first customers arrived. Show or no show, Island Coffee was still a business that needed running. And maybe that was exactly what she needed right now—to stay grounded in what made this place work.

"Coming," she called, heading for the café with Iris.

As she grabbed her favorite coffee pot—the one with

delicate purple flowers that had belonged to Mrs. Watson's mother—Chloe realized something. She didn't need to change who she was for the cameras. She just needed to find a way to share it with a bigger audience.

And she had to figure out a signature product she could produce in the next forty-eight hours.

The morning rush brought its usual parade of regulars, each reacting differently to the camera crew tucked into a corner of the café. Earl and his friends seemed to forget the cameras entirely, falling into their usual debates about the town council's latest proposals. Ms. Myrtle, on the other hand, sat ramrod straight at her usual table, deliberately ignoring the equipment while somehow looking more camera-ready than anyone else in the room. But then, Ms. Myrtle always looked like she'd just stepped out of the pages of a glossy magazine.

Between customers, Chloe flipped through her recipe cards, trying to identify a special treat she could make that would be a signature item at multiple future potential locations of Island Coffee. Nothing felt right, though. She couldn't just bake up a bunch of something and call it a day. That wasn't going to win her the money.

"Have you thought about something that could be prepackaged?" Chris suggested from where he'd been observing. "That might be easier to scale."

"The whole point of Island Coffee is that nothing is prepackaged. Everything is homemade, just like your mother would make," Chloe said, trying not to be combative. "Sorry, I don't mean to sound difficult."

"Don't apologize," Sarah said. "That's exactly the kind of authentic reaction we want. Tell us more about why that matters to you."

Before Chloe could answer, Mrs. Herman appeared in

the doorway to the kitchen. "Oh, I'm sorry dear. I didn't mean to interrupt your filming. I just stopped by to ask if you could make me some red velvet petit fours for my book club next week." She turned to leave, but Sarah waved her in.

"Actually, this is perfect. Would you mind telling us why you chose the petit fours?"

Mrs. Herman's eyes lit up. "Well, they're not just any petit fours. They're made from Chloe's grandmother's recipe, the same ones she used to serve at her Tuesday afternoon gatherings. When I was going through my cancer treatments and nothing tasted right, those little cakes were the first thing that made me feel like myself again." She swiped at the corner of her eye where a tear was forming. "It wasn't just the taste. It was like having a piece of the past, a reminder that some things stay the same even when everything else changes."

Chloe felt something click in her mind. Island Coffee's unique approach wasn't just about the recipes. It was about the stories behind them. The way food connected people to memories, to each other, and gave them a sense of belonging.

"I think I have an idea," she said. She said goodbye to Mrs. Herman, promising to have her red velvet petit fours ready for her meeting.

The next hour passed in a blur as Chloe's concept took shape. She pulled out her grandmother's carefully preserved recipe box, complete with its patina of years of flour and butter stains. Inside were not just recipes but also the stories behind them. There were handwritten notes about who brought what dish to which gathering, little adaptations made over the years, memories preserved on food-spattered cards.

"I'm thinking about creating special boxes," she explained to Chris and Sarah, "where each treat comes with its story. The petit fours Mrs. Herman loves, Ms. Tilley's cinnamon rolls, even my strawberry piña colada muffins. They each have their own story." Her hands moved animatedly as she spoke. "And you can find that in every small town—recipes passed down through generations. We could adapt the concept for each location and preserve local traditions while creating new ones."

Sarah was nodding enthusiastically. "Can you mock-up a prototype? We'd love to film the process."

"Iris," Chloe called. "Could you grab that stack of blank recipe cards from the office? And maybe that nice box my mother gave me for Christmas. The one with the rose pattern?"

While Iris gathered supplies, Chloe began assembling an assortment of treats. She chose items that represented different aspects of Island Coffee: her grandmother's petit fours, a lemon-lavender cake made from Ms. Grover's recipe, and the strawberry piña colada muffins.

"Each card will tell the story behind the treat," she explained as she wrote. "Like how Ms. Grover's lemon-lavender cake started as a happy accident when she was baking for her daughter's wedding and grabbed the wrong extract." She smiled at the memory. "But it was such a hit that she kept making it that way."

"It's like edible history," Chris said.

"Exactly." Chloe carefully arranged the treats in the box, tucking the cards with their respective stories alongside them. "Food is about more than just nutrition and taste. It's about connection, and memory, and belonging. That's what makes Island Coffee special, and that's what these Story Boxes could bring to other communities."

She could see it clearly now. The Story Boxes would celebrate local traditions in every location, featuring baked goods and memories from that community's families. It wouldn't just be about franchising her café—it would be about helping each place create its own version of what made Island Coffee special.

"I think we're ready to film your presentation," Sarah said. "But first, could we get some shots of you sharing the prototype with your regulars? See their reactions?"

Chloe nodded, already knowing exactly who she wanted to ask. If she was going to tell Island Coffee's story, she needed the people who'd helped write it.

She assembled a small group at one of the larger tables: Mrs. Herman, Ms. Myrtle, and Earl and his wife, Gwendolyn, who'd stopped by to say hi on her way home from a volunteer shift at the library. The camera crew positioned themselves as unobtrusively as possible while Chloe presented her prototype Story Box.

"It's about preserving traditions," she explained, opening the box to reveal the carefully arranged treats. "Each card shares the story of the person behind it, how the recipe came to be, and what makes it special."

Ms. Myrtle picked up the card next to the lemon-lavender cake, adjusting her reading glasses. As she read, a smile softened her usually stern expression. "I was there that day, when Catherine accidentally grabbed the lavender extract," she said. "We all told her it was divine, but I don't think she believed us until the wedding guests started asking for the recipe."

"Look at this, Gwendolyn," Earl said, showing his wife the petit fours card. "It mentions your mother's Tuesday afternoon gatherings with Sophie." He turned to the camera. "My mother-in-law and Chloe's grandmother were thick as thieves. Always trying out new recipes on us menfolk."

Gwendolyn dabbed at her eyes with a napkin. "It's like they're still here with us, in a way."

Chloe felt a lump form in her throat. This was exactly what she'd hoped for. Not just preserving recipes but keeping memories alive.

"And you'd adapt this for other locations?" Sarah asked from behind the camera. "How would that work?"

"Every town has its own food traditions and its own stories that deserve to be preserved," Chloe explained. "We'd work with each community to create Story Boxes that celebrate their unique heritage. It's not about copying Island Coffee. It's about helping other places capture what makes them special."

The next hour was spent filming her official presentation. They set up in the kitchen, where Chloe had arranged Story Boxes in various stages of assembly. She walked through the concept, demonstrating how she'd source local recipes and stories, explaining how the boxes could be both grab-and-go items and special orders for events. They could even offer them by mail order to people who'd moved away and wanted a little taste of Big Dune Island wherever they were.

"The Story Boxes solve two challenges," she said, looking directly into the camera like Sarah had coached her. "They give us a product that can be replicated across locations while highlighting what makes each community unique. But more importantly, they give people a way to share their own stories, to feel like they're part of something bigger."

She held up one of the recipe cards. "This isn't just about selling baked goods. It's about preserving traditions, celebrating connections, and creating a place where everyone feels at home, whether they're visiting our café or enjoying these treats at home."

"And cut!" Sarah called. "That was perfect, Chloe. We got everything we need."

Chris nodded in agreement. "You really brought it all together. Great job today."

As the crew began packing up their equipment, Chloe sank into a chair, finally feeling the weight of the day. She'd done it. Whether it was enough to impress the judges remained to be seen, but she'd stayed true to what made Island Coffee special while finding a way to think bigger.

"Here," Iris said, placing a fresh cup of coffee in front of her. She'd used the delicate blue-and-white cup that somehow always found its way into Chloe's hands when she needed comforting. "I'd say you earned this."

"Thanks." Chloe wrapped her hands around the warm cup. "I just hope it was enough."

"It was more than enough," Iris said firmly. "You showed them exactly who you are, and that's always enough."

Looking around at her café, at the regular customers who'd stayed late to support her, and at the Story Boxes that represented everything she loved about this place, Chloe smiled. Win or lose, she'd found a way to be true to herself and her community while taking on this new challenge.

Now she just had to wait and see what the judges thought when the episode aired the following week.

~

"I can't believe they turned this episode around in less than a week," Reagan said as she arranged a platter of chocolate chip cookies on Gigi's granite-topped kitchen island. They were Chloe's grandmother's recipe, of course. It seemed fitting for tonight.

"I can't believe they edited it down to an hour," Chloe said. "They filmed an entire day with me."

Chloe's phone buzzed with an incoming text.

Good luck tonight! I'm rooting for you!

Chloe smiled as she typed a reply to Brianna.

And I'm rooting for you! I can't wait to see your salon.

She heard the front door open as she hit send on the text. Luke's excited voice carried down the hallway. "Mama G! The pizza's here!" Luke had started calling Austin "Dad" fairly soon after he'd adopted the boy, because he'd never known a father. Gigi hadn't wanted him to call her "Mom," however, as he was still healing from losing his mother several years earlier. So they'd come up with "Mama G," and it still made Chloe smile. Gigi wasn't someone who had been in a hurry to have children, but the name seemed to fit perfectly.

"And apparently so is Michael Russo," Austin said, appearing in the kitchen doorway with a surprised expression. "Did you invite him?"

Chloe shook her head, her heart doing a little flip. She hadn't seen much of Michael lately. He'd had meetings in New York, then when he was back down on Big Dune Island, he was often running down to Jacksonville to deal with issues on the warehouse project.

"I did," Gigi said, brushing past them to help Luke with the pizzas. "I ran into him at the courthouse yesterday. We got to talking about the show, and he mentioned how proud he was of you, so I told him about the viewing party and invited him."

Reagan shot Chloe a look that clearly said, *I told you so,* but Chloe pretended not to notice.

"Well," Austin said, "this will be interesting. I don't think I've ever seen the guy in jeans."

But there was Michael, following Luke into the kitchen wearing jeans and a white button-down with the sleeves rolled up. He looked more relaxed than usual.

"Hi," he said, smiling directly at Chloe like she was the only person in the room.

She could feel a blush rush into her cheeks. "Hi yourself. Thanks for coming."

"Wouldn't miss it, and I brought wine," he said, holding up two bottles. "And Luke here tells me to get my phone ready to vote."

"I already saved the number you text to vote in Dad's and Mama G's phones," Luke said. "I can save it in yours too if you want. Did you know the audience vote counts for twenty-five percent of the score?"

"Speaking of voting," Reagan said, "Nellie over at the tourism office posted the number on their Facebook page, and we sent it out in our office newsletter this week. We're going to show the judges that Big Dune has Chloe's back."

"I sent the link to the entire Junior League email list," Gigi said. "Callie's going to share on her social channels too, right?"

Callie and Jesse had called to say they couldn't make it because the baby hadn't slept in nearly twenty-four hours. But Chloe had already had this conversation with her, thanking Callie for offering but declining.

"No." Chloe shook her head. "I asked her not to. I want

to win this on my own merits, not because a big celebrity campaigned for me."

Michael frowned. "I know you didn't want Callie to throw her weight behind you when it came to getting on the show, but you should take advantage of everything at your disposal to win. You got yourself on the show, now let your loyal clientele—especially the famous ones—show their support."

Gigi nodded in agreement. "Callie would never promote something she didn't feel strongly about. She loves the café, Chloe, and she loves you."

"It's just not how I want to win. I want to walk away knowing that I won because I earned it, not because I have a famous friend."

Austin squeezed her shoulder. "Don't cut off your nose to spite your face," he advised.

"Don't you think I can win on my own?" Her big brother always believed in her. Of all the people in this room, he should understand more than anyone about wanting to have something that's your own.

"Of course I think you can win on your own. I just think you should use all the tools at your disposal. But this is your thing. Play it however you want."

"Five minutes!" Luke called out from the living room. As they shuffled out from the kitchen carrying pizza-laden paper plates and napkins, Chloe could see Luke already settled in front of the massive television.

Everyone found spots on the sectional sofa and over-sized chairs. Chloe ended up on one end of the sectional with Reagan beside her. She was hyperaware of Michael settling into the armchair just to her right.

"Here we go," Austin said as the show's logo filled the screen.

As the opening sequence introduced the judges and explained the show's format, Chloe heard the words but didn't absorb them. Her mind was racing, outpaced only by her heart. Clips of the contestants filled the screen first, and Chloe barely recognized herself talking about Island Coffee. Had her voice always sounded like that?

"You look amazing," Reagan whispered. "That dress was perfect."

The camera began following three people from behind, two men and a woman. Rapid-fire photographs showed them at multiple businesses she recognized as some of the other contestants she'd just seen on the screen. She was surprised when the next photo showed them seated in the café.

"Look, it's Island Coffee," Luke said, pointing at the screen.

Had the show sent secret shoppers? Before Chloe could react, the three people reappeared on camera sitting in makeup chairs. As they began removing wigs and peeling off layers of prosthetics on their faces that disguised their identities, a collective gasp went up in the room. It was the judges!

"That was fun," Andie said, leaning forward in her chair to look at the other two judges, who were nodding in agreement.

Nathan laughed. "I don't think anyone suspected us."

"You learn a lot when no one knows you're watching," Thad added.

The judges went on to explain that they had indeed visited all the contestants prior to filming to get a feel for their locations, test their products and services, and experience their customer service firsthand.

"One thing's for sure," Nathan said, "these contestants have some stiff competition."

"Do you remember them coming in?" Gigi asked.

"I think so, but I didn't wait on them," Chloe said.

She tried to remember details of the threesome's visit. They looked familiar now that she'd seen the photo, but she wasn't sure what they'd ordered because they'd been at Iris's table. Not knowing anything more was nerve-racking, but Iris would have taken good care of them just like everyone who dined there.

The murmurs in the room died down as the first segment began with Carson's kombucha chain. He was younger than Chloe had expected—late twenties at most—dressed in a sharp suit as he demonstrated his automated brewing system. Screens displayed real-time analytics about customer preferences and inventory levels. It was impressive, if a bit sterile. He even had robot waiters that delivered drinks and small bites to tables.

"Well, that's terrifying," Reagan muttered.

Then came Brianna's segment. They'd texted after filming the first episode about their nerves and the stress of waiting for the show to air. Neither had divulged any details on the challenge, but it had been nice to have someone to talk to who was going through the same experience.

Brianna's salon was beautiful, all soft colors and clean lines. She'd created a training program for stylists that could be replicated across locations, standardizing her high-end service while still feeling personal.

"She seems nice," Gigi said. "Like she actually cares about her employees and customers."

"She is," Chloe said. "We met at the interview in New York."

It seemed like their businesses had similar vibes until

Brianna started demonstrating how she was using augmented reality and artificial intelligence to allow people to "try on" hairstyles and colors before they committed to them.

Chloe wondered if she needed to integrate more technology into her own business. She wasn't even sure what that would look like. She didn't want customers ordering on kiosks or tablets. Personal service was the bedrock of her business.

Several other contestants flew by in quick segments before they reached Island Coffee. Chloe's stomach clenched as she watched herself struggle with the initial baking shots, but then came Mrs. Herman's visit, and everything clicked into place.

"Look at that," Austin said proudly as the Story Box concept unfolded on screen. "That's my baby sister."

Chloe felt tears prick her eyes watching Mrs. Herman and the others share their stories. The editors had woven the footage together beautifully, capturing the warmth and connection that made Island Coffee special. At the end of her segment, a graphic on the screen gave the code the audience could use later in the show to text their vote for Island Coffee.

"I'm voting for Chloe," Luke said matter-of-factly as Chloe's segment ended, making everyone laugh.

At least she knew she had the vote of every person in this room. Nothing was more important than her community, and the segment reminded her that she was already a winner when it came to that.

Chapter 12

Michael

Michael had watched Chloe's reactions to the show more than the program itself. She wore her heart on her sleeve, and her face and body language telegraphed her every thought. Her foot had bounced nervously leading up to her segment, then quickly stilled as her eyes grew large and round, like a deer caught in the headlights, as Island Coffee filled the screen. When her customers began to appear in front of her, she relaxed, finally smiling.

Both Chloe and Island Coffee had looked great on television. He'd been afraid they'd portray her as some small-town stereotype. Instead, they'd captured the genuine warmth that made Island Coffee special. The editing emphasized how she preserved traditions while creating new ones, making her business model feel both timeless and innovative.

He couldn't help comparing it to the sterile efficiency of Carson's kombucha chain. While Carson's analytics and automation were impressive, there was something cold about watching robots deliver drinks to customers. His overhead was probably low with fewer human employees, but that kind of tech didn't come cheap either, meaning he was either independently wealthy, had significant debt, or had already given up part of his company to investors. The camera had scanned one of his stores quickly, and Michael had caught the empty chairs where people might have lingered to chat if it had been a more inviting space. It had clearly been designed for maximum efficiency.

Brianna's salon struck a better balance, preserving the personal connection of a stylist-client relationship while using technology to enhance the experience rather than replace it. The augmented reality features were clever, and they supported rather than replaced the human element like Carson's technology had.

The remaining contestants' segments ran, including a boutique pet food company that specialized in fresh-made meals, a custom sneaker designer who'd built a cult following on social media, a mobile bike repair business, a subscription box service for children's STEM projects, a candle company that created signature scents for hotels and other businesses, a vintage clothing curator who'd pioneered a rental model for special occasions, and a food truck owner who'd created a line of authentic Mexican sauces.

Michael found himself mentally categorizing each business based on scalability and potential profitability. The pet food company had strong systems, and no doubt the audience would be swayed by the cute labrador puppies that had featured prominently throughout the episode. The vintage clothing curator clearly understood her market but needed better inventory management. The sneaker designer had an impressive social media presence, but it was hard to tell if he was riding a trend that would eventually fade.

What Chloe needed was a way to demonstrate that community connection and profitability weren't mutually exclusive. He'd seen it himself in how Island Coffee had revitalized Main Street, drawing both tourists and locals to spend more time downtown. There was value in that beyond just coffee and pastry sales, but she needed to help the judges see it.

When the judges began their deliberation, he noticed Chloe start bouncing her foot again. Her friend Reagan reached over and grabbed her hand, squeezing it tightly.

Andie praised Chloe's authentic approach and community connection, but Thad quickly joined in to question whether the Story Box concept could scale.

"How do you maintain quality control across multiple locations?" he asked. "What's to stop someone from just printing cards and sticking them in a box of grocery store cookies?"

"Is he serious?" Gigi asked, rolling her eyes.

Chloe glanced over at Michael, her eyes seeming to ask what he thought. He gave her a reassuring smile. "You did great. Don't get hung up on anything they say. Remember that it's a television show. It wouldn't be good TV if all three of them praised every contestant."

Michael hoped she would notice how the judges chimed in with questions and criticism for each of the other contestants.

The show went to commercial to tally the audience votes, which had been coming in since the final contestant's segment had aired. The judges would combine their votes to come up with a ranking of all ten businesses, which would be revealed before the audience vote was added.

Chloe's phone started buzzing, and she moved to the desk that sat along the living room wall as she asked Austin to turn down the television. She had explained to them all earlier that the show wanted live reactions from the contestants without forcing them to travel away from their businesses every week for a live show. So instead, each contestant had to join a live video call during the commercial break so their reactions could appear on screen as the votes were revealed and the lowest person was dismissed.

Chloe had set up a small tripod with a ring light earlier, a kit the show had sent her, and Michael watched her now as she answered the call on speaker, setting her phone on the desk. She was told by a producer to mute her phone and that she would only unmute if she was the released contestant, who would have a minute to receive feedback from the judges.

As soon as she confirmed that she understood and pushed what was presumably the mute button on her phone, the group began with their predictions.

"A hundred bucks says the mobile bike repair guy is toast," Gigi said.

"How can you tell?" Austin asked. "It seems like a good business idea."

"He's one guy trying to do it all himself," Gigi said. "You can tell he doesn't trust anyone else to do it, so he'll never be able to scale."

"I think it's the candle one," Austin disagreed. "I don't think she did a good job explaining what makes her business different. It sounds exactly like the woman who sells candles down at our farmer's market."

"He's got a point," Reagan said. "Michael, what do you

think? You invest in businesses all the time. Which one doesn't make the cut?"

They all turned to look at him, and for the first time since he'd started visiting Big Dune Island, he felt like he was part of their inner circle, not on the outside looking in. When he'd first arrived in town, he knew they'd all been suspicious of his motives for investing in Thomas Construction. And it wasn't beyond his notice that he dressed and talked differently than them at times. But slowly over the years, without him even noticing, he'd somehow become one of them.

"I agree with Gigi. It's the mobile bicycle guy. He's the kind of person my firm filters out after the first meeting, because we know he's too attached and unwilling to make the necessary adjustments."

"Yes!" Gigi whooped, leaning over from where she sat near Michael to give him a high five.

Chloe sat with her eyes glued to the screen, waiting for the show to come back from the commercial. She seemed oblivious to the conversation the rest of them were having.

"The voting lines are now closed, and the audience tally is in," the host announced as the show's music filled the room. "We're going to bring our contestants in remotely," he said as small tiles of the contestants' faces filled the left side of the screen. "Remember, audience voting counts for twenty-five percent of each contestant's score, with the judges' scores making up the remaining seventy-five percent."

"Let's begin with our judges," he said motioning toward where the judges sat at a boardroom table together. They would each score contestants on a scale of one to ten on categories such as innovation, strategy, profitability, long-term viability, brand vision, and more.

Gigi and Austin had both been right, with the mobile bike repair business and the candlemaker being named the bottom two. They revealed the rest of the tally, with Carson's kombucha chain taking first place, the pet food company taking second, and Brianna's salon coming in third. Chloe landed squarely in the middle of the pack in fifth.

"Good job, Clo," Austin said. "You're right in the mix."

Michael was worried Chloe would be disappointed in fifth place—he was so competitive that he certainly would have been—but she looked relieved.

"And now for the audience vote," the host said. "We have a couple of clear front-runners here, and it seems America feels a little differently than our judges."

A graph appeared on the screen showing audience support. Chloe and the dog food company's bars towered over the others on the chart. Audience comments from social media scrolled on the bottom half of the screen, several about Chloe.

"Take me to Island Coffee immediately!"

"How cute is that coffee shop?!"

"I wish we had a café like Chloe's!"

"Yes!" Luke pumped his fist in the air. "You did it, Clo."

Michael had been watching her reaction. She'd burst into a huge smile at first, but she'd toned it down within seconds. He knew it was because she didn't want to appear boastful on camera. She'd never want to make anyone else feel bad. He, however, had to fight his own urge to run across the room, pick her up, and twirl her around in celebration.

When the final rankings were revealed, factoring in both the audience's and the judges' scores, Chloe moved up one spot to fourth. Apparently, America wasn't as in love with Carson as the judges, because he'd come in second to last in their vote. Once combined with the judges' scores, it dropped him to second place, moving the pet food company into first, with Brianna hot on his heels in third.

The bike repair service was eliminated, just as Michael and Gigi had predicted. As the credits rolled and Chloe was able to turn off the camera, everyone started talking at once about the results. They were all gathered around her now, taking turns hugging and congratulating her.

As he watched, he thought about what she needed to do to improve her standing with the judges. More emphasis on revenue projections, and a clearer franchise strategy, would help them see the business potential without sacrificing what made Island Coffee special. He didn't know what the next challenge would be, but those were universal themes she could keep in mind.

She'd made it clear she wanted to do this on her own, though, and he respected that. Still, watching her chat excitedly with Reagan about next week's challenge, he couldn't help wanting to give her a few pointers. Successful business owners didn't go at it alone. They tapped into the resources and knowledge of others.

"Earth to Michael," Gigi called. "We're debating whether Carson's robots could be hacked. You don't know anyone, do you?"

He smiled, realizing he'd been lost in thought. "Afraid not. Although, I have to admit, I'd love to watch one of them handle a meltdown from an irate customer."

"Cannot compute." Austin imitated a computerized voice, moving his arms robotically.

They all laughed as they began cleaning up, gathering plates and empty wine glasses. Everyone was still dissecting the other competitors and their businesses in the kitchen when Michael noticed Chloe slip out onto the back deck. After a moment's hesitation, he followed.

She was leaning against the railing, looking out toward the water that could be heard crashing against the sand but not seen in the darkness beyond the dunes. Chloe turned to see who was joining her.

"You okay?" he asked, wondering if he'd misjudged what he'd thought had been her relief earlier at placing in the middle of the pack. He moved to stand beside her along the railing.

She nodded. "Honestly, I'm just glad I wasn't the first one voted out." Chloe gave him a knowing glance. "You'd be beating yourself up if you'd come in fourth place, wouldn't you?"

Yes, he would. Second place was the first loser and all that. It wasn't the healthiest mindset, but he'd spend his whole career trying to stay on top so he could provide for his mother and sisters. When he'd helped pay for his sisters to go to college, and when he'd bought his mom that house, those were his proudest moments. When he felt most valuable.

Instead of confirming she was right, he focused on her performance. "You did a great job. You were relatable and endearing, and you executed a good idea for the challenge. But you don't need me to tell you that. All of America already told you that."

Michael thought he saw her blush, but it was hard to tell in the soft light that bathed the back deck from the kitchen on the other side of the sliding doors. A smile played at the edge of her mouth, but she didn't look up at him, her gaze trained on the seagrass blowing in the breeze on top of the dunes.

"It means more coming from you," she said so quietly he could barely make out the words.

He wasn't sure how to reply to that. Did she say that because she thought he was a smart businessman? Or was it something more than that?

"I know what you're thinking," she said.

Heat pricked at his neck. Did she know the effect she'd begun having on him? One that was very unbusinesslike.

"Really?" He cleared his throat. "What am I thinking?"

"That I need to be more strategic. Focus on the numbers. Give the judges what they want to see."

That wasn't at all what he'd just been thinking, but he was relieved she couldn't really read his mind.

"Actually," he said carefully, "I was thinking how impressed I am that you didn't let the judges' comments shake your confidence. That's not easy to do."

She turned to look at him then, surprise clear on her face. "But you must have ideas about how I could improve my pitch. You always have ideas."

"I do," he admitted. "But sometimes the best business advice is knowing when to keep your mouth shut."

That earned him a laugh. "Since when do you believe that?"

"It's something new I'm trying." He turned to face her fully, struck by how the moonlight silvered the edges of her profile.

"I know you're dying to give me advice. So go ahead. What can I do differently this week?"

Michael considered his words carefully. "You already have everything you need. The Story Box concept is brilliant because it's authentic to who you are. But maybe there's a way to show the judges the business value of community connection without compromising it."

"What do you mean?"

"Think about what happened to Main Street after you opened Island Coffee. How many empty storefronts were there before? How many tourists ventured past the beach back then, compared to how many now spend time downtown?"

She nodded slowly. "The tourism board did say foot traffic has tripled since we opened."

"Exactly. Community isn't just about feeling good; it's good business. You don't need to change your approach. You just need to help the judges see that every community needs a place where people feel like they belong."

"That actually makes sense. Thank you." She pushed off from the railing. "For letting me figure it out myself, I mean."

"Of course," he said softly, resisting the urge to reach out and take her hand, pull her to him.

The sliding door opened behind them, spilling light and noise onto the deck. "Hey Clo," Reagan called. "Your parents are on Austin's phone. They want to congratulate you."

"Coming!" Chloe called back. She squeezed Michael's arm as she passed, the brief contact sending warmth through him despite the cool evening air.

He stayed on the deck a moment longer, listening to the sound of the waves and wondering when exactly this small-town café owner had started making him question everything he thought he knew about success.

Michael's phone buzzed at seven o'clock the next morning

as he was reviewing the latest projections for the warehouse project. John's name lit up the screen.

"Tell me you've found a way to make the artist studios work," his partner said without preamble.

Michael rubbed his temples. "Good morning to you too."

"The board meeting is in three days. They're going to want answers."

"I know." Michael clicked through the spreadsheets he'd been staring at since dawn. He'd run the numbers a dozen different ways, factoring in tax credits, alternative funding sources, even a crowdfunding component. But he couldn't make the math work without compromising the project's viability. "We might need to consider—"

"Going with the original retail plan," John finished. "I agree. Look, I know you want to help the arts community, but we have investors to answer to. They're not in this for warm fuzzies."

Five years ago, Michael would have already moved on to the next deal. But now he couldn't stop thinking about the artists who'd lost their workspace when the co-op closed. About how spaces like that brought people together, created something bigger than just square footage and lease rates.

"What if we got creative with the structure?" Michael asked. "I think we could—"

"Michael." John's voice carried a warning note. "This isn't like you. Since when do you let emotions cloud your judgment?"

"It's not about emotions," Michael argued, although he wasn't entirely sure that was true anymore. "It's about the creation of long-term value. Look what happened with Thomas Construction. Everyone said Jesse's historic restoration division would never turn a profit, but now it's their fastest-growing segment."

"That was different. The numbers made sense."

But was it really different? Michael thought about what he'd told Chloe last night, about the business value of community connection. About how her café had revitalized Main Street in ways that went beyond simple profit and loss statements.

"Give me until the board meeting," he said. "I might have another angle."

John sighed. "Fine. But remember, this is business, not charity. Speaking of charity, Alessandra told me about the girl you hired as a consultant for The Perry café. She called her ideas—what was the word she used?—provincial. Should I be worried?"

"No, John," Michael said, trying to keep the annoyance out of his voice. "There's no need to concern yourself with Alessandra's jealousy. She's just marking her territory. The *woman* I brought in to consult," he said, emphasizing that Chloe wasn't a girl but a grown adult who should be treated with respect, "has one of the most successful neighborhood cafés in the country. In fact, she's currently being featured on that new television show, *The Next Great American Entrepreneur*. You know what Park Slope is like. We need to weave ourselves into the fabric of that community if we want to be successful. Alessandra's design is like every other one she's done for us, and it won't work in Park Slope. I know what I'm doing. When have I ever steered us wrong?"

John relented in the end, since there were indeed no examples of Michael ever guiding the firm in the wrong direction.

After hanging up, Michael stood and walked to his condo's floor-to-ceiling windows. The morning sun sparkled off the sapphire-blue ocean, and palm trees swayed in the breeze. The view was different in every way from the glass and concrete towers of Manhattan where he'd built his career.

His phone buzzed again, this time with a text from his sister Maria.

> Steve has an interview this afternoon. Keep your fingers crossed.

Michael's chest tightened. He hadn't told his sister that he was trying to help her husband find work through his contacts. Steve was too proud to accept direct help, but that didn't mean Michael couldn't quietly open a few doors.

The warehouse project and Steve's situation were connected in his mind. They were both examples of how traditional business metrics failed to capture the full picture. Steve's company had failed not because he was a bad businessman but because he'd prioritized people over profits. Michael had always seen that as a fatal flaw in business.

But watching Chloe succeed by putting community first was making him question everything he thought he knew about what made a business valuable.

He turned back to his laptop, opening a new spreadsheet. There had to be a way to make the numbers work without sacrificing the project's soul. Maybe he needed to stop thinking like a New York investment banker and start thinking like . . .

Chloe. He remembered his words to her the night before. *Community isn't just about feeling good; it's good business.*

A few minutes later, he had an idea. What if they designated the artist spaces as business incubators and partnered with the city's economic development office? Every city handled it a little differently, but most had access to both state and federal grants, along with ways to form public-private partnerships between the city and the businesses to fuel urban renewal goals. Yes, that might actually work.

Michael fired off a text to Jesse telling him about his idea and asking if he knew anyone in that office. While he waited for a reply, Michael did a little online research to see if other cities had pulled off similar projects.

His phone dinged with a message from Jesse.

> Four words: Community Development Block Grant.

Although Michael had heard of CDBGs, the only thing he knew about them was that the acronym reminded him of the famous CBGB club that used to dominate the music scene in New York.

An internet search, however, told him enough to know this was a good direction to explore. CDBGs allowed community development offices to allocate funds to projects that could generate economic development, including the creation and operation of business incubators. Bingo.

He and Jesse might be able to pull off a miracle, but they'd have to work fast.

Chapter 13

Chloe

"Today's challenge is all about efficiency," Nathan, one of the judges, announced via video stream from Chris's tablet. Chloe was standing in the kitchen, nervously twisting the corner of her blue gingham apron while Iris handled the guests out in the café. It was the morning of the second week of filming, which was only days after the first elimination episode had aired.

"As your businesses grow, you'll need systems that can handle increased volume," Nathan continued. "Show us how you'll maintain quality while serving an increased customer base."

Chloe's mind raced. She already had a full house most mornings, and the show had brought tourists in from nearby towns trying to get a glimpse of the show filming. Some patrons had even had to go on a wait list the last couple of mornings during the morning rush. How was she going to increase sales even more when she was already at capacity? The café's small kitchen wasn't built for a larger volume. It was one reason she was seriously considering the franchising idea, because there wasn't really any way to increase revenue or grow her business in its current form.

"Each contestant is tasked with finding a way to double their average daily revenue today," Nathan continued. "We want to see both how you would boost your sales and how your operations will handle the stress. Remember, customers may be willing to wait for products they really want, but there's a limit to their patience."

Chloe caught a glimpse of Michael through the kitchen door, where he'd stationed himself at his usual table with his laptop. He'd arrived just as filming began, ostensibly to work, but she knew he was curious about this week's challenge.

She wouldn't let herself get caught up in trying to compete with Carson's robots or match whatever automated systems the other contestants would showcase. She had something they didn't: a community that functioned like a well-oiled machine in its own unique way.

She pulled out her phone and opened the group chat that included all the downtown business owners. They used it to coordinate holiday events and warn each other about everything from approaching storms to tour buses full of hungry visitors.

The responses came rapid-fire.

Gigi: Can we order and prepay today for sandwiches tomorrow? We have a big group for an HOA meeting, and I could bring them food. They're nicer when they're not hungry anyway!

Madison: There's a group of travel writers visiting. I could order breakfast for them to pick up in the morning.

Mack: We could order some cakes and pies for the restaurant and offer them as dessert specials this week.

Gigi: Just called Ms. Myrtle. She said she'll order a dozen pies for this weekend's Tour of Homes and put one in each house.

Austin: The B&B can order some cakes and pies for happy hour this week too.

Chloe smiled as the orders rolled in. This wasn't just about efficiency. It was about the network of relationships she'd built, the way the whole community lifted each other up.

"What are you smiling at?" Chris asked, noting her expression.

"I'm thinking that automation isn't the only way to scale," she said. "Sometimes the best business systems are built on trust and connection."

The orders kept flowing in all morning. The ladies from the garden club pre-ordered treats for their next three meetings. The bank down the street wanted to pre-order coffee service for their weekly staff meeting for the next month.

By closing time, Chloe had more than tripled her usual daily revenue without taxing the capacity of the café since it was mostly pick-up orders. She was practically bouncing as she totaled the numbers for the camera.

"How did you manage such a dramatic increase?" Sarah asked during her interview.

"It's marketing, just with a more personal touch," Chloe beamed. "I didn't need fancy technology or complicated systems. I just needed to tap into the relationships we've built over the years."

"It looks like you took in a lot of orders for cakes, pies, and sandwiches that now all have to be made. How will you handle that with your small staff and limited kitchen space?"

It was a good question that had nagged Chloe all day, like a pesky fly in her face. Every time a new order came in, she was equal parts elated and apprehensive. She'd never baked or prepared so much in such a short period of time. Sure, some of it didn't need to be fulfilled immediately, but much of it was for pick-up in the next twenty-four to forty-eight hours.

An incoming text made Chloe's phone vibrate on the table in front of her. As if reading her mind, Reagan came to the rescue.

> Gigi told me about today's challenge. Need any help baking tonight?

Chloe held up the phone triumphantly. "When one of us needs help, we all step up. That was my best friend offering to come help."

There was a look on Chris's face Chloe couldn't quite read. Like he knew something she didn't. It was unnerving, but she chalked it up to him trying to remain neutral in his role as a producer.

After the crew packed up and left, Iris joined Chloe at

the table so they could start planning out how they'd manage all the new orders, especially all the baked goods. They'd committed themselves to dozens of pies and cakes that needed to be baked over the next couple of days, in addition to their normal daily baking for the café.

"I'm sorry I can't stay tonight," Iris said, "but I'll be back early tomorrow morning. Cassidy said she can head over in about an hour to help you, and she's picking up more fruit for the pies from the market on the way. Thankfully that new supply order came in yesterday."

The supply order had been a lucky break. She'd simply need to make another order for later in the week to compensate for all the ingredients they'd be using up that evening.

Her heart swelled as she thought of how her community had come together for her so quickly today. Increasing sales had been relatively easy and painless. Sure, they had a lot of baking and sandwich assembling ahead of them, but her people were coming to her aid on that front too.

Michael had been right. She didn't have to do this all on her own. Her strength was her community.

Later that evening, Chloe, Cassidy, and Reagan had the first batch of pies baking in the oven when Michael's name lit up her phone. Wiping her flour-covered hands on her apron, Chloe slipped out of the kitchen and into the quiet of the closed café to answer.

"Be right back," she called over her shoulder. "I'll make us some coffee."

"Hi," she said, her heart fluttering as she realized she'd never really talked to Michael on the phone. Was he calling to see how her day had gone? Were they those kinds of friends now?

"Hi yourself," he said, a smile in his voice. "Did you get any flour in what you're baking or is it all on you?"

She looked down at her flour-covered apron. "How'd you know—"

The sound of a knock on the front door to the café cut off her question. She turned to see Michael waving at her.

Shaking her head, she walked over to let him in, ending the call and dropping her phone into the pocket of her apron.

"I was at a planning board meeting and ran into Gigi. She told me Reagan came over to help you with all the orders you amassed today. Need another set of hands?"

"Are you offering to bake?" She couldn't hide her surprise. The idea of Michael Russo in an apron was almost comical.

"I can follow basic instructions," he said, shrugging out of his blazer and laying it on the back of a chair. "And I figure you have an entire evening of baking ahead of you."

"I won't say no to more help. I'm going to brew some coffee before I head back into the kitchen. Can I get you one?"

"Sure," he said, following her across the room, leaning his elbows on the glass countertop while she went behind it. "So tell me about the rest of the day. You must have made your goal?"

Chloe told him about nearly tripling the daily revenue and how the community had come together for her to make it happen. When she got the coffee maker going, she turned back to find Michael staring at her with that look he got when he wanted to say something but was afraid it wouldn't be well received.

"Out with it," she said to him, crossing her arms. "I know that look."

"You know," he said, his tone teasing, "that's the second time this week you've told me you can read my mind."

She shrugged. "Your poker face needs work."

He straightened, his eyes searching hers. "I'm just worried . . ." His voice trailed off.

"About?" She rolled her hand in a circular motion to indicate he should keep going.

"I'm concerned the judges will say you basically borrowed from future sales. That most of those people would have ordered from you anyway, they were just ordering ahead and prepaying to help you win the challenge. They might say it doesn't prove you can generate or sustain higher volume."

The bubble of her earlier triumph deflated slightly. "But isn't that how businesses grow? Building relationships, expanding services?"

"It is," he said, measuring his words. "But they're looking for systems that can be replicated across locations. You can't export your personal connections to a franchise in another town."

She could feel herself stiffen as she got defensive. "No, but I can partner with people like Morgan who have those same kinds of connections in their own towns."

"You're right." He nodded. "The format of the show really limits you, though, because you don't get an opportunity to say that to the judges when they critique your performance."

Chloe's breathing quickened as she pictured the judges tearing her apart on national television while she sat helpless in a room full of family and friends with no way to defend herself. It was too late now to change the outcome.

Would she be the next one canned? Tears stung her eyes as her vision began to blur.

Michael must have seen the panic on her face, because he was around the counter in a few quick paces, placing his hands on her arms.

"Hey, I didn't mean to upset you. Chloe, you should be really proud of what you did today. Not many people can shoot off one text and nearly triple their sales. What you have here is special. You know that. Don't let me or anyone else make you doubt that."

He wrapped his arms around her when she didn't immediately respond, and she let herself sink into it. His chest was firm, and she inhaled his spicy cologne as she fought back the tears threatening to fall.

"They're going to vote me off," she sniffed as she pulled back.

Michael reached up and caught a single tear that was sliding down her cheek with his thumb, brushing it aside. His touch was so gentle it nearly caused her to release the dam she was holding back.

"You tripled your sales. They might point out that your method was unsustainable, but you're not going to get voted off with those kinds of numbers. There were probably other people who couldn't even pull it off. Besides, America loves you. They'll vote for you like crazy when they see how your community rallied around you."

"You really think so?" she asked, looking into his eyes so she'd know if he was telling the truth. He really did have a terrible poker face.

"I know so." He smiled wide, tiny lines crinkling around his warm brown eyes. "And next week, you can anticipate where they might poke holes in your approach and either adjust for that or at least explain to them why it works for your concept, like you just told me about Morgan having her own network."

"Okay, I can do that. And maybe the pre-order thing will take off, with people ordering ahead more regularly." A timer went off in the kitchen, pulling her attention away. "But right now, we've got pies to bake."

"Lead the way," Michael said, gesturing her forward.

Chloe headed back into the kitchen where Reagan was pulling a tray of apple pies from the oven while Cassidy crimped the edges of another batch.

"Look who I found," Chloe announced.

"Hi, Michael," Cassidy said.

Reagan's eyebrows shot up at the sight of Michael, and Chloe could practically hear the commentary her friend was holding back.

"Here," Chloe said, grabbing a spare apron from a hook. "You'll need this. Sorry I don't have anything more manly."

Michael accepted the apron—white with tiny purple pansies embroidered along the edges—and tied it around his waist without a hint of self-consciousness. "I've been told purple is my color," he joked.

Chloe stepped back, pretending to assess him. "I think it really is."

"Alright, you two, let's get back to work," Reagan teased.

"We've got an assembly line going," Cassidy explained as Michael walked over. "Chloe makes the fillings, I do the crusts, and Reagan's on oven duty."

"So what are my marching orders, boss?" Michael asked Chloe.

She fought back a smile at how earnest he looked in the flowered apron. "Let's see how you do with cake batter. Think you can handle a mixer?"

"I'll have you know I used to help my mother make

cannoli every Christmas." He rolled up his sleeves. "Though admittedly, that was mostly just holding the forms while she filled them."

"Ooh, cannoli," Reagan said. "We should add those to the menu."

"Don't give him ideas," Chloe laughed. "He already critiques my tiramisu because it's not exactly like his mother's."

"I do not," Michael protested, then paused. "Although, if you're interested, I could probably get her recipe." He flashed Chloe a grin that had her shaking her head.

Chloe showed him how to measure ingredients for the vanilla cake base they'd use for several different orders. As she demonstrated proper mixing technique, she couldn't help noticing how intently he watched her hands, like this was as important as any business deal.

"So," Reagan said once Chloe stepped away to check on her fruit filling, "what made you decide to join our baking party?"

"I heard Chloe needed help." His tone implied it was obvious.

Chloe's stomach did a little flip-flop at the idea that he'd heard she needed help and come running.

"Less talking, more baking," Chloe said, hoping to cut off any further interrogation from Reagan. "We've still got three sheet cakes, two dozen petit fours, and four more pies to go to stay on track."

"The sheet cakes are easy," Michael said, carefully adding vanilla to his mixer. "But petit fours? Don't those require some kind of special icing? That might be beyond my baking abilities."

"They're not so bad once you know the tricks," Chloe assured him. "My grandmother taught me how to make them efficiently." She found herself sharing not just the techniques but the memories of standing in her grandmother's kitchen, learning to pour the fondant in one smooth motion. How her grandmother would tell stories about the women who'd taught her to bake, passing down their wisdom along with their recipes.

"See?" Michael said quietly while Reagan and Cassidy argued across the kitchen about the best nineties boy band. "That's exactly what your Story Boxes capture. The history and the connections here. Don't forget to emphasize that to the judges. Not just the community support but also how you're creating a framework to preserve and share these traditions, and how that creates something unique and specific to each community."

Before Chloe could respond, there was a loud clatter as Michael's mixing bowl slipped, splattering cake batter across his apron.

"Smooth," Reagan laughed.

"I meant to do that," he said confidently, despite the batter now dotting his rolled-up sleeve.

"Here," Chloe said, trying not to laugh at the batter splattered across his expensive shirt. "Let me show you a trick for holding the bowl steady."

She moved next to him, reaching across to position his hands. "You want one hand here," she guided his left hand to the bowl's edge, very aware of how warm his skin felt under her fingers, "and the other supporting the base."

Resisting the urge to inhale his intoxicating cologne, she tried to focus on the task at hand.

"Like this?" he asked, his voice a little rougher than usual.

"Exactly." She stepped back, immediately missing the

warmth of touching him. "Now gradually increase the speed. Don't just crank it up all at once like before."

Across the kitchen, Reagan was suddenly very interested in studying a recipe card, but Chloe could see her friend fighting back a smile.

"Much better," Chloe said as Michael successfully mixed the batter without creating another explosion. "You might have a future in baking after all."

"I think I'll stick to investing," he said, but he was grinning. "Though I have to admit, this is more fun than a board meeting."

Their makeshift team got another round of desserts in the ovens, taking a break to get off their feet while they sat around chatting about the first episode and the other contestants until the timers started going off again.

"Alright," Reagan announced, checking her phone after the last cake was iced. "It's late, and I have to get into the office early tomorrow. We've got the last of the pies in the oven. You two can handle the petit fours without us, right?"

Cassidy was already untying her apron. "Yeah, I still need to study for a statistics exam I have this week."

Chloe walked them to the door, giving each of them tight hugs. "Thank you both so much. I couldn't have done this without you."

"You'd do the same for us," Cassidy said.

Reagan lingered a moment after Cassidy left. "Still think he's just a guy who hired you for consulting?" she asked with a meaningful glance toward the kitchen where Michael was washing mixing bowls.

"No, now I also think he's an excellent baking assistant," Chloe said, laughing as she hugged her friend goodbye. "Thanks again for all the help."

When she returned to the kitchen, Michael had not

only washed the bowls but had them arranged neatly on the drying rack. "Okay, boss. What's next?"

"Last thing is the petit fours. I baked the layers earlier, so we just need to cut and ice them."

For the next hour, they worked side by side at the steel prep table, shoulders occasionally brushing as she showed him how to cut perfect squares and apply the poured fondant. Despite his earlier mishap with the mixer, his hands were surprisingly steady and precise.

"You're actually pretty good at this," she said as he carefully centered a sugar flower on top of each petit four.

"Don't sound so surprised." He gave her a sideways glance. "I do have four sisters. I've helped with my share of birthday cakes over the years."

"Really?" She tried to picture a younger Michael decorating cakes in a cramped Queens kitchen.

"Well, mostly I just held things and cleaned up, but I picked up a few tricks." He finished the last flower with a flourish. "Though none quite as impressive as your grandmother's petit four technique."

Chloe stepped back to survey their work. Rows of perfectly iced little cakes filled every available surface. "We did it," she said, feeling the exhaustion of the long day settle in. "Thank you for staying to help. You didn't have to."

"I wanted to." His voice was soft, and when she looked up, he was watching her with an expression that made her breath catch.

The moment stretched between them, full of possibility, until the timer buzzed for the last pie. Chloe jumped, breaking the spell.

"I should get that," she said quickly, turning toward the oven. "And you should probably get some sleep. It's late."

"Right." He untied his apron, now spotted with fondant

in addition to cake batter. "I don't suppose there's any hope for this shirt?"

"Consider it your official initiation into the Island Coffee baking crew." She smiled, trying to restore their usual easy banter.

"I'll wear my badges of honor proudly." He hung the apron on its hook before turning to give her a hug. "Good night, Chloe. Try to get some rest yourself."

The hug ended far too quickly, and then he was gone. Chloe pulled the final pie from the oven and set it on the cooling rack. The kitchen felt strangely empty now, even surrounded by evidence of their shared work. She touched one of the petit fours he'd decorated, remembering how it felt to guide his hands at the mixer.

What was she doing? She couldn't afford to be distracted by whatever was building between them. She had a competition to focus on, a business to run. A point to prove.

But as she cleaned up the last of their baking marathon, she couldn't quite shake the memory of his smile in the flowered apron, or the way he'd listened so intently to her grandmother's stories, or how natural it had felt working beside him in her kitchen.

Tomorrow she'd worry about the judges and the show and everything else. Tonight, she'd let herself enjoy the lingering warmth of having someone who believed in her enough to spend his evening covered in cake batter just to help her succeed.

Chapter 14

Michael

"Let me get this straight," Monica Chen from the Jacksonville Community Development Office said, leaning forward in her chair. "You want to turn prime downtown real estate into subsidized artist studios?"

"Not exactly," Michael said, clicking to the next slide in his presentation. "We're proposing a mixed-use development that would include a business incubator program focused on creative enterprises. The upper floors would still be market-rate residential units, but the ground floor would provide affordable workspaces for local artists and entrepreneurs who've been displaced by rising rents."

"Like the artists from the Adams Street Co-Op," Jesse added from beside him. They'd spent the past week speaking with a couple of the co-op members about what they needed in a workspace.

"And how does this pencil out?" Monica's colleague Dave Torres asked, frowning at the financial projections on the screen. "Even with the CDBG funding, you're looking at significantly reduced returns compared to standard retail."

"Initially, yes," Michael acknowledged. "But we believe investing in the creative community will increase the property's overall value. Look at what happened in Brooklyn's DUMBO neighborhood, or the Arts District in LA. When you give artists and makers space to thrive, they transform neighborhoods."

"Into neighborhoods where they can no longer afford to live," Monica pointed out.

Michael adjusted his tie. He'd come prepared for this line of questioning.

"That's exactly why we're structuring this as an incubator with locked-in affordable rates," Michael explained. "We're not just creating new workspaces, we're also building a pathway for creative entrepreneurs to build sustainable businesses."

He clicked through slides showing potential floor plans, community gathering spaces, and examples from other successful incubators. One of the photos had an indie coffee shop on the corner of the building, and he thought of Island Coffee. Could a franchise go into this development one day? Maybe it could be the third location after Morgan's over in Cypress Shores.

"The numbers are tight," he admitted, "but we've identified several grant opportunities beyond the CDBG funds. And we're willing to accept lower margins to create something meaningful for the community."

Monica and Dave exchanged looks.

"That's not what we expected to hear from your firm,"

Monica said carefully. "Your other projects have been more focused on luxury development."

"People and priorities change," Jesse said, giving Michael a knowing smile. "Sometimes it takes seeing things from a different perspective. We've seen very positive returns and response to our historic preservation services up on Big Dune."

Michael thought of his brother-in-law Steve and all the families he'd helped even when it hurt his business. If Steve had told him sooner, could he have helped him work out a plan that didn't bankrupt the business?

"We'd need buy-in from the arts community," Dave said, but Michael could tell he was warming to the idea. "They're pretty skeptical of developers after losing the co-op."

"That's why we want to involve them in the planning process," Jesse said. "Make sure we're creating spaces that actually work for their needs. We have a meeting with a group tomorrow afternoon to kick things off."

"And your firm is fully on board with this approach?" Monica asked Michael directly.

There it was. The question he'd been dreading. "They will be," he said, ignoring the little voice in his head that said they still might not be. "Once they see the complete picture."

Once they were in the elevator alone, Jesse shook his head. "You know, when you first showed up on Big Dune Island, I never would have believed you'd be arguing for reduced profits to support local artists."

"Yeah, well, don't spread it around," Michael said dryly. "I have a reputation to maintain."

"I don't know. I kind of like this new you." Jesse punched him playfully in the arm.

"Don't you have somewhere to be?" Michael asked pointedly, trying to hide a smile. "Like home with your wife and baby?"

"Why, are you trying to get rid of me so you can rush off to see Chloe?"

At this, Michael felt his cheeks go hot. He wasn't, but it didn't mean a big part of him didn't want to. Just to check in and make sure she'd finished off the rest of her orders. Unfortunately, he needed to go straight home to work on his proposal before he sent it to the firm's board for final approval.

"It's not like that," he told Jesse.

"Not yet at least." Jesse gave him a knowing look.

As they approached where they'd parked next to one another, Michael opened the door of his Audi. "'Goodbye, Jesse. I'll see you tomorrow."

Jesse smirked, no doubt noting that Michael hadn't protested any further.

Michael's phone rang just as he settled into the driver's seat. Dan O'Sullivan, an old colleague who now ran a construction management firm in Manhattan, greeted Michael when he answered.

"Hey, got your message about your brother-in-law. We can definitely find a spot for him."

"That's great, Dan. Thanks for—"

"I mean, we'll have to create something. We're not actually hiring right now. But for you? I can make it work. Maybe a special projects manager or something."

Michael's enthusiasm dimmed slightly. "I don't want you to create a position just as a favor to me. Steve's got serious experience running his own plumbing company. Twenty years of—"

"Hey, I trust you. If you say he's good, he's good. Just

pass along my info, and we'll get him all set up."

Michael's stomach twisted. Put that way, it sounded less like helping and more like manipulation. "Could you do me one more favor? Don't tell him you're doing it for me. He's legit. He's earned a position like this."

"Got it. Just have him call me. You're a good brother-in-law, Michael. Sorry, I gotta run. Let's catch up soon."

The line went dead before Michael could respond. He sat there for a moment before he started up the car, wondering if he'd just made things worse instead of better. But Steve needed work, and his family needed stability. There was nothing wrong with using the connections you had. Life was all about who you knew and all that.

Pushing away his doubts, Michael pulled out of his parking spot. Right now, he had a board to convince and artists to win over. He didn't have the bandwidth to second-guess himself on one more thing right now.

Back at his condo an hour later, Michael spread his laptop, tablet, and phone across his desk, surrounding himself with three different versions of the warehouse projections. There had to be a way to make this more palatable to the board. Maybe he could squeeze a little more out of the oversized condos planned for the top floor. Add some little touches that didn't cost much in materials or labor but demanded a higher purchase price. That wasn't going to make up much ground, though.

His phone lit up next to him with John's name. Michael groaned before answering it.

"I just got off the phone with Theo," John said without preamble. "We need retail on the first floor. Preferably some higher-end stores and a fine dining establishment. Even with the grants, this artist co-op idea is a loser financially."

Michael ran a hand through his hair. He pulled up his

latest spreadsheet. "If you look at the ten-year projections—"

"I'm looking at them right now. These returns are barely half of what we typically target. The partners aren't going to go for this."

"But the community impact—"

"We're not a non-profit, Michael." John's voice had an edge he rarely used with Michael. "Look, I've given you a lot of latitude with the Florida projects because you've always delivered. But this feels personal. Like you're trying to prove something."

Was he? Michael stared out his window at the darkening sky over the ocean. When had making money stopped being enough?

"What if I can get the returns up to seventy-five percent of our usual target?" Michael asked. "Would the board consider it then? Consider the positive press we could get for working with the neighborhood like this."

There was a long pause. "If you can make the numbers work, I'll back you. But they need to be real numbers, Michael. Not creative accounting or best-case scenarios."

After hanging up, Michael turned back to his spreadsheets. He'd learned over the years that there were always places to find efficiency, to trim costs, to optimize revenue.

But as he stared at the numbers, he couldn't help thinking about the artists and about their need for affordable space to create and collaborate. What would Chloe say? She'd probably tell him that some things were worth more than maximizing profits. But she also had her brother's support to keep Island Coffee's rent affordable while she focused on building community.

His phone buzzed with a text from Jesse.

Just got off the phone with the co-op director. They're expecting a full house tomorrow for our meeting. Pick you up at 2?

Michael typed back a quick confirmation, then returned to his projections. He had to find a way to make this work, and not just by forcing the numbers to tell the story he wanted but by proving that doing good could also be good business.

~

The next afternoon, Michael walked into the Adams Street Playhouse, which sat next to the space the artists had formerly occupied. He noted that the once-vibrant theater was in desperate need of a coat of paint and some routine maintenance inside, basic tasks that were casualties of rising downtown rents.

Gwendolyn Carver, a painter and one of the co-op's leaders, sat at a table near the window, surrounded by other artists. Her silver and black hair was pulled back in a messy bun; paint stained the sleeve of her cardigan. Michael had met her during their initial outreach, and she'd been direct about her doubts.

"Mr. Russo," she said as he approached, reaching out to shake his hand. "Right on time."

"Please, it's Michael." He pulled out a chair, noticing how the others already in the room whispered to one another. "Thank you all for meeting with us."

Jesse arrived moments later with Monica from the development office, whom he'd waited outside the theater to greet. Michael could feel Gwendolyn studying him as he greeted everyone and laid out the updated plans, no doubt sizing him up. Her skepticism was palpable, but he was used to that kind of reaction. Jesse and his father had been the same way the first time he'd met with them all those years ago.

"The incubator model means subsidized rates for the first three years," Michael explained. "After that, rent increases would be capped at—"

"Until the next developer buys the building," one of the younger artists cut in. "We've heard all this before."

"Mr. Russo has promised the deed restrictions would be permanent," Monica added. "Legally binding for any future owner."

"And what's the catch?" Gwendolyn asked. "There's always a catch with developers."

Michael hesitated. He wanted to be up-front with everyone.

"The catch is that we need this to be financially viable," he said finally. "We've got investors to answer to, and they're used to higher returns. I won't pretend this is pure altruism, but we believe there's value in preserving creative spaces and in building something that matters to the community."

"Pretty words," Gwendolyn said. "But why should we trust you? Your firm isn't exactly known for prioritizing community over profits."

"You're right." Michael leaned forward. "A few years ago, I wouldn't have even considered this project. But I've seen what happens when you build spaces that bring people together, that give them a chance to create something mean-ingful. I'm not asking you to trust me based on words alone. I'm asking for a chance to prove it through actions."

"Let me cut in for just a minute," Jesse said from where he sat nearby. They'd talked before they arrived about remaining seated through their presentation so it felt like they were part of the group, instead of standing in front of them trying to sell them on something. "I felt exactly like all of you when Michael's group first made their investment in my business. In fact, we only said yes because we were out of other ideas for how to save things. And I won't lie to you; we didn't always see eye to eye in the beginning. But now I'm proud to be his business partner, and I can tell you, he's made my business and my town better. If you'll give us a chance, I promise we won't let you down."

A tall man with paint-splattered jeans spoke up. "We need more than promises. We need specifics. Square footage, lease terms, build-out allowances."

"Of course." Michael pointed to his laptop. "I have the detailed plans right here. But first, I want to hear what you need. Not what we think you need, but what would actually make this work for your community."

Gwendolyn's expression softened slightly. "That sounds like a good place to start."

For the next hour, Michael mostly listened and took notes. Marcus Taylor, a painter who'd been at the co-op for fifteen years, spoke about how his father had learned to paint with one of the original Florida Highwaymen, self-taught Black artists who sold paintings from the trunks of their cars. They often painted quickly on inexpensive materials like Upson Board or Masonite, framing paintings with discarded crown molding.

"That space wasn't just studios for us," Marcus said, gesturing to his fellow artists. "It was one of the few places Black artists could find community, could mentor the next generation. My daughter was just starting to use the co-op space for her photography when we lost it."

Delia Washington, a sculptor whose work Michael had seen featured in the local paper, nodded. "We understand business is business. But when the co-op closed, we lost more than our workspace. Those studios connected us to fifty years of Black art history in this city. Every displacement pushes our community further to the margins."

"The Highwaymen had to make their own opportunities," James Cooper added. He was older than the others, his hands weathered from decades of working with clay. "Now here we are, still fighting for space to create, still having to prove we belong."

Gwendolyn folded her hands on the table. "What we're trying to make you understand, Mr. Russo, is that this isn't just about square footage or lease rates. When spaces like the co-op disappear, we lose pieces of our cultural heritage that can't be replaced."

Michael thought about what Monica had said about neighborhoods transforming. He'd always seen it as progress, but sitting here, he was beginning to understand the true cost of that change. This wasn't a simple real estate deal. It was about preservation of both space and history.

"I understand what you're saying, but I'd like to be clear about one thing," he said as the meeting wound down. "This won't be exactly like the co-op. We can't replicate everything you had there. But if we work together, maybe we can build something new that preserves what mattered most and paves a path for the future."

Gwendolyn studied him for a long moment. "You're different than I expected, Mr. Russo." She gathered her things, then paused. "Don't make me regret taking a chance on you."

After the artists left, Jesse clapped him on the shoulder. "That went better than expected."

"Think they bought in?" Monica asked.

Michael cringed at her wording, although he didn't

think she meant anything by it. "It wasn't about them buying anything. It was about us listening." He just hoped the board would be willing to do the same.

His phone buzzed with another message from John asking for the updated projections to share with the other partners. Reality came crashing back in like a wave during a storm. Michael had promised both the artists and his board things that seemed increasingly difficult to deliver simultaneously.

Back in his condo that evening, Michael barely noticed the sunset painting the ocean in shades of gold and pink in front of him. His desk was covered in spreadsheets and grant applications, his laptop screen filled with zoning regulations and tax incentive programs.

The problem wasn't just making the numbers work. It was making them tell the right story. He needed to show the board that community investment could drive long-term value. Artists had proven in other cities that they could reinvigorate underdeveloped or forgotten areas, attracting new residents and tourists—now he had to prove it to the board.

Michael worked uninterrupted until his cell phone rang hours later, and he looked down to see Jesse's name.

"Sorry to phone so late. I was on baby duty while Callie took a break to work on a new song she couldn't get out of her head. Gwendolyn called earlier, and she's got the others on board, but they want everything in writing. Locked-in rates, build-out allowances, the whole package."

"How soon?"

"They need it before the city council meeting next

week. Guess they want to voice their support, but only if we've got a solid agreement."

Michael glanced at his watch. Ten hours until the firm's board meeting. "I'll have something for them to review by Friday."

"You okay? You sound—"

"I'm fine. Just juggling a lot of moving parts."

After hanging up, Michael turned back to his laptop. He'd done plenty of all-nighters in his career, but they'd always been about maximizing returns. This felt different. This time, he wasn't just trying to make money. He was trying to make a difference.

The question was whether he could do both.

Chapter 15

Chloe

Cars were lined up on the street in front of Callie and Jesse's Victorian home when Chloe and Reagan arrived after walking the short distance from the café for the second watch party. Blue hydrangeas billowed up like balls of cotton candy from large bushes planted in a row in front of the wraparound porch.

"Jesse did such an amazing job restoring this house," Reagan said. "Remember how long it sat empty after Callie's parents passed? The paint was peeling and the porch was falling apart after that last hurricane. It made me sad every time I walked by."

"It's the prettiest house on the block again," Chloe agreed. Now it looked like it had when Callie's mom had painstakingly cared for it, the house having been in her family for generations.

Callie's uncle Lonnie lived just down the street, and Austin and Chloe's childhood home was a short walk a couple of blocks down. Her mother said she was too nervous to watch the show with everyone at the party chattering away the whole time, so she was watching at home again this week with Chloe's father. Chloe would head down to say hi after it was over tonight.

Baby Clara's cry pierced the evening air as they climbed the porch steps. Inside, they found Gigi alone on the couch bouncing the infant on her shoulder.

"Thank goodness," Gigi said when she spotted them. "Maybe one of you can get her to settle down. I've tried everything. Babies hate me."

"I'll take her," Chloe offered, reaching for the baby. Clara's cries softened to whimpers as Chloe cradled her against her chest. "Maybe she's hungry?"

"I'll go get Callie. She's up there hiding in that sound-proof studio of hers," Gigi said in a teasing tone. "Jesse and Austin ran next door to help Mrs. Goodwin move something, but they said they'd be back before the show starts."

As Chloe rocked the baby, she glanced over to where family photos on the mantel chronicled the house's journey from Callie's childhood home to the place where she and Jesse were now raising their own family. Chloe caught a glimpse of their wedding photo, remembering how Callie and Jesse had ostensibly lured the whole town to Gigi's parents' vow renewal, only to surprise everyone with their own wedding instead to make sure it stayed private.

Soon it would be time for Austin and Gigi's wedding, and Reagan was in a long-distance relationship with a guy she'd met while he was vacationing on the island. Meanwhile, Chloe hadn't even been on a date in years. She was married to the café.

As if the universe was teasing her, Michael walked through the door next. Callie had texted everyone to just come in so they didn't ring the doorbell and wake the baby on the off chance she actually went to sleep.

Like the week before, Michael was dressed casually again, in dark jeans and a soft yellow button-down shirt that brought out the warm brown of his eyes. He greeted Reagan first, but then his gaze lingered on Chloe with Clara, and she felt heat rise in her cheeks.

"I swear, her legs are six inches longer than last time I saw her," Michael said, leaning over to wiggle her foot. "Hi, sweet Clara. Remember me? I'm your uncle Michael. Anyone messes with you, I'm the one you call."

Chloe watched the interaction with surprise. Michael didn't exactly seem like a kid person. She'd always figured he was more like Gigi, with a heart of gold protected somewhere behind layers of steel and determination. He did have four younger sisters, though, she reminded herself, and several nieces and nephews.

"You sound like an old mafia movie," Callie joked as she descended the stairs with Gigi and Piper. "But seriously, you have permission to protect my baby at all costs."

"Uncle Michael isn't going to let her date until she's twenty, isn't that right?" he asked the baby in a sing-song voice.

"Make it thirty," Jesse said as he and Austin entered from the foyer.

"I tried that," Austin said, nodding toward Chloe, "but they were never afraid of me."

They all laughed at that. Austin was six foot two, but he was the definition of a golden retriever in human form.

"Try having *four* sisters and being the man of the house," Michael shook his head and let out an exaggerated sigh like his sisters had been a handful. "I'm lucky they all ended up married to nice guys, but there were some real losers along the way."

"I got lucky," Austin said, reaching over to ruffle Chloe's hair. "Mine's only had the one high school sweetheart, and he was a decent guy."

Chloe felt her face grow hot at the disclosure that she'd only had one boyfriend her entire teenage and adult life. Tucker Barton had been her high school sweetheart, and they'd dated long-distance when he went off to college. Grandma Sophie had fallen ill during her senior year, and she'd stayed in Big Dune and switched her college enrollment to online courses to help take care of her.

She didn't regret spending her grandmother's final two years with her, but Tucker's visits home grew less frequent, and then his parents moved away and he stopped coming back at all. He'd always wanted to leave Big Dune and live in a bigger city, and when she hadn't joined him in Atlanta after her grandmother's passing, they'd had to acknowledge they wanted different things out of life.

Chloe was saved from having the spotlight on her nonexistent love life by the food arriving. Callie had ordered a catering-sized portion of fajitas for dinner, and soon everyone was helping unpack boxes on the dining room table and filling their plates while Callie took Clara upstairs to bed.

Piper had volunteered to make margaritas for those who wanted one, and Chloe followed her into the kitchen to help.

"Are you sure you don't want me to do anything more to promote your appearance on the show?" Piper asked. "Even if you don't win, we can use this to boost your visibility.

Have you thought about doing mail-order cookies or cupcakes or something like that to expand your business? I'm sure Callie would be happy to share it on her socials too."

"I appreciate it," Chloe said. "Maybe after the show is over. But I really want to do this part on my own. I'm not sure what comes next. I guess some of that depends on how the show goes."

The front door opened, and a male voice Chloe recognized as her brother's friend Wyatt carried down the hall. It was nice that he'd also come to support her this week. She noticed Piper perk up at the sound of his voice too.

They were almost done filling two small trays with margaritas when Wyatt came into the kitchen. "Hey, Clo," he said, hugging her. Like Jesse, he was another surrogate big brother.

"Piper," he said, nodding toward her. "I was hoping maybe you'd be in town."

What was that in his tone? Was he flirting with Piper?

"You were, were you?" she practically purred. "I guess it's your lucky day then."

Chloe looked back and forth between them. Did these two have something going on she wasn't aware of? She probably should have taken her tray of drinks into the living room and given them some privacy, but she was too curious to leave.

Of course, any single guy in his right mind would be interested in Piper. She had rich auburn hair and skin that looked like it was made of porcelain, with green eyes that drew your attention immediately. She was always wearing the latest fashion trends, and she was one of those women who was so good at her job that she exuded confidence that spilled over into the rest of her life. She and Gigi were alike in that way.

"Two-minute warning," Austin called out.

"Here, let me take those," Wyatt said, reaching for Piper's tray.

"Why, thank you, kind sir," she said, practically batting her eyelashes at him.

There was definitely something going on with these two. Chloe would have to ask Gigi later.

Chloe was disappointed to find Michael in a dining room chair that had been pulled into the living room for extra seating. Piper and Wyatt claimed the loveseat, which left Chloe sitting on the couch with Reagan and Gigi, on the far side of the room from Michael.

"It's time," Luke said from his seat on the floor as the show's intro began.

"Thanks everyone for coming to support me," Chloe said as everyone quieted down.

"The whole town is ready to text in and vote for you," Reagan said, reaching over and squeezing Chloe's hand.

"I may need it this week," Chloe said.

Reagan gave her a questioning look, but the host's voice filled the room and they all turned to watch.

Chloe's stomach churned as she watched the other contestants tackle the volume challenge. Carson had offered a coupon code through a delivery app, investing a little money to have it send out a push notification to everyone within a five-mile radius. The dog food people offered a discount as well, blasting out an email to their newsletter list of 300,000 people.

"They all had to cut their prices to increase their sales," Gigi said, leaning forward so she could see Chloe around

Reagan, who sat between them. "You didn't have to give up any of your profit to make your goal."

Chloe gave her a tight smile. Michael's words were stuck in her head on repeat.

I'm concerned the judges will say you basically borrowed from future sales.

Brianna was next. She called a client who was a well-known reality star and asked her to post about Brianna's product line since that was easier to scale than her services. She offered a free gift with purchase but explained that the gift was excess inventory she needed to get rid of anyway before it expired.

"That was clever," Reagan said. "People love feeling like they're getting something for free, and it helped her unload something she didn't need anymore."

Chloe wondered if she'd been wrong to turn down Callie's offers of social media support. After all, Brianna hadn't hesitated to work her celebrity connection. Chloe wanted so badly to own this win herself, though.

"I like her haircut," Piper said, fingering her own long red locks. "I've been thinking about chopping mine off and doing something shorter like that."

"No," Callie and Gigi both said in unison.

"Your hair is gorgeous," Callie said. "If my hair was thick and straight like yours, I'd never cut it. I hated when I used to have to wear extensions."

"Seriously," Gigi said. "You look like Ariel from *The Little Mermaid*. Your hair is to die for."

"I'm with them," Wyatt said. "Don't change a thing. It's working for you." He winked at her and Chloe wondered if anyone else saw it. If they did, they didn't say anything.

The conversation was cut short when everyone heard

the host mention Island Coffee. As her segment began, Chloe's heart raced, and she was glad she hadn't eaten anything yet. She wasn't sure she would keep it down. The room was suddenly quiet, other than the television and the blood pounding in her ears.

To her eyes, the editing made her community approach seem quaint compared to the others' solutions. Even the shots of her regulars rallying around her came across as small-town rather than scalable.

"While Ms. Beckett's loyal customer base is admirable," Thad said during the judges' deliberation, "her solution relies too heavily on personal relationships. There's no system, no scalability."

"The community support is touching," Nathan added, "but I agree with Thad. It's not a sustainable business model. What happens when she expands beyond her hometown?"

Even Andie, usually her champion, seemed concerned. "I love the heart behind it, but I'm not sure it really answered the challenge in a way that's repeatable."

Chloe retreated to the dining room table so she could answer the video call from the producers. She couldn't see the television from the other room, but she was grateful for that this week. There was a very real chance she'd be one of the bottom two who had to speak with the judges, and she'd rather do that without her friends and family watching her.

When the rankings were revealed, Chloe had dropped to seventh place this week. Only the strong audience vote kept her from ranking lower, but she was thankful to stay out of the bottom two. The candle company got the axe this week after landing in the bottom two for a second time.

"That's ridiculous," Reagan protested as the credits

rolled and Chloe rejoined everyone in the living room. "They completely missed the point."

"The audience gets it, though," Gigi pointed out. "Look how high her public support still is."

But Chloe couldn't shake the judges' words. Maybe they were right. How could she franchise Island Coffee if everything depended on her personal touch? She looked around the room at her friends' encouraging faces. Connection, community, and making people feel like family was what mattered to her most. But was that enough to win?

She caught Michael watching her, judging her reaction. It wasn't an I-told-you-so look, but he had forewarned her. For the first time, she wondered if she should ask him for more help. If anyone knew how to make the judges see her vision as viable, it would be him.

"Next week will be better," Reagan assured her, but Chloe wasn't so sure. She'd tried to stay true to herself, to what made Island Coffee special. But maybe that wasn't enough. Maybe she needed to be more like Carson, with his automated systems and standardized processes.

"You know," Callie said quietly as the others began gathering plates and glasses, "this reminds me of when my label wanted me to cross over to pop. They said country music was too niche and that I needed to standardize my sound to reach a bigger audience. And yeah, those songs charted higher at first, but I was miserable. I lost myself trying to be what other people thought I should be." She squeezed Chloe's hand. "Just remember that success doesn't mean much if you sacrifice who you are to get there."

Chloe nodded, but inside, she wasn't so sure. Music was different. Callie's authentic country sound had already proven successful before she tried to change it. Island

Coffee was still just a small-town café. Maybe she needed to evolve to reach that next level.

As she helped clean up, she couldn't stop thinking about the judges' words. What if staying true to herself meant staying small forever? She might have been okay with that a few months ago, but now she wanted more. She really wanted to franchise Island Coffee and help make Morgan her first successful franchisee.

Chapter 16

Michael

Michael arrived at Sandy Bottoms early, choosing a weathered picnic table with an unobstructed view of the ocean. The casual beachfront restaurant was a local favorite, known for fresh seafood served in plastic baskets and cold beer in frosted mugs. It wasn't fancy, but that had been Michael's intention in choosing it.

He checked his watch, though he knew he was still fifteen minutes ahead of their agreed meeting time. Chloe had texted earlier asking if they could meet for dinner to discuss strategy for the show, and he'd suggested Sandy Bottoms, partly because it was casual enough that this wouldn't feel like a date, even if part of him wondered what it would be like if it were.

The sun was just starting to sink toward the horizon, painting the sky a fiery orange. From his vantage point he could see almost the entire beach stretching north toward the pier. Families were packing up after a long day, while a few determined kids squeezed in one last game of cornhole before dark.

His phone buzzed with an email from John. More questions about the warehouse project and the artist studios he'd proposed. The board had been skeptical during his presentation yesterday, questioning whether the positive PR was enough to justify the ding to their financial goals. It was a battle he once wouldn't have thought worth fighting but now found himself deeply invested in.

"Sorry I'm late!"

He looked up to see Chloe approaching, slightly breathless, as if she'd hurried from the café. She was wearing a blue-checkered sundress, her brunette hair bouncing as she hurried over.

"You're not late," he said, standing. "I was early."

She slid onto the bench across from him, her smile not quite reaching her eyes. "Thanks for meeting me. I really needed to talk to someone who understands both business and . . . this place." She gestured vaguely toward the town behind them.

"Rough day?" he asked.

"Just questioning everything after watching the show last night. I keep replaying what the judges said about needing systems and scalability."

A server appeared to take their drink orders, and he ordered a local craft beer, while Chloe opted for a glass of rosé. Michael waited until the server was gone before responding.

"The judges have a certain vision of success," he said carefully. "But that doesn't mean it's the only vision. Or even the right one for you."

"That's just it, though." Chloe leaned forward, her arms folded on the wooden table between them. "Maybe they're right. If I want to franchise, I need proper systems. Technology. Ways to standardize everything across locations."

The server returned with their drinks and took their food order. Michael wasn't surprised when Chloe asked for the fried shrimp. It was what all the locals ordered here. He got the same, plus an order of hushpuppies to share.

"Tell me more about your franchise vision," he said once they were alone again. He needed to focus on being objective, on giving her the business advice she'd asked for. Not on how the setting sun caught the golden highlights in her hair.

"Well, I've been thinking about what Carson and Brianna are doing with technology and how I could adapt things like that for Island Coffee." She launched into ideas about online ordering systems and inventory management software. With each suggestion, her natural enthusiasm seemed to dim slightly, like each was a compromise that turned down the bulb lit inside her until her eyes looked empty.

"What about the Story Boxes?" he asked. "And the community connections that make Island Coffee special?"

"I can still do those things," she said, but the enthusiasm was gone. "Just with more efficiency. More structure."

Michael hesitated, torn between what he knew would impress the judges and what made Island Coffee special. He leaned forward, lowering his voice as if sharing a secret.

"Look, you want my honest opinion? Give them what they want in the presentation. Talk about standardized processes, quality control metrics, centralized training programs, all the buzzwords. Throw in some tech jargon about customer data analytics."

"But that's not really my vision," she frowned.

"It doesn't have to be," he said. "It's just a strategy to get through this round. Tell them what they need to hear, then once you've won, you can implement your own vision. The judges want to see that you can speak their language. You already have a profitable, successful business, it's just not what they're used to seeing. So now you need to put it in terms they understand."

She seemed to consider this, nodding slowly. "So you're telling me I need to play the game? Just until I win?"

"Exactly," he said, glad she understood. "It's like when I'm pitching to investors. Sometimes I emphasize different aspects of a project depending on who I'm talking to. It's not being dishonest; it's just strategic communication. Besides, they're not investing in your business and becoming long-term partners. The prize money is yours to keep, and then you can franchise or do whatever you want your own way."

He could see her turning the idea over in her mind. "I guess I could talk about streamlining the Story Box concept. Make it sound more like a replicable system than a community tradition."

Something about the corporate sanitization of her words made him uneasy, but he pushed the feeling aside. She'd asked for business strategy, and sometimes strategy meant making compromises. It was just for the show, he told himself. Only to get her through to the next round.

The food arrived and they dug in. Their hands brushed occasionally as they reached for the same hushpuppy, each touch sending little sparks through him that he tried to ignore. He was doing his best to listen to some of the explanations she was practicing for the show.

"What do you think?" she asked finally. "Is that more what the judges are looking for?"

Michael carefully wiped his hands on a paper napkin, buying time to choose his words. "It sounds very . . . professional."

"But?"

"But it doesn't sound like you." He met her eyes across the table. "Where's the story in all of this? The connection?"

"That's the problem, though, isn't it?" She pushed away her plate. "The judges don't think stories and connections can scale. Maybe it's time to be more practical."

"You mean more like me?" He meant it as a joke, but it came out more seriously than he'd intended.

She studied him for a moment. "You've changed, though. The Michael I first met would never have proposed artist studios in that warehouse project."

He'd told her about the warehouse project while they were baking together. "Sometimes I think you're rubbing off on me," he admitted. "Making me see there's more to success than just numbers."

"And sometimes I think I need to be more like you," she said softly. "More strategic and less emotional, at least about my business."

"Trust me, you don't want to be like I was." He thought of all the deals he'd done where community impact was just a box to check. "There's nothing wrong with caring about people."

The sun had dipped down below the trees now, casting shades of pink and purple into the clouds. The beach had mostly emptied, just a few silhouettes still visible along the shoreline.

"Want to walk?" Chloe asked as they finished their meal. "The beach is right there, and it's such a beautiful evening."

He knew he should say no. Keep things professional. But he was already standing and following her down the wooden steps to the sand. They stopped at the bottom and took off their shoes, putting them in a line of shoes left behind while people strolled the beach.

They walked in comfortable silence for a while along the water's edge, the warm breeze carrying the salty scent of the ocean. Chloe occasionally stepped into the surf to let the waves wash over her feet.

"Do you ever find out anything about the next challenge before the day you film?" he asked, trying to steer his thoughts back to the reason they were there.

"Chris gives me little hints," she said. "He mentioned it would involve creating a formal business pitch. Something that would work in multiple markets."

"That plays to your strengths, though. You already figured that out with the Story Boxes and how you could adapt it to each community's unique history."

Chloe's gaze was fixed on something farther down the beach. A teenage couple walked along the waterline, hand in hand, their silhouettes backlit by the setting sun. The boy scooped up the girl suddenly, spinning her around as her laughter carried on the evening air.

"Young love," Chloe said with a smile. "Do you ever miss being that age?"

Michael watched the couple, trying to imagine what it would have been like to have those experiences. "I didn't really date in high school," he said finally.

She turned to him, surprised. "Really? I would have thought girls would be lining up for someone like you."

Sure, he'd noticed girls when he was that age—what teenage boy didn't?—but his sense of obligation to his family had been far stronger than his hormonal urges. "I was too busy working. After my dad died when I was ten, I became 'the man of the house' overnight. While other guys my age were going to football games and dances, I was picking up shifts at the grocery store and making sure my sisters did their homework."

"That's a lot of responsibility for a kid," she said quietly.

"It was what my family needed." He shrugged, uncomfortable with her sympathy. "What about you? Austin mentioned you had a high school sweetheart."

"Tucker." She nodded. "We were together from sophomore year until about a year after graduation. He went away to college, but I stayed to help with my grandmother when she got sick."

"Long-distance is tough."

"It wasn't just the distance. He never planned to come back to Big Dune. He wanted the big city life, and I"—she gestured to the beach—"well, I wanted this. This is my home."

Michael nodded, understanding better than he'd expected. "And since then?"

"Nothing serious," she admitted. "The café takes up most of my time, and there aren't exactly a lot of options in a town this small. Everyone's either someone you've known since kindergarten or just passing through." She glanced at him, then quickly away. "What about you? I'm sure New York offers more opportunities."

"More doesn't always mean better." He thought of the string of brief relationships he'd had that had all faltered because he couldn't prioritize them over work. About Alessandra, and how she was the exact opposite of the type of woman he could be interested in long-term. "There was someone about seven years ago," he told her. "We were together for almost two years, but she said I was too focused on work, that I didn't know how to 'turn it off.'" It was then that he'd opted for the casual relationship Alessandra provided and written off settling down with someone.

"Was she right?"

"Probably," he admitted. "I've spent my whole life equating professional success with security. Building my identity around being the provider and protector. It doesn't leave much room for anything—or anyone—else."

"What about Alessandra?" she asked in a tone that said she was nervous about the answer.

"Ahh, Alessandra," he paused, deciding how much to share. "We dated very briefly years ago and quickly realized it's not that much fun to date yourself." He chuckled. "We were a bit too much alike at the time."

"I don't think you're anything like her," Chloe said matter-of-factly.

He supposed that was true now, and he was only glad Chloe hadn't gotten to know the guy he'd been back then.

The teenage couple had disappeared up a boardwalk that snaked its way through the dunes, leaving them alone on their stretch of beach. The pale outline of a crescent moon was emerging as the sky grew more dim. Chloe stopped walking, turning to face the water.

"Do you ever wonder what your life would be like if you had made different choices?" she asked, her voice almost lost in the sound of the waves. "If you weren't always trying to take care of everyone else?"

"Sometimes," he said, moving to stand beside her. "But then I wouldn't be who I am now."

"I like who you are now," she said softly, looking up at him.

Something shifted in the air between them, like a magnet drawing him to her. She was close enough that he could see the slight flush on her cheeks, the way the breeze moved strands of hair across her face. Without thinking, he reached out to tuck a strand behind her ear, his fingers lingering against her skin.

She swayed toward him slightly, and suddenly he couldn't remember any of his reservations. The desire to kiss her was stronger than his resolve to keep things professional.

"Chloe! Michael!"

They jumped apart as Tammy Perkins approached, her labrador straining at the leash. "Lovely evening for a walk, isn't it?"

"Beautiful," Chloe managed, her voice slightly breathless. "How are you, Mrs. Perkins?"

Michael half-listened as they chatted, his heart still racing from the almost-kiss. What had he been thinking? This was exactly what he'd told himself not to do. She was ten years younger, at a vulnerable point with the show, and looking to him for business advice, not whatever this was becoming.

"Well, I should get this old boy home for his dinner," Mrs. Perkins said finally, tugging on her dog's leash. "Good luck with your show, dear. The whole town is rooting for you."

As Mrs. Perkins headed back toward the boardwalk, an awkward silence fell between them. Michael shoved his hands in his pockets, unsure what to say.

"It's getting late," Chloe said finally. "I should probably head back. Early morning tomorrow."

"Right," he nodded. "Let me walk you to your car." Whatever had almost happened wasn't something he wanted to risk happening again by staying out with her any longer.

They made their way back toward Sandy Bottoms, the tone of their conversation shifting. They talked about much safer topics, like the next episode's air date, the weather forecast for the weekend, and a new boutique opening on the north end of the island.

As they reached the parking lot, Chloe paused. "Thank you," she said. "Not just for dinner, but for all the advice."

"Anytime," he said, meaning it more than he should.

She hesitated, then stepped forward and hugged him quickly, pulling away before he could fully react. "Goodnight, Michael."

He watched her climb into her car and drive away, knowing he was in deeper than he'd ever intended to be. The worst part was, he wasn't sure how badly he even wanted to fight it anymore.

Chapter 17

Chloe

"Our standardized recipe database with digital production schedules will reduce food waste by twenty percent while maintaining consistent quality across all franchise locations."

Chloe practiced the line in front of her bathroom mirror, trying to inject enthusiasm into words that felt foreign in her mouth. It was like the first time she'd tried to eat sushi and couldn't bring herself to swallow it.

It was the afternoon of the third challenge—a formal business pitch to the judges—and she'd been up late the previous evening rehearsing the presentation. Michael had helped her develop it after she'd received the instructions by email forty-eight hours before filming.

She'd spent hours creating sleek slides filled with graphs, charts, and bullet points outlining her five-year expansion plan. The Story Boxes were still there but were reframed as a "scalable system for community engagement" with "standardized implementation protocols." She'd even added a mock-up of a mobile app where customers could browse location-specific offerings and share their own stories digitally.

It was professional. Strategic. Exactly what the judges had been asking for.

So why did every word feel like a betrayal?

Sighing, she turned away from her reflection and picked up her phone. There was a text from Michael.

Good luck today. You've got this.

Her thumb hovered over the screen, unsure how to respond. Their almost-kiss on the beach a few nights ago had been playing on repeat in her mind, alternating with memories of his business advice.

Tell them what they need to hear, then once you've won, you can implement your own vision.

Was that really how business worked? Saying one thing while planning another?

She settled for a simple "Thanks" in reply and set the phone down. The camera crew would be arriving in an hour to film her preparations for the pitch. She needed to pull herself together.

Downstairs in the empty café, Chloe spread her notes across the counter. Today's filming was taking place after the café had closed. The afternoon sun cast long shadows across the floor, pooling in the worn spots where customers had traveled the same paths for years, since even before it had been a cafe, when it had still been a general store. Her eyes caught on the china displayed along the opposite wall, above the mirror that stretched the length of the café. Each piece had a story, a connection to someone who'd shared a portion of themselves with this place. How did you quantify that in a business plan?

A tap on the glass door made Chloe look up. It was Iris, who'd had today off.

"Thought you might need moral support before the cameras get here," she said as Chloe let her in, tossing her bag on a chair.

"That's so sweet of you," Chloe said, gratitude washing over her like a wave smoothing out the sand. "I'm so nervous I can barely think straight."

Iris studied the papers strewn across the table. "Are these your notes for the presentation?" She picked up one of the pages, scanning the bullet points. "Centralized procurement protocols? Standardized training modules?" Her eyebrows rose. "This doesn't sound like you."

"It's what the judges want to hear," Chloe said, repeating Michael's words. "I need to show them I understand how to build a scalable business model."

Iris set the paper down carefully. "I see."

Something in her tone made Chloe look up. "What?"

"Nothing, dear. I'm sure you know what you're doing."

But the doubt in Iris's voice echoed Chloe's own misgivings. Before she could respond, there was another knock at the door as the camera crew arrived.

The next few hours passed in a blur of filming. Chris directed shots of Chloe preparing her presentation, reviewing notes, and practicing key points. Sarah kept asking her to elaborate on terms like "quality assurance metrics" and "standardized operational procedures," which only made Chloe more painfully aware of how unnatural they sounded coming from her. Luckily, she'd looked most of them up as she was preparing for today.

"Let's get a shot of you explaining the standardized Story Box template to Iris," Chris suggested.

"Oh, um, I don't actually have one yet," Chloe admitted. "It's still in development."

Chris and Sarah exchanged glances. "Okay, no problem. Let's move on to filming your pitch."

By the time they wrapped, Chloe felt exhausted and oddly hollow. The pitch had been as polished as she could make it, but she couldn't shake the feeling that she hadn't said the right things.

She caught herself looking at her phone, half-hoping for another message from Michael. He'd come over to help her when she received the instructions from the judges, but they hadn't talked about what had happened on the beach. The memory of his face inches from hers, the warmth of his hand as he'd tucked her hair behind her ear, had made her stomach flutter.

It was probably for the best that Mrs. Perkins and her dog had inadvertently interrupted. Chloe needed to focus on the competition, not on whatever was developing between them. Besides, the awkward way they'd parted at the beach suggested he'd had second thoughts.

"You okay?" Sarah asked, catching her staring at her phone.

"Just nervous about the pitch," Chloe said quickly.

"Don't be. You're giving them exactly what they're looking for." Sarah patted her shoulder.

After the crew and Iris left, Chloe sat alone in the quiet café. It was the first week she didn't feel good when they'd wrapped filming. And shouldn't she feel the opposite because she was giving the judges what they were looking for?

Her phone buzzed with a text from Reagan.

Are you done filming? I haven't had dinner
yet, and I want to hear all about it.

Chloe smiled, grateful for the distraction.

Yes, please. Takeout at my place? I'm too
tired to go out.

Later that evening, sprawled on her couch with takeout containers littering her coffee table, Chloe confessed her doubts to Reagan.

"I just don't know if I did the right thing. The pitch felt so corporate. So not me."

Reagan twirled her fork in a bowl of seafood alfredo. "Whose idea was it to go this direction? Did the producers push you to do it?"

Heat crept into Chloe's cheeks. "Michael suggested I give the judges what they want to hear. That it's just strategy, not being dishonest."

"Mmm," Reagan hummed around a mouthful of noodles. "And how did that conversation come up?"

"We had dinner at Sandy Bottoms the other night. I asked for his advice."

"Dinner like a date or just dinner?" Reagan arched an eyebrow.

The almost-kiss flashed in Chloe's mind. "Just dinner," she said, immediately feeling guilty. "We walked on the beach after, though. There was kind of a vibe."

"A vibe, huh? Is there more to this story?"

"No. Walking on the beach at sunset just sets a certain tone. But it was nothing."

Reagan pursed her lips and seemed to be considering whether to poke around further before sighing. "Look, I know Michael is successful and all, but are you sure his way is right for you? This is your business, your vision."

"But what if my vision isn't enough?" The question that had been haunting her finally spilled out. "What if I'm just too small-town and too stuck in my ways to ever build something bigger?"

"Don't you dare," Reagan said sternly. "Island Coffee is special precisely because it isn't like every other chain. It's the heart of this town."

Chloe wished she could bottle her friend's confidence like perfume and spritz a little on whenever doubt crept in. "I just want to make it through this round. Then maybe I can find some middle ground."

Reagan didn't look convinced, but she dropped the subject. They spent the rest of the evening watching a reality dating show, a welcome distraction from the far more stressful reality show Chloe was taking part in.

That night, Chloe dreamed of china cups floating away into the distance while she stood behind a sleek counter, surrounded by identical baristas in matching uniforms, all serving coffee from automated machines.

It wasn't a dream. It was a nightmare.

"Welcome back to another round of *The Next Great American Entrepreneur*," the host's voice boomed through Gigi's living room. "Tonight, our contestants face their most challenging task yet. Each entrepreneur will present a comprehensive business plan to expand their companies nationwide."

Chloe sat rigidly on the edge of Gigi's couch, sandwiched between Reagan and Austin. The living room was packed with supporters, including her mother, who'd changed her mind about watching the show alone, her father, Luke, Callie with baby Clara, Piper, and Wyatt. Michael had texted earlier that he and Jesse were stuck in Jacksonville at a meeting about their warehouse project.

Maybe it was better that way. She didn't have a good feeling about tonight's challenge.

The episode began with a montage of each contestant preparing their pitches. She cringed seeing herself on screen, practicing those corporate phrases like she was trying to speak a foreign language.

"Look at you, all business," her dad said proudly, smiling across the room at her. "You look like a real CEO."

She forced a smile, though something about the comment rubbed her the wrong way. Had he not seen her as a leader before?

The presentations began with Carson, whose slick delivery was accompanied by animated graphics showing his automated kombucha bars popping up across a digital map of the United States. The judges nodded approvingly at his detailed five-year plan and proprietary technology.

Brianna followed with an equally polished pitch about her salon franchise and styling school concept. She'd even secured a letter of intent from a major outdoor shopping mall developer interested in housing her locations. Chloe texted her friend a quick congratulations.

When it was finally Chloe's turn, she barely recognized herself on screen. Gone was her usual animated gesturing and warm smile, replaced by a poised, almost stern demeanor as she clicked through slide after slide of business projections.

"As you can see from this chart," her on-screen self said, referring to a tablet the production crew had provided during filming while the slide she'd created appeared on the television, "our centralized recipe database will ensure consistent quality, and the digital production schedule will reduce food waste by twenty percent across all franchise locations."

Reagan leaned over to whisper, "I have no idea what you're saying, but it sounds fancy."

Another slide appeared on the television as the recording of her pitch continued. "We've also developed a standardized training program to ensure quality control across all locations, with digital tracking of key performance metrics."

The real Chloe felt her stomach twist. Who was this person? She had the same warmth as that robot server at Carson's store.

When the pitch reached the Story Box concept, she watched herself explain it not as a heartfelt community tradition, but as a "proprietary engagement system" with "scalable implementation protocols." The words sounded sterile, stripped of all the warmth and connection that had inspired the idea in the first place.

Thad filled the screen now, nodding approvingly. "I'm impressed. This is exactly the kind of strategic thinking we've been looking for from Ms. Beckett."

"She really stepped up her game," Nathan agreed. "I'm much closer to believing she has what it takes to build a national brand after that."

Thad nodded. "She's finally thinking like a real entrepreneur."

"I'm impressed by her willingness to embrace standard-ization and technology," Nathan added. "It shows adapt-ability."

Only Andie seemed less enthusiastic. "I worry she's losing what made her business special in the first place," she said, frowning. "Those personal connections were Island Coffee's unique selling proposition."

"But personal connections don't scale," Thad coun-tered. "She's wisely pivoting to a more sustainable model."

When the audience votes came in, Chloe's stomach dropped. Where she'd previously enjoyed strong support, she'd now fallen to the middle of the pack. The social media comments scrolling on the screen broke her heart.

"What happened to Chloe this week?"

"Island Coffee sounds like every other chain now."

"I liked Chloe better when she didn't just sound like everyone else."

"Well, that's surprising," Gigi said, frowning at the screen. "I thought you did great."

"It's just because they didn't understand what you were trying to convey," her dad added supportively. "Those busi-ness terms can be confusing to regular folks."

But Chloe knew the truth. The audience hadn't misun-derstood at all. They'd understood perfectly. She'd aban-doned what made Island Coffee special in an attempt to impress the judges. And while she'd succeeded with two of them, she'd lost the connection with the very people who had supported her from the beginning.

When the final rankings were revealed, Chloe had climbed two spots in the judges' ranking, landing solidly in third place. But her audience score had dropped signifi-cantly. Still, the combined score kept her safely in fourth place overall, well away from elimination. The subscription box for children's STEM projects had failed to show how it could grow and diversify in a way that satisfied the judges, and they hadn't seemed to get much audience buzz either.

"Third with the judges!" her mother exclaimed. "That's amazing, honey."

"You're a shoo-in for the final four now," Austin said, squeezing her shoulder.

As everyone celebrated around her, Chloe felt strangely hollow. Yes, she'd improved her standing with the judges, which was exactly what she'd set out to do. But at what cost?

When the episode ended, her friends and family lingered, offering congratulations and predictions about the next challenge. Chloe smiled and nodded in all the right places, but her mind was elsewhere.

"Hey, you okay?" Reagan asked quietly, joining her in the kitchen. "You don't seem too thrilled about your big success with the judges."

Chloe glanced around to make sure no one else could hear them. "Did that person on screen seem like me to you?"

Reagan hesitated. "You were very professional."

"I was corporate and bland," Chloe corrected. "I sounded like I was reading from a business school textbook."

"But the judges ate it up," Reagan pointed out. "And that's what matters for winning, right? Michael said you just had to play the game, and then after you win, you can do what you want."

That was the question, wasn't it? What mattered more, winning or staying true to herself?

"I'm just not sure anymore," Chloe admitted. "I got into this wanting to prove I could stand on my own, buy Austin out, help Morgan open her own café in Cypress Shores. But if I have to become someone else to do it, I'm not sure it's worth it."

"So what are you going to do for the next challenge?"

"I honestly don't know." She leaned against the counter. "Part of me thinks I should just keep giving the judges what they want. I'm so close now. But another part . . ."

"Wants to just be yourself?" Reagan finished for her.

"Is that naive? To put authenticity over strategy when there's so much at stake?"

Reagan considered this. "I can't answer that for you. But I will say this—the people here love the Chloe who welcomes everyone in with her warmth and hospitality. That's the Chloe who built Island Coffee in the first place."

While everyone was saying their goodbyes, Chloe snuck out to Gigi's back deck to have a minute to herself. The sound of waves breaking on the shore carried on the night breeze, instantly soothing her soul. A bright moon cast silver light across the dunes.

She pulled out her phone, thumb hovering over Michael's name in her contacts. Part of her wanted to call him, to hear him say she'd done the right thing. But another part held back.

What would he say? He'd helped her craft that corporate version of herself, believing it was what she needed to win. And he'd been right; the judges had responded exactly as he'd predicted. He wouldn't have seen the episode yet, anyway.

Only she could answer the question gnawing at her like a pesky mosquito: Did she want to win by pretending to be someone else or risk losing by being true to herself?

She thought of Morgan, so eager to open her own café. Of Austin, who had believed in her enough to fund her dream. Of all the regulars who counted on Island Coffee being a place where they felt at home. What if she really could bring that feeling to other communities?

The whole drive back home, she thought about authenticity, and success, and what really mattered. Had she lost her way trying to be what she thought others wanted?

She had to decide whether to continue down the current path and secure the win or risk everything by returning to her roots.

Chapter 18

Michael

Michael slumped onto his couch, exhausted from the meetings in Jacksonville and the long drive back. The meeting about the warehouse project had run late, with the city officials raising more questions about his artist studio proposal than he'd anticipated. Despite Monica's support, there was still significant skepticism about whether a private developer could be trusted to maintain affordable spaces long-term.

He'd missed the watch party at Gigi's but had recorded the episode to watch later. Picking up the remote, he hesitated before pressing play. Something about seeing Chloe's pitch made him nervous, though he couldn't pinpoint why. He'd helped her craft exactly what the judges wanted to hear. Her presentation was sleek, professional, and focused on systems and scalability.

So why did it feel like he'd pushed her in the wrong direction?

The show began with its usual fanfare, and Michael watched as each contestant presented their expansion plans. Carson's kombucha chain looked like something straight out of Silicon Valley, all automation and analytics. Brianna's salon concept was equally polished, although she had far more personal touches by nature of the services she provided. They were consistently the front-runners every week, which meant they were the ones to beat.

When Chloe appeared on screen, Michael leaned forward, his stomach tightening. Gone was her usual warmth and animated enthusiasm, replaced by a poised, almost mechanical delivery as she went through slides of business projections and standardized systems.

"As you can see from this chart," she said on screen, her voice flat and professional, "our centralized recipe database will ensure consistent quality, and the digital production schedule will reduce food waste by twenty percent across all franchise locations."

Michael winced. The words were technically correct—exactly what they'd practiced—but they sounded all wrong coming from her. The Chloe who lit up talking about her grandmother's recipes and community traditions was barely recognizable beneath the corporate veneer.

When she described the Story Boxes as a "proprietary engagement system with scalable implementation protocols," Michael actually groaned out loud. He'd helped her write that line, thinking it would impress the judges with its business savvy. Now it just sounded hollow, stripping all the heart from what made the concept special.

When the final rankings were revealed, Michael felt a

complicated mix of relief and guilt. She was safe from elimination, which had been the goal. But at what cost?

He turned off the TV, the room suddenly silent except for the distant sound of waves through the open balcony door. Had he done her a disservice by encouraging her to speak in a language that wasn't her own? He'd only wanted to help her succeed and show the judges she could play at their level. But watching her on screen, he couldn't shake the feeling that he'd pushed her to betray something essential about herself.

His phone buzzed with an incoming call from Maria. He smiled, assuming she was calling with an update about Steve's new job. It had been a week since he'd passed along his friend's information, and Michael had been waiting to hear how it went.

"Hey, what's—"

"How dare you!" Maria cut him off, her voice sharp with anger. "Who do you think you are?"

Michael's stomach dropped. "Maria—"

"Steve found out you told them to create a position for him." Her voice cracked. "Do you have any idea how humiliating that was for him?"

"I was trying to help," Michael said, hearing how weak it sounded. "I didn't tell them to create—"

His sister's raised voice cut him off. "By going behind his back? By making him feel like he can't provide for his family without his rich brother-in-law pulling strings?"

"That's not what I—"

"You can't just throw money at everything and expect it to fix people's problems, Michael. Life isn't just one big business venture, and my husband isn't a failing company that needs your investment."

The line went dead. Michael sat there with the phone

in his hand, the AC running cold against his face. Since when did helping someone make him a villain? If he had the ability to solve a problem, why wouldn't he?

A text came through from his mother.

> Give Steve some time. He's a proud man.

Before he could respond, the phone rang again. Cristina's name lit up the screen. Obviously, Maria had already shared her feelings in the group text they all had that didn't include him and was mostly used to communicate plans when he was in Florida. He hesitated, then answered, bracing himself for more anger.

"Hey, Cris."

"Hey," she said, her voice softer than he'd expected. "I talked to Maria."

"And you're calling to tell me I'm a controlling jerk too?" He tried to keep his tone light, but his hurt seeped through.

"Actually, I'm calling to check on you." There was a pause. "You okay?"

The unexpected concern loosened something in his chest. "Not really. I was just trying to help. And for the record, I did not tell my friend to create a position for him. That was his idea."

"I believe you." He heard her sigh. "But you've always had this thing about fixing problems for everyone, Mike. Ever since Dad died."

"That's what I'm supposed to do," he argued. "Dad told me to take care of everyone."

"You were ten years old," Cristina said gently. "Dad didn't mean for you to carry the whole family on your shoulders forever."

Michael closed his eyes, feeling the weight of three decades of responsibility pressing down on him. "It's who I am, Cris. The big brother, the provider, the protector. If I'm not that, then what am I?"

"A brother. A son. A friend." She paused. "Maybe something more to that coffee shop owner you keep mentioning?"

He felt heat rise to his face. "It's not like that."

"Mom says her name comes up every time you call lately." There was a smile in Cristina's voice. "So what's going on there?"

Michael found himself telling his sister about the show, about how he'd coached her to be more corporate and less herself. "You should have seen her, Cris. It was like watching someone put on a costume or alternate personality. It got the job done, but it was terrible to watch, and I'm the one who told her to do it."

"Because you thought you knew what was best for her business," Cristina said, not unkindly.

"Yes." The parallel to the situation with Steve hit him.

"You know what your problem is? You think caring about people means solving their problems for them. Sometimes it just means being there while they figure things out for themselves."

The words sank in slowly. "I don't think I know how to do that."

"Maybe it's time to learn," she said softly. "For Chloe's sake. And your own."

His sister's words were still echoing in his head ten minutes later when his phone lit up with a text from Chloe.

In case you didn't catch the show, I made it to third with the judges! Thanks for all your help with the pitch.

He started to type a response with suggestions for her next challenge, then stopped, his finger hovering over the screen. He'd just watched her transform herself to follow his advice, becoming almost unrecognizable in the process. And now his sister was furious with him for inserting himself into her husband's life, thinking he knew best.

Maybe it was time to learn when to step back and let people find their own way, as Cristina had suggested.

He typed a simple response instead.

Congrats on moving up. You did exactly what you needed to do.

It was true, but why did it feel so gross? Before he had time to overthink it, he sent another text.

I'll be tied up in Jacksonville with the warehouse project the next couple of weeks. Good luck with the next challenge if I don't see you before then.

It wasn't entirely a lie. The warehouse project did need his attention, especially with the artist studios hanging in the balance. But he also needed space to think, to figure out who he was beyond the role he'd been playing his entire life. And being around her would only trigger his protective instincts.

~

The next morning, Michael spread financial projections across his desk, trying to focus on the warehouse numbers rather than thoughts of Chloe or his sisters. His phone buzzed with an incoming call from Aidan, a colleague at his firm whom he also considered a friend.

"Hey, man," he said as he answered the phone.

"Hey. I was just looking at the new projections on the warehouse and wanted to check in and see how it's going."

"The numbers are tight," Michael admitted. "But I think I can make it work."

There was a slight hesitation on the other end of the call. "Did I ever tell you my mom is an artist?"

"No, what medium?"

"She's a painter," Aiden said. "Her parents steered her away from art school when it was time for college, but she started dabbling with painting again as us kids all got old enough to go to school. In the beginning, she did it just for her, but then she started selling at festivals and eventually got into a gallery. Now she's a full-time professional artist."

"Wow. Good for her. You'll have to show me some of her work sometime."

"I just wanted you to know I've got your back on this. I'd like to see us do more of these types of projects."

"Thanks, I really appreciate that. I know this is probably going to sound hypocritical, given what we do for a living, but living down here part-time has shown me that real estate shouldn't be just a financial investment, a way to build wealth and security. It can also be an opportunity to preserve or create something meaningful, to look beyond profit margins."

"Don't worry," Aidan said with a little chuckle, "I won't tell anyone you said that." He paused. "Seriously, though, I'm with you. I'm getting a little burned out doing the same deals over and over. If you ever need a hand down there, let me know. You're lucky you've gotten to be so hands-on and try new things with that construction company."

Aidan made him promise they'd grab dinner next time he was in New York, then they hung up. He didn't have plans for his next visit, and at the moment, he wasn't sure he was in any rush to go back. Of course, he always missed his mother and sisters, but right now, it was probably best he lay low and give Maria and Steve some space anyway.

The call with Aidan had him thinking about how the assignment on Big Dune had truly changed not only his career trajectory but also, it seemed, his entire outlook on work and life. In the beginning, visiting Big Dune to supervise the recapitalization of Thomas Construction and steer them toward new residential developments on the island had felt like a demotion. Like he was getting shipped off to the boonies as punishment.

Instead, it had allowed him to explore new avenues like historic preservation and now community redevelopment. And all while living on the beach. He stared out his floor-to-ceiling windows and admired the wide sandy beach, how the sun reflecting off the navy-blue water made it look like diamonds danced across the surface. Not many people in his profession had it this good, he thought.

The Michael who'd first come to Big Dune Island would have looked at the warehouse project solely through the lens of ROI and exit strategies. That Michael would have advised Chloe to streamline, standardize, and scale, without a second thought as to what might be lost in the process.

But he was beginning to realize that the island had changed him. Had changed his definition of success. Now it wasn't just about financial security, or at least it shouldn't be. It was about creating something meaningful, something that mattered.

He thought about his conversation with Cristina, about his lifelong assumption that caring meant fixing. About the way he'd pushed Chloe toward a corporate vision that didn't reflect who she really was or what made Island Coffee special.

As he returned to the projections, trying different approaches to make the numbers work for the artist studios, Michael couldn't help drawing parallels between this warehouse and Chloe's situation. In both cases, he was trying to balance commercial viability with preserving something authentic and valuable. The difference was that with the warehouse, he was fighting to protect that authenticity, while with Chloe, he'd encouraged her to compromise it.

Helping Chloe shouldn't be just about winning a competition. It should be about supporting her vision, not reshaping it into what he thought it should be.

His phone buzzed again, this time with an email from John with the subject line: "Board concerns re: warehouse." Michael closed his eyes, not ready to read another list of reasons why his plan wouldn't work. Instead, he pulled up the recording he'd made of the artist meeting and listened to Marcus Taylor describe how the co-op had connected him to fifty years of Black art history in Jacksonville.

"That space wasn't just studios for us," Marcus had said. "It was one of the few places Black artists could find community and could mentor the next generation."

It reminded him of what Chloe had built at Island Coffee. It wasn't just a business but a place where people felt they belonged. Where traditions were preserved, stories were shared, and connections were made. That was what made it special and set it apart from chains or Carson's automated kombucha bars.

And he'd encouraged her to package all that into corporate jargon and standardized systems, as if the heart of her business was just another asset to be leveraged.

The realization hit him with unexpected force. He'd been so focused on helping her win that he'd lost sight of why winning mattered in the first place. It wasn't about impressing judges or beating other contestants. It was about finding the resources to expand a vision that was already working. One that had heart and soul at its center.

Michael picked up his phone and opened his text thread with Chloe, thumb hovering over the keyboard. He wanted to tell her he was sorry, that he'd been wrong to push her toward a strategy that diminished what made Island Coffee special. But what right did he have to insert himself into her journey again, even if it was to admit a mistake?

No, this was her path to walk. Her business, her vision, her choice. The best thing he could do now was step back and trust her to find her own way forward.

He put the phone down and turned back to the warehouse projections. At least there he might still be able to do some good. That was, if he could find a way to make the numbers work without compromising what mattered to the artists who would occupy the space.

As he worked through the day, one thought kept returning: Sometimes the most helpful thing you can do for someone is believe in their vision, not try to reshape it into your own.

Chapter 19

Chloe

"The numbers seem impressive," Iris said, peering over Chloe's shoulder at the spreadsheet open on her laptop.

They were only open for another half hour, but the café had finally quieted down. With each passing week, more tourists poked their heads into Island Coffee to get a glimpse of Chloe or the film crew. The increased foot traffic was great, especially after lunch when their business had previously been slower. Today, however, Chloe was grateful for the extra time to prepare for the show.

"I have to be honest, though," Iris said. "I couldn't make heads or tails of this 'centralized quality assurance protocol' document you sent me yesterday."

Chloe rubbed her eyes, exhausted from another late night of preparation followed by her usual early wake-up call. The fourth challenge was just two days away, and she was still deciding whether she should double down on the corporate approach that had earned her third place with the judges. After all, their vote was worth seventy-five percent of her final score.

"Basically, it's just standard procedures to ensure consistent quality across locations," Chloe explained, though the words still felt foreign in her mouth. "Every franchise will follow the same steps for everything, from brewing coffee to arranging displays."

Iris raised an eyebrow. "So if I worked at the Island Coffee in, say, Savannah, I'd have to make the petit fours exactly as written in the manual? No adjustments based on what that community might prefer?"

"Well . . ." Chloe hesitated. The question highlighted the mental gymnastics she'd already been wrestling with. "There would be some flexibility, of course. But core processes need to be standardized for the brand to maintain consistency."

"I see." Iris's tone was neutral, but Chloe could sense her skepticism.

The bell above the door jingled, saving Chloe from having to elaborate. She glanced up, surprised to see Morgan entering the café. The young woman's blonde ponytail bounced as she approached the counter, her face alight with excitement.

"Morgan!" Chloe came around the counter to greet her with a hug. "What brings you over from Cypress Shores?"

"I had to come congratulate you in person," Morgan said. "I've been watching the show every week. Third place with the judges, Chloe! That's incredible!"

"Thanks," Chloe said, feeling a twinge of discomfort at Morgan's enthusiasm for her corporate performance. "How are things going with your plans?"

Morgan's face fell slightly. "That's actually the other reason I'm here. The building I was hoping to lease got bought by a developer. They're turning it into condos."

"Oh no," Chloe said, genuinely dismayed. "Have you found any other options?"

"Not yet. Commercial space in Cypress Shores is either too expensive or too far from downtown." Morgan twisted her hands. "That's why watching you on the show has been so inspiring. If you win, and if your franchise idea becomes reality . . ."

Chloe hadn't told Morgan she'd already floated her name around with the show's production team, but she was glad they were on the same page. "You could open the first Island Coffee franchise," Chloe finished Morgan's thought.

Morgan nodded eagerly. "It might solve everything. I'd have a proven concept, training, systems. Everything I've been struggling to figure out on my own. Then maybe I could put together a business plan the bank would approve for a loan."

The implications landed heavily on Chloe's shoulders. This wasn't just about her anymore. Morgan's dreams were now tangled with her success on the show. Not to mention that she could even help Morgan with start-up costs if she won the grand prize.

"Would you have time to sit with me and go through some of these financial projections?" Chloe asked, gesturing to her laptop. "I'd love your input, especially since you've been researching opening your own place."

For the next hour, they worked through spreadsheets and business plans. Morgan's background in finance proved invaluable as she spotted inefficiencies and suggested improvements. With each refinement, the franchise model became more detailed. But it was also less like the Island Coffee Chloe had built.

"This is brilliant," Morgan said when they finished. "The judges will be blown away. You're going to win this thing, Chloe. I just know it."

As Morgan left with promises to return for a watch party, Chloe felt a renewed sense of purpose in spite of her misgivings. Whatever doubts she'd been harboring about her corporate approach, they paled in comparison to the opportunity to help Morgan realize her dream. If that meant speaking the judges' language a little longer, so be it.

"You're awfully quiet," Iris observed once they were alone again.

"Just thinking about everything riding on this." Chloe closed her laptop. "Maybe Michael was right. Sometimes winning means playing the game by other people's rules."

Iris hummed thoughtfully. "Speaking of Michael, I haven't seen him around much this week."

"He's busy with a project in Jacksonville." Chloe kept her tone casual, though she did miss his usual texts and check-ins. "Besides, I need to focus. The challenges are getting harder, and I can't afford distractions."

"Is that what he is? A distraction?"

"I just need to concentrate on the competition right now. All this new jargon is complicated, and I need to stay focused. I have to keep impressing the judges."

"Mmm-hmm," Iris said knowingly. "I seem to remember something your grandmother used to say that seems fitting here."

"'Opinions are like the tides: Sometimes they're high, and sometimes they're low, and you can't control which way they go,'" Chloe finished with a small smile.

"Exactly," Iris said, patting her hand. "All you can

control is what *you* think about you. Now, should we taste test these new standard-recipe muffins? For quality assurance protocols, of course."

Chloe laughed, grateful Iris had lightened the mood. But as they sampled the perfectly adequate but somehow soulless muffins made according to her new standardized recipe, she couldn't shake the feeling that something essential was slipping away.

"All right, entrepreneurs," Andie's voice came through the tablet screen two days later. "For this challenge, we want to see your marketing strategy in action. Create a promotional campaign that demonstrates how you would attract new customers. Show us the materials, the messaging, and the impact on your business. You have thirty-six hours."

As the screen went dark, Chloe felt a surge of determination. She could do this. Marketing was all about presentation, and she loved creating beautiful things.

"Any initial thoughts?" Chris asked as the crew set up their equipment.

"I'm thinking a digital campaign," Chloe said, the ideas already forming. "QR codes that would link to an app, social media integration, personalized recommendations based on customer preferences."

Sarah nodded approvingly. "Very modern. The judges will love that."

"But still incorporating the Story Box concept," Chloe added quickly. "Just more streamlined. More efficient."

Chloe worked feverishly on her campaign in the time they were given. She created mock-ups of digital billboards featuring pristine coffee cups against minimalist backgrounds so the coffee cup would stand out. She found an online app designer with a demo she could use to dummy up an app interface where customers could customize orders, track loyalty points, and browse a catalog of Story Boxes. She even recorded a sample podcast and radio ad with carefully scripted language about "premium coffee experiences" and about how at Island Coffee "tradition meets innovation."

Every decision was calculated to impress the judges, particularly Thad and Nathan, who had responded so positively to her business pitch. She also tried to highlight some of the more community-driven aspects, like being able to order a Story Box from your hometown to get a taste of home, to appease Andie and show her things hadn't changed that much.

When the camera crew filmed her explaining the campaign, the words flowed smoothly from her lips.

"One of our key differentiators is the Story Box concept," she explained, gesturing to a sleek mock-up on her tablet. "But we've refined it for scalability. Instead of collecting unique stories from each community, we'll create templates that franchise owners can customize with local content. This maintains the appearance of personalization while ensuring brand consistency."

The *appearance* of personalization. Had she really just said that?

"That sounds very efficient," Sarah commented from behind the camera.

"Efficiency is key to successful scaling," Chloe replied automatically, the phrase lifted directly from a business book she'd been studying the previous evening.

When filming wrapped late that afternoon, Chloe felt hollow despite another technically successful challenge.

She'd created exactly the kind of campaign the judges had been pushing for: professional, scalable, and thoroughly corporate. If this helped her win, it would all be worth it. Wouldn't it? Morgan's face floated through her mind, reassuring her it would be.

The café was empty now, the late afternoon sun casting long shadows across the tables. Chloe wandered to the wall of china, her fingers tracing the edge of a delicate floral teacup that had belonged to Mrs. Peterson's grandmother. She remembered the day Mrs. Peterson had brought it in, tears in her eyes as she'd shared stories of Sunday teas and family gatherings.

How would that memory translate into a standardized template? How could an app capture the way Mrs. Peterson's voice had wavered as she'd recalled her grandmother's laugh?

Her phone buzzed with a text from Reagan.

How did filming go?

Chloe stared at the message, unsure how to answer. Technically, everything had gone perfectly. She'd executed the challenge exactly as planned. So why did she feel so unsettled?

It went well. Think the judges will be impressed.

Reagan's response came quickly.

But are YOU happy with it?

Before she could reply, another text came through from Austin.

Chloe smiled at the thought of her nephew's unwavering faith in her. He didn't care about standardized processes or scalability metrics. He just loved her and the café that had become a second home to him and so many others. She typed her reply.

She didn't reply to Reagan's last text immediately, however. She couldn't because she didn't know the answer.

That night, as Chloe lay in bed staring at the ceiling, she thought about Morgan's hopes pinned to her success, about the judges' approval she'd finally earned, and about Michael's conspicuous absence. She'd gotten exactly what she thought she wanted. She had what looked like a clear path to winning the competition.

So why was Luke the one she kept thinking about. The eventual owner of the Salty Breeze B&B, he looked up to her. She always thought she'd have lots of entrepreneurial lessons to teach him one day, but would she ever advise him to treat his business like she just had?

She knew the answer, and it settled in her chest like a heavy weight.

~

"Welcome back to *The Next Great American Entrepreneur*," the host's voice boomed through Gigi's living room. "Tonight, our contestants will be demonstrating their marketing prowess as they vie for a spot in the final rounds."

Chloe sat surrounded by enthusiastic friends and family, but she was trapped in her own anxious, internal monologue and felt disconnected. Reagan kept shooting her concerned glances, while Morgan, who had driven over from Cypress Shores for the watch party, practically vibrated with excitement beside her.

"You're going to crush it tonight," Morgan whispered. "I just know it."

On screen, Ronnie, who had the vintage clothing rental business, presented her marketing campaign first. She focused on social media influencers who could act as ambassadors, earning affiliate commissions with their individual codes. She'd enlisted a few to create video shorts as examples, and they were so fun and trendy it made Chloe want to sign up for the rental service.

Carson was next with a tech-focused approach featuring animated kiosks that dispensed personalized wellness recommendations along with kombucha. It was impressive, if somewhat creepy because of the biometrics it collected on customers.

Brianna followed with a campaign centered around using her AI model to solve hair emergencies, like an at-home color job gone wrong. She had a clever hashtag, #HairMergency, that was already trending on social media thanks to her high-profile clients.

When it was Chloe's turn, she barely recognized the polished woman confidently discussing market penetration and consumer engagement. Her campaign looked professional, with its minimalist aesthetic and carefully calculated messaging. But it could have been for any upscale coffee chain. There was nothing distinctly Island Coffee about it beyond the name and a passing reference to the Story Boxes. They'd cut much of what she'd said about those.

"Look how professional you seem," her mother said proudly. "You could work for one of those big marketing firms."

"Totally," Gigi agreed. "You're speaking their language."

But Chloe caught the subtle furrow in her father's brow, the way Reagan winced slightly when the camera zoomed in on the sanitized version of the Story Box concept with its "templates for local customization."

"The app interface is incredible," Morgan gushed. "Did you design that yourself?"

Chloe nodded, though the full truth was that she'd followed a template from the app designer. She moved over to the desk in the corner to field the video call from producers. The first two weeks, the calls had made her anxious but excited. Last week, she'd only been anxious after seeing her robotic delivery. This week? She was completely numb. She wasn't sure how she wanted the judges to react. Praise her for her adjustments? Or encourage her to return to her earlier—more authentic—approach?

When the judges appeared on screen to deliver their verdicts, Thad was effusive in his praise.

"Ms. Beckett has clearly taken our feedback to heart," he said approvingly. "This campaign demonstrates a sophisticated understanding of modern marketing techniques and scalability considerations."

"I'm particularly impressed by the way she's standardized the Story Box concept," Nathan added. "It's a smart evolution that maintains the appearance of personalization while ensuring consistency across locations."

There was that phrase again. *The appearance of person-*

alization. Hearing it from Nathan's mouth made it sound even more nauseating than when she'd said it herself.

Only Andie seemed troubled. "It's certainly polished," she conceded. "But I'm missing the warmth that made Island Coffee special in the first place. This campaign could be for any premium coffee chain."

"That's the point of good branding," Thad countered. "It should be universal enough to work anywhere while still conveying quality."

Andie didn't look convinced, but she didn't pursue it any further.

The audience votes told a different story. Chloe's support had dropped again, with comments scrolling across the bottom of the screen expressing disappointment and confusion.

"What happened to the real Island Coffee?"

"This show has turned Island Coffee into every other coffee chain."

"It's like she's forgotten everything that made her special."

Despite the mixed reception, when the final rankings were revealed, Chloe had climbed to second place in the judges' scoring, her highest position yet. But her audience score had plummeted to seventh, dragging her combined ranking down to fifth overall. Jose, the food truck owner with his own line of Mexican sauces, had been eliminated.

"Second place with the judges!" Morgan squeezed her arm excitedly. "That's amazing progress!"

But Chloe couldn't shake the image of her dismal audience score. These were the same people who had rallied around her in the beginning, who had seen something special in Island Coffee worth supporting. Now they were abandoning her.

"Is something wrong?" Morgan asked, noticing Chloe's subdued reaction.

"I'm just tired," Chloe managed a smile. "It's been an intense few weeks."

As the episode ended and everyone began discussing the remaining contestants, Chloe slipped out onto the back deck for some air. The night was clear, stars sprinkling the sky above the dark outline of dunes.

"Want some company?"

Chloe turned to find Reagan leaning against the doorframe, a glass of wine in each hand. She nodded gratefully, accepting one of the glasses.

"Second place with the judges," Reagan said, echoing Morgan's excitement but with a different inflection. "Is that what you wanted?"

Chloe stared out at the darkness where she knew the ocean lay beyond the dunes. "It should be, right? It's what I've been working toward."

"But?"

"But I don't recognize myself anymore," Chloe admitted, the truth finally spilling out. "All this talk about standardization and scalability and market penetration, I feel like I'm playing a role in some corporate drama. And the audience can tell."

"Of course they can," Reagan said gently. "Because they fell in love with the real Island Coffee and the real you."

"The real me doesn't impress the judges, though," Chloe pointed out. "And without the judges' approval, I can't win. And if I don't win—"

"You can't pay back Austin and Morgan doesn't get her franchise," Reagan finished. "I get it. I really do. But Chloe, if you win by becoming something you're not, what kind of foundation is that for a franchise? What kind of example would you actually be setting for Morgan?"

The question settled in Chloe's stomach like she'd consumed lead weights. What would she be teaching Morgan if she stayed this course? That success meant abandoning your vision? That community and connection were just marketing buzzwords to be standardized and templated?

"I don't know what to do," Chloe confessed. "I've come so far, and we're getting close to the finals. If I suddenly change course now, then what?"

"Look, I can't tell you what to do," Reagan said. "But I know who can."

"Who? Michael?"

"No. *You.* The real you. The one who built Island Coffee from nothing and turned it into the heart of this town." Reagan squeezed her shoulder. "Whatever you decide for the next challenge, just make sure it's a choice *you* can live with, not one you think the judges or Morgan or Michael or anyone else wants you to make."

As they rejoined the others inside, Chloe found herself watching Morgan chatting animatedly with Gigi about franchise possibilities. The young woman's earnest enthusiasm reminded Chloe of herself seven years ago, full of dreams and determination. Would the corporate version of Island Coffee she was creating truly offer Morgan what she needed to succeed?

Later that night, back in her apartment above the café, Chloe found herself staring at her phone. There were no messages from Michael. Had he even watched the show? She'd told herself it was better this way, that she needed to focus on the competition without distractions, but she found herself missing his steady presence by her side.

Now, with doubt gnawing at her certainty, she was missing his perspective. Even when they disagreed, his insights always made her think deeper about what she truly wanted.

Whatever path she chose for the next challenge, she knew one thing for certain. She couldn't keep going as she had been. Something had to change, and the decision was hers alone to make.

Chaper 20

Michael

Michael stood at the window of his condo, watching the waves roll in as he listened to Dave Torres explain Jacksonville's parking regulations for the third time this week.

"The original parking plan was for retail space on the first floor," Dave said over the speakerphone. "The artist studios and event space are considered 'public assembly spaces' under the city code. Whereas retail only requires one space per one hundred square feet, public assembly spaces require one space per forty square feet. You don't have room in your attached garage for that many spaces."

Michael rubbed his temples. "What if we implement a valet service? Partner with nearby garages that are typically empty during evening hours when most gallery events would take place?"

"It's possible," Dave conceded. "Though finding willing

partners might be challenging. Downtown businesses are already protective of their limited parking."

After ending the call, Michael opened his laptop to review the latest proposal. The warehouse project had seemed straightforward when they'd first purchased the property. The plan had simply been to renovate a historic building into upscale lofts. But his determination to include affordable artist studios had complicated everything, from financing to zoning to community relations.

His phone buzzed with a text from Aidan.

> Just wrapped meeting at The Perry. Call me when you can. It's about Alessandra.

Michael sighed. Of course it was. He'd sent Aidan to Brooklyn specifically to ensure Chloe's vision for the hotel café was being incorporated, knowing that Alessandra was an "ask for forgiveness instead of permission" kind of person. She'd do things her way unless he watched her closely.

Michael dialed Aidan's number, bracing himself.

"That bad?" Michael asked when Aidan answered.

"Worse," Aidan said. "She's completely scrapped the community wall concept and the seating arrangements Chloe suggested. She said she set things up Chloe's way but that it looked too cluttered, so she's sending half the chairs and tables back and going for a more 'minimal' look. It looks great if you want customers to grab their coffee and leave as quickly as possible. I took some photos I can send you."

"Which is exactly what we don't want," Michael said, frustration building. "The whole point was to create a space where the neighborhood would feel welcome, where they'd want to linger."

"I tried telling her that," Aidan said. "She told me she had refined Chloe's 'charming but impractical' ideas."

Michael winced at the condescension he could hear in Alessandra's phrasing. "Send me the photos. I'll call her myself."

The photos Aidan sent confirmed what Michael had expected to see. Alessandra had created a neutral-colored, contemporary space that could have been transplanted from any upscale hotel. There was nothing unique about it, nothing that reflected the neighborhood or created the sense of belonging that made Island Coffee work so well.

As he dialed Alessandra's number, he couldn't help thinking about Chloe's latest appearance on the show. He'd watched the episode alone in his condo two nights ago, disturbed by how she'd transformed her warm, community-centered marketing approach into corporate jargon about "market penetration" and "standardized templates."

Seeing the Story Boxes reduced to an efficient system rather than a heartfelt connection had felt wrong in a way he couldn't articulate at the time. Now, looking at Alessandra's sterile designs, he understood what had bothered him so much. Both were examples of opting for something simple and replicable over charming and unique.

"Michael, darling," Alessandra answered, her voice silky. "Aidan mentioned you might call. As I'm sure he told you, things are coming along nicely at The Perry."

"I've seen the photos," he said, keeping his tone professional. "You know this is not what we discussed for this project, Alessandra."

"I've elevated the concept," she said smoothly, unperturbed. "The original ideas were a bit provincial. This is Park Slope, not some small town in Florida."

"That 'provincial' approach is exactly what makes

Island Coffee special," Michael said, feeling defensive on Chloe's behalf. "And it's why we asked for Chloe's input in the first place."

"Please," Alessandra scoffed. "I saw her on that show. Even she has moved beyond the quaint community café approach. Her marketing presentation was all about standardization and efficiency. Did you see that ad she created? Sleek sophistication. She could come work for me if the café thing doesn't work out for her."

The observation landed like a punch to the gut. Alessandra wasn't wrong. Chloe had changed her approach to impress the judges. To follow the very advice he'd given her.

"That's exactly the problem," Michael said, the realization crystallizing as he spoke. "She's losing audience support with every episode because she's abandoning what made her special in the first place. People connected with her authentic vision, not some corporate version of it."

"The judges seem to prefer the corporate version," Alessandra pointed out.

"But the customers don't," Michael countered, thinking of the comments scrolling across the screen during the show. "And neither will the people in Park Slope if we give them another generic hotel café."

There was a long pause before Alessandra spoke again. "What exactly are you asking me to do?"

"Go back to the original concept. The community wall with neighborhood stories. The mixed seating that creates conversation spaces. The display cases for local bakers to showcase their goods. All of it."

"That will delay the opening," she warned.

"Then it delays the opening," Michael said firmly. "I'd

rather open late with the right concept than on time with the wrong one."

His partners wouldn't like it, but construction delays weren't unusual. He'd chalk it up to the usual issues.

After hanging up, Michael stared out at the ocean, reviewing their conversation. How had he not seen the parallel sooner? He'd been fighting so hard for the artists' vision at the warehouse while simultaneously encouraging Chloe to compromise hers for the judges' approval.

His phone buzzed with a text from Jesse.

> Potential solution to parking issue. Marcus Taylor suggested partnering with Trinity Church two blocks over. They have a large lot that's empty except Sunday mornings. Meeting with pastor tomorrow at 10. You in?

Michael typed back quickly.

> Absolutely. Sounds promising.

As he set his phone down, he marveled at how naturally the artists had begun offering solutions rather than waiting for him to come up with something. Marcus had connections in the community that Michael could never have accessed on his own. By stepping back and creating space for others to contribute, better solutions were emerging.

His thoughts drifted to Chloe again. He'd been right to give her space these past two weeks, but for the wrong reasons. He hadn't been avoiding her to let her find her own path. He'd been avoiding her because he was afraid of his feelings and uncertain of his role in her journey.

The truth was, he missed her. Missed her enthusiasm, her warmth, and her ability to see the heart of things when he was too focused on the mechanics. And watching her transform herself into someone unrecognizable on the show had been painful, especially knowing he'd encouraged it.

His phone rang again, and his sister Maria's name flashed across the screen. They'd not spoken since she'd yelled at him. He hesitated before answering, still raw from their last conversation about Steve.

"Hey," he said cautiously.

"Hey yourself," she replied, her tone softer than he expected. "Got a minute?"

"For you? Always."

"I wanted to apologize," Maria said. "I shouldn't have blown up at you like that. I know you were just trying to help."

Michael leaned back in his chair, surprised. "No, you were right. I overstepped. I'm sorry I put Steve in that position."

"Well, you'll be happy to know he found a job on his own," she said. "Nothing fancy, but it's with Catalano Plumbing. They mainly do commercial work for office buildings."

"That's great," Michael said, genuinely pleased. "He's the best in the business. They're lucky to have him."

"That's what I told him," Maria agreed. "Anyway, Mom said you're working on some project with artist studios? That doesn't sound like your usual thing."

Michael found himself gesturing enthusiastically as he described the warehouse project, the challenges with parking, and his determination to create space that would preserve rather than displace the arts community.

"You sound different," Maria observed when he finished.

"Different how?"

"I don't know. Less rigid maybe?" She laughed. "More like when we were kids and you used to build elaborate forts for all of us in the living room. You were always thinking about what would make us happy."

The comparison warmed something in Michael's chest. He couldn't remember the last time he'd approached a project with that kind of joy.

After saying goodbye to Maria, Michael turned back to his laptop, opening a map of the area surrounding the warehouse so he could locate the church and any other potential parking options. They'd likely have to work out financial terms with the church and ensure there were no coverage issues with their insurance, but hopefully it was a workable solution.

His thoughts were interrupted by another text, this time from Aidan.

> Just got off the phone with Alessandra. She says she's contacting artists tomorrow about the mural. When did you become so persuasive?

Michael smiled.

> When I finally started believing what I was saying.

The buzzing of his phone continued with a follow-up.

> By the way, watched that show your coffee shop consultant is on. She's great. I hope she doesn't lose her creativity like the rest of us corporate schmucks.

Michael hesitated before responding.

She's been getting advice from the wrong people.

Including you?

Aidan's reply was unnervingly perceptive.

Especially me.

There was a long pause before Aidan responded again.

So what are you going to do about it?

That was the question, wasn't it?

He thought about the warehouse project, how he'd initially approached it with his familiar playbook of financial models and business plans, only to discover that the most valuable contributions had come from listening to the artists themselves.

Maybe that was what Chloe needed now. Not someone to tell her what the judges wanted to hear, but someone who believed in her original vision, the one that had made Island Coffee special in the first place.

Michael glanced at his watch. If he left now, he could make it to Island Coffee before closing. He wasn't sure what he would say to Chloe or if she even wanted to hear from him. But he knew he couldn't sit on the sidelines any longer, watching her become someone she wasn't just to win a competition.

As he gathered his things, his phone lit up with an email from John about a new project they were bidding on in Brooklyn. His reply would have to wait. For once, he realized that something more important than work needed his attention.

~

The bell above the door jingled familiarly as Michael stepped into Island Coffee just as the last customer was leaving. The late afternoon sun slanted through the windows, casting a golden glow over the empty tables. Chloe stood behind the counter, her back to the door as she wiped down the espresso machine.

"We're actually closing," she called over her shoulder.

"Even for someone who brings news about your café design in Brooklyn?"

She turned, surprise flickering across her face. "Michael. I didn't expect to see you." Her voice held a careful neutrality that hadn't been there before.

"I've been in Jacksonville more than I expected," he said, approaching the counter. He noticed dark circles under her eyes. "How are you doing?"

She shrugged, turning back to her cleaning. "Fine. Just busy with the show."

The stilted conversation felt so foreign compared to their easy rapport of just weeks ago. Had he caused this distance with his advice or with his absence?

"I watched your marketing challenge," he said, carefully.

Her hands stilled for a moment before resuming their work. "What did you think?"

There was a vulnerability in her voice that made his chest ache. "I thought you gave the judges exactly what they wanted."

"But not what you wanted?" She glanced at him, her big blue eyes searching his face.

"It's not about what I want, Chloe." He leaned against the counter. "It's about what makes Island Coffee special. What makes *you* special."

She set down her cleaning cloth. "Now you sound like Reagan. I'm just trying to win, Michael. To prove I can succeed on my own terms."

"Are they still your terms, though?" His tone was gentle, not accusatory.

Chloe didn't answer immediately. Instead, she walked to the front door, flipping the sign to "Closed" and turning the lock. When she faced him again, she was solemn.

"I don't know anymore," she admitted. "I really want to help Morgan open the first franchise, and the judges finally respect me now. But every time I see my audience score drop, it breaks my heart a little." She shook her head.

"I came to tell you about The Perry," Michael said, choosing his words carefully. "I had Aidan check on the renovation. Alessandra had completely ignored your suggestions."

Chloe's shoulders slumped. "I'm not surprised. She made it pretty clear what she thought of my 'quaint' ideas."

"So I called her myself," Michael continued. "Told her to go back to your original concept with the community wall, the conversation spaces, all of it."

Her eyes widened. "You did? But why? It's not like she was wrong. Even I've been moving away from that approach."

"That's just it," Michael said, moving closer. "You've been moving away from the very thing that makes Island Coffee work. And I'm partly to blame for that." He gestured to the china and antiques lining the walls, the mismatched tables where people gathered daily. "This place matters because it preserves stories, because it makes people feel like they belong. You can't standardize that or turn it into a template."

Chloe's eyes glistened. "The judges don't seem to think that's enough."

"Maybe not," Michael acknowledged. "But the audience does. The community does." He paused. "I do."

She looked away, blinking rapidly. "I've come too far to change course now. What would that even look like? 'Sorry, judges, forget everything I've said for the past two challenges'?"

"It would look like courage," Michael said simply. "Like someone who knows what matters and isn't afraid to stand by it, even when it's harder."

A tear slipped down her cheek, which she quickly wiped away. "Easy for you to say. You're not the one who has to face them."

"No, I'm not," he agreed. "And I shouldn't have tried to tell you how to face them in the first place. That was your journey to navigate, not mine to direct." He hesitated, then added softly, "I'm sorry, Chloe. For pushing you toward what I thought would impress the judges instead of trusting you to do it on your own."

She studied him, a question in her eyes. "What changed your mind?"

"The warehouse project, partly," he admitted. "I've come to see that I've been fighting to preserve the artists' vision while simultaneously encouraging you to compromise yours. The contradiction finally hit me when Alessandra mentioned how your approach has changed on the show." He shook his head. "I've spent my whole life thinking the best way to help people was to fix their problems. To provide solutions based on what I thought was best. I'm starting to realize sometimes the best way to help is to just believe in someone else's vision."

Chloe was quiet for a long moment. "So what are you saying? That I should throw away all my careful preparation and just wing it for the next challenge?"

"I'm saying you should be the Chloe who built Island Coffee, not the one you think the judges want to see," Michael said. "Beyond that, the choice is yours. It always has been."

She seemed to be wrestling with something as she looked around the café, her gaze lingering on the objects from the community carefully preserved on shelves across the room.

"I don't know if I can," she whispered finally. "What if I fail?"

Michael took a step closer, close enough that he could smell her familiar vanilla-coconut scent. "It wouldn't be failing. You've made it further than most people who applied for the show. But if you're not the winner, then at least you lost being true to yourself and what you've built. There are worse things."

"Like winning as someone I'm not," she finished quietly.

He nodded, resisting the urge to reach for her hand. "For what it's worth, I think the judges might surprise you. Your authentic vision got you on the show in the first place. It's what made America fall in love with Island Coffee."

Chloe busied herself wiping the counter, and an awkward silence settled between them. Michael sensed Chloe needed space to process and make her own decisions.

"I should go," he said. "You probably have preparation to do for the next challenge."

She nodded, though she seemed reluctant to end the conversation. "Thank you. For what you said about The Perry. For believing in my vision."

"Always," he said simply.

As he turned to leave, Chloe called after him. "Michael?"

He paused, looking back at her.

"I've missed you," she said softly.

He smiled, feeling a tightness in his chest loosen. "I've missed you too."

The moment stretched between them, filled with things unsaid. Finally, Michael nodded toward the door. "Good luck with the next challenge. Whatever you decide, I know you'll be amazing."

As he stepped out into the fading daylight, Michael felt lighter than he had in weeks. He'd said what he needed to say. The rest was up to Chloe.

Chapter 21

Chloe

The café was quiet now, the only sound the gentle ticking of the clock on the wall as dusk settled outside the windows. Chloe stood in the center of the empty room, Michael's words echoing in her mind.

You should be the Chloe who built Island Coffee, not the one you think the judges want to see.

She walked slowly around the space, trailing her fingers along the backs of chairs and the smooth wooden tables that had witnessed countless conversations. Each corner of the café held memories. There was the spot where Colton Ward had proposed to Serena Milton because they'd had their first date in the same spot. The table by the window was where the garden club plotted their seasonal plantings. In the corner, the cozy nook where Luke completed his homework on afternoons when Austin had remote broadcasts for the radio station or was out of town.

Chloe approached a shelf of china, gently touching a delicate teacup with hand-painted violets. Mr. Jenkins had brought it in after his mother passed, explaining how she'd collected violet-patterned pieces all her life because they reminded her of the hillsides where she grew up in Virginia.

On her desk upstairs in her apartment, Chloe had meticulously prepared notes for the next challenge. Twenty pages of corporate strategy, market analysis, and standardized systems, all carefully crafted to impress the judges. She knew the Chloe who wrote all of that wasn't the same person she'd been when she first opened Island Coffee. What she struggled with now, however, was how to know the difference between growing and evolving versus compromising and losing yourself. Which was she doing?

Chloe climbed the stairs to her apartment, her mind still churning. In her small kitchen, she pulled out her grandmother's recipe box. It was the one physical object she'd insisted on keeping out when her parents wanted to put everything in storage after Grandma Sophie passed. The wooden box was worn smooth from years of use, the recipe cards inside stained with butter and vanilla, handwritten notes in the margins detailing adaptations and memories.

You can't standardize that or turn it into a template.

She closed her eyes and selected a card at random. Holding it up she saw it was her grandmother's lemon pound cake. The margins were filled with notes:

Made for Earl's 60th birthday. Used Meyer lemons from Edith's tree. Everyone asked for seconds!

Another notation, in different ink:

Clara's baby shower. Added blueberries. Divine!

Chloe was confused at first. Grandma Sophie hadn't been alive when baby Clara was born earlier that year. Then she realized her grandmother meant a different Clara who was pregnant, Callie's mom, which meant the baby was Callie. Chloe decided that she would make the cake for Callie and give her a copy of the card. It would have been the perfect thing to bring to Callie's baby shower if she'd found it sooner, but better late than never.

As she flipped through more cards, she confirmed that each recipe was more than ingredients and instructions. They were timestamps of community moments, of lives intertwined through food and fellowship. How had she lost sight of that?

Chloe carried the recipe box to her small dining table and began spreading cards out, reading the notes, remembering the stories. Her grandmother's strawberry rhubarb pie that had comforted Ms. Tilley after her husband's funeral. The peach cobbler that had been served at three generations of Watson family reunions. The chocolate chip cookies that had become a tradition for the first day of school for neighborhood children for decades.

Her phone buzzed with a text from Reagan.

> How are you feeling about tomorrow's prep for the challenge?

Chloe stared at the message, unsure how to respond. The corporate presentation she'd planned suddenly felt like a betrayal, not just of Island Coffee but of her grandmother's legacy, of all the stories and connections she'd been entrusted with.

But what was the alternative? To throw away weeks of careful repositioning with the judges? To risk everything she'd worked toward just as she was finally gaining their respect? Their score was worth seventy-five percent of her final tally.

Sighing as she sat back in her chair, she texted Reagan.

> Conflicted. Can you come over?

Reagan's response was immediate.

> On my way.

Chloe returned to her desk and opened her laptop, pulling up the PowerPoint presentation she'd been refining for days. Slides filled with terms like "profit optimization" and "customer life cycle management" stared back at her. There was a chart comparing projected growth rates of different standardized menu items and a mock-up of an app interface that would allow customers to customize orders without human interaction.

It was impressive, professional, everything the judges had been pushing her toward.

And it had nothing to do with Island Coffee.

The knock at her door came just as she closed the laptop, feeling a strange mix of clarity and terror washing over her. It was time to choose which Chloe Beckett would show up for the next challenge.

～

"Welcome back, entrepreneurs," Andie announced from the tablet screen Chris held in front of Chloe. "For your next challenge, we want to see the heart and soul of your brand. Create an experience that embodies your company's core values and mission. This should be something that would make customers say, 'This is why I choose your business over all others.'"

"You'll present this directly to the judges via video call tomorrow afternoon," Nathan added. "We want to see not just what you offer but also why it matters to your customers and community."

"This isn't about market share or profit margins," Thad said, his expression serious. "It's about what makes your business essential. The thing that would leave a hole in your customers' lives if you disappeared tomorrow."

As the screen went dark, Chloe felt the room spin slightly around her. It was as if the universe had heard her internal debate and created a challenge that forced her to choose. There was no way to present standardized systems and customer life cycle management as the beating heart of Island Coffee.

"Perfect timing for your corporate rebrand," Sarah said, making notes on her tablet. "You can really showcase how you've balanced your unique community approach with the efficiency and consistency required for a franchise model."

Chris nodded. "The judges will be looking for how you've evolved from a small-town café to a business with broader appeal."

Chloe took a deep breath. She'd latched onto something Andie said.

We want to see the heart and soul of your brand.

"Actually," she said, her voice barely audible, "I'm thinking of taking a different approach."

"Different how?" Chris asked, looking up from his notes.

"I want to show them the real Island Coffee," Chloe said, her confidence growing with each word. "Not the version I thought they wanted to see but what actually makes this place special."

Sarah and Chris exchanged glances. "Are you sure?" Sarah asked. "You've made such progress with the judges by speaking their language."

"I'm sure," Chloe said, looking around her café at the wall of china and the handwritten recipes framed near the register, the worn spots on the wooden floor where people had stood to tell their stories for years. "This place isn't about standardization or scalability. It's about creating a place where people feel like they're welcome."

"Where they belong," Iris echoed from behind the counter, where she'd been pretending not to listen.

Something clicked in Chloe's mind. "That's it. That's what Island Coffee is. It's a place where we all feel like we belong." She turned to Chris. "Can we film some of the regulars? I want to show the judges what this place means to the community."

Chris looked uncertain. "It's not really the direction you've been heading."

"I know," Chloe acknowledged. "But it's the direction I should have been heading all along."

Over the next several hours, Chloe abandoned all her corporate plans and instead invited a procession of regular customers to share what Island Coffee meant to them. Mrs. Herman spoke of how the petit fours had been the first thing that tasted right after her cancer treatments. Earl and his friends described how their morning coffee group had become a lifeline after retirement. Mrs. Lawson shared how she broke down crying in her kitchen trying to make her mother's peach cobbler after she'd passed, because she couldn't get it to taste right. She'd brought Chloe the recipe, and they'd spent an entire Sunday afternoon in the café's kitchen until they got it just right. Now Chloe sold it regularly in the café.

Between interviews, Chloe worked frantically in the kitchen, preparing special items from her grandmother's recipe box, each with its own story. As evening fell, she transformed the café into a gathering space, with tables pushed together to form one long community table.

"What are you doing?" Reagan asked, arriving with armfuls of fresh flowers.

"Setting the stage," Chloe explained, arranging cups and saucers from different families along the table. "Tomorrow, when I present to the judges, I want them to see what Island Coffee truly is. Not just a business but a place where stories and lives intersect."

Morgan arrived just as Chloe was hanging fairy lights along the counter. "I came as soon as I got your message," she said, eyeing the transformed space. "What's going on?"

Chloe took a deep breath. "I'm changing course for tomorrow's challenge. Going back to what makes Island Coffee special in the first place: community, connection, and belonging."

Morgan's face fell slightly. "But what about the franchise plan?"

"That's what I wanted to talk to you about," Chloe said, pouring them each a cup of coffee in mismatched cups. "I've been trying to reshape Island Coffee into something that would impress the judges, but by doing that I've lost sight of what would actually make a franchise successful."

She guided Morgan over to a corner table. "The truth is,

I don't want to create cookie-cutter cafés. I want to help you build something in Cypress Shores that captures the same feeling as Island Coffee but in a way that's authentic to *your* community."

Morgan studied her, confusion evident in her expression. "But doesn't that make it harder to replicate? The judges keep saying—"

"The judges want a business that will make money," Chloe acknowledged. "But Island Coffee doesn't work because of standardized recipes or efficient operations. It works because it preserves memories and creates connections." She gestured around the café. "That can't be manufactured or templated. It has to grow organically in each community."

Morgan was quiet for a moment, tracing the floral pattern on her teacup. "So, what does that mean for Cypress Shores?"

"It means," Chloe said carefully, "that instead of giving you a franchise manual with rigid guidelines, I'd be giving you the framework and philosophy to create a place where people in your town feel like they belong. The soul of the place would be unique to Cypress Shores."

Chloe watched Morgan process this, afraid she was about to lose her first potential franchisee.

Finally, Morgan looked up, her eyes bright. "That's actually why I wanted to open a café in the first place. I wanted to create a space like this where people could connect. I just didn't know how to make it work as a business."

Relief washed over Chloe. "So you're still interested?"

"More than ever," Morgan said. "But what about the judges? What will they think?"

"I don't know," Chloe admitted. "Honestly, I'm afraid it

might cost me the competition. But I'd rather lose being true to what Island Coffee is than win pretending to be something I'm not." She hadn't told Morgan she wanted to invest part of the prize money in her business, and she only hoped she wasn't wrong to risk that too.

Chloe had called back the crew to ask if they could film some shots tonight while the café was closed, and they'd obliged. As the evening progressed, more people arrived—friends, regulars, even Ms. Myrtle and her Junior League members. Word had spread through Reagan's texts that something was happening at Island Coffee, and people were curious. Chloe welcomed them all, encouraging them to write brief notes about what the café meant to them on cards she'd placed around the room.

There was china from a dozen families scattered down the long table, handwritten recipe cards propped as place cards, photographs of community gatherings tucked between vases of fresh flowers. By the end of the night, the corkboard Chloe had added on a back wall was covered with the notes people had written throughout the evening, creating a tapestry of stories and memories.

As the last of them left, Chloe stood in the center of the transformed space, exhausted but certain. This was her vision. Not the polished corporate version she'd been pushing but a place built on stories, on shared history, on the simple truth that everyone needs somewhere they feel they belong.

This was Island Coffee. This was her grandmother's legacy. This was where she belonged.

Chapter 22

Michael

Michael hesitated on the front porch of Callie and Jesse's Victorian home, his hand poised over the door handle. Through the windows, he could see the gathering already in progress, familiar faces alight with laughter. Everyone was busy, arranging snacks and settling onto couches in anticipation of the show.

He'd missed the last two watch parties, but he didn't want to miss this one. Tonight, he needed to be here, regardless of how Chloe's presentation went and whether his advice had helped or hurt.

Before he opened the door, Jesse walked up behind him balancing a stack of pizza boxes.

"There you are," Jesse said with a knowing grin. "I wasn't sure you'd come tonight."

"Yeah, me neither," Michael admitted, taking half the

pizza boxes. It wasn't a matter of whether he'd wanted to be there, though, but rather one of whether he'd be welcome.

"She'll be glad you came," Jesse said reassuringly as he opened the door and headed toward the kitchen, Michael on his heels.

Conversation in the living room paused briefly as people noticed his arrival. Austin raised his beer in greeting, Gigi offered a warm smile, and Callie waved from where she was fiddling with the baby monitor. Reagan was deep in conversation with a woman he assumed was Morgan since Chloe had mentioned she'd be there that evening. But it was Chloe's reaction he found himself watching for, his heart beating a little faster when she looked up from her conversation with Reagan.

Surprise flickered across her face, followed by something warmer that eased the tension in his shoulders.

After taking the pizzas to the kitchen, Michael made his way to the empty spot beside Chloe on the couch. "Is this seat taken?"

"It is now," she said, patting the cushion.

As he settled beside her, he caught the faint scent of vanilla and coconut that he'd come to associate with her. The proximity was both comforting and unsettling.

"Nervous?" he asked quietly.

"Terrified," she said, scrunching up her face. "I pretty much threw out everything I'd been doing for the past two challenges. We presented to the judges remotely on camera this week, and Thad looked like he was sucking on a lemon the entire presentation."

Michael couldn't help the small smile that tugged at his lips. "That might just be his face."

Her laugh was unexpected and genuine, a sound he'd missed more than he cared to admit.

"You're not wrong," she said, her eyes bright and smile wide.

Michael studied her profile as she chatted with Reagan about something on social media. Whatever had happened during the taping, she seemed different tonight. She was still anxious about the judges' reaction, but she seemed more herself. The polished corporate persona she'd adopted in recent weeks had been replaced by the Chloe from before the show. The woman who was unapologetically enthusiastic and warm with everyone she met.

"It's starting!" Austin called from across the room, and everyone quieted as the show's opening sequence filled the screen.

The couple who owned the pet food company aired first. They had filmed a series of touching stories of peoples' beloved pets that had recovered from serious injuries and diseases while on their all-natural diet, with plans to use the videos in social media ads. Cute dogs and kittens were hard to beat.

Michael found himself only half-listening as the custom sneaker designer, Jacob, featured celebrities and athletes who'd designed their own shoes to raise money for charities.

Next up, Carson introduced customers who attested to how their trial of his biometric data collection and personalized wellness recommendations had increased their energy and made them feel healthier. The concept was impressive but also a little creepy.

Brianna's salon presentation showed more personality, featuring client testimonials raving about their newfound confidence buoyed by the makeovers they'd received. Michael noticed Chloe leaning forward slightly, a small smile playing on her lips as she watched. There was genuine appreciation there, and he knew she wouldn't mind if she lost to the woman who had become her friend through this experience.

When the host announced Island Coffee, Michael felt Chloe tense beside him. She twisted a ring on her finger as the camera panned across her café, transformed for this episode into a community gathering space. The setting was beautiful in its imperfection, with its mismatched cups and plates, handwritten recipe cards, and photographs that told a story of connection rather than commerce.

Then Chloe appeared on screen, standing behind the counter of her café. Gone was the stiff, corporate demeanor from previous episodes. Instead, she spoke with quiet confidence, her voice warm, her eyes bright with conviction.

"Island Coffee isn't just about serving drinks and pastries," she explained to the judges. "It's about preserving memories, creating connections, and giving people a place where they feel they belong."

Pride swelled in Michael's chest as he watched. This was the Chloe who had built Island Coffee from nothing, who had created something meaningful beyond balance sheets and profit margins. She wasn't just pitching a business, but a philosophy.

The camera captured regular customers sharing what the café meant to them, from stories of comfort during illness to friendship cultivated over daily rituals to traditions preserved through recipes and tableware. Each testimonial drove home what made Island Coffee special in a way no corporate presentation ever could.

When Morgan appeared on screen, explaining her vision for bringing Island Coffee's philosophy to Cypress Shores, Michael glanced at the young woman sitting across the room. Morgan's eyes were glued to the screen, her expression a mix of excitement and determination. Whatever Chloe had said to her about the change in direction, it had clearly resonated.

The judges' reactions were mixed. Andie was visibly moved, Nathan looked intrigued but uncertain, and Thad wore his perpetual expression of skepticism.

"I don't understand this change in direction," Thad said on screen. "You've spent weeks convincing us you understand modern business practices, and now you're reverting to this"—he waved his hand like he was swatting a bothersome fly—"small-town approach."

Michaels hands balled into fists. He wanted to grab Thad by his perfectly pressed lapels and shake him. What was wrong with a "small-town approach"? Small towns were charming. The people who lived there were happy. They helped each other.

Holding his breath, Michael waited for Chloe's response on the screen. Would she second-guess herself under pressure? Fall back on corporate jargon to appease him?

Instead, she smiled with unexpected confidence. "I'm not reverting. I'm evolving. I've realized that what makes Island Coffee successful isn't something that can be standardized or automated. The business practices matter, yes, but they have to serve the vision, not replace it."

Michael felt renewed pride for Chloe. She hadn't just rejected the corporate facade; she'd found a way to integrate the practical knowledge while staying true to her vision. He was still learning to strike that balance himself.

As the segment continued, he became aware of movement beside him as Reagan began typing furiously on her phone.

"Are you seriously on social media during my big moment?" Chloe teased, nudging her friend.

"Trust me," Reagan replied without looking up. "I have an idea."

On screen, the judges were delivering their final assessments.

"I'm conflicted," Nathan admitted. "Your passion is undeniable, but I question whether this approach can compete in today's marketplace."

"I'm not conflicted at all," Andie countered. "I think Ms. Beckett has rediscovered what made her business special in the first place, and that authenticity shines through."

Thad remained unmoved. "It's a risky move to change course so dramatically this late in the competition. We'll see if the audience appreciates the sudden U-turn."

As the show moved to the next contestant, Reagan thrust her phone toward Chloe, showing her the post she'd just made that was already garnering likes and comments.

The post featured a photo taken at Island Coffee. A group of locals sat at a long table mid-conversation, everyone smiling and laughing. Mismatched china was visible on the table, vases of fresh pink flowers dotting the length of the table. The caption talked about the importance of places where people belong. Standing out boldly at the end was a hashtag: #WhereWeBelong.

"I don't understand," Chloe said, her brows knitted together in confusion.

"People connect with what you're saying," Reagan explained excitedly. "About needing places where we feel we belong. It's not just about Island Coffee either. It's about all those local businesses that make us feel like we're part of something."

Michael watched as understanding dawned on Chloe's face. Suddenly this wasn't just about competing in a reality show anymore; she'd tapped into something deeper that resonated beyond the competition.

Around the room, others were pulling out their phones, looking at Reagan's post. The energy shifted from nervous anticipation to something more vibrant, more hopeful.

"It's starting to trend," Reagan whispered, gripping her phone tightly as the show neared the audience voting segment. "People are sharing photos of their own favorite local spots, with the WhereWeBelong hashtag."

Chloe retreated to Callie's dining room for her on-camera appearance, and Michael resisted the urge to follow her so he could be by her side for the results.

The judges' scores came first, and Chloe came in fourth behind Carson, Brianna, and the pet food couple. Thad clearly wasn't a fan of Chloe's return to her roots, but Nathan must have been swayed in favor of the shift, alongside Andie. The room let out a collective sigh of relief, confident the trending hashtag was a positive sign for the audience vote.

When the audience vote results appeared on screen, Chloe was in second place, behind Brianna, who'd had a bit of a head start with her hashtag debuting the week before.

The combined scores advanced Chloe to third overall, a solid position that ensured her safety for another week. Ronnie, with her vintage clothing subscription, had been eliminated. She hadn't done anything wrong—she simply hadn't captured the attention or imagination of the judges or the audience.

The room erupted in cheers, everyone standing up to high-five and hug. Michael hung back as Austin lifted Chloe in an enthusiastic embrace when she reentered the living room. Morgan rushed over to congratulate her, and Reagan huddled with Callie and Gigi, showing them the hashtag gaining momentum online. He was happy to observe her triumph from the periphery, content to see her surrounded by the very community she'd championed.

When Chloe's gaze found his across the room, he offered a small smile and a nod of acknowledgment, and she smiled broadly in return. No words were necessary. She'd found her path, not because of his advice but despite it. She'd trusted herself when it mattered most.

"And the student surpasses the master," Jesse joked, handing him a fresh beer.

Michael shook his head. "She didn't need me to teach her anything. This was all her. She knew what mattered all along."

"And yet you look like a proud papa anyway," Jesse observed with a knowing smile.

"Not quite the relationship I'm going for," Michael muttered before he could stop himself.

Jesse's eyebrows shot up, but before he could respond, Reagan bounded over to them, her phone in hand.

"You guys have to see this," she said, showing them her screen. "The WhereWeBelong hashtag is already trending nationally!"

Michael wasn't much of a social media guy, but he knew getting thousands of likes and comments that quickly was unusual. Reagan read out several comments from people sharing their own stories of local businesses that made them feel like they belonged.

"This could make her hard to beat," Jesse mused. "She didn't use Callie's celebrity status to get America behind her, and she still blew up."

Michael nodded, watching as, across the room, Callie hugged Chloe. "It's about more than winning now."

He saw Chloe go into the kitchen alone, and he

followed her there, hoping to take advantage of the opportunity to talk to her privately.

"How does it feel?" he asked as he came up beside her while she poured a glass of wine. "Getting America back on your team again?"

"Terrifying," she said, smiling as she put the wine bottle back on the counter. "But it feels right." She turned to face him, her eyes finding his. "Thank you for helping me see what I was losing."

"I didn't do anything," Michael said honestly. "You knew what mattered all along. You just needed to trust yourself."

"What about you?" she asked after a moment. "How's the warehouse project going?"

"Better," he said. "We found a solution to the parking issue. One of the artists suggested partnering with a church a few blocks away that has a large, empty lot most days."

"So the artist studios are happening?"

Michael nodded. "They will. It might delay the project timeline, complicate the financing, and reduce our profit margins, but it's happening." He laughed. "All things I would have considered deal-breakers a year ago."

"What changed?" Her question was soft, but her eyes told him his answer mattered.

He looked at her then, really looked at her—the woman who had reminded him that there was more to success than spreadsheets and ROI, who had stubbornly held on to what mattered even when it complicated things.

"I did," he said simply.

Her hand found his on the counter, a brief touch that nonetheless sent warmth spreading through him. It wasn't a grand declaration or a dramatic moment, but something quieter, more certain—a recognition that whatever was growing between them had its own rhythm, its own time.

Like the hashtag spreading across social media, some things couldn't be forced or standardized. They had to grow organically.

And for the first time in longer than he could remember, Michael had no desire to control the outcome but was content to let things unfold naturally, to trust that some things were worth the wait.

A few days later, Michael was reviewing final budget numbers for The Perry when his phone vibrated with a new message from Aidan.

> You aren't going to believe this.

The next message came in, containing a link to YouTube. When he clicked on it, Alessandra filled the screen. She was seated in a deep leather chair, elegantly dressed in a cream-colored dress that contrasted with the dark brown upholstery.

As the camera zoomed out to take in more of the room, Michael recognized it. She was sitting in Perk Slope—a play on words they'd chosen for the name of the coffee shop at The Perry—and it looked like she'd actually followed Chloe's suggestions for the furniture layout.

She swept her arms out wide as she said, "Welcome to Perk Slope, soon to be the hottest spot in Brooklyn to grab your morning espresso. I thought I'd share a little sneak peek with you today so you can start counting down the days until we open the doors for the whole neighborhood to enjoy."

With this, she stood and began walking around the space, the camera tracking her as she glided around the room.

"I wanted to create a space that feels both modern and timeless," Alessandra explained, gesturing to the seating areas arranged exactly as Chloe had suggested, with intimate conversation nooks harmonizing with larger communal tables designed to bring strangers together.

"The focal point of our design is what I'm calling the Community Wall," she continued, stopping in front of the large wall where a muralist had already begun bringing Park Slope's story to life. "Every great neighborhood has its own unique history, and I felt it was important to honor Park Slope's rich heritage."

Michael's jaw clenched as he watched her point to one vignette and explain its importance. She was taking credit for Chloe's idea.

"And these display cases," Alessandra said, moving toward the counter where glass cases showcased an array of pastries, "will feature creations from local bakers, giving our neighbors a platform to share their talents." Another of Chloe's ideas, presented as if it had sprung fully formed from Alessandra's own creative vision.

As the tour continued, Michael watched Alessandra describe feature after feature that Chloe had originally proposed, from the subtle lighting designed to make people want to linger to the branded cards that would accompany special menu items, each sharing a piece of neighborhood history, just like Chloe's Story Boxes from the television show.

"Authenticity is the new luxury," Alessandra

concluded, settling back into her chair with a self-satisfied smile as the camera panned out again to show the entire room.

The video ended with a sleek graphic announcing the grand opening date.

Michael stared at his phone, his blood pressure rising with each passing second. Aidan's follow-up text appeared on his screen.

> She's giving interviews about her "community-centered design philosophy" too. Not a single mention of Chloe.

Michael's fingers hovered over the keyboard, unsure how to respond. The rage he felt wasn't just professional indignation. This was personal. Alessandra had taken Chloe's heartfelt vision, the same vision she'd initially criticized, and was now passing it off as her own innovative concept. His protective instincts had him seeing red.

Before he could reply, another text from Aidan came through.

> Want me to say something?

Michael took a deep breath. He had to be strategic, not just reactive. Calling Alessandra out publicly would only make the firm look bad, not to mention damage its relationship with her. At this point, he didn't care if they ever worked with her again, but his partners might not agree. Plus, The Perry was nearly complete, and starting a feud now could delay the opening further.

But letting this stand felt wrong on a fundamental level. He could still salvage this as long as Lexi, the firm's publicist, hadn't sent out the release yet.

> Has the press release gone out yet?

Aidan's response came in quickly.

> No, I'll tell Lexi you want to review it before
> it goes out.

He set his phone down and turned back to his laptop, opening a new document. If Alessandra wanted to talk about authenticity and community, then she needed to practice what she preached. And that started with acknowledging the person whose vision had shaped Perk Slope from the beginning.

Michael wasn't sure yet exactly how to handle this situation, but he knew one thing for certain: He wasn't going to let Chloe's contributions be erased.

Chapter 23

Chloe

"Two minutes to live feed," one of the production assistants called out, adjusting Chloe's microphone pack for the third time.

The lounge off the lobby at the Inn on Cypress Shores had been transformed into a satellite studio for tonight's episode, which would feature a combination of prerecorded segments and a live portion during which Chloe would connect with the judges via video call. This week's challenge had focused on expansion planning, and Chloe had spent the past two days filming with Morgan, walking through the space she'd identified for the first Island Coffee franchise.

Chloe's hands were clammy as she smoothed down her floral dress. The #WhereWeBelong movement had exploded in the days following the last episode, with thousands of people across the country sharing photos of the local businesses that made them feel like they belonged. She'd gone from being an underdog to a genuine contender, which both exhilarated and terrified her.

"You look great," Morgan assured her, squeezing her arm before stepping out of frame. "Just be yourself. Remember, that's what got you this far."

"Thanks," Chloe whispered back, taking a deep breath.

Chris gave her a thumbs-up from behind the camera. "Remember, tonight will determine the final four who will advance to next week's finale in New York. The judges have already seen your prerecorded segment with Morgan, but they'll have questions during the live portion."

"Got it," Chloe nodded, trying to project more confidence than she felt.

"Thirty seconds!" the producer called.

A few of Morgan's friends and family had gathered behind the cameras to support her, but they fell quiet as the lights dimmed in the background. On a large screen set up to Chloe's right, she could see the studio in New York where the host and judges were seated at their long table. The other four contestants would be joining from their own locations around the country.

"And we're live in five, four, three . . ." The producer counted down silently with his fingers for the final two seconds.

"Welcome back to *The Next Great American Entrepreneur*," the host's voice boomed through the speakers. "Tonight, one of our five remaining entrepreneurs will be going home, leaving our final four to battle it out in next week's grand finale in New York City!"

After introducing the judges and explaining the night's format, the host turned toward the camera. "Let's check in with our contestants, who have spent the week developing expansion plans for their businesses. First, let's see how Chloe Beckett's Island Coffee is planning to grow beyond Big Dune Island."

The screen switched to the prerecorded segment of Chloe and Morgan walking through the empty storefront in Cypress Shores a few days prior. The footage showed them discussing layout options, pointing out where the community wall would go—Chloe had loved the idea for The Perry so much that she thought it would work well here too—and talking about how they would adapt Island Coffee's concept to reflect Cypress Shores' unique character.

"The key," Chloe's voice explained in the voiceover, "is maintaining the core philosophy that made Island Coffee successful—creating a place where people feel they belong —while allowing each location to authentically reflect its own community."

When the clip ended, the screen returned to the judges' table, where Andie was smiling warmly.

"Chloe, I love how you've managed to create a framework for expansion that doesn't sacrifice authenticity," she said. "Can you tell us more about how you'll maintain quality across locations while still allowing for local variations?"

Chloe launched into her response, explaining the systems she'd developed to ensure consistent coffee quality and service standards, while giving each franchise owner flexibility in its community engagement and local partnerships.

Then Thad leaned forward, his expression neutral but his eyes sharp. "Before we continue with technical questions, I'd like to address something that came to my attention earlier today."

A screen behind the judges flickered to life, and Chloe's

stomach dropped as she recognized Alessandra's face filling the frame. It was a clip from her promotional video for Perk Slope, the coffee shop at The Perry.

"I wanted to create a space that feels both modern and timeless," Alessandra's voice rang out as the camera panned across a café that looked disturbingly familiar to Chloe. "The focal point of our design is what we're calling the community wall . . ."

Chloe's cheeks burned as she watched Alessandra describe—almost word for word—the vision Chloe had shared with her and Michael during their Brooklyn visit. Even the name "community wall" had been Chloe's idea. Was this why Michael hadn't come tonight? He'd said he had business out of town, but was that the real reason?

"Ms. Beckett," Thad said, his voice cutting through Chloe's stunned silence, "I find it interesting that while you've been championing this small-town, community-focused approach on our show, a high-end designer in Brooklyn has already implemented these same concepts at scale in an urban market."

The implication was clear. Thad believed either Chloe had copied Alessandra, or her ideas weren't as unique as she'd claimed.

"I—" Chloe started, but her voice caught. The café in the video was built from her vision, right down to the local baker display cases and the story cards accompanying special menu items. Yet Alessandra was taking full credit, and Thad was using it to undermine Chloe's entire approach.

Her heart was pounding. Michael's face flashed through her mind. Did he know about Alessandra's video?

"Would you care to comment, Ms. Beckett?" Thad pressed.

Chloe took a deep breath, forcing herself to focus despite the hurt and confusion swirling in her mind.

"Actually, I consulted on that project earlier this year. Those were my suggestions for the space, and Alessandra is the designer who implemented my plan." She wanted so badly to add that Alessandra first belittled her ideas and then stole them, but she feared it wouldn't sound very professional.

Thad's eyebrows rose slightly. "You consulted on a high-end Brooklyn hotel project? You haven't mentioned that before."

It was like walking on a tightrope. Chloe wasn't sure what to say. She didn't want to mention Michael or make accusations on live television, but she also couldn't let this mischaracterization stand. "I did a site visit the same weekend I auditioned for this show, actually," she said, desperately channeling some of her cool professionalism in earlier episodes. "I was invited by the developer to share my perspective on creating a space where the entire community felt welcome."

"Well," Thad said with a slight smirk, "it seems your approach can work in urban markets after all, though perhaps it required a professional designer to refine and scale the concept?"

His implication stung, but Chloe forced herself to maintain her composure. "Community isn't limited by geography, Mr. Windemere. Whether it's a small island or a big city, people need places where they feel they belong. That's the principle behind both Island Coffee and now Perk Slope."

Andie leaned forward, a supportive smile on her face. "I think what we're seeing is that Ms. Beckett's philosophy resonates broadly, which only strengthens her franchise potential. I'm sure you've seen how the hashtag is trending." Andie directed this final remark at Thad, who frowned in reply, but Nathan concurred that the buzz was impressive.

The judges moved on to questioning the other contestants, each joining via video feed from their respective locations. Chloe tried to focus on their presentations, but her mind was stuck on the video of Alessandra taking credit for her ideas.

For this penultimate episode, the producers had decided to reveal the audience scores first. As the timer for audience voting ticked down, Chloe watched nervously as the numbers fluctuated on the screen, where voting was being revealed live for the first time. The #WhereWeBelong hashtag appeared repeatedly in the comments scrolling at the bottom, alongside messages defending her against Thad's insinuations.

Finally, the timer stopped, and the host announced the results. "America has voted, and our producers have combined those numbers with our judges' scores. The four entrepreneurs advancing to next week's finale in New York are . . . Carson!" A cheer went up from his remote location. "Brianna!" Another cheer. "Jacob!" The sneaker designer pumped his fist in excitement.

Chloe held her breath as the host paused dramatically.

"And, our small-town sweetheart, Chloe!"

The small crowd at the inn erupted in applause and Chloe smiled in excited relief, but the thrill of making it to the final was soured for Chloe by Alessandra's act of betrayal. How had this happened?

After the broadcast ended and the cameras stopped rolling, Chloe moved through the local crowd on autopilot, accepting congratulations and dodging questions about the Brooklyn project. Brianna had texted how excited she was they'd both made the final, but Chloe hadn't answered her yet. She just wanted to escape, to process what had happened without an audience.

She had almost reached the exit when her phone began buzzing in her hand. It was Michael. Stepping outside, she considered sending him to voicemail, but she decided to face the situation head-on and took the call.

"Chloe, I'm so sorry. I was going to tell you," he said quietly when she answered.

"So you did know about it?" she asked, unable to keep the hurt and accusation from her voice. "And now you want to talk about it, after I had to defend myself on national television?"

She walked to the side of the inn so no one would come out of the front door and interrupt the call. Palm trees swayed gently in the evening breeze, and the sound of waves crashing on the nearby shore provided some privacy for their conversation.

"I found out a few days ago," Michael admitted, his voice full of regret. "Aidan sent me the video. I was going to tell you, but I wanted to get the press release with the firm saying you were the person behind the concept out first. I didn't want to bring you a problem, I wanted to show you the solution, and I never imagined Alessandra's video would come up on the show."

"I'm a big girl, Michael. You don't have to treat me with kid gloves. But as a result of you not telling me, I got blindsided on national television," Chloe said, pacing back and forth, the crushed shells that made up the walkway crunching beneath her sandals. "Do you have any idea how humiliating that was? Having Thad imply I copied someone else's concept when it was actually stolen from me?"

"I'm sorry." His voice was pained, pleading. "I should

have warned you as soon as I saw it. I just didn't want to upset you right before a crucial episode."

"I'm not one of your sisters. I don't need you to protect me."

"You're right," he admitted. "You're not. And they don't need me like that anymore either. I messed up. Again. I'm sorry. I keep trying to protect people by controlling situations, and it keeps backfiring."

The genuine regret in his voice softened Chloe's anger slightly. "How did this even happen? What were you planning to do?" she asked after a moment.

"Alessandra posted the video without prior approval from the firm, and she refuses to take it down. Ever since I found out, I've been working with our publicist, Lexi. The press release for the opening fully acknowledges you as a consultant. I've already called Alessandra, and she knows that you're getting credit in the official release. We'll also be putting up some content on The Perry's social media channels, all of which will credit you. And, if you're open to it, Lexi will pitch you for some media interviews about your vision for The Perry, which of course you can also use as an opportunity to plug Island Coffee."

"I appreciate all of that, but I have to ask, when were you going to tell me about all of this?"

"After tonight's episode. I knew you needed to focus on the competition without added stress. I thought I was helping, but I should have known better after everything that's happened."

"I'm still upset," Chloe said finally. "But I believe you were trying to help. In your own misguided way."

"That should be my tagline: 'Michael Russo: Helping in Misguided Ways Since 1985.'" His tone was lighter now.

Despite herself, Chloe felt a laugh bubble up. "Don't try to charm your way out of this."

"Nope, not trying to charm at all. I'm genuinely sorry, Chloe. You deserved better, both from Alessandra and from me."

"So, what happens now?"

"Now, we make this right," Michael said, determination replacing the guilt in his voice. "Together, if you're willing. No more of me trying to handle things behind your back. We can go through everything I've gathered, decide how we want to approach it, and move forward. Your ideas, your call."

Chloe considered his words. "Okay," she said finally. "I'll look things over, but after that, I need to focus on the finale. The rest can wait until after next week."

"Of course. Whatever you need," Michael said, then added softly, "For what it's worth, you were amazing tonight. The way you handled Thad's ambush was incredibly poised and professional."

"I was in shock, and terrified," Chloe admitted. "But I've learned something important through all this. I know who I am and what Island Coffee stands for. Nobody can take that away, not even Alessandra."

"That's what makes you special, Chloe. Not just your business ideas but your unwavering belief in what matters."

The sincerity in his voice made something warm unfurl in her chest, despite the lingering hurt. Whatever was growing between them had hit a rough patch, but it wasn't a roadblock, just a speed bump.

"The finale films in New York, right?" he asked.

"It does. I fly out in a week."

"Perfect. The Perry will be almost ready to open. I'll

come up too, and we can go in person to see your master-piece. Would you like that?"

A smile spread across her face. "Yes, I would like that. Sounds like a perfect way to cap off the show, win or lose."

They said goodbye, making plans to touch base once she got her itinerary from the show. As she drove home, the emotions of the evening swirled through her mind: the shock of seeing her ideas claimed by someone else, the hurt of feeling betrayed, the pride of advancing to the finale, and then the complicated comfort of knowing Michael had been trying, in his own flawed way, to protect her.

By the time she reached her apartment above the café, one thought floated above all others like a buoy on the ocean: She'd made the finale by being true to herself and her vision. No matter what obstacles arose going forward, she would face them as herself, not as someone else's version of who she should be.

And, she thought with satisfaction, that certainty was its own kind of victory.

Chapter 24

Michael

Michael made it to New York for the finale, but his schedule once there was packed tighter than the subway at rush hour. Between the warehouse project, the impending launch of The Perry, and the handful of preservation projects they had on Big Dune, he barely had time to breathe. Coupled with how anxious he was to see Chloe, this trip to New York wasn't going as he'd planned.

The morning had started with an emergency call from John about budget issues with the artist studios. That "quick call" had expanded into a three-hour video conference, during which Michael had defended—successfully, he hoped—the various expenses required to convert the space.

"The enhanced ventilation is necessary when artists are working with oil-based paints," he'd explained, during what he felt was a ridiculous argument as they went through the budget line by line. "We don't want to end up on the front page because someone got sick from the fumes. Let's all remember there are luxury residences above these artist studios."

John hadn't looked entirely convinced, but he'd relented. "Just make sure it doesn't turn into a money pit."

Now, Michael was standing at the window of his condo in Manhattan, watching as yellow taxis zigzagged through traffic while he waited for Aidan to join him for their final check on The Perry. His phone buzzed with a text from his mother.

> Will you be stopping by while you're in town? The girls want to know if we should plan dinner.

He grimaced, a pang of guilt settling in his stomach. He'd waited until the last minute to tell his mother he was in New York, texting her after he'd arrived that morning. Between the finale and finishing up at The Perry, he'd convinced himself there wasn't time for a family dinner. But the truth was, he was avoiding a get-together because he wasn't ready to talk to them about Chloe. From fielding the knowing looks to fending off the probing questions that would inevitably follow, he didn't feel quite up to it.

> Just a quick business trip, Ma. In and out. I'll be back soon, promise.

No sooner had he sent the message than his phone rang —Maria's name lighting up the screen. Of course his mother had immediately texted his sisters.

"Hey, what's going on?" he asked, trying to sound casual.

"Seriously, Mike? You're in New York and didn't tell us?"

He sighed, pinching the bridge of his nose. "It's just for a few days. I've got meetings back-to-back."

"Mmm-hmm." Her skepticism radiated through the phone. "And this has nothing to do with the finale of that show your coffee girl is on?"

"How did you—"

"Mom and I watch it," Maria said matter-of-factly. "So do Angela and Gina and Cristina. We have a group chat going. We're all rooting for her, by the way."

Michael felt heat rising to his face. "She's not 'my coffee girl.'"

"Sure, and you're definitely not flying to New York specifically to watch her compete in the finale." The sound of a door shutting came through the line, and Maria's voice dropped. "Listen, I won't tell Mom if you don't want me to, but at least be honest with me."

Michael hesitated, then relented. "Fine. Yes, I'm here for the finale. But I am totally slammed with meetings as well, and I also have business to take care of at The Perry. It's the final checks before we open the café."

"The one that snooty designer tried to take credit for?" Maria asked.

"You really have been watching, huh?"

"Like I said, group chat. We might have done some online investigating after that episode."

Michael couldn't help but smile at the thought of his sisters and mother huddled around their phones, digging up information on Alessandra. She wasn't the kind of woman he would ever bring home to meet his family, so they were unaware of his personal history with her. "She's been put in her place, trust me."

"Good," Maria said with satisfaction. "So, when do we get to meet her? Your coffee girl."

"I told you, she's not—"

"Yeah, yeah. Answer the question."

Michael ran a hand through his hair. "I don't know, Maria. It's complicated."

"Is it?" His sister's voice softened. "Because from what we can see, she makes you happy. And that's not complicated at all."

A knock at the door saved him from having to respond. "That's Aidan. I've got to go."

"Fine, but this conversation isn't over. Call Mom, at least. She's worried you're working too hard."

After saying goodbye, Michael let Aidan in. His colleague looked surprisingly relaxed in jeans and a casual button-down shirt.

"Ready for the grand unveiling?" Aidan asked, handing Michael the coffee he'd brought him.

"As ready as I'll ever be," Michael said, grabbing his jacket. "How does it look?"

"Better than we had any right to expect, considering the last-minute changes. Alessandra might have taken credit for Chloe's idea, but she also managed to execute the vision pretty faithfully."

Michael nodded, relieved. "And the press release?"

"Went out this morning. It clearly attributes the community-focused design concept to Chloe, with quotes from you about the importance of creating spaces where people feel they belong."

"Good." Michael checked his watch. "We should head over. I want time to review everything before the afternoon meeting with the hotel manager."

The ride to Park Slope was filled with updates on

various projects and office gossip from Aidan. Michael tried to focus, but his mind kept drifting to Chloe. She'd texted an hour before to say she'd arrived in the city. The network had a dinner scheduled for the finalists that evening before the big day tomorrow, which began with press interviews and ended with the filming of the live finale. He'd wished her luck without offering any of the advice that bubbled to his mind every time he thought about what the press—or the judges—might ask her.

He was still finding his footing in this new territory, where he cared about someone's well-being without trying to control the situation. Maybe it was like when you put on a new pair of leather shoes—uncomfortable at first but a perfect fit if you gave it a little time.

When they arrived at The Perry, scaffolding still surrounded parts of the entrance, but the interior was nearly complete. The lobby gleamed with restored marble floors and fresh paint, the original crown molding brought back to its former glory.

When Michael stepped through the doorway of Perk Slope, he felt a surge of satisfaction. The space was warm and inviting, with comfortable seating arrangements that encouraged conversation. The community wall dominated one side of the room, a beautiful mural depicting scenes from Park Slope's history, with blank spaces scattered across it where photos and stories from local residents would eventually be displayed.

"Not bad," he said, wandering farther into the space.

"Not bad? It's amazing," Aidan corrected. "The lighting, the layout, the sense of flow, it all works together perfectly. Chloe has a real talent for spatial design."

"Yes, she sure does," he said, unable to hide his smile when he thought of her. He hadn't discussed his personal feelings for Chloe with Aidan, so he hoped Aidan wouldn't notice what he was sure was a dopey grin as he moved toward the service counter to see the display cases that would hold goods from local bakers.

"Did the manager find any local suppliers yet?" Michael asked.

Aidan nodded. "Three bakeries have already signed on, and they're talking to a fourth. Plus a coffee roaster in Gowanus. The space won't open to the public for another two weeks, but they're planning a soft launch for neighborhood residents next weekend."

"Good. I want this to feel like it belongs to the community from day one."

They spent the next hour inspecting every detail of the space, making a punch list of final adjustments needed before the opening. Michael found himself channeling Chloe's perspective, focusing not just on the aesthetics but on how the space would function as a gathering place.

Next up was their meeting with the hotel manager. It went smoothly, with only minor adjustments needed to the final plans. The woman was enthusiastic about the café concept, having herself lived in Park Slope for many years.

"This neighborhood has changed so much in the past decade," she said as they wrapped up. "We've gained a lot, but we've lost some of that sense of connection too. I think Perk Slope could help bring that back."

As they left The Perry, Michael felt a sense of pride that had nothing to do with profit margins or investment returns. This project represented something different. It was a space designed primarily to foster community rather than maximize efficiency and profit.

As he headed to his next meeting, all Michael could

think about was seeing Chloe's face when she saw Perk Slope.

His phone buzzed with a text from John.

Warehouse numbers look better than expected. The church parking agreement helped. Moving forward with artist studios as proposed.

Michael smiled, tucking his phone away. Another victory for community over pure profit. The warehouse project wasn't over, but he'd won a crucial battle.

Later that afternoon, Michael was back at his condo reviewing his notes before a meeting with a couple of his partners over at the Astoria project. His phone buzzed with an incoming call from his sister Angela.

"Let me guess," he said by way of greeting. "Maria told you I'm in town."

"Of course she did." Angela laughed. "We're all dying to know about the finale. Cristina's betting you'll be sitting front row."

Michael pinched the bridge of his nose. "I don't know where I'll be sitting."

"So you admit you're going?"

"Yes, fine, I'm going to the finale. It's important to Chloe, and she's . . ." he hesitated, knowing he'd never hear the end of it, then plunged ahead. ". . . important to me."

There was a brief silence on the other end. "Wow," Angela finally said. "That might be the most straightforward thing you've ever said about a woman you're interested in."

Michael smiled despite himself. "Don't get used to it."

"Seriously though, we're happy for you. Even if you won't introduce her to us yet."

"I'm not hiding her," Michael protested. "I'm protecting her."

"From what? Your crazy family?"

Michael hesitated. "No, just from unnecessary anxiety. The competition is stressful enough without adding our family dynamics to the mix."

Angela's sigh was audible. "Always the protector. Ever think maybe she doesn't need protecting? That woman stood her ground on national television when that designer tried to steal her ideas. She seems pretty capable to me."

The observation hit uncomfortably close to home. "It's not that simple."

"It never is with you," Angela said, but her tone was affectionate. "Mom says to call her tomorrow. No excuses."

After hanging up, Michael stared into his coffee, Angela's words echoing in his mind. Was he still trying to protect Chloe when she didn't need it? Or was he actually protecting himself, afraid of what might happen if he fully opened up his life to her?

His phone buzzed again, this time with a text from Jesse.

> They're opening up the community playhouse so everyone can watch Chloe together tomorrow night.

Michael smiled at the thought of Big Dune Island rallying around Chloe. She had built something special there, a business that truly mattered to people. And now she was one step away from the resources to expand that vision.

Regardless of the outcome, Chloe had already succeeded in the most important way. She'd stayed true to her vision and to what made Island Coffee special. She'd learned when to stand firm and when to adapt, finding her own path forward rather than following someone else's blueprint.

Michael was learning through this experience too. Learning to care deeply about something beyond financial success. Learning to support without controlling. Learning that sometimes, the biggest risk wasn't losing money but missing the chance to be part of something meaningful.

His phone buzzed with a final confirmation of his ticket for tomorrow night's taping. He'd be there to witness whatever came next in Chloe's journey. Not as her adviser or protector but simply as someone who believed in her vision. Someone who was proud to know her, whatever the outcome.

The thought filled him with anticipation that had nothing to do with business metrics or investment returns. For perhaps the first time in his adult life, Michael was allowing himself to care about something simply because it mattered to his heart, not his balance sheet.

And that, he realized, might be the most valuable lesson Chloe had taught him yet.

Chapter 25

Chloe

Chloe paced her hotel room floor, trying to expel nervous energy, Manhattan looming large outside her window. People moved along the sidewalks with purpose as yellow taxis weaved through traffic, and the buildings stretched endlessly in every direction.

Being back at the same hotel she'd stayed at for her audition had her thinking about how much had changed since that first visit. She'd arrived uncertain and intimidated, desperate to prove herself worthy of the judges' attention. Now she was back with a clearer sense of who she was and what made her business special. She didn't need to win to prove she'd created something successful that was her own —she knew that now.

The welcome packet on the desk contained a detailed schedule, which began with dinner that evening and then a full day tomorrow, including hair and makeup call times, rehearsal slots, and the filming schedule. The finale would be taped in front of a live studio audience, with the winner announced at the end. Family and friends had been invited to attend, and Chloe knew Reagan, Austin, Gigi, Luke, and her parents would all be there.

And Michael. Her heart did a little flip at the thought of him watching from the audience.

Chloe sank onto the edge of the bed, suddenly overwhelmed by it all. The competition, the potential prize, her complicated feelings for Michael, and the uncertainty of what came next were a lot to process.

Her phone buzzed with a text from Brianna.

> You here yet? Can't believe we made it to the finale!

Chloe smiled as she replied.

> Just arrived! Want to meet for coffee before dinner?

Brianna responded instantly.

> Yes please! Lobby in 30?

With plans made, Chloe headed into the bathroom to apply makeup. She played Callie's latest album on her phone, which was full of upbeat, uplifting tunes. The familiar ritual of getting ready calmed her nerves.

Thirty minutes later, Chloe headed down to the lobby. Brianna was already waiting, her face lighting up when she spotted Chloe.

"There she is!" Brianna stood to hug her. "My favorite competitor."

Chloe laughed, returning the embrace. "Right back at

you. You look amazing." And she did. Brianna's hair was freshly colored and styled, her outfit casual but perfectly put together.

"Had to make sure I was finale-ready," Brianna smoothed her skirt. "There's a cute coffee shop around the corner. Not as good as Island Coffee, I'm sure, but it'll do in a pinch."

As they walked, they fell into easy conversation about their experiences since the last challenge. Brianna had been busy preparing her final presentation, but she'd also managed to secure interest from two potential investors who'd reached out after watching the show.

"It's crazy," she said as they found a table in the small café. "Even if I don't win tomorrow, I've already got more opportunities than I ever expected from being on the show."

"That's amazing," Chloe said sincerely. "Your salon concept is brilliant. You deserve all the success."

"So do you," Brianna insisted. "That whole WhereWe-Belong movement has people talking. I've seen it everywhere on social media."

Chloe still couldn't quite believe how the hashtag had taken off. "It's been surreal," she admitted. "But also validating, you know? To see that my vision resonates with people beyond just Big Dune Island. You must feel that way too after your HairMergency hashtag took off."

Brianna nodded. "It's definitely fun to see how invested people are in the show. Are you nervous about tomorrow?"

"Terrified," Chloe confessed. "You?"

Brianna blew out a breath. "Carson's going to be tough to beat. And Jacob has that whole social media following behind him. But honestly? I'm just proud we made it this far."

"Me too," Chloe agreed. "Although . . ." She hesitated,

then decided to confide in her friend. "After that ambush with the Brooklyn café last episode, I'm a little worried about what Thad might pull tomorrow."

Brianna shook her head sympathetically. "That was awful. I couldn't believe he did that to you on live television." She reached across the table to squeeze Chloe's hand. "But you handled it like a pro. And the audience loved how authentic you were."

"I just hope the finale focuses on our businesses, not drama."

"Speaking of business," Brianna said, her expression turning serious, "have you thought about what you'll do if you win?"

Chloe took a sip of her latte, considering the question. "I want to help Morgan open her café in Cypress Shores. Use part of the prize money to buy out my brother's share of Island Coffee. And then, maybe explore more locations. But slowly, and each one tailored to its community."

"That sounds perfect for your concept," Brianna nodded. "True to your vision but still allowing for growth."

"What about you?"

Brianna's eyes lit up. "I want to open three more locations in the next year and develop a training program for stylists who want to learn my method. And maybe develop my product line further. The company that developed the AI technology I use is talking about a branded concept other salons can adopt too."

They continued chatting through their coffee, sharing ideas and offering each other encouragement. By the time they headed back to the hotel for dinner, Chloe felt more centered than she had all day.

The hotel restaurant had been partially closed off for their group, with a large table set for the finalists, judges, and key production staff. Carson and Jacob were already there when Chloe and Brianna arrived, along with Chris and a few other producers.

"The ladies have arrived," Carson stood, his charm on full display as he shook their hands and then pulled out chairs for them at the table. "Now the party can really begin."

Despite his competitive nature, Carson was cordial, even friendly. Jacob was quieter but greeted them warmly.

"Can you believe we're here?" Jacob asked, his usual confidence tempered with genuine wonder. "Final four. Out of hundreds of applicants."

"It's surreal," Chloe agreed, settling into her seat.

The judges arrived shortly after, and Chloe tried not to tense as Thad approached. To her surprise, he offered her a polite nod.

"Ms. Beckett," he said formally. "I appreciate your composure during our last interaction. Not everyone would have handled that situation with such grace."

Before she could respond, Andie swooped in for hugs, her enthusiasm brightening the mood considerably. "My final four! I'm so proud of all of you. No matter what happens tomorrow, you've accomplished something extraordinary."

Nathan greeted them all with handshakes, his usual reserve in place. "May the best entrepreneur win," he said simply.

Dinner was a surprisingly relaxed affair, with conversation flowing easily among the group. The judges shared stories from previous business ventures, and the finalists swapped tales of their most memorable moments from the competition.

"So," Nathan said as dessert was served, "how are you all feeling about tomorrow?"

"Ready," Carson said immediately, his confidence unwavering.

"Nervous but excited," Brianna admitted.

"Grateful," Jacob added thoughtfully, "for the opportunity, regardless of the outcome."

When all eyes turned to Chloe, she took a moment to truly consider her answer. "I'm feeling certain," she said finally. "About who I am and what Island Coffee stands for. That certainty gives me peace, whatever happens tomorrow."

Andie raised her water glass. "To going into tomorrow with peace, then. And to four remarkable entrepreneurs who remind us all why we do what we do."

As glasses clinked around the table, Chloe felt an unexpected calm settle over her. She was ready for the finale, for the next chapter of Island Coffee, and for whatever came next.

Back in her room later that night, Chloe stepped out onto the small balcony, the city lights stretching out before her. Her phone buzzed with a text from Michael.

> Can't wait to see you shine on that stage tomorrow. Remember, you've already won by staying true to your vision.

She smiled, typing back.

> Thank you for believing in me, even when I forgot to believe in myself.

His response came quickly.

Chloe leaned against the railing, letting the cool night air wash over her. Tomorrow would bring challenges, nerves, and, ultimately, resolution. But tonight, standing high above the city that had once intimidated her, she felt only anticipation.

Win or lose, she already had the place where she belonged.

The morning of the finale dawned clear and bright, sunlight streaming through the gap in the curtains of Chloe's hotel room. She'd been awake for hours already, too keyed up to sleep past five. Her body was still on the café schedule, despite being in the big city.

Standing at the window of her room, Chloe watched the streets below come alive. Even at this early hour, the city pulsed with energy. There were delivery trucks making their rounds, people hustling down the sidewalks to their destinations, and steam rising from manholes like something out of a movie scene. New York never truly slept, and last night, neither had she.

"Today's the day," she whispered to herself, leaning her forehead on the cool glass.

Her phone buzzed on the nightstand with an incoming text from Morgan.

Attached was a photo of a handmade banner the locals had created with "Team Chloe" painted in Island Coffee's signature blue and white colors. The image brought tears to her eyes. The same community that had rallied around her during that pivotal challenge was still firmly in her corner and showing her the love.

Last night, Chloe had felt centered and calm. But alone in her hotel room with the finale just hours away, the nerves she'd managed to keep at bay came rushing in like the tide. Today's schedule would begin with a production meeting going over the format of the finale, a brief run-through on stage, and a final interview for the intro package.

In less than eight hours, she'd know if she'd won the grand prize that could transform Island Coffee. With it, she could buy out Austin's share and help Morgan open the first franchise location. But most importantly, she would prove she could succeed on her own terms.

A knock at the door startled her from her thoughts. She wasn't expecting anyone this early.

"Room service," called a female voice.

Puzzled, Chloe opened the door to find a server with a rolling cart bearing a covered tray, a carafe of coffee, and a vase containing four pink peonies.

"I didn't order this," she said, confused.

The server consulted her tablet. "Are you Chloe Beckett? This was pre-ordered for you." She gestured to a small card beside the vase.

After tipping the server, Chloe closed the door and picked up the card.

Because sometimes you deserve to eat a break-

fast made by someone else. Knock 'em dead today.
I'll be there cheering you on. —Michael

Her heart did a little flip as she lifted the silver dome to reveal a perfect breakfast: buttermilk biscuits that reminded her of her grandmother, fresh fruit, and scrambled eggs. The peonies—bright and cheerful against the neutral hotel décor—made her smile. Somehow, Michael had remembered her mentioning once that they were her favorite.

Just as she poured herself a cup of coffee, her phone rang. Her mother's name lit up the screen.

"Morning, sweetheart! Did we wake you?" Her mother's voice was overly bright, betraying her nervousness.

"I've been up for hours," Chloe assured her. "Too excited to sleep."

"Your father's checking us in for our flight now. We should land around two, plenty of time to get to the studio. And Reagan, Austin, Gigi, and Luke are already on their way."

They chatted for a few more minutes about travel arrangements and the weather, her mother's cheerful chatter barely disguising her anxiety. When they finally hung up, Chloe felt that familiar tug between excitement and the weight of expectations. Not just her own but those of everyone back home who was rooting for her.

She picked at her breakfast, her appetite diminished by nerves, but forced herself to eat. Today would require all her energy and focus.

A text from Brianna lit up her phone.

Morning! Want to grab coffee before
everything gets crazy?

Yes please!

Chloe replied instantly, grateful for the distraction.

Twenty minutes later, she met Brianna in the lobby. Despite the early hour, Brianna looked polished and ready for the day in stylish jeans and a chic blouse, her makeup already perfect.

"You look like you've been up for hours," Chloe observed as they stepped out into the morning air.

"Couldn't sleep," Brianna admitted. "I think I tried on every outfit I brought before giving up and just putting on jeans."

"Same," Chloe laughed. "Though the wardrobe team made it clear they've already chosen our outfits for tonight."

They returned to the same café they'd visited the day before, settling into a quiet corner table with their drinks. The morning rush hadn't yet begun, giving them a peaceful moment before the chaos of finale day began in earnest.

"Can you believe we actually made it?" Brianna asked, stirring her latte. "Sometimes I have to pinch myself."

"I know," Chloe agreed. "When I think about that first interview in New York, how nervous I was just to be in the room with the judges, it feels like a lifetime ago."

"You've changed," Brianna observed. "Not in a bad way. You're more confident now."

"I've figured out what matters," Chloe said thoughtfully. "What makes Island Coffee special and what I want it to become. That gives me a kind of confidence I didn't have before."

Brianna nodded. "That's what people connect with, you know. Your absolute belief in your vision. It comes through even on screen." She hesitated, then added with a smile, "Though I still plan to win tonight."

"May the best entrepreneur win," Chloe laughed, tapping her mug against Brianna's.

They couldn't help continuing to talk about the show, dissecting what they knew about the finale—from what challenges they might face tonight to gossip about the production crew to plans for celebrating afterward, win or lose. By the time they headed back to the hotel, Chloe felt significantly calmer, her earlier anxiety replaced by a quiet determination.

The production team had instructed all finalists to be ready by eleven for hair and makeup. Back in her room, Chloe showered and changed into comfortable clothes, knowing she'd be in the styling chair for at least an hour before changing into whatever outfit had been selected for her.

As she packed up her notes and rehearsed key points in her head, a text came through from Reagan.

> Just landed! Can't wait to see you crush it tonight!

Attached was a selfie of Reagan, Luke, Austin, and Gigi making silly faces in the airport terminal, Austin holding a hastily made "Team Chloe" sign drawn on a piece of paper.

Chloe laughed out loud, her heart full. Whatever happened tonight, she had people who believed in her, not because of what she might accomplish but because of who she was.

A knock at the door announced the arrival of the production assistant who would escort her to hair and makeup. "Ready, Ms. Beckett?"

Taking a deep breath, Chloe nodded. "As I'll ever be."

The next several hours passed in a whirlwind of activity. They wouldn't be going to the studio until it was time to film, so the hotel had dedicated an entire floor to the production team, transforming rooms into makeup stations, wardrobe departments, and interview areas. In the makeup chair, the stylist worked magic, bringing out her eyes with subtle color and giving her a glow that would read well on camera without looking overdone.

"You have such a great bone structure," the woman commented as she applied blush. "The camera loves you."

"Really?" Chloe asked, surprised. "I always feel so awkward during filming."

"Trust me, it doesn't show. You come across as very authentic, very warm. It's refreshing."

In wardrobe, Chloe was presented with a knee-length dress in a deep blue that complemented her eyes. The dress had enough structure to look professional while still allowing her to feel like herself. When she expressed concern about the heels they'd chosen for her, the stylist immediately found her a more comfortable option.

"We want you to focus on the competition, not your feet," the woman said kindly.

From wardrobe, Chloe was swept to a small room where she was interviewed one-on-one by nearly a dozen media members in ten-minute increments. It all went by so quickly, she barely had time to process her thoughts.

By early afternoon, all four finalists were gathered in a holding room, each looking polished and camera-ready, though Carson was the only one who appeared truly relaxed, sprawled in an armchair checking something on his phone.

"Alright, everyone," Chris announced, entering the room with a tablet in hand. "We'll be heading to the studio in fifteen minutes. The live audience is already being seated, and we'll do one final sound check when we arrive."

He went on to explain the evening's format—each finalist would have a chance to present their business and vision one last time, followed by questions from the judges. After a commercial break, they'd face a surprise challenge designed to test how they responded under pressure. Finally, after the audience vote was tallied, the winner would be announced.

"Any questions?" Chris looked around at their tense faces.

"Will we have time to say hello to our families and friends in the audience before we go live?" Jacob asked, his usual confidence faltering slightly.

Chris shook his head. "Not until after the show. We want you focused on the judges and the audience as a whole, not looking for familiar faces."

Chloe's heart sank slightly. She'd been hoping for a glimpse of Michael, Reagan, and her family before taking the stage. A reassuring smile from a friendly face would have steadied her nerves.

As they were led to the waiting cars, Brianna fell into step beside Chloe. "Hey," she said quietly. "No matter what happens tonight, we've both won already. Remember that."

Chloe squeezed her friend's hand gratefully. "Thank you. I'm trying to keep perspective."

The ride to the studio was quiet, each finalist lost in their own thoughts. Chloe watched the city flash by outside the window, focusing on her breathing to calm her nerves.

When they arrived at the studio, the energy shifted palpably. Production assistants with headsets hurried around, lighting technicians made last-minute adjustments, and makeup artists stood ready for touch-ups. The atmosphere was electric with anticipation.

They were led to a green room backstage, where platters of finger foods and bottles of water awaited. Chloe couldn't eat, her stomach too twisted with nerves, but she sipped water while reviewing her notes one last time.

A production assistant appeared with microphone packs for each of them. "Ten minutes to places," she announced.

Chloe slipped into the restroom, needing a moment alone to center herself. Staring into the mirror, she took a deep breath.

"You've got this," she told her reflection. "Just be yourself. That's what got you here."

As she returned to the green room, her phone buzzed with a text. Michael's name lit up the screen.

> Just got here. You're going to be amazing. The whole room is buzzing about #WhereWeBelong.

The message steadied her more than she would have expected. Not because she needed his approval or even his support but because she knew he genuinely believed in what she'd built. Not what it could be but what it already was.

"Places, everyone," called a stage manager. "We're on in five minutes."

As they lined up in the wings, Chloe felt a strange calm settle over her. The months of competition, the emotional roller coaster of finding and nearly losing her authentic vision, the unexpected connections she'd formed—it had all led to this moment.

Win or lose, she would walk off that stage tonight knowing she had stayed true to what mattered most. That, she realized, was its own kind of victory.

Chapter 26

Michael

The studio buzzed with excitement, and Michael felt it ripple across his skin as he looked for his seat. The space was small, with about a hundred seats' arranged in a semicircle around the stage. A large screen dominated the back wall, while four podiums for the finalists stood at the front, facing a table where he imagined the judges would sit.

"Michael!"

He turned to see Reagan waving at him from a few rows back, where she sat with Austin, Gigi, and Luke. Chloe's parents were just filing into the row behind them, her father awkwardly side-stepping past other audience members.

Michael made his way over, greeting everyone with handshakes and hugs. Luke's enthusiasm was infectious as he bounced in his seat, wearing a T-shirt with "Team Chloe" emblazoned across the front.

"Did you see her yet?" Reagan asked.

Michael shook his head. "They're keeping the finalists separated until the show starts. I sent her a text, though."

"She's going to crush it," Austin said confidently. "She knows what she's doing."

"I'm still mad about that designer stealing her ideas," Gigi added, her lawyer's indignation evident. "But at least the press release gave her proper credit."

Michael hadn't shared with them the full extent of his efforts to rectify the situation. The press release was just the beginning. He'd also arranged for Perk Slope to be featured in a local magazine alongside Chloe, showcasing how the Island Coffee concept was being implemented at The Perry.

"Nervous?" Austin asked, nudging Michael's arm.

"Me? No. Why would I be nervous?" Michael replied, too quickly.

Austin smiled knowingly. "Because you care about her."

Before Michael could formulate a response that wouldn't reveal exactly how much he cared, a production assistant appeared on stage with a microphone, asking everyone to take their seats. The host would be coming out to warm up the audience before filming began.

Michael found his seat, which ended up being right in front of Austin and Gigi. It was a prime spot with a clear view of the stage. The house lights dimmed, and the host bounded onto the stage, his energy amplified for the live audience. After a few jokes and instructions on when to applaud, he explained the format for the evening.

"Each finalist will present their business one final time, followed by questions from our distinguished judges. Then, we'll give them a surprise challenge to test their quick thinking. Finally, we'll combine the judges' scores with the audience votes to crown our first-ever *Next Great American Entrepreneur!*"

The audience cheered, and Michael found himself clapping along, caught up in the moment despite his typical aversion to reality show theatrics.

"When we introduce the contestants," the host continued, "give them all a warm welcome, but of course, feel free to show extra support for your favorites."

As the production team made final adjustments, Michael surveyed the room. Each contestant had been given ten tickets, and the rest had been sold first come, first served that morning. He spotted several audience members wearing #WhereWeBelong T-shirts and pins and smiled. It was evidence of how Chloe's message had resonated beyond the show. The hashtag had sparked a genuine movement, with people across the country celebrating the local businesses that gave them a sense of belonging.

The floor director began the countdown, and the audience fell silent. Camera operators took their positions, and the screen lit up with the show's logo. This was it.

"Welcome," boomed the host as the cameras began rolling, "to the finale of *The Next Great American Entrepreneur!*"

The judges were introduced first, each walking out to applause. Thad looked as smug as ever, Nathan appeared appropriately serious, and Andie beamed with genuine excitement. They took their seats at the judges' table, and a hush fell over the crowd.

"And now, let's welcome our four finalists, who have survived every challenge to reach this moment!"

The audience erupted again as the first contestant appeared. "The kombucha king himself, Carson Chen!"

Carson strode confidently onto the stage, waving to the

crowd with the easy charm that had helped him dominate the competition.

"The visionary stylist whose AI is revolutionizing the salon industry, Brianna Alexander!"

Brianna emerged next, elegant and poised, her smile warm but professional.

"Sneaker designer and social media phenomenon, Jacob Torres!"

Jacob bounded onto the stage with youthful energy, pumping his fist to enthusiastic cheers.

Michael found himself holding his breath as the host prepared to announce the final contestant.

"And the woman who showed us all where we belong, it's Chloe Beckett!"

The crowd's reaction was deafening. The #WhereWe-Belong faction of the audience jumped to their feet, and Michael found himself standing too, clapping until his hands hurt. Luke was whistling loudly from his seat, while Reagan and Gigi held up a handmade sign.

And there she was. Walking out in a beautiful blue dress that matched her eyes perfectly, her smile radiating both nervousness and determination. She looked stunning, yes, but more importantly, she looked like herself. Genuine. Grounded. Happy.

For a moment, just a fleeting second, her eyes scanned the audience and landed on Michael. He saw the recognition in her expression, the slight softening of her features as she registered his presence. He gave her an encouraging nod, hoping to convey everything he couldn't say out loud: *I believe in you. You've already won, no matter what happens tonight.*

The finalists took their positions, and the host explained the first segment. Each would have three minutes to present their business vision, followed by two minutes of questions from the judges.

Carson went first, his presentation slick and practiced. He showcased impressive growth metrics for his kombucha chain, with analytics demonstrating customer retention and projected revenue across multiple markets. The judges nodded appreciatively, particularly Thad and Nathan, who seemed especially impressed by the automated elements of his business model.

Brianna followed with an equally polished but more personalized pitch. She emphasized how her salons created not just beautiful hair but renewed confidence, showing testimonials from clients whose lives had been changed by her stylists' work. Her AI technology was positioned as enhancing human connection, not replacing it.

Jacob's presentation focused on his brand's authentic street credibility and the community he'd built through social media. His numbers weren't as strong as Carson's, but his passionate fan base gave him a compelling edge.

Finally, it was Chloe's turn. Michael leaned forward slightly, willing his support to reach her across the space between them.

"When I opened Island Coffee seven years ago," she began, her voice steady despite the enormity of the moment, "I wasn't just starting a business. I was continuing a legacy my grandmother started at her dining room table, where neighbors came together to share stories over coffee and homemade treats."

She wove a narrative that seamlessly connected her past with her vision for the future, with a network of cafes, each unique to its community but united by the core principle of belonging.

"What makes Island Coffee special isn't just what we

serve, but how we make people feel," she continued. "We preserve traditions through our Story Boxes, honor memories through heirloom china, and create spaces where everyone feels like they're at home."

Michael watched the judges' reactions. Andie was nodding enthusiastically, clearly moved. Nathan looked thoughtful, perhaps reassessing his previous skepticism. Even Thad seemed less dismissive than usual.

"The WhereWeBelong movement wasn't something we planned," Chloe said, gesturing to the screen behind her where images from social media appeared. "It happened organically because people recognized something they were missing in their lives—places that matter and businesses that contribute to the fabric of a community rather than just existing within it."

As she concluded, the audience erupted with applause. Michael found himself on his feet again, his chest swelling with pride. She hadn't relied on buzzwords or corporate jargon. She'd spoken from the heart about what truly mattered, and he could tell it had landed with the judges.

The questioning began, with Andie leading off. "You've mentioned wanting to help a young entrepreneur named Morgan open the first Island Coffee franchise in Cypress Shores, Florida. How would you ensure that each location maintains this authentic connection to its community while still delivering a consistent experience?"

"That's the beauty of our model," Chloe answered confidently. "We're not trying to create identical cafés. We provide the framework for success—like proven recipes, operational systems, and design principles—but each owner builds their own community connections. Morgan already knows her town. She'll collect her own stories, add in local recipes, and create a space that feels authentic to

Cypress Shores while still embodying the Island Coffee spirit."

Thad leaned forward, his expression analytical. "Your audience support has been impressive, but let's talk numbers. Your profit margins are slightly lower than some of our other finalists. How do you justify this to potential investors?"

Michael tensed, recognizing the trap. Thad was trying to force Chloe back into a strictly financial framework, away from the community values that made her concept special.

But Chloe wasn't thrown. "Those margins reflect our investment in quality and community," she replied. "And they've yielded returns that don't always show up on a balance sheet. That includes customer loyalty that's weathered economic downturns, staff retention that's saved thousands in training costs, and organic marketing through word-of-mouth that's more effective than paid advertising. Island Coffee is sustainable in ways that aren't reflected in profit margins but that benefit everyone involved."

Michael couldn't help the smile that spread across his face. She'd taken the financial question and reframed it without dismissing its importance. It was exactly the balanced approach he'd been learning from her that recognized business success and community impact weren't opposing forces but complementary ones.

After the questioning for each of the contestants concluded, the host announced a commercial break before the surprise challenge. The finalists were ushered offstage, and the audience buzzed with conversation.

"She's killing it," Reagan leaned forward to say to Michael.

"Absolutely," he agreed, still smiling.

When the show resumed, the host explained the

surprise challenge. Each finalist would have to create an ad campaign for their business in just ten minutes, using only the materials provided. They'd then present their concepts to the judges and audience.

The finalists were led to workstations set up on stage and provided with laptops, printers, markers, paper, posterboards, and basic art supplies. The timer began, and the audience watched as the judges walked between stations, stopping to speak with contestants as they worked.

Michael noticed Chloe spent the first minute just thinking, her eyes closed briefly as if visualizing something. Then she began to work with purpose, her movements decisive. As close-ups of their work flashed on the big screen, it appeared Carson had immediately begun creating some kind of logo. Jacob revealed to the judges that he was working on a tagline, and Brianna was putting together a visual on the computer with photos. Meanwhile, Chloe was the only one not working on the laptop, opting for the posterboard and art supplies instead. When the cameras were on her, she teased that the audience would have to wait to find out more.

When the timer sounded, the presentations began. Brianna went first, showing a campaign focused on before-and-after transformations with emotional testimonials. Jacob had created a street art inspired design for a visual ad that captured his brand's urban edge, with the tagline, "Every street tells a story. Wear yours." Michael wondered if anyone else thought it was a bit too similar to Chloe's Story Box idea, but maybe he was just being protective of her again.

Next, it was Chloe's turn. She held up what looked like a simple poster board illustration.

"This isn't just an ad for Island Coffee," she said. "It's an invitation to become part of a movement."

Rather than trying to create elaborate artwork, she'd focused on concept. The board was arranged like a template with spaces marked "Your Story Here" surrounding a central coffee cup logo. From each space, simple lines connected to others, creating a web of relationships.

"When customers visit any Island Coffee location, they'll receive a card like this," she explained, holding up a small index card with "Where I Belong" printed at the top. "They can share a memory, a hope, or a connection that matters to them. These stories will be displayed on our community walls, connecting customers to each other through shared experiences."

She turned the board to reveal the back, where she'd written a simple, powerful phrase: "You belong here."

"This campaign isn't about selling coffee—it's about creating spaces that matter," she continued. "Each Island Coffee location will adapt this concept to reflect its own community. It's simple, scalable, and true to what makes us special."

She'd managed to capture the essence of her business in a straightforward concept that was both marketable and meaningful. Michael wasn't surprised when the audience responded with enthusiastic applause.

Carson went last, presenting a clean, simple visual ad he'd put together with the headline "A kombucha for every-one." A half dozen different kombucha photos were below, each with a word under it like "Balance," "Energy," and "Focus." There was a QR code where people could take a quiz and get a recommendation for their next drink. Despite the assertion that there was something for everyone and the attempt to personalize it, the ad felt cold and impersonal compared to the other contestants.

The judges deliberated briefly before offering their feedback. They praised Brianna's emotional connection and Jacob's brand consistency. When they reached Chloe, Andie spoke first.

"What's remarkable about your concept," she said, "is how naturally it extends from your business philosophy. It's not just an ad; it's a demonstration of your values in action."

Even Thad seemed impressed. "You've managed to create something that's both commercially viable and authentic to your brand. That's harder than it looks."

As the judges concluded with Carson, noting his design had "sleek, clean lines," the host announced another commercial break before the final scoring and winner announcement. Michael checked his phone, seeing a text from Aidan.

> The ceramics artist is in for The Perry. This is really coming together. I think the neighborhood is going to love it.

Michael smiled, tucking the phone away. He'd asked The Perry's new manager to meet with a local artist about creating all the mugs, inspired by Chloe's use of china from the community. Whether Chloe won tonight or not, her vision was already expanding beyond Big Dune Island. The Perry was just the beginning.

When the show resumed, the atmosphere in the studio was alive with anticipation. The finalists stood in a line at center stage, the spotlights intensifying the expressions on their faces. Chloe's was surprisingly the most relaxed. He knew how she usually vibrated with excitement or anxiety.

"Before we announce our winner," the host said dramatically, "let's review the judges' scores from tonight's performances. In addition to our usual categories, the judges were also asked to score each contestant based on their full body of work this season."

Graphics appeared on the screen showing each contestant's score and ranking. Carson led with the judges by a substantial margin. Brianna was in second place, with Chloe close behind in third. Jacob rounded out the group in fourth.

"But as you know," the host continued, "the audience vote counts for twenty-five percent of the final score. And America has been very vocal about their favorites!"

Michael quickly did the mental math—even with the audience support Chloe was sure to have, it might not be possible for her to leapfrog both Brianna and Carson. As much as America loved her, all the other contestants had their own fan bases, with Brianna having also inspired her own hashtag earlier in the season.

"And now," the host announced, "the moment we've all been waiting for. The winner of *The Next Great American Entrepreneur* is . . ."

The customary dramatic pause stretched into what felt like eternity. Michael's heart raced as he watched the four finalists standing under the harsh spotlights. Carson's confident posture never wavered, while Brianna clasped her hands tightly in front of her. Jacob shifted his weight from foot to foot, and Chloe stood with quiet dignity, her eyes briefly finding Michael's in the audience.

In that suspended moment, Michael came to a stunning realization. Whatever happened next, he wanted to be part of it. Not as an adviser or investor but as someone who believed in Chloe's vision so completely that he wanted to see it unfold firsthand. As someone who had come to care deeply for the person who had created that vision.

The host opened the envelope with theatrical slowness. The studio lights dimmed, leaving only the spotlights on the four finalists. A drum roll sound effect built tension as cameras panned across their faces.

Michael leaned forward in his seat, hands gripping his knees. Around him, Chloe's family and friends held their collective breath.

The host took a deep breath, microphone poised. Michael saw Carson subtly shift his weight forward, as if preparing to step into the winner's spotlight. Thad was watching with particular interest, his expression revealing nothing.

The drum roll reached its crescendo.

And then—

The studio lights came back up as the host announced, "We'll reveal our winner right after this break!"

A collective groan swept through the audience. Michael exhaled heavily, tension momentarily broken by the commercial interruption. As production assistants rushed to touch up makeup and adjust lighting, he caught one final glimpse of Chloe's face before she was led offstage.

In that brief moment, he saw neither triumph nor defeat. She was fully present, ready to accept whatever came next. Regardless of the outcome about to be announced, he had no doubt that Chloe Beckett had already found something more valuable than any competition could offer. She had reclaimed her vision, her purpose, and herself.

And Michael, against all his careful planning and

emotional safeguards, had found something unexpected too. Something that made him want to be a better version of himself. Something that felt remarkably like home. Something that made him feel he too had found where he belonged.

Chapter 27

Chloe

"And the winner of *The Next Great American Entrepreneur* is . . . Carson Chen!"

The words seemed to reach Chloe through a fog as the studio erupted in applause. Lights flashed, music swelled, and beside her, Carson's face transformed with shock and joy. She felt her own face arranging itself into what she hoped was a gracious smile as she turned to congratulate him.

"Well deserved," she said, embracing him warmly. "Your concept is amazing."

Carson squeezed her shoulders as he pulled back. "You did a great job, Chloe."

Chloe had come in second, edging out Brianna by a tight margin thanks to America's vote. It did feel good that America had chosen her first. In fact, that vote felt more important than the judges'.

The next few minutes spun by in a blur of activity. Carson accepted his oversized check while confetti rained down, the judges offering congratulations to all the finalists, production assistants herding them through their final moments on camera.

As Chloe hugged Brianna and Jacob, she felt that she was truly at peace with the outcome. Disappointment was there, of course. She'd wanted to win. Buying Austin out didn't seem that important anymore, but she really had gotten excited about the idea of supporting Morgan and franchising Island Coffee in an intentional way. But standing on that stage, watching Carson bask in his victory, she realized she'd gained something else invaluable.

She hadn't compromised who she was or what Island Coffee stood for. She'd stayed true to her vision, even when it meant risking everything. And somehow, that felt like its own kind of winning.

"Chloe!"

Her family engulfed her the moment she stepped backstage, Austin lifting her off her feet in a bear hug while her parents hovered anxiously nearby.

"You were robbed," Reagan declared, squeezing her arm. "Absolutely robbed."

"It's okay," Chloe said, surprised by how much she meant it. "Carson deserved it. His kombucha empire is pretty impressive."

"But you're famous!" Luke protested, his young face indignant. "The WhereWeBelong hashtag is still trending!"

Gigi nodded emphatically. "You were America's winner."

"Honestly, that means more to me than anything," Chloe assured them. "It was an incredible experience, even if I didn't win."

Her father wrapped an arm around her shoulders. "We're so proud of you, sweetheart. Second place out of hundreds of businesses is extraordinary."

"And you did it your way," her mother added, her eyes suspiciously bright. "On your own terms."

That was it exactly. She'd done it her way. Not by following someone else's blueprint or trying to be what she thought the judges wanted. She'd rediscovered what made Island Coffee special and stayed true to that vision, even when it seemed like the riskier path.

As her family continued to shower her with praise, congratulations, and reassurance, Chloe's eyes scanned the crowded backstage area, looking for one face in particular. She spotted him standing a respectful distance away, hands in his pockets, waiting for her family to have their moment before approaching.

Michael.

Their eyes met across the bustling space, and something in her chest squeezed. The quiet confidence in his gaze told her everything she needed to know. He wasn't disappointed. He was proud.

Austin nudged her shoulder with his. "I think someone else wants a minute with you."

She blushed. Was her protective big brother actually encouraging whatever was happening between her and Michael?

"Birds of a feather flock together, but opposites attract," Austin quipped, mixing his metaphors but making his point. "Go on."

Smiling at her brother, she excused herself from her family, making her way over to Michael.

"Hey," she said, stopping in front of him.

"Hey yourself," he replied, his expression warm. "You were amazing up there."

"Even though I came in second?"

"Especially because you came in second being authentically you, instead of first as someone else."

She laughed, the tension of the day finally releasing. "That's a very philosophical way of looking at it."

"I've been learning from the best." His smile softened. "How are you feeling? Really?"

Chloe considered the question. "Oddly okay. I mean, I wanted to win. Of course I did. But I feel like I already got what I needed from this whole experience." She gestured vaguely at the chaos around them. "I reaffirmed what makes Island Coffee special. And in the process discovered what makes *me* special."

"That's what I saw up there tonight," Michael said quietly. "Someone who knows exactly who she is and what she stands for."

A production assistant appeared, apologizing while informing them that they needed to clear the backstage area and directing all finalists to the official network dinner in thirty minutes.

"We should probably join your family," Michael said, gesturing toward where Austin was animatedly recounting one of Chloe's responses to the rest of the group.

Chloe nodded, feeling a rush of gratitude that all these people had come to support her. "You're staying for dinner, right?"

"There's nowhere else I'd rather be," Michael said, smiling.

The way he looked into her eyes when he said it had her heart thudding so loudly, she was sure the whole room could hear it. She turned her attention to her family, hoping no one could see the blush that heated her cheeks, and got swept up in their recounting of the entire episode. It had all gone by so fast, she could hardly remember what had even happened.

A short while later, Chloe found herself seated at a large round table with her family, Reagan, Gigi, Michael, and surprisingly, Andie, who had asked to join them rather than sit with the other judges. They'd all walked the few short blocks from the studio to the restaurant, where the network had reserved a private room.

"I hope you don't mind," Andie said, sliding into the seat beside Chloe. "I wanted to tell you personally how impressed I've been with your journey."

"Of course I don't mind," Chloe said, the warmth of Andie's words touching her to her very soul. "To be honest, your feedback always meant the most to me."

"That's because she was the only one with any taste," Reagan chimed in, earning a laugh from everyone at the table.

The dinner was everything Chloe needed after the intensity of the competition. The food was delicious, the conversation was light and lively, and she was surrounded by the people she cared about most. Her disappointment at coming in second place faded further with each toast and story shared around the table.

"To creating places where we all feel like we belong," Austin said, raising his glass in the final toast of the evening. "No one does it better than my little sister."

"Hear, hear," echoed around the table as glasses clinked.

As the evening wound down, Chloe found herself beside Michael at the coat check.

"You still have some time before your flight tomorrow to go see The Perry, right?"

"I do. What time should I meet you?"

"Ten? I'll meet you in your hotel lobby."

"Perfect," she replied, unable to keep from smiling. "I'll be there."

Later, as she lay in her hotel bed staring at the ceiling, Chloe reflected on the day. Second place wasn't what she'd dreamed of, but the competition had given her something far more valuable. She had renewed confidence in her vision, and the knowledge that it resonated beyond the borders of Big Dune Island validated it even further. And tomorrow, she'd see that vision realized at The Perry.

With Michael.

That thought carried her into dreams filled with possibility.

~

Morning sunshine found its way through the crack in the curtains as Chloe finished packing. Her flight back to Big Dune Island wasn't until late afternoon, giving her plenty of time to visit The Perry with Michael before heading to the airport.

A knock at her door revealed Brianna, already dressed for travel in sleek jeans and a silk blouse.

"I wanted to say goodbye before I head to the airport," she said, pulling Chloe into a hug. "My flight's in a few hours."

"I'm so glad you stopped by," Chloe said, inviting her in. "I was hoping we'd get to talk before leaving."

"Second and third place," Brianna said, shaking her head with a smile. "Not too shabby."

Chloe laughed. "Honestly, I'm okay with how things turned out. This whole experience gave me exactly what I needed, even if maybe I went into it wanting something different."

"Me too," Brianna agreed. "Plus, I've already had three more potential investors reach out since last night."

"That's amazing!"

"What about you? Any big plans now that the show's over?"

"Actually, yes," Chloe said, feeling a flutter of excitement. "I'm visiting The Perry this morning to see the coffee shop design I consulted on."

"With tall, dark, and handsome?" Brianna asked, wiggling her eyebrows.

Chloe felt her cheeks flush. "Maybe."

"I knew it! The way he looked at you last night," Brianna fanned her face with her hand. "Girl, that man is smitten."

"He's older than me," Chloe said, "so I never really thought he saw me like that. But I think maybe that's another thing this whole experience changed."

"Who needs a cardboard check when you can go home with a sexy man like that?" Brianna let out a low whistle. "You go girl."

As they continued chatting, they made their way down to the lobby.

"The AI hair styling thing is definitely worth the trip to Atlanta," Brianna insisted as they parted in the lobby. "And you can show me around Big Dune Island in the summer. I haven't been since I was a kid."

"It's a deal," Chloe promised.

They promised to visit each other soon before sharing one final hug.

As Brianna's taxi pulled away, Chloe spotted Michael entering the hotel lobby. He looked relaxed in dark jeans and a light blue button-down shirt, no tie in sight. Her heart did a little flip at the sight of him.

"Good morning," he said, smiling as he approached. "Ready to see Perk Slope?"

"More than ready," she replied. "I've been looking forward to it all night."

The drive to Brooklyn was filled with comfortable conversations about their dinner the previous evening, Andie's surprising support, and how the rest of Chloe's family planned to spend their day in the city before their evening flight.

As they crossed the Brooklyn Bridge, Chloe gazed out at the water sparkling in the morning sun. "I'm glad we're doing this during the day. I want to see everything clearly."

"The light in the space is pretty spectacular in the morning," Michael said. "That's another thing we got exactly right."

Soon they were pulling up in front of The Perry. In daylight, the restored brick facade was even more impressive than she remembered, its architectural details highlighted by the morning sun.

"They're still putting the finishing touches on the lobby," Michael explained as he led her inside, nodding to a construction manager who greeted him by name. "But the café is essentially complete."

He guided her to a separate entrance to their left with "Perk Slope" written in elegant gold lettering above the door. Producing a key, he unlocked it and stepped back to let her enter first.

Chloe's mouth dropped open as she stepped inside. The space was flooded with warm morning light streaming through the large windows and illuminating every detail, just as she'd imagined during her consultation with Michael and Alessandra months ago.

The seating areas were arranged exactly as she'd suggested. There were comfortable clusters that encouraged conversation, a mix of tables for different group sizes, cozy corners where someone could linger alone with a book. The counter along one wall gleamed with polished wood and glass display cases ready for pastries.

But it was the wall behind the counter that truly took her breath away.

The community wall dominated the space, a beautiful mural depicting scenes from Park Slope's history interspersed with blank spaces where photos and stories from local residents would eventually be displayed. It was everything she'd described during that first visit. It was the essence of belonging, translated through art.

"It's perfect," she whispered, turning slowly to take it all in. "I can't believe it."

Michael stepped beside her. "You made this happen, Chloe. Every detail that makes this place special came from you."

"But Alessandra—"

"Was directed to implement your vision, exactly as you described it." His expression hardened briefly. "We've made it very clear in everything we've pushed out that the credit for the concept belongs to you."

Chloe wandered farther into the space, running her hand along the counter, picturing the conversations that would unfold there, the connections that would form between neighbors over coffee and pastries.

"There's more," Michael said, leading her to the register area. He pulled out a small framed document and handed it to her.

It was a certificate, elegant in its simplicity. At the top, it read, "The Perry's Community Partners," and below that was a statement: "The concept for Perk Slope was created in collaboration with Chloe Beckett, founder of Island Coffee, Big Dune Island, Florida. Community, connection, and belonging are the foundations of this space."

Tears pricked unexpectedly at her eyes. "Thank you," she said, her voice thick with emotion.

"Don't thank me," Michael said quietly. "This is just giving credit where it's due."

Chloe set the certificate down and turned to face him fully. In the golden morning light streaming through the windows, with her vision realized all around them, everything felt heightened, more vivid somehow.

"I mean it, Michael. Thank you. Not just for this but for believing in me. For pushing me to be better without trying to change who I am."

His eyes met hers, something shifting in their depths. "That goes both ways, you know. You've changed how I see success, what I value in business and in life."

The air between them seemed to hum with possibility. Chloe was acutely aware of how close they were standing, of the way the morning light caught in his eyes, of her heart thundering in her chest.

"I may not have won the competition," she said softly, "but standing here, seeing all this, I don't feel like I missed out on anything that matters."

"You didn't lose," Michael said, taking a step closer. "You chose a different path. The one that was truer to your vision."

"Our vision now," she corrected, gesturing to the space around them. "Perk Slope is proof that it works beyond Island Coffee."

"It works because of you," he said, his voice dropping lower. "Because you understand that business isn't just about transactions. It's about connections."

His gaze dropped briefly to her lips, and Chloe felt the world narrow to just this moment, just this space between them.

"Connections matter," she agreed, in a husky tone of voice she hardly recognized as her own.

Whether she moved first or he did, Chloe couldn't have said. But suddenly, the space between them vanished, and his lips were on hers. The kiss was gentle at first, questioning, but quickly deepened as Chloe responded, her hand finding its way to his shoulder, then the back of his neck.

She felt his arms encircle her waist, drawing her closer, and she went willingly, everything else falling away. In that moment, there was only Michael and the certainty that this, too, was exactly where she belonged.

When they finally broke apart, both slightly breathless, Michael rested his forehead against hers. "I've been wanting to do that since that night on the beach," he admitted.

"Me too," she whispered. "I was so disappointed when Mrs. Perkins interrupted us."

He laughed softly, the sound vibrating through her. "Remind me to thank her someday. If she hadn't, I might have kissed you then, before either of us really knew what we wanted."

Chloe pulled back slightly to look at him. "And now?"

"Now," he said, his gaze steady on hers, "I know exactly what I want. *Who* I want."

Her heart soared as he leaned in to kiss her again, this time with more certainty, more promise. There in that space that embodied everything she valued, with a man who had challenged and supported her in equal measure, Chloe felt a deeper sense of victory than any competition could provide.

Second place had never felt so much like winning.

"There's someone else you should meet," Michael said after they'd spent another half hour exploring the café and all its features. "There's a Puerto Rican bakery down the street run by a woman named Valentina. She's going to be providing pastries for Perk Slope, and she reminds me a little of Iris. I think you two will hit it off."

"I'd love that," Chloe said, already thinking about how Morgan could build similar relationships in Cypress Shores. "Maybe we could even arrange a recipe exchange between her and Island Coffee."

Michael smiled broadly, but with a warmth she hadn't seen before. "See? That's what makes you so special. You're already thinking beyond boundaries. That's why this whole thing works."

They left Perk Slope hand in hand to walk down the street to Valentina's bakery. Chloe took one last look at the space, her imagination painting it filled with life—customers chatting at tables, baristas crafting drinks, stories being shared on the community wall.

"It's going to be magical," she said.

"It already is," he replied, squeezing her hand gently.

And as they walked through the sunlit streets of Park Slope, Chloe knew that wherever this journey led next—whether expanding Island Coffee, helping Morgan open in Cypress Shores, or navigating this new relationship with Michael—she would face it all as her most authentic self.

That was a prize worth more than any oversized check or television show could ever offer.

Chapter 28

Michael

Six weeks later, Michael stood in the cavernous space of the Jacksonville warehouse, surveying the transformation taking place around him. What had once been an abandoned industrial building was now buzzing with activity as workers installed track lighting, artists mapped out their future studio spaces, and community organizers planned the layout for the ground-floor gallery.

"What do you think about moving these partitions another two feet?" Marcus Taylor asked, gesturing to the modular walls that temporarily defined his studio space. "I need good northern light for my landscapes."

Michael nodded, making a note on his tablet. "Absolutely. Let's adjust the layout. That shouldn't be a problem."

Marcus smiled, his weathered hands clasping Michael's shoulder. "Never thought I'd see a developer who cared about the direction of light for painting."

"A year or two ago, I wouldn't have," Michael admitted. "I'm still learning."

And he was. Every decision about the warehouse project had become a balancing act that involved weighing the financial realities against the needs of the artists who would occupy the space. A year earlier, he would have prioritized efficiency and profit margins above all else. Now, he found himself considering factors like the quality of light, the flow of visitors and patrons, and the preservation of the building's historical character.

The change hadn't gone unnoticed by his partners either. Just that morning, John had called to review the latest budget adjustments.

"These artist studios are eating into our ROI," John had said, though his tone lacked its usual edge. "But I have to admit, the press coverage has been exceptional. Three different publications calling us 'visionary' in one week is a record."

Michael had smiled at that. "Sometimes doing good is good business."

As he made his way through the building, stopping to consult with the electrician about the gallery lighting, his phone buzzed with a text from Chloe.

He smiled, quickly typing back a reply.

"Mr. Russo?" A young woman with bright blue hair approached, a clipboard in hand. "I'm Tara from the Downtown Arts Alliance. Do you have a minute to go over the program for tomorrow's preview?"

"Of course," he said, following her to a makeshift desk set up in what would eventually become the gallery café.

Tomorrow's event was more than just a preview of the artist studios; it was a statement about the kind of developer Michael wanted to be moving forward. He'd invited city officials, arts patrons, and community leaders to see the space before construction was completed so he could build excitement not just for the physical space but for the concept itself.

Chloe would be there, of course, but he'd also decided to fly in his mother and sisters to see the new space and meet Chloe for the first time. He knew if his family saw this project, and the woman who'd inspired so much of it, they'd see his own transformation too.

"We've confirmed fifteen artists will have demonstrations set up," Tara explained, reviewing her list. "Marcus will be painting live, Delia's bringing a pottery wheel, and James Cooper has agreed to display some of his sculptures. The Jacksonville Heritage Society is also excited about the historical exhibition they're setting up on the east wall."

As he wrapped up the details with Tara, Michael's phone rang. Jesse's name flashed on the screen.

"How's it looking?" Jesse asked when Michael answered. "Still on track for tomorrow?"

"Just finalizing the details now. It's coming together better than I expected."

"Sorry I can't make it," Jesse said. "Callie's got that music festival performance, and Clara's got a cold."

"No problem," Michael assured him. "We'll do a proper tour once the whole space is finished. How are your projects going?"

"Busy. Those Victorian restorations on the north end of the island are taking longer than expected. Historical accuracy is a pain in the—"

"But worth it," Michael finished for him, smiling.

"Hey," Jesse laughed. "I'm the one who's supposed to say that while you grumble about the 'hysterical committee.'" Jesse was poking fun at how Michael used to refer to the Big Dune Island Historical Preservation Committee.

After ending the call, Michael took one final walk through the warehouse, mentally checking off items on his to-do list. The space was ready, and he couldn't wait to show it to everyone in his life whose opinions meant the most.

By the time he pulled into his condo's parking lot a few hours later, night had fallen. Exhausted but satisfied with the day's progress, he sent Chloe a quick text.

> Just got back to the island. We're all set for tomorrow. I'll pick you up at 9?

Her response came as he walked through his front door.

> Perfect. I'm baking something special for the artists. Can't wait!

Smiling at her enthusiasm, Michael kicked off his shoes and walked to the balcony. The ocean stretched dark and vast beyond the dunes, stars scattered across the clear sky. The constant rhythm of waves breaking on the shore had become a comfort, so different from the city noise he'd grown up with.

Standing there, with the salt breeze on his face and

thoughts of tomorrow's event in his mind, Michael realized something important. This place, once just a convenient location for overseeing investments, had become home in a way New York hadn't felt in years.

~

The following morning, Michael pulled up outside Island Coffee just as Chloe was locking up. She wore a cheerful yellow sundress with a lightweight cardigan, her hair falling in neat curls to her shoulders. A large basket covered with a checkered cloth sat at her feet.

"Morning," he called, getting out to help her. "What's all this?"

"Just a few things for the artists," she said, smiling as she handed him the surprisingly heavy basket. "Muffins, cookies, and those petits fours Mrs. Herman loves. I figured everyone could use some fuel during the preview."

Michael shook his head, smiling as he loaded the basket into the back seat. "You didn't have to do that."

"I wanted to," she said simply, sliding into the passenger seat. "Besides, baked goods are the universal language of 'welcome to the neighborhood.' My grandmother taught me that."

As they drove north toward Jacksonville, Michael filled her in on the final preparations. He described Marcus's paintings, Delia's sculptures, and the temporary exhibition documenting the warehouse's history.

"It sounds incredible," Chloe said, her eyes bright with excitement. "I can't believe how quickly you've pulled this together."

"Don't get too excited yet," he cautioned. "It's still a construction zone. The finished space is months away."

"Still," she insisted, "the fact that you fought for this project says everything."

Michael's phone buzzed with a text notification. He glanced at it quickly at a red light and chuckled.

"What?" Chloe asked.

"My family. Apparently they finally got in the air." He showed her the last of several messages Maria had sent using the plane's Wi-Fi after his family had been delayed trying to leave New York that morning. They'd miss the beginning of the event, but the important thing was that they'd be there.

Hope you're ready for the invasion. See you soon!

"I'm so excited to finally meet them," Chloe said, smiling.

Chloe asked questions about his family as they drove, and Michael found himself relaxing as he described his sisters' personalities, warning her about their tendency to gang up on him with questions.

They arrived at the warehouse to find the parking lot already filling with cars. Local news vans were setting up near the entrance, and a small crowd had gathered by the doors.

"Quite a turnout," Chloe observed, impressed by the number of people milling around.

"The arts community has been waiting for this for a long time," Michael explained as he parked. "When the old co-op closed, a lot of these artists had nowhere to do their work."

Inside, the transformation was even more apparent than the day before. The previously empty space was now alive with activity. Artists had set up temporary displays throughout the ground floor, with Marcus already at work on a canvas near the center of the room, his brush moving confidently across the surface.

Tara spotted them immediately, rushing over with clipboard in hand. "Mr. Russo! Everything's ready for the official welcome at eleven. The mayor just arrived, and the Jacksonville Arts Commission wants a word when you have a moment."

"I'll be right there," Michael assured her. Turning to Chloe, he added, "Let me give you a quick tour before things get too hectic."

As they moved through the space, Michael explaining the vision for each area, he found himself watching Chloe's reactions more than the space itself. Her eyes widened at the soaring ceilings and original brick walls. She paused to admire the way the morning light streamed through the tall windows, creating pools of sunshine on the polished concrete floors.

"It's perfect," she said, stopping in what would become the community gallery. "I can already imagine the exhibitions, the opening nights, the conversations that will happen here."

"That's what I was hoping you'd say," Michael admitted. "When I first looked at this building, all I saw was square footage and potential rental income. Now I see possibilities for connection."

They continued the tour, stopping to introduce Chloe to various artists setting up their demonstrations. At each interaction, Michael noticed how quickly Chloe established rapport, asking thoughtful questions about their work and sharing stories about Island Coffee's community wall.

When they reached Marcus's station, the painter set down his brush and extended a paint-speckled hand to

Chloe. "You must be the famous Chloe Beckett. Michael's told us all about you and your café."

"All good things, I hope." She laughed, shaking his hand.

"More than good," Marcus assured her. "He credits you with showing him how community-centered spaces can transform a neighborhood. That's why many of us agreed to take a chance on this project."

Chloe blushed, glancing at Michael. "I think he gives me too much credit."

"I doubt that's true," Marcus countered with a smile. The canvas started on his easel displayed the beginnings of a vibrant landscape depicting the St. Johns River at sunrise.

Tara appeared again, informing Michael that the mayor was ready to begin the formal welcome. With a quick squeeze of Chloe's hand, he followed Tara to the makeshift podium near the entrance.

The next hour passed in a blur of speeches, applause, and handshakes. Michael kept his own remarks brief, emphasizing that the project was about preserving Jacksonville's artistic heritage while creating a space for future generations to connect and create. He acknowledged his firm's partners, the city officials who had streamlined permits, and most importantly, the artists who had trusted their vision.

Throughout his speech, he found his gaze turning to Chloe, who stood near the back of the crowd. Her encouraging smile gave him confidence, grounding him in the purpose behind the project.

After the formalities concluded, the event shifted to a more casual open house format. Visitors wandered between artist demonstrations, sampled food from local vendors who would eventually have permanent spaces in the building, and engaged in conversations about the neighborhood's future.

Michael was deep in discussion with a city councilwoman when James Cooper, the elder sculptor whose weathered hands had created some of the most striking pieces on display, approached with Chloe beside him.

"Mr. Russo," James said, his deep voice commanding attention despite its softness, "your young lady here has been telling me about your work on The Perry in Brooklyn. Seems you're making a habit of creating these community spaces."

"I'm trying," Michael acknowledged, feeling a flush of pleasure at the phrase "your young lady." "Though I still have a lot to learn."

"That's the best kind of man," James said with an approving nod. "The kind who knows they don't know everything."

As the conversation continued, Michael noticed Chloe slipping away toward the refreshment table where the baked goods from her basket had been set up. Several artists had gathered there, sampling her offerings with obvious appreciation.

The councilwoman was called away to another group, and Michael seized the opportunity to rejoin Chloe, who was laughing at something Delia, the sculptor, had said.

"Your petit fours are divine," Delia was exclaiming. "You must share the recipe."

"Family secret," Chloe said with a wink. "But I'd be happy to teach you sometime."

"These remind me of the ones my grandmother used to make for church socials," James added, joining them with a napkin filled with cookies. "Same care in them."

"That's the highest compliment I could receive," Chloe beamed.

Michael's phone buzzed in his pocket, and he took it out to see a text from Maria.

> We're here! Where are you hiding?

"They're here," he said to Chloe.

Before she could respond, a familiar voice carried across the warehouse. "Michael Anthony Russo, where are you hiding?"

Michael turned to see his mother entering the space, followed by all four of his sisters. Maria spotted him first, waving enthusiastically, while his mother looked around the warehouse with wide eyes.

"Ma!" Michael called, making his way over to them with Chloe close behind. "You made it."

"We wouldn't miss this," his mother said, reaching up to hug him tightly. "Though you could have warned us it was going to be this impressive." She gestured around the space.

"I'll show you around, but first I want you to meet Chloe."

"Mrs. Russo," Chloe said warmly, extending her hand. "It's so wonderful to finally meet you."

"Oh, none of that," his mom said, pulling Chloe into a hug instead. "Call me Sylvia. And it's about time we met properly. Michael talks about you constantly."

"Ma," Michael protested, feeling his cheeks heat.

"Don't 'Ma' me," she said, stepping back to look at Chloe appreciatively. "You're even prettier in person than you were on TV."

"You know what they say. The TV adds ten pounds." Chloe laughed.

"Nonsense," his mother said. "In fact, you look like you haven't been eating enough. Don't worry, I'll see you get fed while I'm here."

His sisters crowded around, introducing themselves with the kind of enthusiasm that had always made Michael feel simultaneously grateful and slightly overwhelmed. Angela commented on Chloe's dress, Cristina asked about Island Coffee, and Gina wanted to know if she'd brought any of her famous baked goods.

"Actually," Chloe said, "there's a whole spread over by the refreshment table. Help yourselves."

As his sisters dispersed to sample the food, his mother linked her arm through Chloe's. "Walk with me, dear. I want to see what my son has been up to."

Michael watched nervously as Chloe led his mother through the warehouse, stopping to admire various artist displays and introduce Ma to the artists. Maria fell into step beside him.

"She's perfect for you," Maria said quietly. "I haven't seen you this relaxed in years."

"You think so?" Michael asked, trying to sound casual.

"I know so," Maria replied. "And this place . . ." She gestured around the warehouse. "Dad would have been so proud. You're building something that matters."

Across the space, Michael could see his mother deep in conversation with Chloe, both women laughing at something. His chest tightened with emotion at seeing two of the most important women in his life connecting so naturally.

When they reconvened near Marcus's station, Ma was beaming. "Michael, this is extraordinary." Turning to Chloe, she said, "And I've seen Perk Slope. You two make quite a team."

"We do," Michael agreed, catching Chloe's eye.

As the event wound down and the visitors began to leave, Michael found himself surrounded by his family, all talking at once about restaurants and dinner plans. Marcus approached them, wiping his hands on a paint-stained rag.

"Your family?" he asked Michael.

"Unfortunately," Michael joked, earning swats from his sisters.

"Don't listen to him," his mother told Marcus. "We came all the way down from New York to see what he's been working on. And to meet this young lady we've heard so much about."

Marcus smiled. "Well, you raised a good man, Mrs. Russo. This project is going to mean so much to our community."

"I can see that," she said, looking around the space one more time. "I always wondered what would make my son finally settle down somewhere. Now I know."

As they gathered their things and prepared to leave, Michael caught Chloe's hand.

"Too much?" he asked quietly, nodding toward his animated family ahead of them.

"Not at all," she assured him. "I love seeing where you come from. They're wonderful."

"They love you already," he observed. "Almost as much as I do."

Back on the island that evening, the family dinner extended well into the evening, with stories shared, embarrassing childhood anecdotes told—mostly at his expense—and plans made for future visits. When they finally said their goodbyes in the restaurant parking lot, his mother pulled Chloe aside for one final hug.

"I can tell you're taking good care of my son," she said softly. "I like who he is down here with you. Reminds me of his father." She turned to wink at her son, and he fought back the tears stinging his eyes.

As Michael's family piled into their rental to head over to the beach house he'd rented for them near his condo, he and Chloe stood together under the streetlights.

"Well," he said, "that went better than I expected."

"They're amazing," Chloe said. "I can see where you get your determination. And your protective instincts."

"And my inability to keep my mouth shut?" he asked, laughing.

"That too." She reached up to straighten his collar. "Thank you for inviting me into more of your world today," she said, standing one step above him on the restaurant stairs so they were eye to eye.

"It's our world now," he corrected. He leaned forward, his mouth meeting hers for a kiss that was over too quickly. He missed the warmth of her lips, which always tasted like her favorite cherry lip balm, the instant they left his.

Her smile was the last thing he saw as he drove away, and he instantly felt like a piece of him was missing when she disappeared from view. But for the first time, that emptiness didn't feel like a permanent condition.

It felt like the space before something new began.

Chapter 29

Chloe

The morning rush at Island Coffee had finally eased, leaving Chloe with a rare moment to catch her breath. The summer tourist season was in full swing, and she'd also spent the past few days getting to know Michael's family between shifts at the café. Island Coffee had been busier than ever since her appearance on *The Next Great American Entrepreneur*. Despite coming in second place, the exposure had been incredible, with visitors frequently mentioning they'd seen her on the show.

"Another group just asked for a selfie with you," Iris said, refilling the sugar dispensers. "They're sending it to friends with the hashtag."

"WhereWeBelong." Chloe nodded, smiling as she finished arranging a fresh tray of blueberry scones in the display case. "It still amazes me how that caught on."

"Not me." Iris shook her head. "You touched on something real. People need places where they feel they belong, now more than ever. We should probably make T-shirts or something and capitalize on it."

"Now you're starting to sound like Thad," Chloe teased. "Seeing dollar signs everywhere you look."

The bell above the door jingled, and Chloe looked up, ready to greet another customer. The words died on her lips as she recognized the elegant woman entering the café.

"Andie?"

The judge from the TV show stood just inside the doorway, taking in the café with obvious appreciation. Her signature sleek bob and designer dress seemed almost out of place among the café's cozy mismatched tables and vintage china and the other patrons' beach-vibe attire.

"Surprise!" Andie spread her arms wide, laughing as Chloe rushed around the counter to greet her. "I hope you don't mind an unexpected visitor."

"Of course not!" Chloe embraced her warmly. "What are you doing on Big Dune Island? Not that I'm not thrilled to see you!"

"I had some business in Jacksonville, and I thought—well, I couldn't be this close and not see the famous Island Coffee for myself." Andie's gaze swept around the café, taking in the wall of china, the community board filled with local announcements, and the regulars settled comfortably at their usual tables. "It's exactly as charming as I remember from my brief reconnaissance mission before the show."

"Well, I'm just glad this time I know who you are." Chloe laughed, leading Andie to a table by the window. "Can I grab you something to eat or drink?"

"I hear your grandmother's buttermilk biscuits are legendary," Andie said. "And whatever coffee you recommend."

"Coming right up." Chloe hurried back behind the counter, her mind racing. What had brought one of the judges all the way to Big Dune Island?

As she prepared a pour-over of their special island blend and warmed a freshly baked biscuit, Chloe watched Andie interacting with Mrs. Herman, who had approached her table with undisguised curiosity. The two women were chatting like old friends by the time Chloe brought over the food.

"These china patterns are just exquisite," Andie was saying as Chloe set down a delicate cup with hand-painted violets. "Is there a story behind this one?"

"This was Mrs. Jenkins's mother's favorite pattern," Chloe explained, placing the biscuit on a matching saucer. "The violets reminded her of where she grew up in Virginia. When she passed, Mr. Jenkins brought me the entire set."

"That's what makes this place so special," Mrs. Herman told Andie. "Every cup of coffee comes with a memory." She patted Chloe's arm affectionately before returning to her table.

Andie took a sip of her coffee, closing her eyes momentarily. "Divine," she pronounced. "And this view of Main Street is perfect for people-watching."

"It's my favorite spot," Chloe admitted, hesitating. "Would you like me to leave you to enjoy your coffee, or—"

"Actually, I was hoping we could talk." Andie gestured to the empty chair across from her. "I didn't just come for the biscuits, though they are incredible."

Glancing around to make sure Iris had the counter covered, Chloe slid into the seat. "Is everything okay?"

"Better than okay," Andie assured her, leaning forward conspiratorially. "I've been watching what's happened since the finale. This WhereWeBelong movement really struck a chord with people, and I still see it popping up in my timeline."

Chloe nodded, still slightly amazed by the response herself. "I know, it's been incredible to see how many people connected with the idea."

"It's more than just a hashtag now," Andie said, pulling out her tablet. "Look at these."

She scrolled through a series of social media posts showing small businesses across the country. There was a family-owned bookstore in Maine, a neighborhood bakery in Chicago, a community garden project in Portland, all using #WhereWeBelong to share their stories.

"People are celebrating places that create community, that preserve traditions, that make them feel like they belong," Andie continued. "And it all traces back to you and Island Coffee."

"I'm honored," Chloe said, genuinely moved. Had Andie come all this way just to show her some social media posts?

Andie set down her coffee cup, her expression turning more serious. "After the show ended, I couldn't stop thinking about your vision. About how you managed to create something both financially successful and deeply meaningful to your community."

"Thank you," Chloe said, touched by the praise.

"I also couldn't stop thinking about Morgan and how many other female entrepreneurs might have similar visions but lack the resources to make them reality." Andie reached into her bag and pulled out a sleek folder embossed with her company's logo. "So I decided to do something about it."

She slid the folder across the table. Chloe opened it to find a professionally designed proposal titled "The

Belonging Initiative: A Grant Program for Women-Owned Community-Focused Businesses."

"You're starting a grant program?" Chloe asked, scanning the document with growing excitement.

"I am," Andie confirmed. "Focused specifically on women entrepreneurs whose business models prioritize community connection. And I want you to be on the board that selects the recipients."

Chloe looked up from the proposal, stunned. "Me? But I—"

"You embody exactly the values this initiative seeks to promote," Andie said firmly. "You've proven that a business can be both profitable and purposeful. That it can preserve traditions while embracing innovation. That's the perspective I need on this board."

The bell above the door jingled again as Morgan entered the café. Spotting Chloe, she waved excitedly and headed toward their table.

"Morgan!" Chloe stood to greet her. "Perfect timing. This is Andie Matthews, one of the judges from the show."

"I know," Morgan said, smiling. "She asked me to meet her here." She shook Andie's hand. "It's a pleasure to meet you. I watched every episode."

After Andie motioned for Morgan to join them, she turned to her. "How are your plans coming along?"

Morgan's expression dimmed slightly. "Still working on financing. The building I was hoping to lease is available again, but the banks are hesitant to take a chance on a first-time business owner with no collateral."

Chloe felt the familiar pang of disappointment she got whenever she was reminded that coming in second on the show had put her dream of helping Morgan on hold.

"The usual catch-22." Andie nodded sympathetically.

"Can't get funding without experience, can't get experience without funding."

Morgan shrugged, forcing a smile. "I'm not giving up. It's all just taking longer than I'd hoped."

Andie glanced at the proposal still open in front of Chloe, then gave Morgan a considering look. "Tell me more about your vision for this café. What would make it special to Cypress Shores?"

As Morgan described her plans—the community space she wanted to create, the local history she hoped to preserve, the gathering place she envisioned for her town—Chloe watched Andie's face. The judge was nodding thoughtfully, occasionally making notes on her tablet.

"It sounds like you've put a lot of thought into this," Andie said when Morgan finished. "And you're planning to follow Chloe's model, adapting it to reflect your own community?"

"Exactly." Morgan nodded enthusiastically. "Island Coffee has shown that a café can be more than just a place to grab coffee. It can be the heart of a community. Cypress Shores is missing that kind of place."

Andie turned to Chloe with a smile. "What do you think? Does Morgan's vision align with what you had in mind for the first Island Coffee franchise?"

"Absolutely," Chloe confirmed. "She understands exactly what makes our concept work. It's not just about copying a formula but really connecting with her specific community."

"In that case," Andie said, reaching back into her bag, "I believe I might have a solution." She pulled out another folder and handed it to Morgan. "Consider yourself the first official recipient of The Belonging Initiative grant program."

Morgan stared at the folder in her hands, then at Andie, her expression shifting from confusion to disbelief. "What?"

"It's a grant," Andie explained. "Not a loan. Enough to secure your lease, complete renovations, and cover operating expenses for your first year. All we ask is that you document your journey for future grant recipients to learn from."

"But, how?" Morgan's voice was barely above a whisper, her hands trembling as she opened the folder to see the grant details. "I haven't even applied."

"Consider this a pilot program," Andie said with a smile. "And who better to test it on than someone already connected to the movement that inspired it?" She turned to Chloe. "Assuming you're willing to serve as Morgan's mentor and on our selection board for future recipients."

Chloe felt tears welling in her eyes as the full impact of what was happening hit her. "I'd be honored," she managed to say.

Morgan was openly crying now, clutching the folder to her chest. "I don't know what to say. You're like a fairy godmother."

"I like that title." Andie smiled. "Just promise me you'll take good care of that building in Cypress Shores and turn it into a place where people feel they belong."

"I will," Morgan promised fervently. "You won't regret this."

As Morgan excused herself to call her parents with the news, Andie turned back to Chloe. "There's one more thing," she said, her expression softening. "Coming in second on the show may have felt like a disappointment initially. But I believe this is a far better outcome for you."

"How so?" Chloe asked. She didn't disagree, but she was curious to hear Andie's thoughts.

"If you'd won, you'd have expanded on your own. That would have been wonderful, of course," Andie acknowledged. "But this way, your vision gets to spread through others like Morgan. Through the businesses this grant program will support, the impact will be exponentially greater." She leaned forward and said more quietly, but with a wink, "And you don't have to listen to input from Thad anymore."

Chloe laughed, watching as Morgan paced excitedly outside the café window, phone pressed to her ear, gesturing animatedly as she shared her news.

"You're right," she agreed. "This feels more authentic to what Island Coffee is about. Not just growing bigger but reaching further."

"Exactly." Andie nodded approvingly. "And as a board member, you'll help select future grant recipients, shaping the initiative to truly reflect the values you've championed."

By the time Morgan returned, her face glowing with happiness, Iris had joined them, bringing fresh coffee and a plate of Chloe's special cookies reserved for celebrations. Chloe excitedly filled Iris in on what had just transpired.

"I need to document this moment," Iris declared, pulling out her phone to take a photo of the three women. "The beginning of something special."

As Iris captured the image of Chloe, Morgan, and Andie smiling together around the table, Chloe felt like her heart was so full it might burst from her chest. This unexpected turn of events felt more aligned with her vision than winning the competition would have been.

Later, after Andie had departed with promises to email the full board details and Morgan had left to meet with the building owner in Cypress Shores, Chloe found herself alone in the café as closing time approached. The late afternoon sun slanted through the windows, casting a golden glow across the worn wooden floors.

She moved through the space, straightening chairs and wiping tables, her mind still processing the day's remarkable developments. She'd tried to call Michael earlier, but he'd been seeing his family off that morning and then heading to Jacksonville for a meeting, so he hadn't answered. He'd texted later, letting her know he'd call her as soon as he could. When her phone buzzed and Michael's name appeared on the screen, Chloe nearly dropped the phone, she snatched it up so quickly.

"Hey you," he said warmly.

"Hey yourself," she said, smiling at the sound of his voice. "You'll never guess who showed up today."

"Let me think," he teased. "Your secret admirer? The Queen of England? That guy who keeps trying to sell crystals out on the sidewalk?"

"Close." She laughed. "Andie Matthews. From the show."

"Really?" His surprise was evident even through the phone. "What brought her to Big Dune?"

Chloe settled into a chair by the window, watching the last rays of sunlight paint Main Street in amber hues. "She's starting a grant program for female entrepreneurs with community-focused business models, and she wants me on the selection board." She filled him in on all the details.

"Chloe, that's incredible," Michael said, his pleasure for her evident in his voice. "Though I can't say I'm surprised. You made quite an impression."

"That's not even the best part," she continued, excitement bubbling up again. "Morgan is going to be the first grant recipient. She can finally open her café in Cypress Shores."

"So the first Island Coffee franchise is happening after all," Michael observed. "Just not quite how you imagined."

"It's better," Chloe admitted. "This way, I get to mentor Morgan, help other women through the grant program, and still maintain what makes Island Coffee special. It feels right, Michael. Like this is what I was meant to do all along."

"Sometimes winning isn't about coming in first place in someone else's contest," Michael said thoughtfully. "I'm really proud of you, Chloe."

Warmth spread through her at his words. "How's everything going with the warehouse project? Are the artists still talking about the preview event?"

"It's all they can talk about," Michael laughed. "Marcus has already sold three paintings based on connections he made that day, and the city council approved our final permits this morning, so we're full steam ahead."

"That's wonderful," Chloe said, hearing the genuine excitement in his voice. She knew how much this project meant to him, how it represented so much of his evolution as a developer. "When are you back on the island?"

"Tomorrow afternoon," he replied. "I was thinking maybe we could have dinner? I'd love to hear more about Andie's visit and the grant program."

"I'd like that," she said, smiling into the phone. "Text me when you get in."

After they said goodbye, Chloe remained by the window, watching as the streetlights flickered on along Main Street. Families strolled past on their way to dinner, locals called greetings to each other across the street, and the first stars appeared in the deepening blue sky.

She thought about all that had happened since that first interview in New York—the challenges, the setbacks, the moments of doubt, and, ultimately, the rediscovery of what truly mattered. Coming in second had felt like a disappointment in the moment, but now she could see it had opened a door to something that better aligned with her values.

Island Coffee would grow, not through rapid expansion or standardized processes but through mentorship, through sharing its philosophy with entrepreneurs like Morgan who understood the value of community and connection. The Belonging Initiative would extend that impact even further, helping women create spaces that mattered in their own communities.

And through it all, Michael had evolved alongside her, finding his own path to creating meaningful spaces like the warehouse project and Perk Slope in The Perry.

As Chloe finally locked up the café and climbed the stairs to her apartment, she felt a deep sense of contentment settle over her. Tonight's conversation with Michael had confirmed what she'd been feeling more strongly with each passing day—that what had begun as a business connection had deepened into something much more significant.

Tomorrow, Chloe would share the exciting news about the grant program with her family and Reagan. She would start planning how to help Morgan bring Island Coffee's vision to Cypress Shores. She would begin this unexpected new chapter that felt, somehow, like exactly where she was meant to be all along.

But tonight, she would simply savor the knowledge that sometimes, the best outcome isn't the one you initially imagined but the one that leads you to exactly where you belong.

Epilogue

Six Months Later

The early morning sunlight filtered through the windows of Cypress Shores Coffee, illuminating the space Morgan had created with such care. Much like Island Coffee, the café featured mismatched tables and chairs in organic groupings, creating cozy conversation nooks throughout the space.

But Morgan had made it distinctly her own, incorporating elements that reflected Cypress Shores' history as a fishing village. Vintage nets adorned the walls, shadow boxes displayed antique fishing lures, and old black-and-white photographs of boats lined the hallway to the restrooms.

Chloe stood behind the counter, arranging the display of pastries they'd been baking since four in the morning. Today was the grand opening, and everything needed to be perfect.

"Do you think we made enough scones?" Morgan asked, appearing from the kitchen with another tray. "I'm worried about running out before noon."

"We made twice what I typically go through on a busy Saturday," Chloe assured her, making room in the display case. "And we can always bake more if needed. That's the beauty of having the kitchen right here."

Morgan nodded, though she still looked anxious. "I just want everything to be perfect. The whole town's been watching the renovation. Everyone's curious."

"And they're going to love it," Chloe said, stepping back to admire their handiwork. "Look at what you've created here, Morgan. It's beautiful."

It truly was. The long counter was crafted from reclaimed wood from an old fishing pier, polished to a warm glow. Behind it, the community wall was already taking shape, with spaces marked for local stories and photographs, adorned at the top with the same WhereWeBelong hashtag Island Coffee now had painted atop one of its walls. China pieces donated by Cypress Shores families lined shelves along the walls, each with a small card noting its history.

Morgan had taken Island Coffee's philosophy and adapted it perfectly to her own community. It wasn't a copy. Instead, it was a sister space, connected by shared values but unique in its execution.

"I couldn't have done it without you," Morgan said, beaming as she stood in the center of the café that was her dream. "And the grant, of course."

"You did the hard part," Chloe insisted. "You had the vision for what this place could be for Cypress Shores."

The bell above the door jingled, and they both turned to see Michael entering, carrying a large coffee urn.

"Special delivery from Island Coffee," he announced,

setting it on the counter. "I've got one more in the car. Iris said these should keep things running smoothly if the espresso machine gets backed up."

"She's a lifesaver," Morgan said gratefully. "I should have thought of that."

"That's why we're here," Chloe reminded her. "First day support team at your service."

Over the previous months, as Morgan had prepared to open Cypress Shore Coffee, the bond between the two women had deepened from mentor-mentee to genuine friendship. Chloe had shared everything she'd learned from her own experience, from practical advice about suppliers and scheduling to the more intangible elements that made Island Coffee special.

Michael had become an unexpected adviser as well, offering insights on the business plan and helping Morgan negotiate favorable terms on her lease. His experience with Perk Slope had proven invaluable in transforming the former hardware store into a warm, inviting space that honored its history while creating something new.

"Is everything set for the ribbon cutting?" Michael asked, checking his watch. "The mayor said she'd be here at nine, right?"

Morgan nodded, adjusting a stack of napkins emblazoned with the café's logo—a stylized coffee cup with waves inside. "Everything's ready. I just can't believe it's actually happening."

Chloe squeezed her hand. "Believe it. You did this."

As Morgan went to double-check the seating arrangement for the ceremony, Michael slipped his arm around Chloe's waist, pulling her close.

"You look happy," he observed, dropping a kiss on her temple.

"I am," she confirmed, leaning into him. "Seeing everything come together like this, it's even better than I imagined."

The past six months had been a whirlwind of activity. Between mentoring Morgan, serving on the board for The Belonging Initiative, and managing Island Coffee's growing popularity, Chloe had barely had time to catch her breath. And, of course, she wanted to spend every spare minute with Michael as their relationship continued to blossom. Some days, she could hardly believe it was her life, because it was beyond her wildest dreams.

The Belonging Initiative had already selected three more grant recipients: a cooperative bookstore in Arizona, a community kitchen in Michigan, and a textile arts studio in Georgia. Each business embodied the same philosophy that had made Island Coffee successful. They were all creating spaces where people felt they belonged while preserving local traditions and stories.

Michael had been busy as well, dividing his time between the Jacksonville warehouse project, now entering its final phase of construction, and his increasing presence on Big Dune Island. Last month, he'd finalized the purchase of a Victorian house near her parents. It was a commitment to putting down permanent roots on the island that had made Chloe's heart soar.

"Have I mentioned how proud I am of you?" Michael asked, his voice low enough that only she could hear.

"Only about a dozen times this week." She laughed. "But I don't mind hearing it again."

"Well, I am," he insisted. "Watching you mentor Morgan, seeing how you've shaped The Belonging Initiative. You've created something that's going to outlast all of us."

Before Chloe could respond, the door opened again, and a steady stream of people began filing in—Austin and Gigi with Luke in tow, her parents, Reagan, Jesse and Callie with baby Clara, and Morgan's family and friends, who were eager for their first look at the new café.

The next hour passed in a blur of introductions, exclamations, and heartfelt congratulations. Morgan moved through the crowd with growing confidence, sharing her vision for the space and how she hoped it would become a gathering place for the community. Soon, the doors would officially open to the public, but for now, Morgan could enjoy praise and congratulations from her support network.

At precisely nine o'clock, the mayor of Cypress Shores arrived, accompanied by several town council members and a photographer from the local paper. As Morgan positioned herself for the ribbon cutting, she surprised everyone by beckoning Chloe to join her.

"I wouldn't be standing here without Chloe Beckett," Morgan announced to the assembled crowd. "Not just because of her guidance and support but because she showed all of us what's possible when a business truly serves its community."

Chloe felt tears threatening as Morgan gave her one handle of the oversized scissors and they began cutting the blue ribbon together while cameras flashed. The cheer that went up seemed to lift the very roof. As the celebration continued inside, with free coffee flowing and pastries being sampled at every table, Chloe found a moment to slip away to the small office at the back of the café. She needed a minute to compose herself, to fully absorb the significance of what was happening.

A soft knock at the door revealed Michael, two cups of coffee in hand.

"Thought you might need this," he said, offering her one of the cups. "It's been quite a morning."

"Thank you," she said, accepting the coffee gratefully. It was served in one of the special cups Morgan had commissioned for the café. They were ceramic mugs crafted by a local artist, each one slightly different. She couldn't take credit for that one, as it was an idea of Michael's from The Perry.

Michael settled into the chair beside her, his free hand finding hers naturally. "What are you thinking about, hiding back here?"

"Just taking it all in," she admitted. "When I first applied for the show, all I wanted was to prove I could succeed on my own, to buy out Austin's share and maybe help Morgan open a café. But this"—she gestured vaguely toward the celebration happening beyond the door—"this is so much more than I imagined."

"That's what happens when you stay true to what matters," Michael said, squeezing her hand. "It grows into something bigger than yourself."

They sat in comfortable silence for a moment, sipping their coffee and listening to the happy buzz of conversation from the main room. Through the partially open door, Chloe could see Morgan showing Andie some of the local fishing artifacts displayed on the walls. The judge had flown in specifically for the opening, both to support Morgan and to document the first success story for The Belonging Initiative's promotional materials.

"Have I told you lately that I love you?" Michael asked suddenly, his voice soft but certain.

Chloe turned to him, warmth spreading through her chest. Those words, still new enough between them to make her heart skip, never failed to amaze her.

"Not since last night," she teased gently.

"Well, I do," he said, setting down his coffee cup to take both her hands in his. "And being here today, seeing all of this, just confirms what I've known for a while now."

"What's that?" she asked, though something in his expression made her breath catch.

"That I want to build a life with you," he said simply. "I want to be by your side for all of it—the café, the Initiative, whatever comes next. I want to create our own place where we belong, together."

Chloe felt tears welling up again, but these were different from the emotional tears of the morning. These were the kind that came from a heart so full it couldn't contain itself.

"I want that too," she whispered, leaning forward to kiss him softly. "More than anything."

The door swung open wider as Morgan peered in. "There you two are! Everyone's asking for—" She stopped, noticing their linked hands and emotional expressions. "Oh! Sorry to interrupt."

"You're not interrupting," Chloe assured her, standing but keeping one hand firmly in Michael's. "We were just coming back out."

"Well, hurry up," Morgan urged, her excitement palpable. "Andie wants to make a toast, and she insists you both be there for it."

They rejoined the celebration, moving through the crowded café that hummed with conversation and laughter. Andie clinked a spoon against her coffee cup, attracting everyone's attention. When the room quieted, she raised her cup in a toast.

"To Morgan, for bringing Cypress Shore Coffee to life,"

she began. "To Chloe, whose vision inspired a movement. Here's to Cypress Shore Coffee, a place where we belong."

"To where we belong," someone in the crowd shouted out, everyone else echoing the motto, cups raised high.

As Chloe looked around the room—at Morgan's proud smile, at the Cypress Shores residents already claiming favorite tables, at Michael beside her, his eyes filled with love and promise—she knew she had found exactly where she belonged.

Not in winning a competition or proving herself to judges but in staying true to what mattered most. In creating spaces, both physical and emotional, where people could connect, share stories, and feel at home.

"We're so proud of you, sweetheart," Chloe's mother said, coming over to hug her as the crowd went back to mingling.

"Very impressive," her father added, resting a hand on her shoulder. "I guess I have to start treating you more like a grown-up now. Just remember, though, you'll always be my little girl." He leaned down and kissed her forehead.

Later, as the last customers finally departed and Morgan began the process of closing after her first official day, Chloe, Michael, and Chloe's parents lingered to help with the cleanup.

"I think we can call today a success," Morgan declared, her earlier anxiety replaced by a satisfied exhaustion. "We sold out of nearly everything."

"I told you," Chloe said, gathering empty cups from a table near the window. "People in Cypress Shores have been waiting for a place like this."

As they worked together to restore order to the café, Chloe noticed Michael pausing by the community wall, studying the spaces waiting to be filled with local stories and memories.

"What are you thinking?" she asked, joining him.

"I'm thinking about what a privilege it is to create spaces that matter," he said, his arm sliding around her waist. "Whether it's a café like this, the artist studios in Jacksonville, or Perk Slope in Brooklyn. They're all part of the same story now."

"Our story," she agreed, leaning into him.

"Honey," her mother said, coming up behind them, "I think we're going to head out."

Chloe hugged each of her parents and thanked them for coming.

"We wouldn't miss it for the world," her mother said, beaming with a pride that made Chloe's eyes sting with tears.

"You've got it from here, right?" Mr. Beckett asked Michael.

"I do, sir."

Chloe thought she caught them exchange a look, but she wasn't sure what it was about. She was just glad her father and Michael had developed their own relationship over the past several months, even going out to golf together the past couple of weekends.

"Hey, let's go for a walk. It's beautiful out there, and we've been inside all day," Michael said after her parents left the café.

"Sure," she said, taking his hand and following him outside.

The early evening air was warm and fragrant with jasmine, the sun beginning its slow descent toward the horizon. A few doors down from the café was a pocket park, a small green space with a couple of benches nestled between two of the historic buildings that lined the street. Michael led her there, his hand tightening slightly around hers.

"This is nice," Chloe said as they sat on a bench beneath a flowering dogwood tree. Music from a restaurant down the block mixed with the gentle lapping of water at the nearby shore to create an atmosphere that felt warm and comforting.

Michael turned toward her, his expression suddenly serious. "Do you remember the first time we met?"

Chloe smiled. "You came into Island Coffee with Jesse. You ordered a soy latte with an extra shot of espresso, and you barely looked at me." The moment was etched in her memory, because she'd thought Michael would never really look at her, at who she really was.

"I was a different person then," Michael admitted with a sheepish smile. "But knowing you has made me a better person in every possible way."

He reached into his pocket and pulled out a small velvet box, causing Chloe's breath to catch. "Over the years, I've watched you build Island Coffee into something special. I saw how you created a place where people truly belonged. And then somewhere along the way, I realized something important." He took a deep breath, his eyes never leaving hers. "I realized that where I belong isn't a place at all. It's with you, Chloe."

Michael slid from the bench to one knee before her, opening the box to reveal a vintage ring with a delicate sapphire surrounded by smaller diamonds. "This was my grandmother's. My mom gave it to me last month. I told her I'd found the person I want to spend my life with."

Tears filled Chloe's eyes as she looked from the ring to Michael's face, seeing all the love and certainty she felt reflected there.

"Chloe Beckett, you've shown me what really matters in life. You've changed how I see success, how I value community, how I build spaces. Now I'm asking if you'll build a life with me." His voice grew softer, more intimate. "Will you marry me?"

The question hung in the air between them, full of possibility and promise. Chloe didn't need time to consider her answer. She felt as though she had been moving toward this moment since that first kiss at The Perry. Okay, maybe even since that first day she'd seen him and couldn't take her eyes off him, even if he'd never given her a second glance back then.

"Yes," she said, her voice breaking with emotion as joy bubbled up like the finest espresso. "Yes, Michael. A thousand times yes."

As he slipped the ring onto her finger, she marveled at how perfectly it fit, how right it felt. Then he was beside her on the bench again, gathering her in his arms for a kiss that sealed the promise of their future together.

When they finally broke apart, both smiling too widely to maintain the kiss, Michael rested his forehead against hers. "I love you, Chloe."

"I love you too, Michael," she whispered, taking his hand. "And this is exactly where we belong. Together."

Acknowledgments

Dear reader,

Thank you for reading Michael and Chloe's story! My greatest wish is that it took you on a little mental vacation where you felt safe and happy. If you haven't read the rest of the Big Dune Island series, I hope you'll go back and read the other stories set in this little town where my mind loves to live.

As always, my first thank you is to Jenny Hale at Harpeth Road for continuing to believe in me and for allowing me to continue the story on Big Dune Island with a third book set there. To my Harpeth Road editors—Sarah Bauer, Lara Simpson, Kamille Parkinson, and Emma Sherk —thank you for helping make this book shine! And Lara, we'll always have Valentina!

I also have some of the best author friends a woman could ask for! Thank you to my author bestie, Lindsay Gibson, for always being just a text away and to my Kiss Pitch 2022 group and the 2024 Debuts Discord for their continued advice, cheerleading, and support.

To Olivia, my alpha reader, I can't imagine doing this without you! As always, thank you for finding the holes in my story and helping make it stronger in so many ways.

Also to Kelsey, my author assistant, thank you for everything you do for me! When I get asked how I do as much as I do, I always say your name first. So grateful for you! (And readers, go check out Kelsey Whitney's books too!)

ARC team, you are amazing! Forget the Dallas Cowboys Cheerleaders . . . I have the best cheerleaders around! Every social media post, like, share, comment, and DM means so much to me. I absolutely could not do this without you. And thank you to Ashley for all your marketing help!

So many of my friends offer constant cheerleading and support through each and every one of my books. Shout out to Teresa, Maggie, Stephanie/Twinny, Michelle, Scarlett, Allyse, Noreen, Kristin, and Zoe!

I have the best family anyone could ask for. Thank you to my parents, my brother, Bo and his wife, Nickki, and all my aunts, uncles, and cousins for always believing in and encouraging me. I have some of the most amazing aunts: Shug, Luder Belle, Nank, Mary Ann, and Judy. Also, Nancy, Gail, and Vicky, my bonus aunts!

I also married into the best family! Jane, Scott, Tonya, James, and Julie—I'm so lucky to have all of you!

To my husband, Chadd, make sure you read the dedication. Love on!

And, last but certainly not least, to my readers and reviewers. I appreciate every email, social post and review. I mean this from the bottom of my heart: I couldn't do what I love without you!

A Letter from Savannah Carlisle

Hello!

Thank you so much for picking up my novel, *Where We Belong*. I hope you enjoyed being whisked away to beautiful Big Dune Island on a mental vacation!

If you'd like to know when my next book is out, you can sign up for new Harpeth Road release alerts for my novels here:

https://www.harpethroad.com/savannah-carlisle-newsletter-signup

I won't share your information with anyone else, and I'll only email you a quick message whenever new books come out or go on sale.

If you did enjoy *Where We Belong*, I'd be so thankful if you'd write a review online. Getting feedback from readers helps to persuade others to pick up my book for the first time. It's one of the biggest gifts you could give me.

Until next time,
Savannah